Exordium

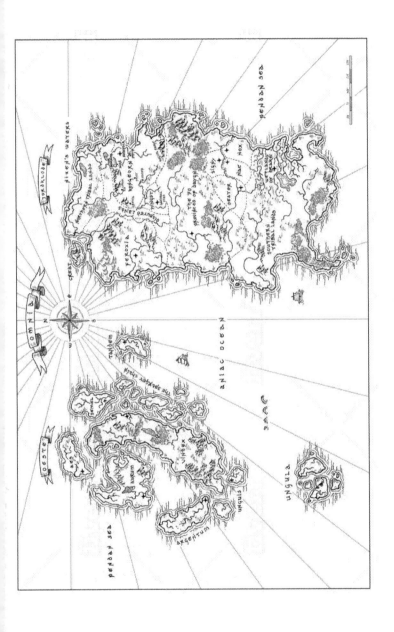

Exordium

S. N. Jones

ZENITH PUBLISHING

Copyright © S.N. JONES 2020

Supervising Editor: Caitlin Chrismon
Associate Editor(s): Charlie Hilfiker
Internal Formatting: Charlie Hilfiker, Alma Basic
Cover Designer: L. Austen Johnson

www.GenZPublishing.org
Aberdeen, NJ

ISBN: 978-1-952919-90-9

For You:

You know who you are

Table of Contents

Preface

First, there was Nothing.

And then, like the dawning of a new day, Light shone over the globe. The Mother spoke, and it was so. Clothed in earth and water, air and fire, her fingers glowed with the Light of Creation. It is said that her skin took on the color of the greenest leaves, and her hair was made of blossoms. She broke off pieces of herself and cast them into Omnia, into her sandbox of creation.

At her call, three shelves of land rose up from the waters, Jordklode in the East, Oeste in the West, and Ungula in the Southwest. In the waters and on the lands, She gave birth to animals of all kinds, blessing each of them, no matter how big or small. Everything She touched thrived, and all creation thanked its Mother, Avani, for Her love and for Her care.

But as the Mother watched what She had created, She was struck with a creeping disappointment, an eternal sadness. She loved all things, but there were none like Her, none to call Her own.

So, out of the pure Light, She made two beings, the Lovers of the Sky. The radiant Luna and her beloved Sol embraced each other in the sky, shining down through the clouds, casting down their light for all the creatures of Omnia, of creation.

And yet, there was still something missing.

So, the Mother used Her own Light, Her own Divinity, to make a son She could call Her own: Jakel. Jakel was far fairer than the Lovers of the Sky, and he knew this. Yet, despite his Mother's encouragement and teachings, Jakel grew jealous, hateful. He envied the Lovers, how they cast light over all. He began to feel cold towards his Mother who had made everything. And so, using the power that the Mother had given him, Jakel ripped the Lovers apart, separating them into Night and Day. But even this was not enough to quench his jealously, his greed; he was still hungry for power.

Some time went by, and the Mother tried to overlook Her son's corruption, but it grew more and more difficult. Distraught, the Mother decided to breathe life into another, a final creation. From the pure soil of the island Creat, the Mother molded woman and man. Unlike Her, they did not possess infinite knowledge and would need to be guided. For this task, three sets of guardians were created and each given their own human charges.

The Dragonae, fierce yet wise, would guard their clans and teach them the lessons the Mother had instilled in them. They would do this in the Southwest lands known as Ungula. Their numbers were few, but their loyalty to their people was great.

The Kinay, giant aquatic serpents, would teach and guide their tribes in the ways they would need for their group of large islands, known as Oeste. Their knowledge of prudence and production gave them an edge, even without limbs.

Finally, the wolves of old, the Luposi, would guide the inhabitants of Jordklode and keep them close until they were no longer needed. The wolves held their humans close, teaching them about family, about trust, and above all else, about love.

Even in all their differences, the guardians were fierce protectors, fair judges, and loving teachers. Above all, however, all the guardians were charged with the duty of implementing six rules among their humans:

1—Trust the Mother and develop a relationship with Her.

2—Treat each other with justice, equality, and compassion.

3—Abstain from greed, hate, and jealousy.

4—If a wrong is done, punish with less severity than is deserved.

5—Remember kindness in all situations, but give the decision to the Mother when it is required.

6—When one has found their soul-partner, they may bond in two ways; first, they may bond publicly, through a wedding, this is optional; secondly, they must bond before the eyes of the Mother with a Total Embrace of Mind, Body, and Soul.

These are the Laws of the Guardians.

However, it was a mere century before the five Luposi, along with their human clans, parted ways. The only two wolf clans remaining in Jordklode's Northeast were Hingst and Kongeorn, the latter being far more powerful in number. These two stayed loyal to the Mother; as history shows, the rest of the wolves, along with the Kinay, strayed from their Mother. Outside of Kongeorn and Hingst lands, chaos and human greed reigned supreme.

And so, four hundred and one years after the Creation, the first war began in the south of Jordklode. Less than a century later, another bloody war took place, this time in the North, where Kongeorn's power continued to grow. Two more northern wars occurred in the following two hundred years. The first gave birth to a new superpower, the kingdom of Feroxia, whose king, Pridbor I, bathed in the blood of his slaves. The second war, the Disputed War, was between Kongeorn—with her ally Hingst—and the new Feroxian kingdom.

This would not be the last conflict between these two.

And it would not be the last time innocent blood was spilled.

But there was, at the end of the eighth century, a rising Sol on the horizon, an icy blue one, whose name would be forgotten.

But her story will never be.

Part One

Chapter 1
All Is as It Should Be

Aboard a mighty vessel, I sail the seas, torching vile cities and raising the pure from the ashes. By my side, and all around me, are the ones I call family, the people who encourage me to keep sailing and searching. Winds from every direction, south and north, west and east, take turns washing my hair with the smell of salt. As the waves crash against the sides of my ship, they sigh, speaking my name as they do,

"Vita…Vita…Vita…" All is well. All is right. All is as it should be.

I awoke to the sounds of clansmen stomping, their boots unnecessarily heavy. Horses neighed from the stables, as if to herald the rising of the great red Sol. I stretched, feeling the muscles in my legs shake as I granted them mobility. Rubbing my eyes, I stood, exposing my skin to the unexpected chill of the room, and felt the cramping feeling in my abdomen. Regretting my decision, I hopped back beneath the blankets.

But then, the tendril reached my nose. That heavenly scent, the aroma of what I loved most about life: breakfast. Weighing the risks and benefits, I finally chose the better option.

As I dressed, my eyes wandered to the fireplace, to its ornate and intricate carvings in the slick and polished wood. Masterfully made, though its maker was unknown. Mine was the only room in the keep with such a treasure. In fact, mine was perhaps the only room in all of Jordklode to hold such history and elegance.

As my mind recalled lesson upon lesson of historical events, it remembered one in particular. Over two hundred years before my own birth, Hamish the Strong arrived at Redefalk—at that point, a much newer keep. He charged through the gates, bearing a message of great importance. But that message would never come from his lips. Hamish the Strong had been mortally wounded, and, no later than he was laid in front of my fireplace, did he pass into the Etter world.

Though he had never spoken it, the message was clear. Death to Kongeorn. In my room, war had been declared on a rising power. A rising power whom we would not soon forgive.

I thought on the story as I readied myself for the day. It was truly astonishing how one corner of the world could hold such importance, how one room could yield such history.

After my hair was tamed into braids, and my monthly visitor attended to, I began to wander the halls in my riding clothes, following the aroma of food, glorious food. When my patience could take no more, I barreled towards the meal hall. Tapestries flew by and weapons on walls became a blur. To my left was a particular tapestry, one of my lineage, or at least, the most formidable woman in my lineage.

The fading burgundy background did her no justice. The fire she brought to life was far brighter, far more eye-catching, like the scars she wore.

Nana had always been proud of her scars. She said each one told a story, and I made it my business to know every one of them. Nana was the only one who didn't mind my nosy nature, mostly because she shared it. The first story I learned was of the scars on her shoulder: islands of pale skin adorning her left shoulder from when she first met my grandfather.

"My papa had been angry with me, so he sent me on patrol. I was out by a creek bed when I heard a rustle in the bushes. Brandishing my short sword, I crept forward ever so slowly." She would always pause at suspenseful points, just as Da did. Like mother, like son. "Unable to be patient any longer, I jumped through the bushes and right onto your grandfather's hunting trap. The porcupine needles went straight through my skin, near through my shoulder. Of course, being the man he was, your grandfather fixed me up, happy enough to be in the presence of a woman, let alone a goddess like myself." Nana enjoyed embellishing.

In the tapestry, her eyes were a deep purple, but when I had known her, they had always been a pale blue or grey. The Kongeorn eyes had skipped her, I suppose. But the fire in her heart was testament to her name as Kongeorn, and testament to why I loved her so. Testament to why, when she passed, my four-year-old self didn't even want to get out of bed. Where my brothers left me and Da didn't have time, Nana had always been there, understanding.

Mother often had to clean up after the boys, and my godfather after Da, so Nana and I, out of necessity, were thick as thieves.

"Miss you," I put a hand to her embroidered one and sighed. After taking a moment, I came back to my senses and again stalked down to breakfast. It enticed me, bringing forward a primal need. Returning to full speed, I gained momentum and burst through the oak doors, shouting,

"*Juede'urjen!*" All the men and women in the hall responded back with the morning greeting. Their faces blended together: people I knew and saw every day. *Familiar.*

Striding towards my place near the dais, I detected movement out of the corner of my eye. Stopping, I waited for him to pounce. As his dark fingertips met my shoulder, I grasped his forearm, and threw his body over my shoulder and onto the floor.

"What are you doing, you *svater*? You know, of all the three hundred and something times you've done that, you've only succeeded in gettin' me to the ground once." With my hands on my hips, I stared down at him mockingly.

"Well, Stormy, I've always kept you on your toes, haven't I?" He reached up and my hand clutched his, pulling him up. His nickname for me was one he had kept since the day we met.

I had had no more than five birthdays when we received word that a ward from the West, from the house of Hingst, our closest ally, would be coming to us.

As the sprinkles of rain misted around us, my brothers and I ran rambunctiously through the stable yards. The youngest and only girl, I was left in the mud. Despite this, I never gave up trying to show my brothers I could run with them.

After being knocked down by all four of my older brothers, I finally exploded in rage at one of them. Luckily for me, it was Amund, who was only ten at the time. As the eldest, he felt he was the most chivalrous of all. Especially so compared to Einar, who was eight, and the twins, Elof and Geir, who were six at the time. Einar was always mean and threw temper tantrums, while Elof and Geir were the ones who caused said tantrums with their bountiful pranking. I was just along for the ride, trying to keep up, as I was that day.

"Leave us be, Vita." Amund ruffled my blond hair. "Playing with swords is for boys." His comment had stung. I knew what was expected of me, but I never wanted to fulfill those expectations. I thought them boring, to say the least. As Amund ran off, sword in hand, my other brothers followed. Elof and Geir flashed by in a whirl, unknowingly knocking me down and into the mud. It caked my face and penetrated my nostrils, causing me to sputter and cough. As I lay trying to get the mud out of my mouth, Einar sauntered by, eying me through slitted lids.

He stopped and turned, as if obligated, and held out his hand to me. I reached out to take it, but was only welcomed with his other hand splattering mud back on my face and into my nose. After that, without a word, Einar stood and calmly walked off. Eyes watering, I only laid in the mud, not wanting to get up. My chunky frame ached in embarrassment. And there, in the middle of the muddy courtyard, my five-year-old self truly felt the part of the forgotten little sister.

I hate him.

Soon enough, I heard the squish of mud underneath boots, prompting me to take my face out from behind mud-caked hair. Peering up, I took in the sight of my godfather, a man who always had time for a fragile little girl named Vita.

"My little Euna," Bjorth knelt to my level, "what has happened ta you?" Picking me up, he did not give me much time to explain before wiping the mud from my face. He smiled one of sympathy before carrying me into our keep. I laid my head against his giant chest, completely nestled in his arms, as Bjorth carried me to a part of the keep I had never been to.

Opening my eyes, I took in the sight of furs all around me. I gazed in delight, wondering what magic could be found in this room of treasures. I grinned a gap-toothed grin as Bjorth took my muddy coat from me. As he covered me in furs, I realized just how cold and wet I was.

"Your Da and I used'a come to this room as boys. When his older brothers decided we was too small ta play with 'em, we made our own fun." Bjorth chuckled and turned away from me. He bent over and opened a trunk that I hadn't noticed behind him. Without getting up, I tried to peer around, but to no avail. When he turned back, he held something in his large hands.

"Believe i' or no', this was mine back in the day." Almost sheepishly, the behemoth of a man offered me the cloth in his hands. Taking it from him, I examined the cloth before unfolding it to see what was inside. When I saw the flash of metal, I jumped to my feet.

"It's a sword! A real-life sword!" I ran to him to give him a hug, but was stopped short.

"Rule number one: no running with it 'til ya learn ta use it." I nodded, proud to have my own sword. For the first time, my very own sword.

I could only imagine what had been going on in Bjorth's head for him to give a five-year old an actual, metal sword. That was, until I realized it was dulled and blunt, so I couldn't actually hurt anyone too badly.

But just because I couldn't hurt anyone didn't mean I couldn't show it off. And boy, did I show it off. Every man, woman, and child who made the mistake of walking by me paid tribute to my new weapon, whom I had named Wolf-tail. After showing my father and receiving his congratulations, I went and showed my mother.

"Mami, look what Bjorth gave me!" I squealed with delight as I held up the dull blade. My mother half-smiled, her eyes barely passing over me.

"That's wonderful, V."

Grumpy at the lack of attention, I stalked away to find Amund. Maybe *he* would appreciate it.

He scrutinized it, balancing the hilt and blade on his pointer finger. After he was finished inspecting Wolf-tail, he made a show of giving it back and shaking my hand before inviting me to play war. After that, I ran after my brothers, trying to hit at least one of them, but was always slower and on the receiving end. Soon, however, I made a plan, the *ultimate* plan.

Covering myself in mud and leaves, I hid in the shrubs next to the paths my brothers always took. When I saw them pass, I jumped out and placed Wolf-tail's point right at Amund's chest.

After finally besting someone, let alone Amund, I squealed in victory, proud of that monumental moment of triumph. That is, until he picked me up and threw me over his shoulder. Though he was only ten, he was strong enough to wield a halberd and carry me without effort. I was paying special attention to the way mud splattered on his boots when I heard the sound of horses.

"Turn me around, Amund, turn me around!" I demanded as I pounded on his back. Without another word, Amund set me down gently, eyes set on what I assumed was a glorious parade of dazzling white stallions. When I turned, however, I only saw a solitary roan mare with two figures on her back. Bored, I focused on something else, a fly, perhaps. In doing so, however, I failed to see the way the second figure was peering at me.

Later that evening, I was finally introduced to Adam of Hingst, the house of Kongeorn's—our—new ward. He was older than me, which I found irritatingly familiar, even if he was friendlier than all my brothers. As our new ward, Adam was to be treated as family, and, though I didn't mean to, I was the first to call him, "brother." After he had arrived, and after we had become friends, I had come to realize that I didn't need to learn to keep up with my brothers. I had my own agenda, and Adam was happy to tag along.

And now, together still, we swaggered to our seats near my mother, who was already eating breakfast. Instead of inquiring about our sleep, she was acting unusually interested in her porridge. When I said her name, she jumped and looked up, startled at the greeting.

"Oh! Hello, Vita, Adam. I was just thinking about the boys and your father…" She trailed off. Ever since my father and four older brothers had left for scouting, my mother had been somewhat nervous. I, on the other hand, kept full faith in them; they had always known how to fight for themselves. After all, my father was the best warrior in all of Jordklode. And he would never let us forget it.

Every opportunity he got, Da would tell us tales of his own conquests or the stories of our nation's creation. The former enthralled and inspired me, while the latter enchanted me beyond all reason. Amund, Einar, Elof, Geir, Adam, and I would spend countless evenings on the rug before the fireplace listening to these tales.

"The wolves of old," he'd begin, "would run through the forest with the first of the aboriginal houses. Each house had their own wolf. The oldest was Hjorth, who hunted the mighty stag of the forests. The second was Ulv, who would slink around waiting for his brothers to slip up, so he could take their trophy. The third was Egern, who would play jokes on his brothers and scare off their kills. The last two, however, were different." It was always at this point that Da would pause for dramatic effect,

"The one was not from the forest at all, but came from the grasslands; he was innovative and free, he was Hingst. The final was no brother at all, but a sister. She was bravest, but cunning and patient, like a bird of prey: she was Kongeorn.

"They ruled Jordklode in harmony, until Hjorth caught the scent of a new wolf. He took charge to investigate and came across a female wolf from the South. He experienced a new kind of love and left his family to live anew." Da always told us that each of the wolves had a spirit that lived within our world, that their will was drawn from an omniscient Creator, who looked after all of us. That theme was forever present in our lives and in Da's stories.

Before long, however, Amund left our stories behind. One day, he told me he wanted glory, not children's stories. Yes, my feelings had been hurt, but I still continued to listen to Da with my remaining brothers.

"One day," he would continue, "after Hjorth had gone away to find his own lands near the mountains, Ulv decided he would rule over his brothers and sister. He wanted to trap them and trick them into fighting each other. It wasn't long before Kongeorn caught on to his schemes and rallied her remaining brothers to chase off their malevolent brother. He slipped off into the shadows and out of sight, but was never far away, always sulking." Amund wasn't the only one who wanted more than history; soon after Amund's departure, Einar left our circle as well.

"The two brothers and their sister remained as a pack and patrolled their family land. But before long, Egern decided he wanted more than just patrol. So, he bid his brother and sister farewell and followed the trail of Hjorth to the South. Only Hingst and Kongeorn remained." It didn't take much more for Elof and Geir to leave after Einar, since they didn't want to be around their sister and the ward.

"When the winters grew harsh and the wolves became cold, they would look to each other for warmth and companionship. Their bond lasted through time and, as their kingdoms emerged, Hingst named Kongeorn his queen, and has bowed to her ever since." The stories of our past, the history of our peoples, were soaked up by Adam and me. We craved the stories, and, had the war not started, we would have still been listening as Da told them.

It had been only days after my twentieth birthday when we received the falcon. It carried a letter of warning: King Alfred of the Feron line and Feroxian kingdom had finally, expectedly, declared war.

Through the years, Adam and I had been well schooled in many subjects, but politics and history were what we studied most. And we knew the evil man Alfred was. In his youth, he had pillaged countless civilian towns in the name of his father. In his mid-life, he conquered towns and took their women as his slaves. And then, he set his eyes on us.

Greedy, slimy, and cruel, King Alfred was the most horrendous king to ever rule over the kingdom to our west. Even Pridbor I had had a cause. Alfred just killed and raped for the hell of it, which made him all the more dangerous. Da, knowing as well as we did, decided to refrain from combat as long as possible. He dreaded the idea of war, especially a war that would mean Alfred's troops on our land, doing Mother-knows-what to our people. So, when the falcon arrived, Da receded from daily life.

He confined himself to his study or the council room, either way, always thinking of strategies, of other ways to go about the situation. This lasted months, even through Amund's wedding. When finally he decided on a plan of action, no one questioned him. He, along with my brothers and other well-trained warriors, were to go scouting along the borders of the Disputed and Feroxian lands. Why Adam and I were excluded, I had no idea, and—in all honesty—it infuriated me. What I wouldn't give to get my axe on a Feroxian soldier; it was any Kongeorn's dream. Regardless of what I wanted, however, Adam and I had been left behind.

The day they left was my twenty-first birthday.

Adam and I sat down in our chairs and began to inhale the food that had been set before us. We had no shame, and would never have shame, when it came to food. Every so often, one of us would decide to say something along the lines of, "How did you sleep?" But no answer was ever given: our mouths were too full. When finally we had eaten our fill, we turned to each other, knowing what the other would say. It was our daily ritual.

"Race you to the stables!" I challenged and began to sprint to the doors, Adam at my heels.

"Wait, Vita," I heard Mother's voice slice through the room, killing the jolly atmosphere, "not today. I would like to have a word with you." Her tone worried me, so I changed course and followed her from the hall, dejected. Adam, assuming I was in trouble, let a smile tug at his lips before turning and going to the stables by himself. I merely rolled my eyes at him and followed my mother, becoming increasingly nervous with every step. We passed some of the same paintings I had grown up making fun of. Many were of brave warriors, others depicted wise diplomats. There was only one woman though, and she deserved all of my reverence.

My thoughts drifted off and away to a different time, one that I wished I could have experienced, one that Da had told us stories about.

The stories, of course, weren't his own, but had come from a book: *The Adventures of Octavia.* It was a collection of stories from the point of view of a fleet commander who shared a name with the title. She had sailed for half a century, and I always wanted nothing more than to do this as well. However, the opportunity for this had never presented itself, and I was left with only my daydreaming and her portrait as fodder for that dream's flame.

When we had finally stopped, I realized Mother and I were in front of her and Da's bedchambers.

"Vita, I…" Before continuing, Mother headed inside her chambers, leaving me to follow and ponder why she wished to speak to me. I closed the doors behind me and prepared myself for the news of some idiot prince wanting my hand in marriage. But this news never came. Mother simply sat on her bed, staring at the floor as if it were the only thing in the room. When I attempted to walk to her, she cut me off, "Vita, there's been an attack…"

"By whom, Mother?" I questioned, suddenly standing stiff.

"By King Alfred the Cruel. He and his troops ambushed your father and his men at their camp." She stopped abruptly. A single tear ran down her cheek and plopped onto her gown.

I tried to process her words. King Alfred had a grudge against us, of that I had no doubt. He and the Feroxian kingdom had lost a war to my family only thirty years before, but for him to show this kind of delayed retaliation—it didn't make any sense.

I shook the confusion from my mind and focused on the next steps.

"Mother, when they return, we shall have our revenge. We are Kongeorn! We will fight back, and those faithless Ferons will know us by fear and blood. Mother, we must prepare for Da and my brothers' return!" I started to pace, planning out strategies for training in my head. We could send scouts, spies, feign a marriage proposal to the king's son. I'd be damned if I wasn't going to do something.

I thought my mother would whole-heartedly agree. In many ways, she was far more skilled than Da, far more daring.

It had been soon after Adam's arrival many years before that my brothers had revoked their promise to play with me. Distraught, and not yet trusting the new ward from the West, I went to my mother, head hanging low.

"Mami, why won't the boys play with me?" My lip trembled as I spoke.

She immediately stopped what she was doing and straightened, only to crouch down to my level a few moments later. She sighed heavily and shook her head.

"Because they believe themselves to be better than you." There was a type of shame in her voice, the kind that came with knowing something was your own fault.

"But why?" My eyes were tearing up and my chin quivered.

"Because I have not raised them the way I should have. I am sorry, V. The world has overwritten my lessons."

"Then who will I play with?" I hadn't quite understood her answer, yet I persisted in my pursuit of understanding.

"Why don't you play with Adam? I am sure he would love a friend."

"Will you play with us, too?" The words sprang from my mouth without warning, surprising both my mother and me. She nodded hesitantly before taking my hand and leading me out of the keep.

It was months later that I saw just how similar we were.

"Again, you two!" She shouted at Adam and me as we trained. Instead of playing war, like I had thought we would do, Adam and I were training nearly as hard as members of the legion, though we were only six and nine. My mother had been the one to train us, to tell us which moves to do, which steps to make, which breaks to take. After hours of training, the temper within me burst forth.

"Mami! We train, and we train, and we train! Why do we do so much? I do not see my brothers out here for half of it!" I had thrown down my dulled blade and stormed towards her. My cheeks were red, no doubt, just as Da's got when he was angry.

My mother simply eyed me, one eyebrow raised. She inhaled before looking at me pointedly.

"I train you harder because that is how your life will be. You are far too young to understand, but you will have to fight, tooth and nail, for respect. For any kind of it. Your brothers will always have it easy, and they know it, though I've tried to tell them. But you, Vita, will have to work twice as hard to get what you want."

"Why? Why is it so much more difficult for me? And Adam, too!"

"As I said, you cannot possibly understand it, but you will always be discriminated against, because you are female, and Adam, because he is a foreigner."

"Well," my temper had subsided, and the gears in my young mind were turning quicker and quicker, "why don't we just change that, then?"

"Vita," my mother scoffed, "it isn't that easy."

"Then I will just have to work as hard as you say." And with that, I turned on my heel, picked my sword back up, and commenced to sparring with Adam again.

My mother leaned against the fence as my father walked up and gently shoved her.

"She's your daughter, through and through." My mother muttered, still watching Adam and me.

"Whatever do you mean?" My father grinned, scratching his stubbled chin.

"She's far too sensitive as to what people think of her." My mother turned her head to address my father directly.

"Well, at least she's got enough of you in her to do something about it." My father chuckled as he said the words, before my mother punched him in the chest.

"And don't you forget it."

To tell the truth, the only reason my mother wasn't on that scouting mission same as Adam or me was because we were still judged. We were still pinned as too controversial to aid our own nation. But I knew, just as much as I knew that the Luna would rise at night, that my mother would go into battle beside my father if she needed to; after all, she had done it once before.

As I looked at my mother then, I knew that, despite the judgment, she would be ready to fight alongside my father, just as she had taught Adam and I to do so long ago. She had shown her tenacity in teaching us, in training us, and I knew she would not hesitate to join the rest of our family on the battlefield when we responded to this ambush.

"Vita! Stop it! Your father is dead!" I froze, the present dashing back to me, giving me whiplash. *Dead? There is no way: Da is the strongest man to ever live, the wisest to ever rule, he can't die. She is mistaken.* "V… They were ambushed in the night while Einar was on watch. He stayed in the shadows while your father was flayed; he watched while your father suffered. Geir and Elof were found in their tent, their throats cut from ear to ear. Your oldest brother, my brave Amund, he was able to send a falcon explaining what happened. I received it last night."

My heart stopped, horror crashing over me in waves. I became acutely aware of all my senses. Of the scent of hickory and pine, the chirps of the birds outside, the feel of my cotton leggings. The world spun, making me nauseous. My father and the twins were gone, but there was still hope for Einar, for Amund.

"Mami… what of Einar? Of Amund? What of them? Surely they escaped?" My hands were shaking with fear, with rage. *This isn't possible.* My emotions threatened to burst forth, through my skin and out into the world. *There must be something.* I waited for her answer as silence fought to deafen my ears. My heartbeat thumped again in my throat: *thump, thump, thump.* When finally she spoke, I was unsure I had heard her correctly over the rapid beating of my heart, over the sensory overload I was experiencing.

"Einar is alive." My heart jumped once it understood this revelation. There was still hope; I still had one brother left alive by this massacre.

"Where is he?" I implored, needing to see him for myself. All of the negative thoughts and feelings which identified him in my mind were stifled as I tried to hold onto him, the last piece of normalcy in this surreal nightmare.

"He has been confined to his room, guarded."

"Why, Mami?"

"When I met him at the door, he just—he just handed me a piece of parchment. He just stood there and let—he let me read it. When I called the guards and Bjorth, he let them take him away. All he did was look at me." She trailed off, her voice wavering, thick with emotion, though she tried to hide it.

In her hand, I noticed for the first time a crumpled sheet of parchment. Slowly, cautiously, I made my way to her. I took the letter. It read:

Mother,

If you would, think back,
To all the times you neglected me, ignored me,
Thought of me as just another son.

You underestimated me, Mother;
You always have.

Even when I told you that Amund was weak, that he
Would never rule the way I could,
You dismissed me.

Even when I tried to tell you all the power I had been given by the real *god we*
should be worshipping, you laughed.

You laughed at me, Mother.

But you will see.
You will see that I have the divine right to rule.
And I have used it.
With it, I was able to make an ally out of our greatest enemy.

With it, I was able to skin the man I once called "Father," murder the boys I once called "brothers," and crush the heart of the only one in my way.

I have come back now, Mother, for you.
I want you to see me.
I want you to see your true son, all that he has become.
And I want you to fall to your knees and beg.

For your life.
For forgiveness.

And, believe me, once you see my power, you will beg.

I crumpled the letter in my hands and threw it with all my strength into the brazier, where a harsh fire burned red. All I wanted to do was thrash and scream and spit, but none of that would do anything. I stared into the flames, letting their heat encourage my fury. It was then that Mami spoke.

"V, what are we going to do?" She squeaked like a child asking its mother for help. The fury stuttered. I was not the ruler; I had only some knowledge of how to handle the situation, yet she was asking *me*. She was the experienced one, the trusted one. She was the one who knew how to deal with times of crisis. She looked at me as if I had the answers, as if I would come through with some solution. I held my breath, suddenly feeling the weight of the world on my shoulders, as if she had passed it to me with a single question. *I don't know what to do.*

After a few moments of fearful silence, I heard my mother, gaining her trademark composure, exhale slowly: "The news will be announced tonight, and at dawn, he dies."

An execution? Another death? How—why—I can't—no… she's right. Justice must prevail.

At the thought, my core grew hot, and I needed to get out into the cool air, so I sprinted out of the room, ran down the halls and out to the gnarled forest. Dashing between trees, and jumping over rocks, I let the tears come. Moss and fir trees whirled by, streams of green and auburn encompassing me. I felt the coming acid and stopped, stooping over at the nearest tree trunk. I hurled the contents of my breakfast, unable to stop it from coming up. Wiping my mouth on my sleeve, I breathed deep and put my forehead against the cool bark. After a few moments, the rough wood began to dig into my skin, so I stepped back. My eyes looked down at my boots, boots that Da had made me for my birthday. He had made them from my first Sorve kill.

Not long after my fifteenth birthday, Da had taken me, and only me, on a hunt to the North. I had been nervous, but as I saw the herd of elk-like creatures approach, the adrenaline kicked in. I notched the arrow and pulled back, just as I had been taught. I released and exhaled, hitting one of the female Sorve in the ribs. It wasn't a great shot, but it did the job. That, and the time it took Da to make the boots of the Sorve's grey pelt, were his gifts to me that year.

As I watched him shape the pelt into boots, he told me of the delicate balance within our world.

"V, in times of peace, we can feel the presence of the Mother. She creates life and gives us the opportunity to do the same. But you must understand," he paused briefly to cut the excess sinew, "She expects us to return to Her after we have lived. Just like this Sorve, we die as well. To break that cycle takes great and terrible power."

I didn't understand.

"Break the cycle? You mean to come back from death, from the Etter?" I asked, leaning forward.

"Yes. To come back from the dead is something only the power of the Mother or Jakel can achieve," Da explained, continuing to work on my boots.

"But what about the Northern Tribes? The stories say they have magic, that they can bring back animals from the dead. The rumors even say that their leader is immortal, that he cannot be touched by death." I found myself whispering as I raised my question and obliged my curiosity.

Da chuckled.

"You should really spend less time with Gyda. She's going to make you believe that Kinay and Dragonae still roam Omnia."

I didn't speak.

Da sighed, setting down his knife and cord, before looking at me.

"Okay, okay, I'll tell you about the Northern Tribes, but *don't* tell your mother I told you, okay?" I nodded eagerly, waiting for him to continue. "The rumors of magic are true. When the Mother still walked Omnia, She bestowed on the Northern Tribes, well, one in particular—the Ordliqt—a gift of her power. Their leader, the

Sapien, is immortal because he is our bridge to the Mother. When we have questions about what She wants, we ask him."

I looked at Da, trying to process all of this information, trying to compare it to what I already knew. Before he could start working on my boots again, I piped up,

"What about the other magic? I've heard of magic being used in the Seventy Provinces of Daygn, and in Feroxia, too!"

"Let me be clear: any magic that does not come from the Northern Tribes is derived from Jakel's power. It is unnatural. You must stay away from it." His tone was serious, and his face was hard, authoritative. I recoiled slightly.

"But how can I tell the difference?"

"You'll know it when you see it. You'll feel it here." He pointed to my heart, and all I could do was nod.

I exhaled. *This isn't real. I'm going to wake up and none of this will have happened. I'll eat breakfast and race Adam to the stables. Mami won't cry, no one will have died. I just need to wake up.* I pinched myself on the arm. Nothing changed. Shifting some, I pounded my head against the tree. *Ouch.* But still, nothing changed. I stooped for my knife, desperation bubbling. *Maybe you have to draw blood.*

I turned my head and jumped. Frozen, I stood with my hand still slowly inching towards my dagger. A she-wolf with eyes of ice, graceful and silent, had snuck up on me. She studied me as I did her.

Why hasn't she killed me yet?

Her coat was white and gray, smooth in pattern until the tip of her tail, which was black as night. We both stood unmoving, taking in the other. Without warning, she started towards me, head lowered. Instinct told me to reach for my dagger, to throw it, but a voice somewhere inside convinced me otherwise. The she-wolf stopped before me and lay down, head still bowed. In return, my knees bent until I found myself kneeling in the grass as well. It was then that she looked up.

In her eyes, where I had seen the icy blue before, I now saw so much more. I saw the stories Da told us as children playing out in real time; I saw my brothers dying in the night, and I saw a woman wearing the skin of a wolf, rising above all, letting out a battle cry, and riding into the sun. When the visions ebbed away, the she-wolf's eyes faded and her head fell to my lap. The rise and fall of her chest ceased, and a great wind shook the trees.

I sat for a moment, taking in the events which had just transpired. It could have just been the grief, but I couldn't shake the feeling of another presence. I took another deep breath and exhaled, trying to breathe out the crazy. I shook my head and did as I felt I should. It was then that I pulled my dagger from my boot and skinned the she-wolf. And so, I sat until dusk, shaping her fur into a cloak, with her head protecting my own. When I finished, I donned my cloak, avoiding the teeth that remained on the hood, and hiked home, still trying to understand that which I could only explain as a trip.

The forest seemed still, as if no creature dared to move or cry out in my presence. The trees remained static, their branches rigid and frozen in the cool night air. In the stillness, a burden began to weigh down upon me, cloaking me like the furs on my shoulders. It sobered me, taking my attention away from the visions and cynical thoughts, and plopped me right where I would stay. I could not hide from it, nor—I found—did I want to. My duty to my people, to my name, bore down on me, and I refused to shake it.

Chapter 2

The Song of a Mother

As a child, Einar had never wanted to play, even when Da made him. He never liked swordplay, nor horse riding, nor even studies with Adam and me. In fact, no one ever knew where he was, for he was always by himself.

It didn't matter who it was. After his twelfth birthday, Einar just stopped interacting with us. At first, Amund tried to talk to him, to get him to train, but Einar would always turn away and walk off by himself.

Elof and Geir tried to rouse him with their pranks; they hoped that he would chase them after finding his riding boots stuffed with horse manure. Instead, he would just look at them, his face void of emotion, and cast the boots into the fireplace.

Adam and I were the last ones to try to help Einar. We'd offered to go out riding with him, or to train with him, but his response was always the same—in that there was no response. Einar would ignore us completely, acting as though we didn't even exist.

Years passed and we stopped trying to help him, to befriend him. I didn't want to give up on him, but he gave me no choice.

From then on, Einar lived a life shrouded in mystery to all but himself.

The only clue we had ever gotten that Einar was harboring violent tendencies was when Elof and Geir walked in on Einar, only fifteen at the time, cutting open the corpse of a blue-bird in his room as he chanted foreign words over it. The twins told Adam and me in hushed whispers of how the bird's bones floated from its body, only to turn to ash. When they told us, I could feel the fear, the apprehension in my heart and knew that the magic Einar practiced was derived from Jakel.

Einar never explained himself, and we never asked. Perhaps we thought that pushing something like that away would make it disappear; it seemed we were horribly mistaken.

The Mourning Fires had been lit for my lost brothers and father. As I made my way to the center of the fort, I noticed many a mother with her child staring speechless into the flames. None of them looked up to watch me walk by. They stood motionless, like sentinels. Shadows behind them flickered and danced to and fro to their own somber melody.

Each woman had the same look on her face, the same kind of numbness painted on. It was as if the only living things were the fires themselves.

One woman, different than the rest, looked as if she might throw herself into the same flames which reflected in her golden eyes. She was the only one to look up, and, as she watched me walk, I saw her move her hand to a pendant at her chest.

Watching them, I realized that I was not the only one betrayed. A party of eighteen warriors left that day, and only one traitor had returned. Other sisters had lost brothers, children lost fathers, and so many wives had lost their beloved husbands. As I arrived at the fort, I saw, through a second landing window, the silhouette of one of those such wives.

Amund's wife, Karina, was of Hingst blood, but always considered herself one of us. She loved Da, Mami, my brothers, Adam, and I as if we were her own kin. She treated me as sister, showing me a type of bond I had never known before. When their betrothal was announced, I could not have been happier. Their wedding had been one of the best nights of my own life. And now, she was left without the man she pledged herself to, a man whom I had seen look at her with such adoration and love and respect.

They had only been wed six months.

Drifting down the hall aimlessly, still clothed in my she-wolf cloak, I began to wonder if Adam knew. *When I didn't come to the stables, what did he do? When I didn't show up, did he look for me?* Not wanting to be alone in my own head, I made my way to his room instead of mine. I knew the path by heart; I had walked it countless times. My feet moved on their own accord, for my mind felt too numb to direct them. Not even the portraits could stir me to a conscious mind.

When I came upon his doors, I saw they were open, beckoning me. Turning the corner, I removed the cloak and set my eyes on the bed where Adam lay sleeping. He knew I would come. After something like this, after a test of faith, I always came to him.

Wordlessly, I closed his doors, took off my boots and vest, and got in beside him. I turned on my side and watched as his dark chest rose and fell peacefully. I could only wish for that kind of peace then. At the thought of it, a single tear rolled down my cheek and plopped onto the pillow. Adam, hearing the small squeak that came from my lips, opened his eyes and turned over on his side to face me.

"It didn't take long for me to realize something was wrong," he whispered, reaching out a calloused hand to wipe the tear path from my cheek. "I knew where you'd go. So I hiked out there and saw you." He trailed off, assuming I knew what he would say if he continued.

Things like this had happened before. When Nana died and had passed into the Etter, everyone had told me to be happy, that she was in a better place with the Mother. But, even as a child, that had never made much sense. Yes, I believed in Heaven. But that still meant I couldn't be with the people I loved, like Nana. For weeks after Nana's passing, I had seen her everywhere, but had kept it from everyone for fear that they'd think me crazy. Everyone, that was, but Adam. He'd believed me, he said, because *he* had seen her, too.

But then we stopped seeing her, and people forgot about her. And I didn't want anyone to forget about Da, or Amund, or Elof and Geir. And I didn't want to be away from them. The thought of not seeing them every day, not playing victim to a prank, never hearing a story ever again—it broke my heart.

"Da, and Amund, and Elof and Geir, they—they're—" A crack in my chest cut me off, sending a sob through my body. Adam pulled me into his bare chest, where the smell of pine and horses and him engulfed me. There were no more words between us, only tears. I felt wet drops land in my hair, giving away Adam's own grief. He was just as much a Kongeorn as I was. He had sat through the stories and been on the receiving end of pranks and been bested in the training grounds. He knew what it felt like. He always did. Before long, between my sobs and the warmth of Adam around me, and the flames crackling in the fireplace, I drifted off into another world.

The song of a mother, sweet and loving, fills my ears. I look over to see a woman clothed in a purple tunic singing to a swaddled bundle. She croons and smiles as the child's fingers intertwine with her hair. The mother gives off a twinkling laugh, then looks up at me.

"I thought children were nothing more than tiny monsters to you," her voice echoes in the air. "Come on, she's just a baby. I'm sure you'll get along just fine."

I walk over to the mother, and now I see who she is: Karina, my brother's bride. Who is this child then? The child of my brother? The heir of Kongeorn? I am given no time to think before she thrusts the baby into my arms. Then, there is no doubt; the eyes staring back up at me are the same as my father's, as Amund's, as my own. She is a child of Kongeorn.

From my dream, I awoke in Adam's bed, the first traces of sunlight streaming in through the windows. He was already dressed and washed, seated beside me, waiting for my emergence from sleep. He was looking down at his fingers as they fiddled. I rubbed my eyes and propped myself on one elbow.

"So, I really do have to be there then, when my mother kills him." It was more statement than question.

"Yes, you will, Stormy." He looked down at the blanket under him. "But I will be there too. Always will be."

"*Svatus kud*," I whined, covering my face with a pillow and covering up the emotional appreciation below the surface. It was a defense mechanism that I knew he could see through, but I used it nonetheless. In the wake of being vulnerable, I couldn't let myself break again, even if the emotion was only gratitude.

Ignoring my groans, Adam pulled me from the bed and dragged me to my own room, with me fighting him the entire way. When I was inside my own room, he waved and closed the doors, leaving me to myself. I laid there, on the stone floor, refusing to get up. Before long, I gave in and got up, stretching. I nearly stumbled on my way to the cherry wardrobe, where all my clothing hung.

Unlike many of the older women, I always wore trousers instead of skirts or gowns. They just proved far too restricting for how I lived. Among the various furs and tunics, I found the one set that I never wanted to wear, and had hoped against all hope that I wouldn't have to. *But here I am.*

I put on the dark clothing of mourning: a black skirt, black bodice, and a black cloak. The cloak was to symbolize my own involvement in Einar's execution. Though I wasn't to be the executioner, I was of the same family, and had to act as a shadow, shrouded in darkness.

Once I had donned all of these garments, I strode to the courtyard, where, at dawn, my mother would remove my brother's head. Adam joined me as I arrived, taking my arm firmly, leading me through a crowd of friends, as if to keep me in check, secure. He knew me too well. The scene before me, however, was enough to make me want to turn and run.

Ahead of us was the Altar of Motus, where all executions took place. They were to be humane, no torture, and were to be paid witness by any and all, as well as the Mother. She named this altar for its purpose, for the compassion which was to be shown in the punishment. The sight of this stone, onyx and stained, was anything but compassionate. I could only remember one execution, and it was one Adam and I had snuck into.

All my life, Da had told us about the love of the Mother, how She cherished every one of Her children. All love came from the Mother, Da told me, and all hate came from Her fallen son, Jakel. Our job was to love others and accept them for their differences.

One of those differences was whom they loved. One of my father's friends and warrior, Oliver, was always there for Adam and me. When my mother wasn't around to teach us fighting stances or moves, Oliver would volunteer his time. He was patient and kind, always giving us ways to improve in constructive ways.

One day, Oliver brought another man to help us train. His name was Jesse. Before we began our lesson for the day, Oliver explained that Jesse was his husband. I was young and had yet to be exposed to the hate of the world, so I happily welcomed Jesse. Adam did the same.

For weeks, Oliver and his husband helped train Adam and me when my mother didn't have the time. On a few occasions, Jesse even let me test out his broadsword, which was far too heavy for me. I came to idolize both Oliver and Jesse; Adam and I even talked about how excited we were to one day fight alongside the two men.

Unfortunately, as we came to learn, there are those in this world who do not understand love and, instead, preferred hatred.

Da explained to Adam and me one day that Jesse had been killed and was in the Etter with the Mother. I asked him why Jesse had been killed, and my father could only look at me, complete defeat in his eyes.

"The woman who killed him does not believe that two men can love each other. She feels so much hate that she does not understand the ways of the Mother; she does not understand that their love was no threat to her."

"That makes no sense," I said, unable to comprehend how someone could go as far as to kill another simply because of whom that person loved.

"No, it doesn't. But—both of you, listen to me closely—you will find that there are people in this world that let hate blind them.

You must always remember to choose love, even when all the hatred of the world is bearing down on you."

Da told us that the woman who killed Jesse would be executed, as was the law. He told us to stay home. Of course, we didn't listen. In cloaks, Adam and I, still children, snuck past Bjorth and into the crowd of spectators gathered at the Altar of Motus.

The woman sneered at all who came to witness justice. As I looked at her, I felt hatred bloom in my heart. This woman, right in front of me, had killed my friend, a good man, just because he had a husband and not a wife. For the first time in my life, I *wanted* to hurt someone. I wanted her to feel the pain that I felt, that Oliver felt.

My father gave the woman a swift death, though still an execution. After seeing the woman's head roll, I vowed to never attend another execution. It was not the blood that scared me, nor the death, but the feeling I had gotten. Even as a child, I could feel how much I wanted this woman to bleed. I wanted her dead and out of the world. In retrospect, those feelings had terrified me, and I told myself to stay away from them. Funny how things like that work.

But then, I had no choice but to witness yet another execution, and this time, it was far too close to my heart, where the anger was already boiling. The crowd around me was still, waiting. Bjorth, holding his own battle axe, had rings around his eyes. They trailed on the ground, looking at nothing.

Da and Bjorth were cousins, the closest in age of any in our family; they shared a birthday. Bjorth was everything my father needed him to be and more: his best friend, his counsel, his partner in crime. Da had only ever met my mother because of a hunting trip Bjorth had set up. And after Mami's father had passed, Bjorth had escorted my mother down the aisle.

All these memories were no doubt playing through my godfather's mind. The pain was evident, there in the way his eyebrows drooped and his chin wavered. I had known the man all my life, and this side of him was brand new to me.

Then there was my mother. She stood, in all black, a hood shielding her face, to the side of the altar. In her hand, my father's favorite sword, one which he only ever took to the greatest battles: Videm. *Maybe that was why he perished; he was without it by his side.*

My mother paid no mind to the large crowd of people, men and women alike, who came to watch justice prevail. She only looked at the blade in her hand. *It would seem that she has died with him.* The words came across my mind, and I stepped forward, only to be pulled back by Adam, whose look told me what I already knew. *There is no touch in the world but of steel to skin that would comfort her now.*

As I thought this, the drums began to beat, signaling the arrival of the fiend who ripped my family apart.

My heart thumped faster and faster, and memories flooded forth.

Einar sitting in a corner by himself, unwilling to socialize at a family dinner. His grey eyes flitted between each family member, but when they landed on me, still young enough—still lonely enough— to reach out, they stopped. I stood up and jumped down from my chair. My plaited hair swung over and onto my shoulder as I waddled over to him.

"Einar, come to the table," my small voice spoke, full of the confidence only an untested toddler could wield.

"No," his voice, just as small as mine, was cold and harsh.

"But we miss you." I reached out a pudgy hand to help him up from his spot in the shadows.

"Vita, look at them" I turned briefly, doing as he said, but I still couldn't understand. "They don't care. Mother and Father haven't even noticed me here. They didn't even look away from Amund when you got up." My eyebrows furrowed, trying to make sense of it. I didn't understand then, but later, I began to.

Perhaps ten years later, when I was on the cusp of being a teenager and Einar an adult, I had a similar encounter with him, one that I hadn't wanted to have in the first place.

I had just finished sparring with Adam, who had been my best friend for eight years at that point. He was beginning to stop looking lanky and awkward, and starting to pack on muscle and confidence. All of which made my sparring victories few and far between.

After Adam had departed to wash off, I decided to walk around to the back side of the stable, just on a whim.

But, as I rounded the corner, I saw Einar there, slumped over, head in hands and *crying*. I had never seen him emotional; no one had. Something within me told me to just leave him be, that he needed to be alone. *But he's* always *alone.* I had reasoned with myself, finally making the decision to approach and sit next to him.

Like my other brothers, he was tall and lean with light eyes. Though his were grey and not blue. He wore his auburn hair shaved close to his head, much like Amund.

"Leave—leave me a—alone." He managed through hiccups. Though he meant the tone to be cold and mean, it merely came out as sad, almost like a cry for help. So, against my gut, I didn't get up and leave.

"I told you to get away!" His head rose from his hands, where I could see a large red burn on his right temple. "I don't want you here! No one does!" I breathed in and out, but still refused to move.

"*Svatus kud*, you little freak! Don't you know how to listen? When someone older than you tells you to do something, you do it! You do it and you don't question it. You don't ask why, you don't voice your opinion, you don't ignore them." His tone changed from angry to something indescribable. It was almost as if he began to address himself instead of me.

"You do what you are told, or you get punished. You don't question it. You don't question it." His eyes, ringed with red, stared through me, searching for something else, searching for something to fear.

That was enough for me: I couldn't sit through his rambling. All I had wanted was to help him, but I came away with more sorrow, more empathy, in my heart than I had thought possible.

The crowd stared at him, shackled and, disturbingly, smiling. His malicious eyes crinkled in satisfaction as he opened his mouth to reveal sharpened teeth. Blood, from his lips, stained their points.

My jaw clenched at the sight. This was a far cry from that day I had seen him in tears. Since that day, I had never seen him with any emotion other than smug pride or simmering fury. *What changed?*

Men and women around us held their breath as Einar stopped in front of my mother and turned to face her, all while Bjorth put a hand on the shackles at his back.

"Why so melancholy, Mother? You have so much to be thankful for. I did not fight when you set your dogs on me. I offered safety, peace, with going oh-so-willingly into custody. I offered you a chance to beg forgiveness. And yet, you still insist on this folly." His voice was quiet, steady, the way a snake slithers through the grass. He smiled as he stared her down. His attitude sickened me, and I felt that pushed down malice bubbling to the surface. *Do it, Mami. He does not deserve to breathe this air.* My skin increased in temperature as I watched, encouraging my mother wordlessly.

When my mother only looked down, Einar sighed and clucked his tongue. *Tsk, tsk.* This caught my mother's attention, and her head snapped up to take him in. To this, he merely sneered.

"So you still refuse to acknowledge my power?" My mother only peered at him. I could see a faint reflection of light under the shadow of her cloak. What had her son become? There was no doubt she blamed herself. Again, Einar inhaled.

"Do you see all these souls? Do you see them, Mother?" He snapped at her, attempting at intimidation. Knowing my mother, however, I knew he was failing. Yet, he persisted, "They are but grains of sand to be washed away by a great wave. A great wave," he turned then to address the crowd, looking everyone in the eyes before stopping at me, "which will decimate every man, woman, and child who has the nerve to proclaim the false name of this 'Creator.' It is coming, and I have been promised a place among them. Their god is far greater than yours, and he has made your blade nothing— "He was cut off as my mother swung Videm, separating head from shoulders and silencing him.

In the midst of her action, my mother's hood fell from her head, revealing red-rimmed eyes and dark circles, which made her appear far older than she was. I let a smile escape onto my lips, but it disappeared when I saw my mother's hands continue to move. The blade trembled in her hands as her eyes rose to meet my own. Without a single word, she turned the blade on herself, thrusting it into her ribs. As she fell, I found myself unable to be held back. Adam released me; I met her just as her head was about to hit the stone.

"Mami," I started, not knowing what to say. I could have asked why, but I already knew her answer. As I looked down into her eyes, it was as if I could see her memories flood to the surface. Einar, a toddler, running up to her, arms up, asking to be held. Einar, a boy, coming to her with a scraped knee, only to be turned away. Einar, almost a teenager, crying, asking her for help, for a hug, and her turning him away, telling him to 'stop crying; boys don't cry.' Her regrets, her memories, flooded from her mind into mind, and I knew. In her mind, she had murdered my father. In her mind, she had slain my brothers.

Yes, she had made mistakes. Yes, she could have done more, but no one could be blamed for the evil in his heart. None of this, I wanted to tell her, could have been changed. I was only silent, though, as she opened her mouth to speak.

"Fall to rise higher." With those words circling around my ears, she smiled a sad smile and drifted off to the next world. I sat there, on bloodied stone, unable to move, unwilling to move. I did not even cry. The only feeling in my heart was fury.

Mami. Tears would change nothing.

I shouldn't have been so callous. Nothing would change the past.

I am so sorry. But I needed to do something, anything, to deal with this new future.

"Bjorth," I reluctantly called to my godfather with uncomfortable authority, "see to it that my mother receives a funeral worthy of a Kongeorn," With nothing else to say, I gingerly laid my mother's head on the stone, placed a kiss on her placid forehead, and walked past, to the clearing where I first saw the she-wolf.

Fire engulfed my heart. An anger unlike any I had known surged through my veins. Einar had ruined the lives of so many with one letter. With one decision, he thought to see my people crumble. But it would not be. Yes, I had lost my own blood. Yes, I had watched my mother die in front of me. No one, not even a Guardian, could change that. Running away, sobbing until my tears turned to ash, none of that would help.

I stopped.

Running will not help. Crying will do nothing. Then what can I do?

Suddenly, the clearing I stopped in became blurred, warped. Grass-covered dirt sloped up and trailed down where it hadn't before. The ground below me became unstable. Around me, trees bent down, reaching for a piece of me, trying to scratch and scrape me. Looking down, I saw vines twisted around my fear-bound body. *There is nothing I can do.* They contracted, tighter and tighter, draining my strength, extinguishing my breath until I swayed, and fell to the ground. As my head met rock, the vision cracked.

Regaining my sanity, I sat up, taking in the reality before me. I had indeed been to this clearing before, but not with the she-wolf. I had been here as a child, with Da. It was here that Da had explained to me why the Mother could not meddle in human affairs; it was here that I began to understand our world.

"When the first clans were created," he began, "the Mother walked with them. She spoke as a friend, as a loving mother. It was Her intention to have a relationship with each of Her creations, Her children. Before the Great Creation, She was alone. Can you imagine, V? She had almighty and everlasting power, but no one to share it with. That was why She created us, and all of the clans.

"Every day, She would commune with the clans, but was sad to see that many people were unhappy. Just like when I see you upset, She was sad to see Her children upset. The more She saw of this, the sadder She became. Finally, when the clans went their separate ways, She could see that they did not want Her with them anymore. All, except Kongeorn. Our ancestors begged Her to stay, and for a while, She did. And Kongeorn prospered.

"Well, V, the other clans saw this and grew very angry, so you know what they did? They asked Jakel, the Prince of Darkness, to expel the Mother from Jordklode. And, well, he did."

"But Da," I asked, "how could Jakel hurt the Mother like that? I thought that was his *Mami*." My childhood curiosity knew no bounds.

"Jakel had stolen some of the Mother's power, long before your—and my—birth. He was jealous, and jealousy, like hate, can destroy hearts. He used that power to hurt the Mother, which is why She cannot walk among us anymore, V."

"But Mami says that the Mother is always with us," I pointed out, feeling proud at finding a hole in my father's story.

"Yes, your Mami is right. But she means in spirit. She can talk to us if She wants, but She can never actually be here. Just like when we die. V, when your Nana died, she went into the Mother's care, but she is still with us sometimes. Do you understand, V?" At that point, he was kneeling before me, eyes level with my own.

"Yes, I do, Da." I didn't, really.

Everything my father had tried to explain that day, in this clearing, had to have a point. Nothing ever just happens. Rubbing my aching skull, I pondered the thought. My mother's words then returned back to me. *Fall to rise higher.* There was no way I could just let the hate of my brother harden the hearts of my people. How, though, I had no clue.

Chapter 3
The Most Important Question

Without an answer, I returned to the keep, where I found the halls empty and myself drawn to the council room. On my journey there, I found my eye drawn to the walls, to the portraits. Each represented an important event in our history. An image of our first king, Gauthier, stood proud and tall. Down the line, I saw a depiction of my Nana killing an assassin before he was able to get to my great-grandfather. After that was a funeral for seven. My father's six older brothers and his father had been killed in the Battle of Tears during the Hateful Wars. It was because of that battle that my father had become king.

I suppose a new mural will be added soon enough. As the only remaining child of Andor and Dagmar, I was the only lawful claim to leadership. And, though I had never wanted this, I could not stand to disappoint my people. I would be the first queen of Kongeorn, the first woman to officially rule on her own, without a husband. The thought was both empowering and intimidating.

As I grew closer to the council room, where I had taken part—albeit a small one—in several matters before, the sound of argument grew increasingly loud. There were no men at the doors to bar an entrance, so I took the chance and pushed through the giant doors and into the council room.

Inside, four old men sat bickering. The leader, the ruler, of Kongeorn would make the number of council members five, a number sacred to the followers of the Mother, like us Kongeorns. As I stood, waiting, the four men continued still to quarrel. I caught snippets of their arguments.

"War is imminent, there is no denying that," Hakon insisted, voice scratchy, white hair corkscrewing out from his wrinkled head.

"But can we win it? Surely, with a *woman* at the front, we will fail," Rasmus interjected, loud and ignorant of my presence.

"She is the daughter of Andor, and she is stronger in mind and body than most men," Trond responded, ever faithful to me as my first teacher.

"Perhaps we should ask her ourselves," Simon, the quietest and oldest of the bunch, spoke for the first time. He turned his gaze to me before offering a welcoming smile. The rest of the men followed his line of vision and stopped their clucking immediately. Their conversation would need to be addressed, particularly Rasmus' quip about my ability to lead. Stepping down into the bowl-like stage, I remained silent. Hands behind my back, I met each set of eyes.

Hakon had been loyal to my father to a fault. When my father, at age ten, had been falsely charged with treason by his uncle, Hakon had vouched for him and had championed for him at his trial. For this, Hakon was rewarded with a life-long position on the council, but lived without his left hand thanks to Great-Uncle

Adolf's sword. He had always been kind and respectful to me, but only for my father's sake.

Rasmus had been my father's military trainer when he was still able to wield a sword. He believed in strict forms of masculinity, like those in the West and South believed. His favor would not be easy to gain. He favored even Einar over me.

Trond had been my teacher for as long as I could be taught. Through him, I learned the names, histories, and customs of far-off places, as well as the languages of some. He had also taught me the ways of war strategy. I already had his favor, and knew he would champion for me if the need arose.

Simon was the oldest man in our history, even though he was from the far south, where dark men such as he learned their way in the world. At one hundred twenty-four, he had the most cumulative amount of wisdom and knowledge to offer. He had seen parts of history that the books refused to tell. To him, my womanhood would not matter, but I would still have to prove myself, nonetheless.

As I eyed each man, I felt my confidence swell. Although these men were intimidating—winning each man's support would be its own obstacle—they had been my father's confidants. And, whether I liked it or not, they would be mine as well.

"I understand the doubts you may feel towards me and my potential leadership," I circled the council, stopping briefly at Rasmus, who didn't try to hide his scoff at "leadership." Each man reacted differently to my words. Rasmus, with his apprehension, then Hakon, who studied me, one eyebrow raised. Trond looked on me with a small smile on his lips; and Simon, who watched intently, devoid of telling emotion.

"I also understand that this council has been loyal to my father, may his soul rest." I stopped in front of them, standing proudly. "Be that as it may, I have decided to offer you all a proposition. If you are uncomfortable with being led by a woman, you have my leave to go." All the men, save for Simon, stiffened. "You will be removed from the council permanently. That being said, I believe it is also best to make additions and revisions to the way this council is run. I want to make this land a shining light for the future, and that cannot be done by those who prefer the past." My eyes rested on Rasmus, who visibly shrank under my gaze. I turned on my heel and mounted the stairs to leave. Turning my head briefly, I added,

"This meeting is over; we will convene again tomorrow after the lunch hour with our new members." Departing from the council room, I made my way to the stables, where I would ask the first of my four additions to join me. As the adrenaline of defending myself left my body, I felt strings of doubt tangle in my mind.

Where did that come from? Svat, *what if I was too forward?* Svatus kud, *Vita.* I shook my head at myself, marveling at this different side of me. I had no idea how I had done it, and it had all happened so quickly. But, looking back, I felt I had done well. Well enough, anyway.

Though the atmosphere was devoid of human sound, the animals of winter—white Sparx sparrows, Nickeroon crows, and common Pidges—sang into the brisk air. The horses neighed and whinnied in response. My own horse, Dagny, a brown and white filly, grew restless as I approached. The stall next to her, where Adam's black horse, Tyr, resided, was empty. Knowing Adam and knowing where he'd go, I mounted Dagny and headed further east, to the Evig-wood.

Adam and Tyr's tell-tale tracks were left in the mud. I sped Dagny to a gallop. Adam and I had once played in the woods to the East. It was far from my brothers and far from the real world we lived in. When I was fifteen and Adam eighteen, we would ride out every day, exploring to the edges of what we saw as the edge of Jordklode. And, to our surprise, it was.

About thirty miles from Redefalk, we found, one day, a sharp drop off where land stopped. The cliff went down into a type of rocky canyon, where mountains blacker than night rose and fell for countless more miles. To look upon it was to see the place where Death was born, or at least that's what we told ourselves. We came back to that secret spot every day for a year until a growing crimson light on the horizon scared us away. And here we were, returning.

I stopped Dagny about thirty feet from the edge, where Tyr, grazing, was secured to a tree. From there, I walked to the edge, looking for my friend. He was, however, nowhere in sight. For a moment, I stopped, heart pounding, wondering if he had jumped, yet another of my family to die. I peered over the edge, but to no avail. It was too far down; I could not see the bottom. Confused and worried, I backed away from the edge, afraid of the height. To my left, a bush shook and, to my relief, Adam emerged, carrying a medium-sized wooden box. The wood was peeling and the lock which secured it closed was broken. Adam stopped, seeing me.

"I remembered that we buried it, and I thought now would be a good time to, well, unbury it." He walked towards me, box in hand. It had been two days after finding the Edge when we hid the box. In it were some of our favorite story books, the kind that take one back to when the world around them was bright and innocent. Among these were action stories, like *The Adventures of Octavia, Dead Waning,* and *Glass Keeper.* The first was our favorite. At one time, I wanted to be just like Octavia, exploring the whole of Jordklode. But, it seemed, that the dream was not to be.

Adam set the box down in between us as we both found a spot in the grass. He opened the box to find only two books, not the three we had buried for safekeeping. Confused, Adam and I inspected the hole in which it had been buried. The missing book, *Dead Waning,* was nowhere to be found.

"Perhaps an animal got into it?" Adam raised the question, which I figured was probably the most likely option. Looking down at the dug-up earth, we both grew silent. So much had happened in such a short time. It was nice to return to a place of peace, if only for a moment.

"Adam," I said, snapping out of the silence, "I met with the council members earlier." He looked at me expectantly. Nosy as he was, he'd never admit it. "And I told them I have decided to add new members to the council. Four old men and a young queen are not going to be a very balanced team."

To this, Adam raised an eyebrow. If he wasn't talking, it was either because he was lost in thought, I was talking, or he knew what was coming. I imagine this case was the last.

"And, I would like you to be one of the additions." Finally, he broke his façade and smiled. This news seemed to make him genuinely happy. Adam had, just like me, always enjoyed sitting in on the meetings, finding out what was going to happen before it did. With one of my four additions added, I felt content. However, that meant I had to go onto the next one and leave the peace of the Edge.

Adam and I rode the thirty miles back to Redefalk together, our two remaining books in tow. When we arrived at the stables, we dismounted. I took Dagny to her stall, but was in a hurry to leave and could not unsaddle nor brush her down. So I promised her I would be back with treats if she'd let Adam do it. As for Adam, he was right at home. Besides the Wetland region to the far southeast, the Hingst lands were the most famous for horses, and for their care: Adam certainly added to the stereotype.

And so I left the stables, searching for the second of my four additions. It did not take me long to find Bjorth in his room of furs and treasures, where I had so long before received Wolf-tail. It was there that I found Bjorth, studying the flames with intensely hazel eyes. The red beard he often wore had begun to turn white, and the lines on his face had become more profound, perhaps even more so in the past night and day. After all, Da had been his cousin, his best friend. When Da's brothers had been killed in battle, Bjorth was the one who got Da through; he was the one who made sure Da came back home, alive, to Redefalk. His devotion, however, cost him dearly.

On the right side of Bjorth's head ran a scar, from cheekbone to scalp. His right ear was missing its top half, and so, he had a ragged look about him from that side. When asked why he was not married, he always pointed to that scar. To him, it seemed as though no woman could love a *deformity* such as his, even if the reason for it was enthralling. He had fought off one of Da's attackers during the same battle that killed my uncles. And for it, he earned his scar.

Bjorth did not look up as I came around to face him, blocking the fire. I could feel its heat on my back as I took one of my godfather's large, calloused hands in mine. I could see then that his eyes were watery with tears. Never had I seen him so forlorn. Never had I ever seen him without his jolly warmth. I understood, for warmth was hard to keep in times of frigid loss, especially those like the one we felt then.

"I don' know how I could've let him leave me here," Bjorth whispered, almost to himself. "He said, 'Now, Bjorth, you take care o' V un'il I return.'" He hung his head in shame. It hadn't occurred to me that he felt like that. "Maybe if I'da been there, he wouldn' be dead. Maybe, if I'da gotten another scar…" He trailed off, tracing the line of knitted tissue with his free hand. I could have told him it wasn't his fault, or that there was nothing that he could have done, but he would not accept the words. Instead, I changed the subject the best way I could.

"I want you to sit on the council," I said, searching his face. The tone hadn't been profound or ceremonial, nothing like how it should have been for bestowing such and honor. And yet, the hurry in my voice, the urgency, seemed right in that moment.

Bjorth's eyes rose up from the floor, reflecting to me his surprise. They grew wide, accentuating the lines under them and along his forehead.

"I—I've never been good at that kind o' stuff." He shook his head, trying to make me doubt my decision. He didn't understand.

"That doesn't matter. I need trustworthy people to aid me, people whom I know will bring real solutions and ideas to the council, people who want what is best for Kongeorn's future, people like you." I tried to smile, to show him I meant it, to show him the request was genuine. Finally, Bjorth nodded, accepting the invitation.

"My little Euna, I am most honored to serve you."

"And I am most pleased you have accepted my request. I will see you tomorrow, in the council room, after lunch." I squeezed his hand before offering a small smile and turning away.

I then left Bjorth to his thoughts, both mourning and rejoicing. And I found myself searching for a small healer's hut, where my next addition resided. When finally I arrived, I knocked thrice before entering the small abode. Inside, the ceiling was low, but my short frame fit without issue. Above me hung various herbs and potted plants whose names I did not know. On the floor, numerous furs softened the step of my boots. The wooden walls themselves were the canvas for hundreds upon hundreds of healing recipes and symptoms and diagnoses. Perhaps the most captivating part of this seemingly simple home was the lack of a bed; that, and the large polecat which slinked in the shadows.

The polecat's eyes burned yellow from the shadows where it lurked. To most, the ferret creature was scary and unpleasant—a mere pest to others. That was why I usually kept my distance. If I had not learned to do this, it would have been hard to enter this abode without receiving a few scratches from Emile. He just wanted sleep, which I could relate to, so I let him be and continued my search for the healer.

In the far corner, I saw her. She was bent over, ruffling through a large trunk filled to the brim with bottles and the like. When she found what she was looking for, she stood up and turned, only to nearly jump from her skin.

"*Svatus kud*, Vita! You nearly scared me soul from me skin!" She clutched at her heart, feigning an attack. I rolled my eyes. Gyda could be dramatic, but I suppose I deserved it for sneaking up on her. She pointed at me with her good hand, "You have gotten far too quiet, young missy. Too quiet for these old ears to hear ya, anyway." She paused for a moment, then her eyes lit up, "Oh, is't that time a'ready? I have your poultice made here." She scuttled over to a window sill and handed me my monthly savior, which I could already feel I would need. She then turned her attention to the flask she held in her two remaining left fingers. She turned around and put it back, again cursing. Almost forgetting that I stood behind her, Gyda again rummaged through her trunk.

"I wish to ask you a favor." Though she didn't respond, I assumed she had one eyebrow raised, waiting for me to proceed, "I want you to attend the council." She stopped rummaging and slowly straightened before turning back to me. She stood akimbo, eyebrow raised.

"Well it's about damn time," she exclaimed. "For years, I've been trying ta get your bastard of a father to let me on that damned council. And finally, finally, I get to show those old bastards why I've lived through four—five—kings!" She whistled, and I watched, not knowing what else to say. I knew she'd accept, but I had never expected her to be so *enthusiastic*. The thought made me smile.

"I will see you tomorrow after lunch, then." And so I left her to celebrate, placing the poultice in my pocket. For my last addition, I would have to circle back to the western end of the keep, where Amund used to reside with his young wife, Karina. As I climbed the stairs, I wondered about my final choice. She was kind and thoughtful, well read in her history, and she was like a sister to me. Upon arrival, I knocked on her door. When there was no answer, I cracked open the door. I could have done the polite thing and left, but that just wasn't in my nosy nature.

Inside, a fire burned bright in the fireplace, offering light as the Sol had been blocked out by the burgundy curtains. The bed was empty, and the couch was vacant. In front of the window, however, stood my sister-by-marriage. Her raven hair fell like a waterfall to the small of her back. She stood straight, as if she had become a sentinel. As I observed quietly from the shadows, I realized that my own reaction to the death of my loved-ones had been quite understated.

I inflected, focusing on my memories. It had taken less than a full day cycle to move out of mourning. Guilt flooded through me like a crashing wave as I took in a sharp breath. Karina would never be the same; she would forever be mourning the loss of her husband, of the possibilities, and there I was, already moved on to the next plan, to the next decision. How could I do that?

Just because you do not cry does not mean you do not mourn.

What? The emergence of the unknown voice confused me. The fact that it resonated from within my own mind made it all the more unsettling.

Death is dealt with differently, you see. Some isolate themselves and drown in their sorrows. Others erase their emotions with drink. And others still, like yourself, hide their agony in order to do what needs to be done. Just because it doesn't show, doesn't mean it isn't there, Vita. The voice, probably a figment of my imagination, there to provide an excuse for my conscience, allowed me to see the differences, and in doing so, helped me greatly in taking a step forward, toward what needed to be done.

As I approached, I began to see that Karina was not exactly standing completely still. Instead, soft sobs shook her graceful body. Red rimmed, her eyes released pearl tears. Her lips mouthed inaudible words, reflecting my own mind in its inability to form them. Instead, I put my arm around her. And though Karina was taller, she felt so small as she leaned her head into my shoulder. It was then that the sobs became louder and more violent. I led her to her bed, where we both sat, and I held her to me. Looking down at her, I felt a new feeling emerge, one which I never thought I would get to feel. I felt like a mother, soothing one of her children. Never had I soothed anyone before, never had I needed to soothe anyone. But a significant amount had changed since I first had those thoughts.

"Vita, I m—must tell y—you something," She hiccupped, barely able to get the words out. She straightened and looked me in the eyes, "I am w—with child." And suddenly, my dream came flooding back: I saw Karina's chocolate eyes peering at me, asking me to hold the heir to Kongeorn. And I understood. This child, this blue-eyed heir, was going to need me to clean up this mess before they came into the world, before they had to take up the mantle. *Finally, something concrete!*

"Your news brightens my day and makes joyous my heart. But I also have something to tell, or rather, ask, you." Karina shifted, her breathing growing calmer and tears slowing as they stopped spilling from her eyes. "I want you to help rule. I want you with me on the council." To this, she smiled. Placing a hand on her still flat abdomen, Karina nodded.

"I would be honored, Vita, absolutely honored." We hugged, taking in the other's warmth and love. Though we were not blood, my heart certainly considered Karina a sister. After telling her when she was to be at the council room, I departed, off to the library, where I hoped to find answers for Einar's hysteria that I would be able to present to the council on the morrow.

You know already why his heart grew dark. The voice returned to me.

I haven't the slightest idea of what you mean, I answered. I was talking to a disembodied voice in my head, perhaps I was as deranged as Einar.

Don't you dare think such things. You are not him. You are not evil. And I am not a "disembodied voice." The voice's sass was comparable to only Da's or my own, perhaps even Adam's, and yet, I still challenged it.

Show me.

Fine.

I waited for a sign, for a person to step out from behind one of the translucent curtains, but there was nothing. Sighing, I continued towards the library. Upon entering, I saw several books already taken from the shelves. One was *Adventures of Octavia,* which I immediately recognized. Others were family histories, and the final, which was somewhat foreign to me, read *The Family Kongeorn.* I decided to return each to their designated spots, which were indicated on the spine. It was a pet peeve of mine when people did not return the books to the original spots. I started with *The Family Kongeorn,* whose binding indicated it belonged in the second stack to the left, on the right side, two shelves from the top. I walked and reached to put it in its spot, when I saw a face peering back at me.

Hello.

Startled, I flinched, moving backwards and almost bumping into the next stack. The woman was my height, with chestnut colored hair and icy blue eyes. She had a sharp nose and thick brows. Had Da been born a woman, he would have looked like her.

That's exactly right. How smart you are.

Wait, what?

Had Da been born a girl…okay, maybe not exactly. The woman's lips moved, but her voice was still only in my head. *It was expected that Mother and Father never told you about me.*

I did not reply, simply too stunned for words, so she continued.

About a year before Amund was born, I was. Except, I never took my first breath. It seemed I was never destined for Jordklode, but for the Etter.

I thought on her words. *Words? How do you know that* she *is even there? And, even then, don't you think Da or Mami would have said at least something about her?* The doubts pulsed in my mind, but I found myself, incredibly, starting to accept this. Through my limbs, a familiarity spread, offering comfort and certainty. Though all reason claimed that this woman was a figment of my imagination, perhaps she could be helpful. Even then, with the doubt there, she was just so familiar, so much like Da—too much like Da. So I decided to suspend my belief and give into the gray areas of life, the ones that aren't necessarily yes or no, imagination or reality. Tales of ghosts and shades were abundant in Jordklode, where many still believed in the purity of the Etter. The veil between Life and Death was said to be thinner in the places where the Mother had walked, like in Redefalk. Da had even given such experiences a name.

"Chance meetings, V," Da said as he held my hand after Nana's funeral, "your Nana used to tell me about all of hers. I didn't believe her, of course, until I had one of my own.

"My oldest brother, David, died a warrior's death in battle when I was sixteen. He and most of my family died that day, but his death hit me hardest. While my father wasn't much of a fighter, David had taught me everything I knew. I was the youngest, like you, and he always made time for me while the other boys did Mother knows what.

"So after the funeral pyres were lit, I mourned for almost a year. On that last day, as I was preparing to see your Nana, I saw David. He walked into my room as if he were still alive, as if he was still there with me."

Da's eyes brimmed with tears as he looked off into the distance, almost forgetting the little girl, barely old enough to understand, holding his hand,

"He told me that he was proud of me, that the Mother had great things in store for me, and that my rule would lead to peace in our lands. I didn't believe him then, but I believe him now."

"Why now, Da?" I remember saying.

"Because of you and your brothers, V. If I can bring such good things into the world then maybe I can bring peace."

Chance encounters with lost loved ones weren't unheard of. I had even seen Nana after her death, but this was entirely different. This woman could have been the sister I never had, and she was standing before me, radiating an ethereal glow.

Why are you here? I asked, a bit more comfortable with the situation, however unusual.

The Mother has asked me to watch you, and to help you. There is darkness all around you, and I am here to help strengthen the light. Her words were cryptic. Had I not been conversing with a spirit of the Etter Realm, I would have rolled my eyes. I moved away from the stack and back over to the reading table, all the while knowing she was silently following me. I sat down in one of the stiff wooden chairs and waited for her to follow suit. She did. I narrowed my eyes at her, not in a menacing way, but in a challenging, almost mocking way.

Why do you make this face at me? she inquired, genuinely worried.

I believe you know very well why I make this face at you, Sister Whose Name I Have Not Yet Been Told. She rolled her eyes, and I saw her lower the wall of divinity that had prevented us from conversing the way I would converse with family. If that was what she was, then I wanted to feel comfortable treating her like it.

Ahava, she stated, as if I would know what she meant.

Um, bless you? I replied, not knowing how to respond.

Ahava, it is my name, you whimsy. My name is Ahava. After she explained, I finally understood. And "whimsy?" How sister-like of her to refer to me as such. I felt more comfortable all ready.

In all seriousness, Ahava, *why are you here? Why are you not in the Etter with Mami and Da and our brothers?*

I have already told you: because I am to guide and protect you. I thought on her words, as they were again somewhat cryptic and like that which one would read in a novel. Again, I narrowed my eyes.

Why? Truly curious, I asked.

You see, Vita, Einar was not the only one to be touched by evil. I am here to guide you on a path that will allow you to expel the rest of the evil from Jordklode.

Why? An idea popped into my head. A game which I had played with my brothers, one which agitated them, crept into my mind.

As I said, there is an evil here. Jakel, the Dark Prince, has taken hold of many and will not stop until he has achieved his goal.

Why? I smiled inwardly, anticipating the coming explosion.

There is no way to know Jakel's motivation, only to know that his heart is filled with hate and jealousy for the Mother.

Why? It was almost too much as I hid my smile and restrained my chuckle.

Svatus kud, *Vita! Knock it off!* She finally saw the game I was playing with her and grew annoyed, chastising me. As soon as the words left her mouth however, she began to laugh. Before long, we were both snorting, with tears of laughter running down our cheeks.

Were you always this obnoxious? she asked me, calming herself and wiping the tear from her eye absentmindedly.

This and much more, I assure you. We settled back into a calm atmosphere, which soon began to chill as Ahava quickly changed the subject, as if snapping a bone back into place.

Vita, in all that is serious, what I said to you is true. Einar was not the first to receive Jakel's touch. You cannot let them carry out his agenda.

So what do I do? I asked, detecting a new sound in her voice. Was it fear? Or authority?

You wait. Wait until a sign is given. We do not have all the information at hand, and cannot let Jakel know that we know of his intentions. Do you understand me?

I nodded.

Good. With that, my sister faded from sight. As she disappeared, the room dimmed, but also grew warmer. As I sat, pondering her words, her orders, I wondered if I was capable of waiting. Patience is a virtue, but it was one I never practiced.

I turned from the empty room, aware of every noise and especially aware that the Sol was about to set. The funeral pyre would begin its burning at dusk. But I didn't want to watch. Yes, I had told Bjorth to make the proper arrangements, but seeing my mother's body go up in flickering flames made me sick to my stomach. I had had enough death for the time being. And, as I felt the pains in my abdomen grow from the attention, I decided I needed to use the poultice I had been given.

Chapter 4

A Speech for the Books

I half ran, half limped to my room, where I knew a cozy fire would be blazing. Svat *on a stick, that hurts.* After rubbing the poultice on my abdomen, I climbed into bed and assumed the fetal position, waiting for the herbs to kick in and ease the cramps. I was thankful that my Luna-blood only came every other month. But it was still awful anyway. The night followed in excruciating lag, during which I found no sleep and no rest to help me in the day to come. Even after my body had been pacified with the poultice, my brain refused to give into sleep. Thoughts of significance and trivia alike swirled around, stupefying sight as if it were fog on a dim day. All around me, the sheets were far too warm, far too sticky. Their material began to attach to me, unyielding as I tried to throw it off in tossing and turning about. When finally sleep came, it was not restful, but that place half-way between dreams and wakefulness, where every noise jolts one awake and every tingle is an insect on the skin. Needless to say, the day ahead was not properly prepared for.

The sweat from my own skin, wet and sticky, woke me the next morning at sunrise. The taste in my mouth, though familiar, was more pungent than usual, and required my immediate attention. I rolled to the side and found myself plummeting to the wooden floor below. The reverberations from my fall echoed along the room, until finally it met with the door, which was still half open.

Wonderful, just what I need: some passerby sees their leader on the floor in a tangle of sheets. I quickly gained my footing and, realizing that in the night I had shed my clothes, decided it truly was best to see to the door, sheets clutched to my chest. Luckily, it seemed, no one had seen my act of clumsiness, which absolutely no one could see.

After donning the best tunic I owned and taking care to replace the poultice, I made my way to breakfast with unusual disinterest. The thought of food, for once, did not hold my mind in its delicious and addicting grasp. Instead, I found my mind wrenched away to another time. A time of nothing.

At only thirteen years old, I was curiously rough for a girl. Whenever insulted or teased, my first thought was violence, the second was usually some form of regret at not analyzing my opponent. Of course, if Amund was the one to inflict fun on me, I would find myself in an unrelenting headlock, forced to give in when I could take no more. With the twins, well, there were two of them and only one of me, so I usually found myself covered in some sort of brown substance, either manure or mud, and sulking harder than before. With Einar, however, I learned to never talk back.

"I love the way you dress like a boy, even though you're a girl." Einar said one day, as if itching for retaliation.

"I can dress however I want. Girls can like boy things, and boys can like girl things, Mami said so," I tried to sound confident, but his glazed glare shook me. I tried to open my mouth to further my argument, but no words formed in my throat. To my surprise, as I struggled to explain and defend myself, Einar began to smile coyly. To him, this was all a game.

"You're so stupid, you know that?" Again, I found words dying in my throat, before they even experienced their first breath. He began to circle me, hands clasped behind his back. "Do you know what they do with stupid girls in the West?" I shook my head, "They sell them to brothels. Maybe I should persuade Mother and Father to sell *you* to a brothel." There were no brothels in Redefalk because of the belief that it stained one of the Mother's bonding laws. Besides that, I had heard about the bastards born to the women who sold their bodies, and the thought of that for myself made my blood run cold. Einar could see the fear in my eyes and relished it. He leaned in closer to me, breathing heavily. Minutes passed, with Einar still standing, like a statue, far too close for comfort. Finally, I found the courage to break away and run, faster than I knew I could, away and away from my brother. I made a promise as I doubled over to catch my breath. It was a promise never to talk to Einar, nor make eye contact with him, again.

I had done my best, for eight years, to avoid him. After a while, it had become easy. I had learned his schedule: breakfast in the hall at sunrise, training after until lunch, lunch in the hall at high noon, then he retreated to his room until dinner. I had built my routine off of his, ensuring that I never hear his cruel words, nor see his hateful stares. I promised myself that staying away from him was best, and I had kept it for so long.

But all promises end up broken, whether we realize it or not.

The hall was far quieter than was usual. I could sense the sobriety in the air as I walked to my seat near the dais. As I began to sit, however, I was interrupted.

"Stormy, that's not your seat anymore," Adam stopped me. It then occurred to me that I belonged on the actual dais, in the actual seat where my father had eaten breakfast, lunch, and dinner for countless years. It would never be, no matter who said it was, my seat. That elegantly carved wood was only ever meant for Da, and it would always be his.

But I was still expected to occupy it.

And so, I made my way to the rise, where I had a view of the entire hall. I looked to the seat beside me and furrowed my brow. How long was that seat to be vacant? It was meant only for the secondary ruler, of which there was none, for the time being, anyway. My eyes shifted to Adam, but he was not allowed on the dais, as he was not my husband or king. Looking back to the seat, I began to feel a loneliness building inside me.

Breakfast passed with only silence coming from my lips. For once, my food was barely touched. It seemed that the previous night's encounter and lack of rest had left me in an introverted mood. As if a snail, my mind shrank back into the shadows of thought, where I could not access my thoughts and be present in the same moment. So, preferring one to the other, I resigned myself to my room for quiet self-interaction.

A draft from the western-facing window infiltrated the room, pushing comfort aside and supplanting it with a sense of unquestionable fear. Just outside my window, glaring up at me, were Emile's yellow eyes. He sat, unmoving, as if waiting for me to acknowledge him. Unlike most animals, Emile always had a way of making me somewhat uneasy. His eyes bore into mine, never backing down, waiting for me to back off as, believe it or not, I always ended up doing. Moving away from the window and back towards my fireplace, I elected to zone out, to inspect the carvings instead of think about the day and its decisions ahead.

The color of cinnamon, the wood brightened up the room, sometimes more than the fire it surrounded. The legs and headers told a story, a story I had never had the idea to pay attention to. The bottom left corner depicted a birthing scene. A young woman, beside her a great bearded man, lay in a bed, her bump profound and ready. The artist had been so meticulous as to painstakingly include the droplets of sweat which matted her hair.

The next image, above the former, showed a magnificent tree, whose roots spiraled skyward, beckoning the coming Sol and Luna above it. Facing each other in tender embrace, the faces of the Sol and his bride completed the other. But, like most happy times in life, it was not to last. They were soon forced apart, farther and farther away from one another, until night and day, their respective dwellings, became polar, forever opposites.

Their story, however, was to continue. The Sol left his love with drops of sunlight in the stars, which guided lovers to one another to live out the story which could not be for the celestial beings. One of these such stories was that of the first recorded king and queen of Kongeorn.

Gauthier, a leader of great renown, found a woman weeping on the side of the road on the way to his destination, modern day Redefalk. He asked the woman, long of hair but sad of smile, why she was crying. But then he saw. Her cheeks were swollen with bruises. And her eyes, her icy blue eyes, they were afraid of what her father would do to her next. And Gauthier, wanting to rescue her, earnestly asked her name. She replied, in a voice stronger than before, that the name which she had chosen for herself was, "Adelaide."

Gauthier vowed to help her, but she implored him to only do as she asked. And what she asked, he did.

And so, the following night, he met her in the same place, blood staining her hands, the hands of justice. The Luna shone her light down upon them, seeing the story begin under her eye, and to continue under that of her own love.

And continue it did, but that was where the engravings ended.

Realizing I had spent some time engrossed in the midst of an artist's retelling of the first love story, I snapped out of it to find myself cross-legged on the carpet, face only inches from the polished wood.

I scooted back, almost afraid to break my gaze upon the art. As I widened my frame of vision, however, I noticed something strange, something I had failed to notice before. In each image, there was a symbol artfully hidden. It was the symbol "kai," which was the old way of saying "thirteen." It was a circle with a gap at the top and a line horizontally drawn through the middle. The image where it was most obvious, and was actually in several different spots, was in the last depiction. My head reeled as it tried to comprehend what the meaning or purpose for this could possibly be. I found none. Dejected, I turned away from the wooden work of art.

From the dimmed sunlight that streamed through the cursed window, I told the time to be only an hour to lunch. And after that, my first true council meeting. The first of many tests for my rule. And in all honesty, I revealed to myself, I was not at all ready.

What if that isn't the only thing I am not ready for? What if I am not meant to rule? What if Rasmus was right? There had never been only a queen to rule by herself. It would set a precedent, and some would no doubt disagree with its message. But more importantly, what if I ended up like Einar, what if I began to crave power, to obsess over it? A ruler's job is to protect those they are bound to, but what if those people did not want to be protected by their ruler?

It seems you will just have to ask them yourself.

I was unsure if the thought was suggested by another or by myself, but I found it was the best option for the time-being.

The chamber room was nearly filled to the brim with onlookers and my own councilmen, minus one. Meeting each set of eyes, both old and young, I resolved to begin the meeting. Standing, I let the room grow quiet, attentive. When their attention was secured, I felt the courage of my father return, and I began to speak.

"There have been many times in our history that the step of Kongeorn has faltered, but—I say to you with a sure voice—it has never stopped, never been knocked down.

"In the past days, many events have transpired. We have all experienced loss. And, while those we have lost must be honored, we must also honor and protect those we still have." Many of the mothers looked down at their children, ignorant of the weight which would be put upon them in their own time.

"And so, a decision must be made. With our king, our commander, gone, who shall reign in his stead?" The room grew quiet, stale, confused.

"One of the member seats is vacant, as many of you have no doubt noticed. The wise and long-trusted Rasmus resigned in light of the tragedy, not out of grief, but out of doubt. He did not wish to be ruled by, or work alongside, a woman. He believed a woman's 'reliance' on her emotion would be damaging to a ruler." To this, though spoken in a calm voice, many in the crowd visibly took offense to. "And yet, I would wonder if this thinking," I raised my voice slightly to reign them back in, "is shared among those whom I have been charged with leading." I paused, taking a deep breath, and truly wondered what my mind had gotten me into this time.

"If this opinion is shared, if you do not deem me fit for rule, then I will gladly step aside for someone who better fits your vision." The silence in the room, though thick and palpable, was sliced by the sound of a chair scooting back, and by an old man struggling to gain his feet.

"In all my years," Simon mustered, "never have I seen one more worthy of the crown and more reluctant to receive it." Beside him, Gyda also stood.

"Aye, and should anyone question this, I'll contest 'em to me last breath. Besides, this 'motion nonsense' is pure *svat*."

"Agreed."

"There is no doubt."

"And so it must be."

One by one, all of my fellow councilmen stood, giving to me their approval, but it was not only theirs which I required. Looking past them, and into the crowd of witnesses, I voiced the question again.

"Would you have me as your queen?" For several moments, there was only silence. And then, a young girl, perhaps twelve or thirteen, began to clap. Her actions were replicated by those around her, each of them individually giving me their consent to govern them, to lead them, to protect them.

Fluttering wildly, my heart soared, filled to its limits with relief, with happiness. My people wanted to be *my people*. And it wasn't the thought of power that elated me, but the prospect of leaving the world better than I found it, better than I could not believe it was. But in order to do that, more decisions had to be made.

Grinning broadly, I raised my hand and waited for the roar of voices to quiet. Once it had, I began again:

"There are no words to thank you, all of you, but I can start by getting straight to work. Any of you, council member or citizen, who has a concern, comment, or issue, please, speak now." Nothing. Again, the room was still, as if there were not three score people inhabiting it. And, for the second time that day, Simon came to my rescue.

"My Queen, I suppose it would make the most sense to start with that which applies to you, yourself, and your assumption of royal power." He took a breath, gathering his thoughts, carefully placing them onto his tongue, "Like Rasmus, there are those who do not trust the rule of a woman, and, no matter how wrong they may be, their absences will certainly be missed. Upon hearing of the deaths in your family, all of our eight allies to our south have revoked their pledges of alliance. That being said, one of those provinces, Oster, was our chief market for exports. Without it, we either find another ally to trade with, or we find a new way to earn coin." After his speech, many of those in the crowd began to whisper amongst themselves, no doubt panicking and, perhaps, wondering if their decision had been the best one.

Ignore the voices; they will ruin you if you cannot block them out. Good. Now, what do we still have as an asset? I thought on it for some time, until the room was buzzing with conversation, conversation which I had blocked out, of course. I surveyed the room; many of the men, and even some of the women, I recognized from the practice fields, from sparring and parring and training. If there was one thing Kongeorn boasted, it was the quality of its warriors, both male and female. I took out my trusty dagger, and banged its butt against the tired wood repeatedly until the room again grew quiet. Gaining confidence, I shared my idea.

"Are you sure?" Karina asked, knowing well that those who agreed to be a part of the squadron would be putting their lives in danger, those like me. I nodded, almost excited about the potential. With no more questions, I called for a vote.

"All in favor?" Trond asked. Eight hands found themselves in the air, though two of them rather hesitantly.

"And so it shall be: henceforth, the primary income of the government of Kongeorn is the title sellsword, to be hired out by other governments, both large and small, for missions such as retrievals, battles, and diplomatic matters. This meeting is now adjourned."

Instead of staying and mingling with the crowd, I quickly and quietly made my way out. There was a pull in my heart to my father and mother's bed chambers. An urgency grew in my being, begging me to get away from the crowd. *They can't see me like this.* The halls were empty before me, but I could hear the buzz of conversation approaching from behind. Feeling the emotion bubbling up, I hurried to the doors. The buzzing grew louder and, as I reached the doors, I felt as if I was being chased. Once inside, however, that feeling of urgency melted. My throat tightened as I walked to my parents' bed, where I used to come after having nightmares.

But I couldn't wake up from this nightmare. I had just replaced my father as our ruler. I had confirmed his absence. There was nothing else to do, to say. It had all happened so quickly.

They can't be gone. There's no way. I tried to picture them, to see them in front of me, reaching out, telling me it would be okay. But no matter how hard I tried, I just couldn't remember what they looked like. In my mind, I knew the laugh lines weren't in the right place, nor the messy cowlicks. It was wrong. All of it, wrong. *What I wouldn't give...* And then I felt it. It started off as a tightening in my chest, then it grew stronger. It was desperation. I found myself clawing back through memories, trying to think of ways I could have saved them. *I shouldn't have let Adam hold me back. I should have seen this coming. I should have gone with them. Why didn't I go with them?* Round and round, these thoughts flew, faster and faster. I held my hands to my heart, trying to keep my chest from ripping apart.

"Creator," I mustered, "please. I can't do this on my own. I shouldn't be here. It should be Da or Mami or Amund. I can't. I'm not them." I felt my knees buckle and moved my elbows to the bed, like a child ready to say nighttime prayers.

"I have no right. I have no right to be alive when they are not. Please, take me and bring them back. Take me. Please." There was no answer. I hadn't expected one, really, but hearing the silence only made the desperation turn, morph, into the ugly head of doubt. My toes tingled in my boots, while the feeling of disappointment spread. It oozed through my limbs, cold and slow, agony. They weren't coming back. They never would be. I would have to do this on my own.

The news of our newest diplomatic decision spread throughout Jordklode, and before long, our old allies began to contact us once again. Some for trading, some for a neutral intermediary, and a few for retrieval. These allies and contacts brought in more profit, both monetary and political, than I could have hoped for. The most intriguing of all these events and adventures was that which was done for an international group of scholars known as the Heri Scholares. They were diplomatically immune, as they had ties to every province and were almost as old as the lands themselves. That being said, their vaults were full of coin, from all nations, to fund their scholarship.

The truth and science of our beginnings, to many, is worth so much more than gold.

The Heri Scholares were a testament to this truth, and so, had no trouble offering a sizable sum for the retrieval of artifacts from the birthplace of all of Omnia, from the island of Creat.

Instead of giving us a time frame to work within, the Scholares asked only that we bring back anything on the island that was not naturally occurring. For them, time was of no complication. They had waited eight centuries; they could wait another month.

When that month was up, however, we were prepared for the journey. The group was to go, without any of the Scholares in tow, to Creat, only with the directions given to us on a quite old, *almost* unreadable map.

Pidges, small, black birds with fierce and sharp calls, squabbled above in the clearing spring sky, announcing another day was at hand. To the stables, I walked with purpose, ready to lead the search party into the far reaches of the North. It was early spring, the coldest time for Kongeorn. And we had prepared. We being myself, Adam, three younger warriors—all men—and six horses. We would mount five and use the last as an extra for carrying the artifacts; that was, if we were to find them.

And so, we set out in search of items, of objects, that may have held the secret to our pasts, and to our futures. The entire trip to the Northern edge of Jordklode took our small group a total of six days and a half night, all of which were pleasant in weather and easy on our bones. The sight, however, of the sea which separated our continent from the primeval island of Creat was, no doubt, going to be much harder to endure.

We arrived at the cliffs of Jordklode just as the Luna was rising in the eastern sky. Its brilliant colors marked the clouds with their own temperaments. From the golds and yellows of dwindling daylight in the West, to the purples and midnights of impending night, the view drew our eyes and painted the individual waves, each with their own majesty. And there, far off in the distance, was the place where the first guardians had been birthed into this world.

"In the very beginning, the Mother was completely alone, watching over Nothing, and wishing for something to call Her own," Da said, "and so, She decided to act." Da stood, towering over us kids and shielding us from the brightness of the crackling evening fire. "First, She ignited the light of our Sol, and of our Luna. And, in those times, the radiant Luna and her devoted Sol would stay together in the sky, watching over all. Together, they gave birth to the winds and the clouds and the stars. But it was not to last.

"For the Mother was still alone. She had created two lovers, a pair, a couple, and yet, She was still the only of Herself. So She created Her own companion, a son, of sorts, and called him Jakel—"

"But he was bad!" I would pipe in, always wanting to be the center of attention.

"Shut up," Einar ordered, hating me and every word which escaped my lips.

"Einar, you mustn't be rude to your sister; she just wants to be heard," Mami chastised him, leaving him be only with a roll of her eyes and a sad attempt at a smile. Da continued.

"Yes, Jakel was very, very bad. But the Mother loved him anyway, because parents always love their children, and we choose to ignore their faults." How right he was. "Anyway, with Her very own son, the Mother decided to continue to create more. First, the seas, both roaring and tranquil, and then, the creatures within were birthed and given names. And to go over them, She created the lands, both Jordklode and Oeste, as well as the Etter, far above us. And to those, She gave each their own animal inhabitants. But something else was missing."

"Us!" I shouted, all too excited at knowing the answer, but grew small again under Einar's hateful glare.

"Yes, my love, it was missing *us*. And so, on the Island of Creat, the Mother brought to life the wolves of old, and the serpents, as well." That was new. Da had never before mentioned the serpents, only the wolves. It was strange to me, but I refused to speak up again for fear of Einar's hatred.

"And with the guardians sent out, preparing the world for the first men, the Mother rested, content with Her success. But She failed to notice what Her beloved son was doing to His first creations. You see, Jakel had grown jealous of the Sol and Luna's power and love, and so, he drove them apart, further and further. The Sol wept drops of his majesty, and they stayed with the Luna, accompanying her in the absence of his love."

And that was where the story ended. But there we were, staring at the place where our ancestors had come from, the place where the first guardians had emerged. And, with awe in our eyes, we descended the cliffs, leaving two of our men behind to care for the horses. The descent to the rocky shore below caused my stomach to turn, just as the mist slicked the rocks we repelled down. Every few feet, different colored rocks would appear before my face, testifying to the beauty of even the most hostile places.

When finally we had reached the bottom, the hard, black rock had given way to grey-blue pebbles, and the waves crashed and ebbed several feet out. The question of how we were to get to the island was answered as I scanned the beach. Just as the scholars had promised, a section of stone rose up out of the surf, only noticeable because of the break in height. I motioned for Adam to follow me as I began towards the path.

Chapter 5

Thirteen Items and Some Burned Fingers

"You're sure this is it?" Adam questioned of me, already knowing my answer.

"Of course I'm not sure, but a stone path matching the exact description given by the scholars bares decent chances of being what we're looking for." He rolled his eyes in reply. Though the twilight had set in, the Luna would still give light to our way, and I was far too curious, far too antsy, to wait out the night.

"Jaque," I called back, "Adam and I are going to cross; if we do not return by midday tomorrow—well—I'll leave that to your judgement." After the best instruction I could leave was left, my boots found the first step to the stone pathway. Adam followed close behind.

As we ascended the strange stairs, I realized just how high we were. Even at the highest tide, no crashing wave would be able to reach us, and if the wind were to pick up, the journey would be far more perilous. Lucky for us, the night was calm, lit by the waxing Luna and her stars above. And because of that light, I began to detect images in the stone beneath my feet. Like my fireplace, they told a story, the same story I had come to know by heart, except it was upside down. The story was meant to be told leaving the island, not going to it. Still, however, I gave pause to show Adam.

"I was wondering when you were going to mention them," he replied, poking me in the ribs. I only glared at him and continued walking. Soon enough, under the light of the Sol's lover, we saw where the path dropped off, where we could descend onto the Island of Creat.

We had been told to look for specific items: they would be the ideal artifacts, however, anything not naturally occurring was acceptable, too. When we started the search, our feet sunk into white sand, ethereal in the moonlight. We had been told that any of the *special* items would be further inland, near a great mountain which was the only break in the flat skyline. Contrary to what we were told, however, the island was not heavily wooded. In fact, it was hardly inhabited by any plant, leaving a flat, dry landscape, and a visible path to the mountain we were asked to trek to.

"Mayken," Adam exhaled the word, gazing at the great rock in the distance. Cloaked in shadow, the lands around it were black, hidden from the light above. And so, our destination in sight, we began to walk, eyes glued to the massive landmark.

Like so many of the tales of our world, my father had introduced us to this one.

Mayken was the mountain of creation, the spot where the Mother, Herself, touched down onto Omnia. The ground had risen up to meet Her, rejoicing in Her kindness and power. It was from the peak of this mountain that She could see the canvas of Omnia, then a blank and barren waste.

It is said that when She stepped down from the mountain, setting foot into charred ash, the rocks and dirt became lush and green with life. With every step She took, the earth came alive.

And when it came time to make the Guardians, the Mother perched at the summit of Mayken and spoke them into being. Yes, this island was sacred to all who believed in the Mother, but Mayken, itself, was the centerpiece of that faith.

As we grew closer, I saw that the mountain was not completely rock; instead, it was made of the same gem-like stones I had seen in the cliffs. And, near its bottom, there was an opening—surprisingly—with light coming from it. Adam and I paused, both noticing the queer sight, and gave the other a look. I raised an eyebrow at him. He returned with a shoulder shrug, and we continued on. Soon, we were in the shadow of the behemoth, getting closer and closer to the lit opening. It was obviously strange, so there was no need to state the evident as we prepared ourselves for what lay inside, if anything.

I extracted my dagger from my boot as Adam took out his favorite chain. We both took a deep breath and crept into the cavern.

Colors. Light. All refracting toward us, through us. I dropped my dagger, completely stunned at the spectacle. Beside me, I heard Adam's chains hit the lit floor, followed by his knees. Looking over, I saw him, his hands clasped, mouth whispering a silent prayer. I would have done the same, if not for what caught my eyes next.

"Adam," I whispered. He did not reply, still lost in prayer. "Adam," I spoke louder. This time he looked up and, taking the hint, followed my gaze. There, in the center of the cavern, lay a pile of artifacts. On top, however, was the sword I had only heard about in stories.

"After Gauthier had wed his beloved bride, he founded Redefalk, and was given a sword by the Mother to prove his worth." Da had said one night after I had begged for more stories. Adam sat beside me, and we both swung our young legs back and forth in anticipation. "The sword was engraved with the words, '*Kadit n'qu surjatis a sup'riori.*' or, as we know it, 'Fall to Rise Higher.'" We all had sat stunned, minds completely blown at this monumental truth.

It made sense to me that the blade would carry our words. Gauthier had been the first true king of Kongeorn, the first to coin that phrase. And the blade that the Mother had given him was a testament to those words.

Only those who knew what it was to truly fall, only to rise again could wield that blade. Or at least, that's what Nana had told me, oh so long ago.

As I padded closer to the infamous blade, I could see that it was not only one color, but, like the cavern, a myriad of them shining out, reflecting. And along the blade itself, as pure as light from the sun, were the same words I had internalized in my heart, seared into my soul. All the other artifacts, the other treasures, paled in comparison beneath it, as if they weren't even there.

I reached out, aching for the legendary blade, for the pommel in my palm, and to see my own distorted reflection in its gleaming face. Behind me, Adam said something, but it was lost on me in its entirety. Instead, I only saw the sword, and its colors swirled around me, surrounding my fingers, reaching out, just as I was to it. And when our tendrils met, I felt a warmth. It began in my fingertips and continued throughout, snaking through the veins of my hand, then arm, and to my heart, where it was sent out to every corner of my body. I felt my head fall back, as if I had been lifted from the ground and into the air, now glimmering with life.

Encompassed in clouds of security, I allowed my eyes to close, and blocked out the rest of the world.

Vita stayed that way, suspended in the air before me, for what had to be several moments. Her eyes moved vividly beneath her eyelids, indicating a dream of some sort, but I was not too sure. Her flax hair splayed out around her, as if floating in a clear pool beneath the moonlight. Her lips were just slightly parted, catching my eye, as always.

All around her were figures, tall and ethereal. Like many of the spirits I had seen, they floated along, unable to be held down by gravity. There were three of them.

The first was a man with flowing dark hair, a circlet upon his head. His eyes were trained on the sword in Vita's hand. I scoured my memory before realizing that this spirit was King Gauthier.

The next was a woman, long of hair. It flowed out behind her as she gracefully danced behind King Gauthier. Her eyes were the bright, icy blue of Kongeorn. She, too, wore a circlet; it didn't take long for me to come to the conclusion that this woman was Queen Adelaide.

The final spirit was another woman. She also bore the icy blue eyes of the Kongeorn royal line, but her face was more familiar. Her hair was dark, and her nose was aquiline. She turned in a circle before looking directly at me.

"Kongeorn will always need her Hingst. Two parts of one soul. The sword and the shield. There must always be one to serve the Mother."

I stepped back slightly as the woman's words began to echo in my head. The spirits resumed their dance around Vita, and my focus shifted again to my queen, my best friend.

Beneath the glow and the ethereal scene, I began to miss the sight of her eyes looking back at me, of her voice calling me an idiot, of everything that transfixed me day after day. She was right in front of me, and I missed her.

In the last seconds of her levitation, the light in the cavern began to dull, to dim, and the sword itself looked as if it were becoming but air. I wanted to speak, but the sight before me was too stunning to speak over.

I felt my feet hit the ground again, with a soft thump. But when I opened my eyes, the cavern had darkened, leaving only the moonlight, faint and pale, to guide my eyes. Looking down, I searched for the sword, for any sign of its majesty and imperfection. Instead, I only saw scrolls and bracelets and a medallion.

"W—where did it go?" I asked, worried that it had all been a dream. Adam did not answer immediately; instead, his eyes, still vibrant in the dim cave, were tacked on me, unmoving. For once, I could not detect his emotion. His eyebrows were raised, but not necessarily in surprise. And his lips were slightly parted, but he looked as if he were incapable of speech. Suddenly, it dawned upon me what he was feeling. And from that, I surmised that the events I had experienced and those flares which I had felt within my soul were indeed real, and he had felt and seen it all as well. *But what is "it?"* Before I could further ponder, Adam found his voice.

"It—well, there really is no sensible or sane or reasonable way to put this, but—it kind of—that is, to say, it *did*—became a part of you. As in, the sword just became air and, it just, went into you." He continued to babble, repeating his own words over and over again as I attempted to grasp the concept myself. Oddly enough, what Adam described actually made sense to me. *The warmth, it must have been the sword itself.*

Wrong. Ahava chose that moment to chime in.

Okay, then what *was it?* I retorted, both annoyed and thankful for her sense of timing.

Not the physical sword, Sister, but the spirit *of the sword, its essence, went inside you, intertwining with your soul.* She sounded as if she was trying to explain complex economic strategies to a child, which she might as well have beenbecause her words were mostly lost on me.

So, I began, feeling dumb, as usual, *did the Sword of Gauthier choose me?* Though she hadn't made herself visible to me, I sensed an eye roll.

Absolutely not. Vita, you are most certainly not the chosen one. *You just happen to fulfill the sword's requirements for its gift. And, because I know you are going to ask, I will just list them out for you.* At that point, I genuinely thought about making a snide remark regarding her abundance of sass, but I figured it may not have been the smartest idea for me, at that time. So I made a mental note to do it later. *The sword was placed here directly after Gauthier's death by the Mother, Who still walked among men. She made it so the sword would gift the first person who came in contact with it who had a believing heart, a fierce loyalty, and a strong mind with the wisdom to make peace in times of war. It contains the Mother's Blessing.*

And you just happen to have been the first to even find it. Though I'm sure the fact that you couldn't keep your grubby paws away from it helped it choose, too.

"Hey," I reacted out loud, a bit too loud to sound sane. Luckily, Adam was still having somewhat of a mental breakdown. However, my exclamation had snapped him out of it, and he looked at me questioningly. "Oh, forget it," I said. *And forget you, too,* I came back at Ahava, albeit pathetically, since every trace of her voice had disappeared. After gaining partial understanding of what had just occurred, I decided to take inventory of what we still had in the cavern.

In comparison to the sword, the other items were knickknacks, mere trinkets. However, I pushed the sword out of my mind for the time being and gave them my time as well. Only this time, with the sword's light gone, I had to squint to see each item.

There were thirteen of them. The first was a shining green emerald, which, taken out of the small shaft of Luna light, turned milky gray. I handed it to Adam for him to inspect as well. It seemed he had gotten over the confusion of before, at least on the surface. The next item was the holy symbol "letum," which took the form of a circle, but with a raised lightning bolt down the middle, giving the illusion it had been cracked. I handed this to Adam as well. There was another letum symbol, but pieces were crumbling away, and there was no lightning bolt. Next was a crystalized bough of barley, symbolizing drought. Then, a ship in a bottle, cemented in place by some sort of sand around it.

The sixth item was a golden noose, and the seventh was a pure white cloth with a baby blue stain; the eighth was a baby figurine swaddled in the darkest black cloth, while the ninth was a black crown made of nails. The tenth item was a map, foreign to me in both language and the countries it depicted. Four of the nations in the map had been blotted out in crimson ink. The eleventh was a blue globe of gemstone, which looked as if it were made of waves from the sea, ebbing in and out forever over all lands.

The twelfth was a set of two gemstones, sparkling white like stars, fused together in an eternal dance. I almost didn't hand that one to Adam. The final item, which I could scarcely call an item, was a small ball of fire. Its tendrils snaked back and forth, revealing ash and, what looked like, water beneath. My eyes were trained on the flames, breath scarcely coming to my lungs as awe crackled through my bones. For the second time that night, my hand reached out. Looking back, I realize that reaching your hand out for an open flame isn't the smartest or sanest idea, but I can say that there was no thinking involved.

Instead, I felt drawn to it, and, as my fingers met the flame, I felt pain in them. I cried out, bringing my hand back to my chest, cradling it and regretting life decisions. Adam only laughed at me.

Why is it that I am both able to name the successive leaders of each world power and actually reach into a fire simultaneously? I gave Adam a look that could cause a puppy to exit a room whimpering. He kept laughing. I merely rolled my eyes and decided that the sword wasn't the only thing we wouldn't be bringing back intact.

"Let's go," I ordered, trying to sound as menacing as possible. "There's no way to safely transport that *thing* so we will just have to leave it." I took some of the other items from the still howling Adam and stomped out of the cavern.

By the time we had made it back to the foot bridge, I decided to speak to Adam again. But, as usual, he already knew what I was going to say.

"I won't mention what happened with the sword." He leaned in closer, as if someone of the desolate island would suddenly appear and hear his words. "Besides, I could always just tell them about the fire!" He chuckled again and hurried up and onto the bridge, just out of the way of my icy glare, which soon began to melt at the coming of the rising Sol.

As I mounted the stairs and found my feet on the storytelling stone, I found the pictures blazing in oranges and pinks, actually reflecting the orb coming out of the horizon. Soon enough, however, it wasn't the light which pulled my mind in. Instead, I began to recognize the glyphs.

A young woman, beside her a great bearded man, was giving birth, and above them, was a mighty tree, roots extending farther and farther up. As I walked, continuously looking down, I saw the stories of Gauthier and Adelaide, followed by all of those I had ever heard come from Da's mouth, and then some I didn't recognize.

About one hundred paces from the end of the bridge, I saw a particularly intense picture. A woman was being tied to a large piece of wood, flames chasing up around her. Her eyes were the only part which remained in color, and I could see that they were a startling gold as they gazed upward. The image chilled me, and I kept walking. The images grew more and more vivid, meticulous in their craft. The last stone before the steps depicted the burned woman standing to the left of a woman with curly hair, who held in her hand a dark gem. To her right, however, the image was completely scratched out, which I hadn't noticed from before. *Perhaps it had been the lack of light, idiot.*

With one last sigh, I stepped down back onto the white sand, where Adam and the rest of my party were patiently waiting for their oh-so-wise and fearless of a leader.

Chram 7th, the year 527, From the Diary of Octavia Tesifa—

Today, we sailed to the Northernmost point of Jordklode, an island Zelith calls Creat. I was amazed to find that there was a stand-alone mountain in the precise middle of the seemingly desolate island. Even in brilliant sunlight, my crew and myself could detect a strange light, an aura, surrounding the landmark. I wanted to go in, to investigate what gave the rock such magical properties.

Zelith, of course, said no.

He may be my second in command, but he acts as if he might as well be my caretaker, a grumpy grandfather. Still, out of respect for his wisdom, whether it was deserved or not, I acquiesced and we boarded the ship once again.

That is to say, they boarded the ship. I, on the other hand, stayed for another hour or so to investigate. While trekking through the bony brush, my boot caught on an object, half buried, in the ground. And no, it wasn't a rock. Well, kind of, but also not. It was a gem, onyx and containing depth. When my hand reached for it, however, a spark flew out from it and shocked my fingers!

That, needless to say, was enough to send me, back to the ship and the sea, where I belong.

Chapter 6
Alliances Are Hard to Come By

The journey back to Redefalk was uneventful, that is, except for when Adam told the story of the fire for the billionth time, and I gave him a bruised rib to apologize for it. Though he wouldn't repeat the story while I was around, I knew everyone in Jordklode would no doubt hear about it. When we finally journeyed through the gates of Redefalk, we received many cheers, which was common after an outing such as this. We were funding the government after all. However, two things were different.

On the steps of the keep stood three members of the Heri Scholares, and next to them was our bird keeper, who, in his hand, held a roll of parchment. Also noticing this, Adam gave me a look and flitted his eyes to the Scholares. He would deal with them: give them what we found, accept our agreed sum, and see them out of Redefalk. I, however, would see to whatever it was that had Pierre so distraught-looking. Nodding, I rode ahead. I greeted the Scholares first, explaining that it was an honor and Adam would be seeing to them momentarily. Then, I dismounted Dagny, handed her off to a stable girl, and motioned for Pierre to follow me inside.

Though the Sol was still up, the sconces on the walls were already lit, warming the halls as Pierre and I padded to my chambers. Once there, I closed the doors behind me and took the scroll from him. Unrolling it, I strolled over to my lit fireplace.

"Did you read it?" I asked him. Though Pierre was loyal to us, he was sometimes loose with important information. In fact, he never knew how to really act around most people, but it most certainly was not his fault.

"Nope, I did not." He often spoke simply, or with a lisp, something that was just a part of him. But where his speech and social instincts failed him, he more than made up for in geographical knowledge, penmanship, and eloquent writing. I smiled at him then and told him that he was free to go. The middle-aged man scurried out the doors and left me to myself, as I so often was. I finished opening the letter and began to read:

Queen Vita of the Name Kongeorn,

I wish to announce, with both reverence and relief, that my father, King Alfred of the Name Feron, has died.

I now write to you as King Richard of the Name Feron, and as someone who wishes to reassert friendship between our two nations, especially in light of the atrocities committed by my own predecessors.

It would be my eternal honor if you would honor me with your presence in my kingdom, so that we, together, may right the wrongs my people have done upon yours.

I patiently await your response.

King Richard of Feroxia

The first thought which popped into my head resembled joy, in reference to the past king's death. Knowing that such a man was out of the world would make sleeping far easier. The second notion resembled surprise, principally at the new king's, King Richard's, admission of fault, of wrongdoing. To me, such a man who could swallow his pride was worth speaking to. And finally, the third thought, far in the deepest corners of my mind, was caution. *What if he only wants me there so he may kill me?* But then again, I was only a temporary ruler until Amund's son or daughter was born. There would always be an heir to our throne.

I thought back to my realizations of months passed. I was to make way for the next generations of Kongeorns, to make peace in my lifetime so they could make progress in theirs. That must have been the Mother's plan, so I drafted my own response and sent it off to Pierre, who could make my crude words lovely and worthy of a ruler.

I smiled to myself, hoping Da was proud, watching from the Etter.

When I told Adam of the letter, and of my decision, his sense of caution was far louder than my own.

"What makes you think that he *won't* kill you, or at least try to?" He raised his voice over the crackling of the fire in my fireplace. Though he had a point, I had already gone through this process of thoughts, myself.

"He won't kill me, or try, because he wants to make peace. And one cannot make peace by murdering another country's ruler. Besides, he is different from his father." I spoke with certainty, completely sound in my beliefs.

"I cannot believe how naive you sound, Vita." His voice began to rise again. "Sons learn by watching their fathers. You say he is different? Maybe, but I think you're wrong, and your miscalculation could get you killed and Kongeorn conquered." He had stalked towards me, trying to use his height to intimidate me. Yes, he had a point: quite a few, actually. However, I had faith that the Mother intended for me to go to Feroxia, to find a path to peace.

"At the end of the day," I spoke calmly, a foil to his intensity, "I am your queen, and I have made my decision to go to Feroxia next month." His green eyes burned.

"Then I'm going with you. You'll need people you trust protecting you—"

"I don't need protection; I can take care of myself. I've done it plenty of times without *you*," I shot back, temper flaring. Just because I was a woman, everyone believed I needed help, that I needed a guiding hand or a strong man to keep me safe. But they were wrong. Adam was wrong, and he knew it.

But my comment had hurt him, too. His eyes softened and he returned to his reserved state before leaving the room, and me, all to myself again.

Why couldn't you have just kept your mouth shut? I shouted to myself, feeling ashamed and stupid and everything I had ever felt after a run in with Einar. Adam was my best friend, and I had just hurt him. I had let my own stupid pride ruin a compromise. *Da could never be proud of you: look at yourself.* And I did.

In the reflection of the darkened window, I could see that tears had begun to slide down my cheeks. My nails were biting into my palms, increasing the pain I felt I needed to feel as punishment for what I had done to my best friend. That voice inside was right. Da could never be proud of me. I was so naive; I would never amount to anything. Even as I stood, looking at myself, I knew that I was a disappointment to his memory. Perhaps even the Mother looked upon me in disgust, just as I looked at myself then.

Oh, Vita, I looked up, expecting to see Ahava, there to tell me how clueless, how worthless, I was. Instead, it was my mother in the mirror.

What are you doing here? You shouldn't be here. The words scrambled out of my mind. Her translucent hand reached out, and I whirled around to see her more clearly. Her face looked young, like when I had been five and all of my brothers were alive and the world was okay and Da was alive, too. Her dark hair fell untangled to the small of her back, silky and shiny. But she didn't answer my question. I asked again. Still no reply. Maybe she was just a part of my mind trying to make me feel better. An excuse to stop the tears.

I turned and plopped down onto my bed, face down on the blankets and let the dam break. Thoughts I had pushed back for so long came cascading over me, as if to drown me.

You'll never be a good queen. Everyone can see right through you. They know you're weak. Einar was right; you are pointless. You are stupid. Your family is dead because you weren't smart enough, strong enough. You aren't meant to be a Kongeorn. I hate you. Everyone hates—

No. Mami's voice pushed passed all of the clutter, silencing the other voices in my head. *Vita, you cannot be doubtful of yourself. You cannot take what others may think of you as what you think of yourself.* I felt her hand on my hair, chasing away the demons, the doubts. *You are worth so much. Not just because you are queen now, not because of where you come from, but because you are here, alive. The Mother loves you with all Her heart. I love you with all my heart. But you have to realize that, to achieve all that you aim to, and want to, achieve, you have to take another look at yourself, because the only opinion that matters is the one in that mirror.* She coaxed me up out of the puddle of tears I had created. I shuffled, like a toddler to her vegetables, to the same mirror I had peered in minutes before.

In it, there was a red-faced, teary-eyed, heavy-hearted girl. One that could barely get through the day without feeling her heart break. She was most certainly not a queen, nor was she beautiful. She had her father's sharp, crooked nose and thick eyebrows. She had lips which tended to grow chapped in the winter, and long dirty blond hair that was always ending up on her clothes and floor somehow. Looking further down, she had a strong, able body, but no elegant, long legs. She didn't even look like a woman, let alone a queen.

You're looking wrong, Vita. Try again. This time, don't focus on comparison; focus on what makes you you.

The girl looked back up, studying herself. Her dark eyebrows scrunched, showing animated emotion. And her eyes shone like ice in darkness, emitting a cool blue light which transfixed me. Her crooked nose had a story behind it. Though it had always been pronounced and sharp, it had been broken several years prior. She had been walking to breakfast when her best friend—my best friend—caught her by surprise. He had tackled me to the ground, and the bridge of my nose had caught on the side of the great oak table. A dent had formed there that never healed.

No, my body wasn't feminine. I didn't have Karina's long legs, or Gyda's ample breast, but I had legs that could push a turned-over wagon if needed and arms that could fight off several men at a time in the training yard.

I didn't have to be beautiful. Because I could be smart, or confident, or strong, or passionate. Value isn't in beauty, nor looks, but in how much we give, and who we make ourselves out to be. It is all in our decision. I half-smiled, no longer hearing the voices in the background.

That's my girl, Mami said, kissing the top of my head and disappearing.

Though I couldn't change myself or the past, I could still do something about the future, like my friendship with Adam. So I made my way out of the doors, where, to my surprise, I found him sitting against the opposite wall, head in his hands. I took my place beside him.

"I'm," I started to say.

"No, *I'm* sorry. I knew that you would get mad. And I know that it irritates you when I say you need protecting. I'm the one who should be sorry." He looked over at me and put his head back into his hands. I put my arms around him, like he had so many times done for me. I laid my head on his shoulder. We stayed that way for a long time. A time that I didn't bother to gauge. After, he lifted his head, tears staining his cheeks, but certainty in his voice.

"I am going with you. But not because you need protecting. Because I can't be without my best friend." I smiled, liking that answer, and hugged him tighter.

"I wouldn't have it any other way." And that was how any arguments we ever had usually ended. Fighting with Adam or hurting him was like trying to hurt myself, only far more difficult. There had been so many times that he had saved me from myself, from the pit of loathing and fear of disappointing people that only came from being the youngest, the one with the most to prove. But there had been times when I had saved him, too. Times when he needed me just as much as I needed him. And it was because of events such as those that held us together, bound us in trust and friendship.

I had been fifteen, still trying to gain confidence in myself, and slowly learning that I had to take it, not wait for it. Adam had been eighteen and every bit the level-headed brain to my fickle and spontaneous wills. Wherever I decided to go, he would follow, attempting to keep me out of trouble, while sometimes making it for the both of us in the process.

One afternoon, after a sparring lesson in the training grounds, I had gone to bathe. But when I came back to the training grounds, Adam had disappeared. I asked around and, to my dismay, no one knew where he was. Following instinct, or rather, just guessing, I went to the stables in search of my best friend. When I got there, I found that it was desolate, and only two horses remained in their stalls. Luckily for me, Adam was grooming one of them.

When I opened the stall door, Adam flinched, but then returned to grooming the dapple-gray coat as if I wasn't there. I tentatively placed my fingers on his shoulder, but he shook them off.

"What's wrong?" I asked, wondering of all the horrible things that could have taken place in my absence. He didn't answer. I walked to the other side of the mare, trying to look at his face. When I did, I saw that one of his downcast eyes was swollen and red, the beginnings of what would most definitely be a nasty bruise. As I inspected his face further, I found various cuts: on his bottom lip, above his brow; I found shame, as well, the most alarming.

"What happened?" I reworded my previous question, posing a far firmer tone. His eyes instantly traveled even further downward, suddenly fascinated by the idea of shoes. After a moment or two, he replied.

"Amund and I got into a fight." I waited for him to explain, but he appeared to be closing up again. I had to keep him pried open.

"Why?" I kept any judgement, condemnatory or otherwise, out of my expression and voice.

"It's stupid. I shouldn't have taken it so personally." I rolled my eyes, frustrated that I would have to actively pull teeth to get the answers I wanted from him. I reached over the mare and stopped his hand and the brush he was holding.

"What did he say?" I enunciated each word, making my intent clear. Knowing he couldn't get out of it, Adam decided to confess.

"Nothing," he sighed, "only that my family didn't want me, and that's why they sent me here. And that I wasn't wanted here, either." My breathing caught. Amund knew this issue was to be left alone. I clenched my jaw and nodded, thinking about consequences and actions and how this probably wouldn't solve anything. After a moment or so of pondering the subject, I decided my brain was doing too much work and let my heart step in.

"I'll leave you alone. But come get me if you want to talk." I turned on my heel and walked calmly out of Adam's sight. Once there, I sprinted to Amund's room, where I knew he'd be. I didn't knock before entering to find him taking pleasure in the company of a woman I had never seen. He turned his head to me, not stopping. Irritated, I rose my voice.

"You, leave. Now." Had this been a different day, I would have been kinder to the woman, whom I then realized was with a traveling troop that had stopped in Redefalk. She, horrified, covered herself and ran from the room.

"*Svatus kud*, Vita! What the hell could you possibly want that is so important?" He spat at me, covering himself in his sheets.

"Don't '*svatus kud*' me, Amund. You very well know what the hell is so important." I left the door open, wanting everyone to hear my words. "What *exactly* did you say to him?" Upon hearing these words come from my mouth, Amund, still covered from the waist down, hurried to close the doors I had left open.

"Why should you care? He knows I'm right. He doesn't belong here, Vita, he's not one of us. *We* don't want him here, and his parents definitely didn't want him either. It's time he learned his place, and it is lower than us." Amund approached me, trying to use his height advantage to intimidate me. Usually, that would have worked, but not that day. I shoved him backwards.

"He is family! And *nothing* you can ever say will change that!"

"Vita, he's not your brother! He's not our blood!" Amund raised his voice significantly. My veins burned.

"He's more of a brother than you ever were! Where were you every day when I wanted to spend time with you? Where were you the day I had my first fighting lesson? All of you, Elof, Geir, Einar, you thought that my place was so far beneath you that *I* was never worth your time! Adam would *never,* has never, abandoned me. You place so much importance on blood, but you don't even know what family is, what it does." Amund's face contorted, enraged.

"And how would you know *anything,*" he spat back. "You are nothing, just a little girl." I took a deep breath, calming myself before speaking this time.

"Wow, Amund, I've never heard that one before. Please, forgive my rudeness, my passion, to the future ruler of Kongeorn; I am appalled that my simple girl emotions got into my head." My voice dripped in sarcasm before morphing into a serious tone. "I hope you know that Da would be horrified to know the kind of person his beloved heir is. He's grooming you, but you will *never* be half the man he is, even at his lowest. A king does not extort or use his people; he protects them, loves them, sacrifices for them. The way you're going right now, you'll rule exactly like Alfred the Cruel." His eyebrows raised on their own accord as he tried to come back with something.

"Then why don't you rule?" he shouted back at me. I smiled and turned to leave.

"Because I'm a woman, obviously." I braced myself to leave, hand on the cool oak door, and then I heard a restrained voice, one which couldn't belong to my headstrong brother, speak from behind me.

"Then what should I do?" There was something like defeat, like shame, clouding the tremors of his words.

"Be the king the people need, not the one you're tempted to be. And never," I turned back around, making myself perfectly clear, "speak to Adam like that again, *ever*." I stared at him, expecting him to break the sorry facade, to retort, asking what I would do if he did. Which, I knew, I didn't have an answer to. There would be nothing I could do. But I felt, after staring down the eyes I saw every day in the mirror, I knew he wouldn't dare. And it seemed I was right.

Neither of us forgot that conversation, and Amund made it his goal to be the king and the brother we all needed, including Adam. He finally made Adam feel welcome, the way I had never been. And that seemed to be what made my heart the most happy, because Adam's happiness was my happiness, and I would defend that to my last breath.

Chapter 7
And So It Begins

The next few weeks were filled to the brim with plans upon plans: who would go with me, when we would leave, how long we would be staying. It was the day the leaves began to change that my company and I left for Feroxia's capital city of Ferida. It would take a total of seven days. We packed accordingly, bringing ample food and provisions. Gyda snuck me a jar of her magical poultice, knowing I'd need it while I was gone. And Adam packed extra cloth for me as well. We were all set.

The first night, we made camp and sat around a fire, ever vigilant, as the first signs of cold began to creep into our bones. I looked around, taking in the faces of those around me.

Bjorth stared into the flames, his scar shining, an acute reminder of those we had both lost and the things he had been willing to do to protect them. In past months, I had seen the patches of white spread throughout his red beard, and the top of his bald head, where hundreds of freckles called home, was beginning to show age spots. And yet, he could not stand to be left behind. Next to Bjorth was one of Amund's friends, a soldier whose wife had been giving birth when the party left that fateful day. Da had ordered him to stay behind and relish the experience being a father brought. Daniel had never forgiven himself, like Bjorth, for staying behind, for not being one of the dead. He had named his daughter Amanda to honor my oldest brother.

Next to Daniel were the cousins. Engel and Fritz were my age and were proficient swordsmen. When the news of my father's and brothers' deaths came home, they were some of the first to request to be trained. And they worked hard each and every day. From dawn until dusk, they could be found riding or sparring or shooting, always doing something together that could better each of them. As they say, *iron sharpens iron.*

After them was Dana, one of the few women, like me, who actually trained from childhood. She was the daughter of a farmer in the western territories of Kongeorn, and when King Alfred's troops targeted her farm, there was nothing—no one—left except for Dana, who had been out riding at the time. She was twelve. As she sat across the fire from me, nearly fifteen years later, she had the face and the mind of a warrior, of a woman who'd met Death and shook his hand before walking away.

Next to her was Oliver, an experienced fighter from the South who had joined our legion after Da had freed him from wrongful imprisonment.

When Oliver was seventeen, he had fallen in love with his brother's best friend. However, love between a man and another man in the South was highly frowned upon and punishable by imprisonment, as well as death, in several territories. His lover had been executed, and Oliver was next when Da had stepped in, a young diplomat from the North at the time. For the next thirty years, Oliver would serve my Da with everything he had. Da had told him to travel South and rescue others under the heavy weight of oppression. That was where he was when he heard of Da's death.

Finally, in between Dana and I, was Adam. Of course, he had kept his promise and was the first to be waiting in the square, horse packed and ready to leave. Unlike the rest of us, it seemed Adam had no survivor's guilt. Yes, he mourned, but he did not blame himself, as he shouldn't have. In fact, none of us should have felt the blame for Einar's choice, for his evil spirit, but I did anyway, and if I had let it completely eat away at me, I would never have made the journey to Ferida.

Bjorth got up from his seat and moved towards the wood behind us. He stopped and looked down at me before saying,

"Euna, would you walk with me?"

I stood from my spot and followed Bjorth as he walked, seemingly lost in thought. I never liked silences like these, the ones that come before difficult conversations.

"When Da tried for peace, did you ever doubt his decisions?" I asked, trying to start.

"Yes," was all he said.

I nodded, waiting for something else, but getting nothing.

"I always told ya that the reason I didn't marry was my scar. That's not true," Bjorth's voice was quiet, meant just for me to hear, "I was in love once. Her name was Seraphina. Andor and I had just scouted through the Disputed Lands when we found her.

"She was covered in dirt, hiding out in a ravine, but we spotted her."

Bjorth chuckled sadly.

"She was an escaped slave from Feroxia, running as far as she could. We brought her back to Redefalk with us. I taught her how to properly defend herself so she would never be a slave again. I loved her.

"I had planned to ask her to wed when the falcon came. It said she was Alfred's property, that she was his concubine. For every day that we didn't return her, he would kill one of the Kongeorn prisoners in his dungeon.

"Andor told her it was a bluff, that Alfred would kill them anyway, but Sera didn't believe him. She returned to Feroxia, and we never heard from her again."

My face was somber, taking in Bjorth's story, his grief.

"What I am trying to say, V, is that these Ferons can't be trusted. They will promise or threaten you and won't play by the rules. I don't know what Richard has in store for you, but I don't think it is peace."

Bjorth's words stuck with me the rest of the trip, but we had come too far to turn back. Not to mention, turning back would have been seen as a slight towards Richard, which would only make things worse.

I had no choice but to continue down the path I had chosen for us.

When we arrived at the outskirts of Ferida, the first thing to greet us was silence. We all exchanged glances; a city without noise was either dead or deathly ill. There were no vendors selling their wares, no children running around wildly, not even any dogs barking. The city, though it was the capitol, might as well have been abandoned.

We, however, continued on our way, Adam and I in the front, followed by Engel, Fritz, and Dana, and then Daniel, Bjorth, and Oliver. Had anyone been around to see us, they would have thought us simple travelers or merchants, maybe sellswords. I was not there to boast, nor was it in my character to dress like a queen. They would have to learn to accept my hunter's clothing.

While we made our way further towards the center of the city, the silence prevailed, only to be broken every so often by the occasional dog barking or door slamming. We all stayed on our guard, worried by the unusual scenes of this city. Even the smells were strange. In the larger, bustling keeps, the pungent scent of feces and horses permeated the stifling air. In smaller keeps like Redefalk, the smells were often similar to pine and mud. But here, there was an odd *lack* of odor, as if everything had been wiped clean of its personality, its nature. I pondered this as our horses clopped along the pristine cobbled road.

And then we came upon a wall, one we physically could not see above. There was no door in sight, and I wondered if my navigation skills had failed me, which they were known to do at times.

"This is the correct place, yes?" I looked behind me at Oliver, who had previously been to this settlement. He merely nodded, then put a shushing finger to his lips. For him, the silence was normal, but the gesture was not. I followed his gaze upward, craning my neck and attempting to see the top of this grand edifice. Before I could say anything, a voice—and what I was sure was spit—fell down from above.

"Who are you?" the voice asked in a thick Feroxian accent.

"*Nos so'os de Sonheorn. Eu sou a rainha Vita,*" I replied with as much authority and volume as I could muster, all the while peering up at an unseen audience. After my response, I heard several shouts and then a large crack, followed by rumbling, which we could feel underneath us. Dagny nearly spooked beneath me as the enormous stone wall in front of us split along each stone and opened, beckoning.

In awe, we directed our horses through the opening. Realizing my mouth was gaping open, I quickly snapped it shut and looked behind me. Again, Oliver merely nodded, this time with a smug grin on his face. Behind him, the wall began to close, mending itself before our eyes. I stopped Dagny as several stable boys, all scrawny and in need of a wash, descended upon us, offering their services, which we gladly accepted, albeit somewhat surprised at their enthusiasm. Curiouser and curiouser.

We were then led to a single wooden door at the base of a fantastically large stone building, which I assumed to be—and

Oliver confirmed to be—the castle of the Feroxians and the Feron name. Wordlessly, the door was creaked open, and we fell into a line, our stern guide at the front, and another trailing at the back.

Whether it was the strange dampness of the air, or the cramped spaces within the stone stairwell, wont for windows, I was beginning to feel as if we were climbing some sort of stairway to Heaven. *Yeah, 'cause it would look like this…* I rolled my eyes at my own thoughts, the lazy side of me praying for a light at the end of this oh-so-dark, ascending tunnel. Luckily, the training of my years in combat prepared me for the heroic feat of walking up a ridiculous number of steps. How could I have been so lucky?

When *finally* we reached what I hoped to the Mother to be the top, another wooden door stood in our way. Our guide knocked and, upon hearing a voice acknowledge him from the other side, opened the door. As I strode out of the darkness, I found myself and my friends in a low-lit chamber with sconces every few feet on the cold stone walls. There were very few windows, and those that were existent were covered by a dark sheet. Therefore, the light in the room was sensual, at best, and stifling, at worst. To our left was a raise in the stone where, up five or so feet, sat the Feroxian throne. According to history, it had been a crowning gift to Pridbor by one of their "gods." He was their highest god, the god of suffering and death and ambition. And like all that god represented, the throne was twisted. The tarred and hardened bones of Pridbor's enemies had been conjoined for eternity by the god's hands. The polish of the tar could, no doubt, trick one into thinking it a work of art, something to be in awe of. But knowing the price paid for this symbol of power was to know why it was a thing of death.

To the Feroxians, however, especially the Feron line of kings, any work of Dor was sacred, and never—*never*—to be questioned. And, as far as I could tell, it hadn't been for quite some time.

In that throne, that testament to blood and dust, sat the new Feroxian king, the son of Alfred the Cruel.

"Ah, finally," Richard, king of the land, spoke to us, his eyes, however, only on one of us, "I was beginning to think you had lost your way." His dialect of the Feroxian tongue was fluid, fast, but clear and easy to follow, as well.

I replied, "Thank you, sir, we are glad to have made it safely." I nodded my head to him, a subtle sign of respect. Though there was no evidence that he deserved my respect, it was required to keep up the pretense of civility.

"I *respect* your enthusiasm to speak to me, Miss; I would, however, prefer that I speak directly to the Queen of Kongeorn, or a man, at least." I turned to Dana, the only other woman in the group, and shared a look with her before giving a slight nod. *This will be good.* Dana didn't possess many of the renowned Kongeorn traits, such as the blue eyes or the pronounced jawline. If Richard thought that Dana was Kongeorn blood, then he obviously didn't do his research. Still, Dana stepped forward and acknowledged him with a curt tip of her brow.

"So, you wish to speak to the Queen of Kongeorn?" She held her hands behind her back, straight-backed, the way a queen—other than myself—would carry herself. Her long brown braid sashayed behind her as she turned her head, surveying all in attendance. I took note, as well. Three young guards by the main entrance, a set of large wooden doors. Two older gentlemen seated behind the king, of which both looked to be about ninety. And behind us, the two men who had led us up the stairway. If we needed to, we could most definitely make it out of this room alive. Hopefully, that would not prove to be an issue.

Dana continued. "A Queen such as Vita of Kongeorn demands respect. And *I* would prefer that you speak to her with more reverence, as she has most definitely earned it." Dana then turned to me and gestured forward. "My Queen, I hope you are satisfied." I gave her an approving look as I again stepped to the front of the group. *Oh, how passive aggression suits me.* I met the king's eyes, and was pleased to note the not-so-hidden surprise in his eyes. I smirked, waiting for a verbal reaction. Moments later, I got it.

"Well, it would seem that I was mistaken, Your Highness," he paused before adding, "orgive me; I did not know." Other rulers would have been offended, and I won't lie: it only contributed to the idea that I wasn't meant to make a difference. How can someone who doesn't seem like a ruler accomplish things that are expected of a ruler?

My mind was drawn back to the mirror at Redefalk, where I had analyzed myself, for both good and bad. I thought back to the words Mami had spoken, the words I hadn't wanted to hear. *The only person whose opinion matters is the one in that mirror.* I could not say she was right or wrong, but to do what I needed to do, to do what was best for the people I represented, to do what was needed from me,

I had to put away any doubt I still had in myself. And I had to forgive and forget those who would not.

"You are forgiven, Sir." I paused. "You are not the first to assume less of me." I would offer no more. He did not need an explanation from me, and I felt no need to explain myself at all. I only waited, the statement hanging in the cramped air around us. Behind the king, one of the two old men shifted and leaned forward slightly, whispering into his ear. He was no more experienced than I in affairs of state, of that which is expected of those who carry the mantel of a society.

"Ah, yes," he began, not as a reply to my previous declaration, but as a new page to write on, "you must be exhausted from your journey. My men will see you all to your rooms; I only hope they are to your liking. I will make certain that food is brought to you. Feasts are so tedious, and will only serve to drain you more." I merely nodded, gave him a parting gesture of respect before leading my comrades out behind our guide.

The young guard did not speak, and though he was large in body, and quite muscular, he looked as if he were only seventeen or eighteen. I glanced to Bjorth next to me to gauge his thoughts. He nodded, agreeing that the traits of our guide were quite unusual.

We turned down a long hallway, several windows, luckily uncovered, let in the dim sunlight of the afternoon. There were thirteen doors—thirteen rooms—along the wall which faced the windows. Outside the unobstructed windows were trees, all in a neat line, groomed to perfection. As far as sights went, I was impressed by this kingdom, albeit still a bit uncomfortable.

When we came to the seventh door on our right, the young guard stopped and turned, allowing us to see his eyes clearly for the first time. Unlike many young men in Kongeorn's streets and taverns, this one seemed emotionless. His eyes did not search, they did not pry, they did not tell. He only looked to Oliver, opened the door, and gestured for him to go inside. Oliver seemed unfazed, so I took this to be normal Feroxian hospitality. The next four doors were reserved for Fritz, Engel, Daniel, and Dana, respectively. They all entered without hesitation but, I knew, still on guard. When Bjorth's door came next, he looked back at me before entering. In his eyes, I could detect caution, worry. He always worried about me.

Adam's was the next room, and he did not enter when the guard opened the door. Instead, he scrutinized the behemoth of a man and reached out his hand.

"Adam," he offered his name, trying his best to be somewhat friendly. The man simply looked at Adam's hand, not understanding, it seemed. After a few moments, Adam turned to me, shrugged, and entered his designated room. Finally, it was my turn. The man led me to the last door, the only one without a window across from it. He opened, and motioned for me to go inside, where, I noticed, all of my bags had been deposited. *That's not weird...* And when I entered, he followed me in, but did not close the door behind him.

I straightened, slowly moving my right hand closer to my left, whose sleeve held one of my daggers. The man approached me, and alone, I was truly able to gauge just how massive this man was. As a short person, myself, I was used to looking up at people, but I had to crane my neck to see his face, almost as if I was back outside the wall again.

"Um, is there something you need?" I asked, trying be as polite as possible—and not show just how uncomfortable I was. The brute handed me a piece of paper I hadn't noticed had been in his large fist. Before I opened it, I asked him, "What is your name? So that I may tell Richard how good a guide you've been." He did not speak, but his face grew red, and he looked almost sheepish. He opened his mouth into some sort of odd grin, and there, I saw that his tongue had been cut out. I had to stop myself from verbally saying, "Ohhhhhhh." Instead, though, I took one of his massive hands in mine and shook it. He smiled as I did so. "Thank you again," I said, and he walked out, closing the door and leaving me still quite confused.

After staring at the door with a puzzled look on my face for what must have been at least five minutes, I remembered the paper in my hand. Opening it, I read:

My Queen,

I hope that you would be so kind as to speak with me tomorrow morning during breakfast. I will have a seat of honor placed out for you next to me. And do not worry, your men will be close by.

~King Richard

Though well meant, the gesture gave me a feeling deep in my gut I couldn't deny even if I tried. The closest feeling to it I could recall was apprehension, but even that didn't quite fit. The last line particularly made me furrow my brows in confusion, as if there were a reason for danger. *Or he could just be trying to ease any worry you may have.* Either way, I would speak to him the next day at breakfast.

The food that was brought for me to eat in my room was good, but not exceptional. It seemed again that the sights in Ferida overpowered all else it had to offer, including its people's activities, of which I had seen none. After my meal, I felt the ache in my buttocks from riding, and the soreness of my core from being on the move all day, and from having started my Luna's blood on the ride there. And so, after putting the poultice on my abdomen, I resigned myself to the bed covered in burgundy sheets. No sooner had I laid my head down to sleep that I began to dream.

In the midst of a great fog, I stand. It clings to my skin, which is covered by nothing but the air itself. In the distance, I hear the rushing of water. A great waterfall, perhaps. I follow the noise to investigate. My bare feet soon come in contact with warm, tranquil water, and I find myself wading into a stunning pool. The mist surrounding me clears and, on the other side of the large pool, just behind the waterfall, I see a man.

His onyx eyes are glued to me, pulling me forward towards him, towards the rushing water. He smiles a half grin, and my eyes rove over his chiseled body. As I grow nearer, his hand reaches out for me, and I take it, still completely mesmerized. He speaks my name, and I walk through the sheet of warm, life giving water. I join him beneath it. I let him run his fingertips over my face. From the crook of my nose to my lips to my cheek.

His own face is made from marble, always changing colors, and always brilliant. His wet and curled hair reaches just below his ears. But his eyes are what continues to enchant me, to seduce me into growing closer and closer. Those eyes shine darker than nights without stars; there is no protection from their enthralling pull. Soon, my face is but an inch from his. His vice arms hold me to him, unwilling to let me go—and I have no intention of leaving. I would stay there with him forever, do anything for him: die for him, or kill for him. Closer and closer, I move in until our lips embrace and our limbs intertwine.

When I finally pull away to breathe, I open my eyes to look upon him once more. What I see shakes me. Down the center of his face, there is a long scar, a crack, as if the stone he is made out of was hit with a war hammer. Instead of enchanting me, his eyes now bear into me, burning me with their touch. I try to pull away, but he won't let me go. My arms are immobile and my legs carry no strength. Feeling completely helpless, I cry out for Da, for Mami, for Adam, for anyone to come save me.

The being is not pleased; he scowls at me and shows sharpened teeth before pushing me under the water, now boiling with bubbles. I kick and thrash, but to no avail. Darkness moves forward out from my periphery and into my mind, consuming all in its path.

I awoke, caked in sweat, just as Adam crashed through the door. Luckily for him, it didn't break and leave all of us with explaining to do. He rushed toward me and put a cooling hand to my sweat-covered forehead.

"What happened?" he rushed the words from his mouth. "Are you alright?" He looked into each of my eyes, trying to see if I was sufficiently responsive. As the shock from the dream—and that's all it had to have been—cleared away, I began to nod, vigorously at first, then much more slowly as I realized I was, indeed, okay. Adam sighed in relief and collapsed next to me on the bed. As he covered his face with his right arm, I heard heavy footsteps approach from the hallway.

Bjorth overran the door and skidded back, knees almost giving way. Seeing me safe, he took a moment to catch his labored breath. Then, once it was caught, he looked back up and noticed something neither Adam, nor I, had noticed. His face turned the color of his beard and he gingerly shut the door, clearing his throat in the process. As the door thudded shut, I realized what he had seen and looked over at Adam.

He was sweaty, hair tousled, with no shirt and night shorts disheveled, besides. Eyes widening, I looked down at myself. I inhaled as I saw that I, myself, was wearing nothing but burgundy sheet. I rolled my eyes and pinched the bridge of my nose.

"Adam," I spoke, now desperate for Bjorth to know that it wasn't what it looked like, "Adam!" With a lazy exclamation, he lifted his arm away from his face and looked at me. I raised my eyebrows, giving him an authoritative look. Realizing, he looked at me and then at himself before hustling out of the room and down the hallway to Bjorth's room. I listened to the hammering on the door, and then its opening before exhaling and laying back down. The last thing I needed was my godfather thinking I was controlled by hormones. I pulled the sheets back over my face, mulling over the embarrassing scenario before quickly pulling them down again and emerging from the bed.

Naked, I walked over to the window, then retreated, remembering that such *displays* were not proper of a queen, or anyone else, for that matter. Changing my route, I walked over to my small trunk of clothing and opened it. *Wow, so many to choose from, how could a girl ever decide?* Good thing I was good with fast decisions. I quickly changed into one of the two outfits I had packed and tied my hair back before leaving the room, appetite in tow.

Usually, in a new place such as a foreign keep, I would be cautious about using my own instincts to get to a room, but I just followed the sweet aroma of breakfast pastries to a dining hall not far from where my room was. Inside, I saw the king, along with the two old men and a handful of servants, all of whom kept their heads lowered at all times. I added that to the List of Strange Things in Feroxia and strode up to the king.

"Ah, good morning, Highness." He grinned, careful to swallow his food before speaking, "I trust you slept well?" Something in the way he said it, perhaps the look in his eyes, made me think—just for a moment—that he knew about my dream. I shook it off as simply the continuing reaction to the unsettling nightmare. After all, he seemed genuinely interested.

"Yes, I did," I lied, smiling graciously, before returning, "And I hope you did as well." He motioned for me to take the seat across from him, where a silver plate had been set out, along with a silver goblet encrusted with rubies. He really had pulled out all the stops for our visit. I took my seat, and just as I did so, a servant came up on my side, head bowed low, and asked if I should want wine with my breakfast.

"No, thank you," I replied, "water will be fine." I tried to sweeten my tone, still a bit unsettled by how solemn the servants were.

At home, the servants were workers, with families in the town, who had children that any child of higher birth would gladly play with. Many of our servers I had known and talked with and eaten with since childhood. The hall was always buzzing with their conversations amongst themselves and with my family members. It was simply strange to me to observe such standoffish people. Another item for the list, then. I looked down at my plate and saw that it had been filled with various pastries and preparations of breakfast foods, both familiar and unfamiliar. What surprised me most, however, was how it had gotten there without me noticing.

"I take pride in knowing my servants are the quietest in Jordklode," Richard spoke, answering one of my questions. "They are taught to move, to serve, as if they are invisible, as if they do not exist." I nodded, faking understanding. Again, it was a strange notion to me, but to each his own. Before I could try to make myself invisible and dig into the delectable-looking food before me, the king pressed on.

"I trust you received my message yesterday." He didn't wait for me to answer before continuing, "I had an idea as to *how* to solve this little peace predicament between our two great nations, and I wanted to gauge your thoughts before officially presenting it to both of our councils." He had my attention; though, him calling the rift between Feroxia and Kongeorn a "predicament" had almost made me snort aloud. I nodded, and waited for him to speak again.

"If you would accompany me through the gardens, I would be happy to elaborate." Richard didn't wait for my reply. Instead, he stood from the table, walked over to me, and held out his arm.

Reluctantly, and somewhat uncomfortably, I took it, standing.

We left the quiet meal hall through a set of door to the left, which led to a small landing, followed by white marble steps into what I assumed Richard meant as the garden.

By my standards, this was no garden. The only plants I saw were basil plants, giving the entire area an overwhelming odor that, in small doses, would have been bearable. Along the stony path which carved through the forest of basil were statues, most likely of the past kings of Feroxia.

"This," Richard stopped us in front of one of the statues, whose face was harder than the stone it was carved from, "is our founder, Pridbor I. He had a vision of a great nation led by hard work and strong leadership, which I am sure you can admire."

Pridbor built his nation on the backs of slaves. He was a tyrant who killed his wives when they disobeyed him. I thought to myself, fighting to hide my disgust.

Richard looked at me as he spoke. His expression was calm, almost serene, but there was more—deceit, perhaps?—lurking deep below the surface, showing through his eyes.

"You hate, just as much as I do, the death of innocent people," he said, "and I am ashamed to say that this war between our two peoples has caused so many of those deaths. And what for? Can we even remember why this conflict began in the first place?"

I almost recoiled. He couldn't be serious. This 'conflict' had been started thirty years before, when his own father hired mercenaries to attack Kongeorn civilians at the border to the Disputed Lands. When that wasn't enough, they went into battle against Da and his family.

King Alfred himself had killed my grandfather and six uncles before Nana, Da, Bjorth, and my mother forced them to retreat. After that, my father took the throne, only to lead the final battle of that time against the Feroxians. He—like all Kongeorns—had hoped to end the war with that battle.

Unfortunately, while the official war had ended, the Feroxians continued to attack our people, provoking a new war that had ignited with the deaths of parents and brothers.

"Regardless of the past, of the *conflict*, stopping the deaths of innocent people is my top priority." I tried to remain calm, diplomatic.

"See? We found something we can agree on."

We walked further, passing a statue or two, and Richard told me about his life, about the foreign leaders he had met.

"When I was just barely a man, my father arranged a meeting between the leader of the Seventy Provinces of Daygn and myself. I was astonished to see how their people lived. You know, Daygn is divided into seventy city-states, hence the name," Richard continued to, as I resigned myself to annoyed silence, explain to me what I already knew, "and their ruler is this very strong man, Theseus."

Da had been sure that all of his children knew all there was to know about the nations of our world. On command, I could recite the wording of the Tandem Neutrality Agreement of 555—and that was seven full pages of text. Nothing Richard could tell me would be new. *Surely, he realizes that, as a ruler, I know all of this. Wait.* I sucked my teeth. *I'm a woman, so how could I* possibly *know anything of worth, right?*

Richard continued on.

"Anyway, while in the capitol of the Provinces, which is called Anyac, I saw how their people lived. No one starved. There was peace. The streets were clean, and the merchants were thriving. I came home from that trip more optimistic than I had been in a long time.

"All I could think was, 'I want that for our people.' And I know that, as long as this ridiculous, unprovoked war rages on, we will never get that."

For the first time since my arrival, I full-heartedly agreed with Richard. I stopped where I was, prompting the king to do the same.

"That's why I'm here. The sooner we can come to an agreement, the sooner we can end this war. Our people deserve that." I could feel the emotion in my throat as I spoke, eyes pleading.

I had seen how his people were living. The streets were empty. The fear was thick here, and I couldn't help but feel guilty for that. After all, it takes two sides to fight a war.

Richard smiled at me, and I smiled back, genuine and somewhat excited.

We moved on down the line of statues, stopping at each statue so Richard could praise their deeds. I struggled to maintain a neutral face, wondering if he had forgotten the conversation we had just had. Each statue represented hate and war; each face represented death. Why focus on the past when we were there to change the future?

Finally, we came to the end of the line of statues. I'd never seen paintings of the man this statue honored, but I knew by the sharp chin and the cold eyes that this was King Alfred the Cruel.

"My father," Richard said, "was a flawed man. He made mistakes. But he was a good leader, a good king."

Fury began to bubble in my stomach as I looked upon the face of the man who conspired with my brother to kill my family. I could feel the hate radiate off of the cold marble, and the odor of basil seeped through my skin, stinging my nerves. Surely, Richard couldn't be serious. Painting his father in a decent light would do nothing to bring peace between our two nations. He had to know that. I glared up at the statue as Richard continued,

"He wanted what was best for our two nations."

It took everything in me not to spit on the statue.

"Which is why I am sure he would want their union."

The cloud of anger disappeared. I almost snapped my neck with how fast I turned my head to look at Richard, hoping against hope that he wasn't about to say what I thought he was going to say.

"Vita, you and I both know that power is made in connection. Connections with other nations makes your own stronger. Whether it be by trade, by alliance, or, as I propose, by marriage."

"Excuse me?" The question came out kinder than I had thought it in my head, which, in retrospect, was good. I wanted peace. We had just talked about peace, but not this way. *Not like this.* Jordklodian laws dictates that, when two countries are joined by marriage, the man in the union is the primary ruler, and the nation of the woman—if that is the composition of the pairing—is annexed by that of the man's. If I were to marry Richard, the war may end, but the suffering of my people might not. And that was a chance I was *not* willing to take.

"I propose that we wed, and join our kingdoms, while claiming the Disputed Lands. We could rule, we could dominate, the continent of Jordklode." He reached for my free hand, his pale eyes imploring me, begging me, for an answer.

"No," I replied, snatching my hand away from him, removing my arm from his. Amund's child, the child Karina carried was meant to inherit Kongeorn, and I could not give it away to some foreign monarch. My purpose had nothing to do with marrying this king. It was not my right.

Something flashed in Richard's eyes, turning them, for mere seconds, into a far darker color. He quickly regained composure before looking up at the statue next to him.

"Of course," he paused, as if to steady himself, "I completely respect this decision. And I hope this does not put a snag in our efforts for peace." His face was calm, composed, but out of the corner of my eye, I could see the white-knuckle grip he had on the pendant at his chest. Then, I walked past him, back toward the palace, in search of one of my counsels.

"Thank you, Your Majesty," I said, my legs numb as my mind shouted at me to get away, to find an escape so I could breathe and speak to one of my own people about this development, "I promise that we will find another solution. I am sure of it."

Unfortunately for me, I found none of those people in the halls on the way back to my room. Instead, I heard from someone I really didn't want to speak with.

Well, you've made it this far, at least. She sounded smug to me. I didn't like that. She had no reason to be smug. I hated when people were smug.

Yeah, I'm here, but the trip is already a bit ruined, if you ask me. For some reason, ever since her sass in Creat, I just found conversations with Ahava to be really—*really*—draining. As if everything she said was meant to confuse and frustrate me. And it usually did.

Do not be dissuaded because something you could not predict came into the picture, Vita. I still detected smugness. I could feel the string straining, and it was about to snap.

"Okay," I shouted, before remembering only crazy people talk to the voices in their heads aloud, *Seriously, Ahava, you have to stop it with all of the mystic shit, okay? I may not be on the same plane as you, but I deserve to know at least something about my fate if I am to be some puppet for those on high!* And the smugness disappeared. In fact, I thought Ahava had, as well, because she remained silent for so long. I actually got back to my room and closed the door behind me before she replied at all.

Vita, I suppose the only thing I can really say is that I'm sorry. You're right; we are not on the same plane. This is the existence I am used to, and I suppose I just can't understand the confusion you are feeling. Finally, some sort of connection. Something from her that I could trust.

And I am—for the most part—sorry that I snapped at you, I returned, feeling just a tad guilty. But my temper, like my father's before me, could only take so much aggravation. Ahava remained silent again for a while.

Well, though I am restricted from telling you what *to do or* what *is in your future, I suppose it may make you feel better to know that I only know what the Mother tells me, which—for the record—isn't that much.* Her voice was sheepish, more human than ever before. *And you aren't Her puppet; She doesn't have it all laid out on this big table, you know. You make the choices, and She can merely predict what will happen because of them. But there are millions upon millions of possible outcomes, of possible decisions, that you could make true. So, no, you are most certainly not a puppet. You never were.* After that, her voice faded and stayed faded for the rest of the day.

After spending a couple of hours holed up in my room, staring out the window at the small piece of Feroxia that I could see, I decided to share with at least one of my counsels what Richard had proposed.

I knocked gingerly on the door, hoping he would answer. I smiled as the door opened to reveal Oliver's chocolate eyes and tousled black hair. He offered me half a smile before gesturing for me to enter. His room looked identical to mine, in every way except for the window, which painted the picture of another section of the capital city and palace grounds. I stopped in the middle, not wanting to take a seat, and bade him to sit down. After relaying all that had occurred at breakfast, I waited for Oliver to say something, anything. I knew he wasn't much for words, but he was wise when he did decide to speak.

"Vita," Oliver addressed me in his deep timbre, "though I cannot speak for your father, I do speak for many of the Kongeorn people, and they would want you to follow your heart, which I see you have done in turning King Richard down on his offer. And besides, your heart lies only with those you have already chosen." He smirked at me before growing silent, his normal disposition. *Damn, he's good.* I felt my cheeks growing red, so I mumbled my thanks and departed from the room.

By then, it was lunchtime, and my stomach would not forgive me for skipping out on the rest of my breakfast. However, I also didn't want to see Richard again while this awkward phase was still in place, for me at least. I flipped a mental coin and found that food, as always, won out with my priorities. Instead of going to the hall, where I knew Richard was, I made my way to the source, the kitchens.

As I entered, all whispered conversation and bustle stopped. Each cook and maid and servant looked at one another, dropped what they were doing, and bowed. Taken aback, I just kind of stared. Yet another thing I had to add to that pesky list. After a while, one of the bigger cooks spoke, still bowing.

"Your Magnificence, please, we beg of you to have mercy. If you are displeased, we will see ourselves to a suitable punishment." Again, I simply looked at them. Then I realized I would probably need to say *something*.

"Um, I'm not dissatisfied at all." I tried to speak clearly, like someone who could recover in awkward situations. "In fact, I am completely impressed with both your services and cooking." I could see the anxiety lift from the room. "Oh, please, you don't need to bow." They all straightened, but the majority still kept their heads lowered. "I only wanted to know if I could have my lunch in my room; I am not feeling well enough to dine in the hall at the moment." *There ya go, Vita, way to recover.* The same burly cook was surprised, a bit confused, but more than happy to oblige me. I thanked him and took the food back on my own.

After polishing off the delectable lunch, I thought on home, on Kongeorn. Truth be told, I missed it. Sure, Feroxia was extravagant, not to mention disciplined. But it was also strange and unfamiliar. If anything, it made me miss Da and Mami even more, like their spirits were unable to reach me outside of Redefalk. I laid down on the bed and reflected.

Bjorth was there, and that was like home. I had friends here with me, and Dagny, too. And I had Adam. That thought, more so than any fireplace or great hall, made me feel better, more at home. Because where Adam was, home was.

In the midst of a great fog, I stand. It clings to my skin, which is covered by nothing but the air itself. In the distance, I hear the rushing of water. A great waterfall, perhaps. I follow the noise to investigate. My bare feet soon come in contact with warm, tranquil water, and I find myself wading into a stunning pool. The mist surrounding me clears and, on the other side of the large pool, just behind the waterfall, I see a man.

His emerald eyes shine through the mist of the waterfall, beckoning me, drawing me further. Instead of feeling hypnotized, I feel calm, steady, at peace. I pass through the sheet of water and into his arms. I take in his features, the same features I associate with life, with my world, the same features I can never live without.

This time, his arms encompass me, warming me, keeping me alive, keeping me close, exactly where I want to be. Closer and closer, we move, until our foreheads meet, and there is nowhere else I want to ever be. I close my eyes.

Chapter 8
Defenestration of Adam

The sound of a knock at the door caused me to open my eyes abruptly. I looked to the window, black with a Luna-less night. *Jeez, I guess I must have been exhausted.* I got up, still fully clothed from the day, and answered the door. My big friend from before waited outside for me. He beckoned me forward, to follow him as I did before. I cautiously did so, quietly shutting the door behind me.

My big friend led me down several hallways until we found a heavily guarded door. The two guards were bulky, but nowhere near my guide. They both eyed me. Then one knocked three times on the door behind him and, upon receiving a cue of some sort, opened the door. My big friend blocked out my view of what was behind the door, so I simply followed him inside.

Once in the meticulously furnished room, I stepped out from behind the big man's shadow. I looked at him as I did, wondering why he had brought me here; however, he covered his face sheepishly with his meaty hands. I turned my head to take in the sight of King Richard laying in a regally large bed, a naked and collared woman on each side of him.

The doors shut behind us, and my big friend kept his hands over his eyes.

"I do apologize for waking you so early in the morning, or late in the night, depending on how you look at it." His left hand absentmindedly stroked the skin of one of the collared women. Her skin was tanned, glowing, and her hair was long and black, wildly falling around her, down to her waist. The other was of pale skin with freckles and red hair. She looked fragile, with pale grey eyes that looked at nothing. They both, however, shared a single trait. A tattoo of the crest of Feron was inked onto each of their right cheeks. My heart thudded as I realized what they were.

"Do you see my lovely girls? They are quite exquisite, picked especially by myself. Daas," he gestured to the darker one, "was bought from an owner in Toyg. And Daora was born here to one of my father's favorite whores." He kissed her cheek and proceeded to whisper something in her ear. Whatever it was, she smiled at the words and, with no amount of leisure, disappeared below the comforter.

"Perfection." King Richard sighed to the lump under the blankets before turning his attention back to me. "They could be yours as well. I am not against sharing." I wrinkled my nose in disgust, wanting desperately to be anywhere but here. No person should be forced to do anything, let alone *shared*. He took note of my expression.

"Oh well, anyway, I wanted to speak to you about my proposition from earlier. I would greatly appreciate it if you would reconsider. You see, I *need* Kongeorn under my thumb, which means

I need *you*. And oh, how badly do I want what I need." He paused, sighing yet again. "You will agree to marry me, sign a treaty, and hand over all Kongeorn lands to the Feron name, or I will send you home with the heads of your comrades." I physically could not contain the intake of breath at his words. He chuckled at my surprise. *How could you have been so stupid, so naive? Adam was right all along, and now you're going to get him killed.*

"Make a decision tonight. If you join me here before dawn, all will be forgiven; if not…" he trailed off, smiling at me. He then waved a hand, ordering us to leave. The big man, however, still covered his face, so I had to pull him with me out of the doors. We walked a few steps, both of our faces red for different reasons, before I leaned into the big man.

"How quickly can you get me back to my chambers and make sure mine and my friends' horses are saddled to leave?" The big man only smiled at me before swooping me up into his large arms and ambling down the hall. By the time we got to the window-marked hallway, he was out of breath. I bade him set me down. Once he did, I kissed his cheek, and he ran off again, holding a meaty hand to his face.

I sprinted the remaining few feet to Oliver's door and banged on it urgently. After a moment or so, it opened.

"Get what you need, we have to leave as soon as possible. King Richard has promised us death." Oliver obeyed and did as I asked. While he did so, I visited each of the next five doors, relaying the same message each time. And each time, the recipient sprang to get ready. Once we all stood in our traveling clothes in the hall, I directed them further.

"Your horses are saddled, but you cannot leave through any doors; the windows will have to do. Go." All of them picked a window and jumped, landing after ten feet or so. All of them, that was, but one.

Adam contemplated me as I ordered him to jump, the Sol rising behind us.

"No, I cannot leave you, never," He was almost as stubborn as I was, but my eyes and the authority in my voice gave him no choice but to obey.

"You will jump. You will return safely to Redefalk. And you will leave me behind."

"Bu—"

"Go. Now. If you stay, there is no doubt that Richard will have you killed."

"How do you know they won't kill you?"

"Because he cannot afford to." I withdrew my dagger from my boot and gave it to him, knowing he would care for it. Even though he still showed signs of stubbornness, he put the dagger in his own boot. With that, I pushed my consort from the window and into the bushes below. He, along with the rest of my company, would return home. The Feroxian guards would not pursue or kill them, because all they really wanted was me. I stood, in front of the window, blocking the view, as Richard's men came upon me.

"Ay, 'ere she is," the biggest of the men, Benno, exclaimed, "looks like she was too slow to get out of our grasp, she was." I rolled my eyes as the other brutes bound my hands behind my back. While they did so, I felt at least three hard gropes on my backside. In a different situation, they would have lost those hands, but I needed to stall for as long as possible for my company to get away.

"She may not be the pretties', but she's got one fine rump, she does." This time, a gap-toothed fool by the name of Ham—yes, his name was "Ham"—grabbed me. All I could do for the moment was stare straight ahead, only thinking of cutting off certain *extremities* of theirs.

When finally they grew quiet and the crackling of torches was the only sound besides the muffled footsteps upon rugs, we turned down a dark corridor, one which collected more grime and cobwebs than any other that I had seen. It was a clear contrast to the conspicuous perfection of the rest of this city. We traveled down its musty pathways for some time before we stopped at a wooden door that was just slightly ajar. In we walked to find Richard, alone.

"I should have your heads for the unannounced intrusion, but I need you all for a few more hours," he turned, shaven clean, with his chin jutting out, "and it seems you were able to do one thing right." He bid them unhand me, and I walked forward, still bound tightly. Richard examined me, hands hovering just above my skin and clothing. "Now," he concluded, "I do believe there is one thing wrong. You have entirely too many layers on."

I raised my eyebrows. Surely, he wouldn't—then again, the only women he could get along with barely ever wore clothes.

"Benno, your dagger, please." Benno handed the handle to Richard as the king gazed thoughtfully at my trousers and tunic.

Then, he grabbed a handful and slashed down, tearing it from my body. He slashed and tore countless more times, all while I stood, unmoving. When he was finished, my nether was hardly covered, while my breasts, now cold, were exposed. I still stood, unwavering, head up, shoulders back.

"Well look at you, Your Radiance. I would say you glow, but that may be from the new sunlight. Let me have a closer look here." With that, he began to prod and poke, first at my arms, then my shoulders, and around to my chest. One hand pulled me closer to him, while the other explored my flesh. I waited for the opportune moment. As he reached for my left breast, I turned and caught his hand between my teeth.

Clamping down, I heard him howl in pain and delighted in the taste of blood I found in my mouth.

"Y—you bitch!" He squealed as I released his broken, battered fingers. He ordered his men to find a healer, and to bring a woman called Avery with them as well. *Probably one of his whores to boost his ego after that. Not much he'll be able to do with that hand from now on.* I sat down, skin to the cold stone floor, basking in the victory that I had snatched in that moment. I waited calmly, collectedly, for the men and woman to arrive. All the while, Richard whimpered and cradled his bloodied hand. I could feel the anger and pain rolling off of him in waves. *No matter the consequences, the look on his face is well worth it.* I didn't know how wrong I would be.

It appeared Avery wasn't a woman, but a pale man from the southern regions of Jordklode. Avery, as he explained himself to me, was a man of curiosity. He wanted to know how far and how long the human body could be tested. I realized, halfway through his speech, that he was not only a man of *curiosity*, but a member of the southern cult called "Cruor Allicit," commonly known as the "C'All."

They took children and whores and people who would not be missed from their homes to experiment on them. Their goal was to see how long and how much the body could endure. The highest honor was to have a *subject* last through all five stages of the *experiments*, none if which ever involved bones. Of all things, bones were sacred to the Cruor Allicit. They tortured their victims only in skin and tissue, and mind. Still, none survived past stage four.

Looking into Avery's pale, almost translucent, eyes, I felt the first twinge of fear. What would he do to me? I had only ever read about the C'All, and all that I had read, and more, would be in my future. In that moment, I felt small, helpless, and vulnerable. In that moment, I was no longer in control.

"Darling child, it will be my pleasure to examine you. I feel you will be the most exciting patient yet," his voice oozed from his lips like rotten honey as it trailed down his chin and into my ears. His accent was relaxed, and he spoke slowly, like many who called the southern reaches of Feroxia home. With a twinkle in his eye, Avery smiled. It wasn't sinister, no, but a smile of great joy, which, in itself, made my heart drop. Avery bid everyone leave, including Richard, who departed with a sneer upon his face.

After the stone room was emptied, save for myself and Avery, the strange C'All first covered the window with a black strip of cloth and began to ruffle through a sack he had brought with him.

In it, he found chains, which he used to keep me securely in place, several rusted blades, and needles of all different sizes, as well as different jars of liquids. He began with the blades.

The thumping of my own heart drowned out the C'All's accented cooing as a decayed blade grew ever closer to my skin. He started at my abdomen, where he swiped the blade. I cried out, flinching as the gash welled up with blood. Again and again, he did this, each time, going just a bit deeper. Sometimes, he would return to a previously made slash, and open it further. Tears ran down my cheeks as I struggled to hold in the screams.

"My dear, you are quite strong. That is quite promising. But, we will see how you feel after tomorrow." With that, he unchained me, leaving my hands still bound, packed up his instruments, and left me in a pool of my own blood. At that point, the Sol had left the sky, and my first day alone with these monsters had ended. The night winds blew through the window, chilling me to my bones.

Breathe through it. Just breathe through it. Breathe through it, and it will be over. Just get through tomorrow. Get through tomorrow. Creator, give me the strength to get through the night.

I stand in front of that same mirror where my mother's shade had taught me to see my worth, but this time, she is not here. No one is here. I am, in every sense of the word, alone. I cannot look away from those prying, icy eyes. They bear into me, seeking out everything that I cannot stand, that I loathe with my entire being. They are unforgiving. They are unmoving. And they are mine. My reflection reaches out from the glass, emerging into my world, its fingers bony and white, like skin that had been stretched too long.

The hand clasps mine, and I see the familiarity of the back of my own hand. It pulls. I follow. No hesitation; I cannot disobey myself.

Over the following fourteen days, C'All Avery visited me a total of ten times, each "experiment" ending in more pain.

One of the days, Avery marked areas along my body, taking care to mark more sensitive places like my face and fingers. He explained to me, without fail, what he would do to me.

"You see, Vita, these needles will stick into your muscle, the most important parts of your body. They will be inserted with great care, to see if that alone causes you great pain.

"If not, I will use other methods."

The needles were threaded through my skin. They started shallow, just at the surface. Once Avery deemed me 'strong enough' to continue, though, the needles burrowed deeper, through skin and tissue and muscle.

Breathe, you have to breathe.

He took pleasure in slowly teasing my flesh with the tip of the needle, before forcing it through the barrier. He zigged the needle one way before zagging it the other, doing as much damage as possible until he reached bone.

You have to breathe.

When that didn't result in enough agony, the needles were dipped in ester acid, which corroded away at the tissue around it. When the needles burrowed through my skin, all I could feel was the burning away, the death of tissue and the destruction of my nerves. All I wanted to do was scream, cry out, explode with all the pain.

Don't give him the satisfaction.

When I finally screamed, when I finally let go of my dignity, when I finally begged for mercy, Avery only laughed.

You are weak.

He threw his greasy head back and cackled.

You are pathetic.

Cemrebed 31st, the year 568, From the Diary of Octavia Tesifa—

    I have grown tired, my friends: tired and old. I am tired of life, of breathing, of watching and seeing and talking. I have forgotten where I come from, whom I belong to. And the truth is, I do not care. I have, as promised, told you the story of the greatest pirate, the greatest ship captain, to ever sail the waters of this world. And, as promised, I have lived the life of adventure, the Adventures of Octavia.

    Goodbye, my friends, and think of me when the salty winds of the sea are upon you.

Chapter 9
Playing the Game

The worst, and by far the most painful, the instrument which truly broke me, was Mortem, otherwise known as Stage Four. C'All Avery said only three of his subjects had ever gotten that far, and none had survived Mortem. But he, he said, had *confidence* in me.

The day Mortem was used was my thirteenth in captivity. I had been counting by painting lines of my blood every time I saw the Luna, some part of me hoping that was the last night I would ever see. But the Lunas kept rising, and more instruments came. C'All Avery first showed me the instrument, which looked like a hollow cylinder that blossomed out at the top. The bottom was small and looked similar to a needle, but had a hole in it.

First, C'All Avery stuck the small end into the fire. *Let him kill me. Please, just let this be the end.* Then, he stabbed the heated spike into my left breast. Just shy of my ribs, the spike burned and corroded the tissue around it. *Let me die.* Then, the C'All dripped boiling honey into the spike. The honey would ooze from the tiny hole and eat away at the scarred tissue. *Just let me go.* If I let go, I could be with my family again.

Each time, he would twist the spike in further, to keep the pain fresh. *Please.* Each twist brought the Sol closer to me. *Just let go.* Each wiggle increased a bright burning tenfold. *Please.* It seemed I would die then and there, but I was not so lucky. *Just die already!* Instead, I merely lost consciousness.

Halfway through the night, my eyes opened to darkness and to the dim, blurry image of three men. Two were large, and the other was relatively small. The small one approached me, and a vague, tiny thought pushed to get to the front of my mind. But everything was so blurry and my body ached with every breath. To think was too much effort, to see clearly was too much effort. Then, to my muffled surprise, I felt hands on my legs, moving them without my permission. I felt a sharp pain at the joining of my legs, followed by the sting of nails digging into my breasts. It hurt. I felt dirty and used. And there was nothing I could do. Then there was nothing at all.

Nothing. I receded into the safety of my mind as my eyes stared ahead, past the man's head, past the agony of non-consent. *Powerless. You have nothing to stop him. And now you are being ruined.* I felt a solitary tear slip from my eye as my body and mind finally became numb. It wasn't until the man said something that I realized he was finished with me.

When I was still breathing the next morning, C'All Avery was surprised, but incredibly pleased with himself. He bade the guards to only give me water and stale bread for the next three days, for he had an outing that would take as long. He had to tell others of his success and prep for what he called "the Finality," which was Stage Five.

I curled myself up into a tight ball, trying to smother the pain, smother my thoughts.

Da would be so disappointed; he would be ashamed of you.

The voices went back and forth in my head. Ahava was not one of them.

Get up, you have to fight.

Just let go.

No, remember why you have to fight.

Don't listen to them, just close your eyes and let the pain end.

"Fall to rise higher." The last thought forced my eyelids apart. Broken, only to stitch myself back together. That was why I had to fight. Yes, if I let go, then I could be with my family. But I had a job to do. My people, my family, needed me alive. Shifting out of the fetal position, I closed my eyes and waited for something, anything. At first, only staggered breathing and silence; then, Luna, light and clarity.

No one expects me to survive. No one expects me to fight. So I'll give them what they expect.

On the sixteenth day, parched and half dead, I asked to see Richard.

I knelt on the floor, head lowered, hands shackled in rusty chains behind my back. The unbroken neglect, constant torture, and endless nightmares had left me weakened in body, where the separation from my people, my home, and Adam had left me broken in soul. Somehow, it seemed, Richard could sense this weakness. And so decided to make one more trip to see me in my stony prison.

His gilded boots scuffed the floor as he walked. From behind strings of knotted yellow hair, I could see that he was wearing his best garments, those which he believed were "worthy" of a king. Such garments, he told me, were reserved for special occasions. His smug grin added to the annoyance that I associated with this canker-blossom. He circled me in my emaciated state several times before speaking,

"I see you've lost your fire, savage. Lucky for you, my conscience cannot rest at night knowing you are in such discomfort." He squatted in front of me. *Conscience, my ass.* Head still low, I listened to what he said next, "I will give you one last chance to repent for all you have done. If you give yourself up now, all will be forgiven." He sounded like a monk, like someone who could boast righteousness. *Always the hypocrite.* I had to reply, but I didn't know with what. Before I could speak, I glimpsed a ghost in the shadows.

My eyes focused in on him, on the man who had taught me what being a fighter was, the same man who gave me strength with every thought. His icy blue eyes softened once I met them. We had always been told that we shared that trait. Richard saw my gaze and turned to look over his shoulder at where Da stood.

"It seems she's lost it." He chuckled as he bade his men join in. They believed him a comedian, practically a court jester. My father only nodded, as if to affirm my thoughts.

"I wish to be alone with you." The words came out soft and quiet, my voice ragged. Richard stopped his laughing and regained composure. He asked for me to repeat myself.

I did.

With that, he ordered his men to stand outside the room, leaving only the two of us. When all was quiet, I rose from my knees, ignoring every ache in my bones. *Show him just how far you have fallen.* Richard only offered a smug grin to my pain. Keeping my eyes on my father, I slowly limped to the window, barren of any glass or ornament. A summer's breeze, far from the cold winter of reality, engulfed me, giving me only more strength. It was amazing what us human beings could do, when tested. It was amazing what we could be capable of, but Richard wouldn't know that. I thought on all that had been done to me; both Avery and the king had tried so hard to destroy me, but seeing my father gave me something I hadn't felt in so long: hope.

"I will admit: you have played your cards wisely, Your Majesty. However, I must again offer you my answer. I will not, and cannot, give my people to you." I pivoted to take in his expression of frustration and childlike anger. His brow began to twitch as his hands became fists.

"You, you and your kind, know nothing of the ways of life. I have you. You cannot do a thing about it. You will marry me. I have already taken you. You *will* sign over your kingdom to me, no matter what your 'answer' is." Spittle ran down his chin as he spat his words.

"Excuse me, but the last time I checked, the word 'no' means '*no.*' Then again, that never stopped you before." I straightened into a proud posture, into the queen I had to be, the queen my father knew I could be. "You have no power over me. Besides, to marry me would be to break your own laws."

"I know not what you mean, shrew. What laws of *mine* do you speak?" His face grew redder as a vein in his forehead began to pop.

"They are not just your laws, but the laws of all: of all peoples and of all religions. No man may wed, nor take, a woman who belongs to another." He froze, confused. Slowly, his face began to lose its expression as he understood my words.

"You are not already claimed; it cannot be. *I* claimed you!"

"Oh, but it can. Long before I stepped foot here, long before you couldn't deal with rejection, I claimed *myself.* I am not some piece of property, or some legislation, that you, nor anyone else, can claim for their own. I am my own. And you will understand that, or you won't live much longer." My explanation was met only with silence. *And now, we rise higher.* I stood, my head high despite the aches in my bare chest and stained loins, as he contemplated my answer. When it had gone on long enough, I stepped to him, my hands still shackled behind me.

"Richard, I am going to be very clear," I whispered in a silky tone as I grew closer. "What you did to me can *never* be forgotten, but that doesn't mean I'm just going to lay down and die. You've had your fun; now it's time for mine." His face again contorted in anger as I pulled away from his ear. Strength surged throughout my tested bones. It took no more than a solid yank to break the rusted chain which bound my hands. Silencing the king before he could call out, I clamped my hand over his mouth.

"Now listen to me, Richard. This is very important. I am going to render you unconscious, then jump from that window into the ash tree so conveniently planted below. Then, I am going to find my way back to my kingdom, my people, and my home. And if I am going to leave you with anything, it will be this: I will return, next time with my armies, and I will murder you and free your people from your tyranny." Once I finished my speech, I swung my right elbow to meet his temple, causing King Richard to crumple to the floor. I then, rags and all, leapt from the stony window ledge into the tree below.

Crashing down through the branches, the world moved in slow motion. Each barren branch felt soft, like downy feathers. The world around me lagged, giving no force to the gravity which pulled me to the earth below. There was no pain in the impact. Instead, I landed on my feet. How? I did not know, nor did I have time to ponder.

It would be another quarter-hour before the king awoke, and that would be all I had to change clothes and identity. After that, it would be four days' hard riding to the eastern border with the Disputed Lands, but I did not have a mount. *Alright, step two, right there.* Finally, it would be a good four and half more days to Redefalk. Time was of the essence, so I got to work.

I remained on unpopulated paths, where my tell-tale nakedness could not be seen. Even so, these hidden paths did nothing to spare me the sights of the people who called the capital city home. Children meandered around, with no purpose, no joy on their faces. Women wore tattered rags, close to my own, which could never keep out the winter cold. My own skin was numb to the growing chill, ignorant of its bite, by that time.

The only men to be seen were those in the Capital Guard. But they were of no life either. Their swords were rusty and flaking. Their half-helms were cracked and dinged. They paid no mind to the children, nor the women. The only thriving thing was silence. These people were slaves to fear, slaves to their king. They had no hope for life, none at all for themselves. It was no wonder Feroxia was so sullen when its people were being crushed by the weight of fear.

But then I saw it. Over the doorway of each small residence, a symbol was carved: a large "Z" with a pommeled staff down the middle. It was the symbol of the Cruor Allicit. Avery, or men of his same stature, had been to every house. They had done the same torture to innocent people as had been done to me. Knowing this truth, I scrutinized the children further. The skin that showed through their tattered clothing was riddled with scars, much like the ones I would have. The king had tortured the life out of his own people.

Disgusted, I looked away from the scenes of Feroxian life. In my own life, I had never expected to find such horror in one place. Committing atrocities such as these on the enemy? I'd seen it before. I had even experienced it. I knew what it could do to the mind, to the spirit. But to do such a thing to one's own people? It was unheard of.

And it had to be stopped.

Keeping the scars of the children in mind, I trekked on, unseen, looking for any uninhabited place where I could find a moment's refuge.

On the outskirts of the capital city, an abandoned mill stood, looming over the River Rye. I made my way to it, albeit hindered by my many wounds. Luckily, Avery had not touched my legs, so those were only somewhat weak. When I reached the splintered door, I crashed through, losing my balance. Inside, I saw, were the corpses of some seven children, along with four adults. The stench of decaying flesh attacked my nostrils, but was soon pushed aside by my own horrid bouquet. I made my way slowly to a fallen table in the center of what used to be the kitchen. Under it, I found a rusted dagger.

Memories of the razors flashed through my head, wrenching away my grip on reality. The corpses around me began to shift in their cobwebs, rising from Death's hand. Each took their turn in snatching a lock of my matted hair, shearing it off. I could not move, for fear the knife would graze my scalp or ear or cheek. Soon enough, however, the bones stopped clicking, and the corpses stopped laughing, and my body stopped trembling.

One unchanged scene, however, was the many cut locks of hair on the floor below me. Gasping, I took my palm to my scalp, feeling how short my hair had become: my tresses barely fell to my earlobes. And in my own hand was the blade that had done the job.

Looking around, shaking off the vision, I remembered what else I needed to do.

Of the eleven corpses, only the men's clothing would do. I had never been seen as a beautiful woman, but it was true that I carried many of my father's features. The sharp, hooked nose, and the thick eyebrows, coupled with my now-short hair, made the façade a perfect one. The only problem was the two mounds on my chest. Those had to go.

Ripping one of the corpses' skirts, I made a wrap to conceal my breasts beneath the man's tunic, ignoring the pain in the left. After donning the rest of my guise, I made the decision to search for food. I had been completely ignoring the constant emptiness in my stomach, but then it grew too profound. In the past, I had always had enough food, enough nutrients; having nothing, being neglected, was something I had never had to deal with. The hunger made me mindful of those who felt that way every day, of the people like those in the mill, who had suffered because of Richard.

No force in Jordklode could stop me then.

Still ignorant of my own pains, I searched and found food in the form of fallen nuts from dying trees surrounding the mill. Further down the narrow road, a farm. Without thinking, I walked up to the door and knocked. A woman, perhaps in her seventies, opened the door. Stout and gray, her face was wrinkled, but she wore a smile.

"*So'o posso te ahudar, querida?*" she asked me in the Feroxian tongue. I smiled and mustered a reply in the same.

"Hello, I was wondering if you would be so kind as to allow me to work for you in exchange for food and a horse of yours?" The old woman squinted at me then chuckled to herself. She nodded and gestured for me to follow her inside. We waddled to the kitchen area, where several children laughed and some wrestled on the floor.

"Those are me grand kiddies," she said, "eighteen in all, though some are working the land as of now. What you say your name was, dearie?" It took no time for me to answer.

"Adam," I said, "my name is Adam." The old woman eyed me up and down. She smiled to herself before asking me to follow her again, this time to the yard past the back façade of the house.

There, she stopped, looking me up and down again before saying, "Yer a terrible liar, sweet girl." She smiled at me, as if to offer comfort. "I understand that you need work and all, and that you must be hiding from somethin' or someone, but if yer goin to work here, I have to be able to trust you." Like many old women from Redefalk, this one had a knack for chastising comfort. My own Nana was particularly fond of this form of teaching.

"I'm sorry, ma'am. I suppose I am a bad liar. My name, my real name, is Vita. I beg of you, I really need this work. I quite literally have nothing else but the shirt on my back at the moment." The woman, whose name I had still yet to learn, pursed her lips, thinking about my fate. She thought particularly long, most likely to keep me on my toes.

"No," she finally said, "I am truly sorry, dear, but if yer so desperate to hide from someone, I can'ot be involved, or bring my fam'ly int'it." I merely nodded. Her reasoning was one I could understand completely. Family, above almost all other things, could decide the fate of someone, whether they be a stranger or lover. I, of course, was the former. And so, without arguing or pleading, I departed from the farm. Kindly, the old woman did give me a few rations of bread and dried fruits for my "wanderings."

I, however, was still without a mount. *I could always just steal one. But that, that my dear Vita, is a slippery slope we don't want to be on.* So, I traveled east on foot, instead. It would more than triple the time, but I would also be harder to track. By then, there was no doubt Richard had men out looking for me. He knew where I would be going, but he couldn't know which route I would take.

Because of the adrenaline, I no longer felt the physical hurt from my wounds. Though they had not completely healed, they no longer bled, and no longer hindered my movement. In fact, all physical restraints had been lifted by the untapped power of my body. The price that was paid, however, was in my dreams. Every night that I tried to find rest, the memories of my time with the C'All came flooding back, in vivid clarity.

Every slash, every drop of acid, every burn, was felt tenfold of the original. I began to sleep with a strip of leather from the clothing between my teeth so I wouldn't scream into the night. Biting down on the leather also kept me from biting my tongue off, which would have made surviving a lot more *difficult.* After six or seven of these nightmarish nights, I came to the Disputed and Kongeorn lands border. I was more than halfway there. But I still had a long way to go.

"Vita, come sit by me." Nana had patted the cushion next to her before returning to her pipe. I did as I was told, knowing that a story was coming. Nana always puffed on her pipe when she wanted to tell me a story. 'It helps to slow me down,' she always said. I believed her. Had it not been for that pipe, Nana's stories would have given my childhood-self whiplash.

"Do you ever dream that you can fly, V? That you have wings and can just take off and do anything?" I nodded enthusiastically.

"Nana, I love to dream! It's my favorite!" She smiled and took a puff of her pipe, waiting to regain my attention. That was an issue sometimes—okay, maybe all the time. Once I had settled down and stopped trying to tell her of my own dreams, she turned to me and breathed deeply.

"Before I met your grandfather, before I was worried about being the heir, I decided to sail across the Pendan Sea, to Oeste. Though my Papa hated the idea of me leaving, he was no match for my resolve." She winked at me, and I did my best to wink back. She continued, "I was so excited. No one in our history had ever done this, and I was about to be among the first. So we set off for Oeste. But," she paused for effect, "we were blown off course." I remember gasping and putting my small, chubby hand over my mouth. To this, she smiled and took a puff of her pipe before continuing.

"We ended up in this place, this beautiful place, that I thought only existed in myth. But no, it was as real as the sand beneath our feet when we came ashore. We were in Ungula, V—the islands of the Dragonae." I sputtered out the juice I had been sipping on. Another puff of the pipe, and Nana went on, "I couldn't believe it either until I saw the Sol shadowed by something so large above us. With wings larger than a sail on either side, followed by smaller ones further down the sleek body. And the neck was long, slender, but mobile and strong. Beneath it, four strong legs, the size of tree trunks, with talons at the claw. When it landed in front of us, we all jumped back. It had a long snout, feathered by a crown of sharp bone. And the eyes. Vita, they glowed gold. The creature lowered its head, and we saw, astride it, a human woman with the same glowing eyes. The woman dismounted.

"We thought she was going to speak with us, ask us why we had come—maybe even order us to leave. But she didn't; the creature did. Out of its fantastic snout came the most musical voice. Instead of warning us, it welcomed us."

"But Nana," I piped in, confused, "that wasn't real." She dropped her pipe and turned her grey eyes on me.

"My, Vita, how like your father you are. He couldn't wrap his mind around something he'd never seen either. That will be the death of us, I suppose. This family has everything, but imagination and faith is not one of them." She had stooped to pick up her pipe then stood and left me on the cushion, still entirely confused.

I began my trek through Kongeorn lands by simply observing the terrain and the living things which called it home. Though it was winter, the air here was still mild, as it would be for a few more weeks. The springs brought most of the cool air. The pleasant weather meant easy walking, even if I was running low on food. I decided to try to find some when I reached the next town. Before I got there, however, I heard the thundering of horse hooves on the padded earth. Fearing it to be Feroxian bounty hunters, I scrambled up a tree about ten feet from the road.

Some would have picked a tree closer to the path, but I knew that that was a, well, stupid idea. All the hunters would have to do would be to look up, and I would be as good as dead. That was why I chose a tree farther off the path, where I could blend in amongst hundreds of branches. *This is why I'm not still back in that stone hell. The intelligence of woman and man's inability to swallow their ego.* I chuckled internally. Despite my jape, the heart in my chest pounded incessantly, causing me to sweat as well. It took most of my mental strength to keep those malevolent voices at bay as I clutched at the trunk of the tree.

Though I couldn't fully see or hear the riders, I could see the red of their silks, which meant I had been right to hide. I had also been right to hide farther off the path, for they rode against the edge of the path, along the tree line. Of course, they didn't detect me. Once they were well past, I fell—yes, I fell—from the tree branches. *Have I always been this clumsy?* It seemed I was much better at getting into trees than out of them.

I walked just off the path, in case more, or the same, riders came along. This would ensure I could not be seen from a distance, because the next stretch was flat where before it had been hilly. The flattening of the terrain meant getting closer to the first town. If my memory served me correctly, the town was called Fere. It was smaller than most towns, meant for trading off goods. Fere had been one of the first merchant-based cities to be established. Lucky for me, it would be crowded with spring on the way.

When finally the first houses and brothels started to pop-up, and more people populated the road, I joined the fray, despite the paranoia in the back of my mind. I knew I had to smell horribly, but no one paid me any mind. In fact, I think it helped me to blend in further. As I pushed along, I saw children running along, free from life's burdens, uncaring of impending war. Their faces were dirty, and their hair was greasy, but they giggled and grinned. The sight sobered me. Was I going to take their fathers, their mothers, away from them with a war? Was I going to lure a monster's legion onto their lands?

I couldn't. I wouldn't.

But if I didn't, Richard could still march on Kongeorn. He could turn these people, these children, into the slaves of horror I saw in Feroxia. And that, above all else, could not be allowed to happen. A decision weighed on the scales and, before I returned home, I would need to find an answer.

Breaking from my thoughts, I smelled fresh-baked breads; the aroma of which caused my belly to rumble. My last ration had been eaten hours before, and it had been minimal. I followed the scent to a door that led into a small hovel. A family would live in such a place, and I would never take food from a family. *Morals, values, always getting in the way of food.* I turned away, hungry, disappointed, but also proud. If I could keep myself from stealing something so small, I could keep myself from stealing bigger things. My mind reasoned with itself. *If I really am able to refrain from hurting others in small ways, I will never have to worry about becoming like Richard.* I smiled at the thought.

And so I walked on, observing city life. Merchants in colorful clothing shouted, selling their wares. A man in purple was selling wines; a man in yellow, perfumes; and a man in green, pears from the South. It was to him that I was drawn to. His face was lined with wrinkles, but he was well-tanned and quite kind. I gazed at the pears, and then, realizing I had no money, I quickly turned away.

"You, there, pleaze. Do you not want one of my pears?" His accent, though reminiscent of C'All Avery, was much kinder, and far smoother in nature. I knew he was speaking to me, so I turned around to face him.

"Sir, I am sorry, I was just looking; I don't have any money." My eyes met his, and a note of recognition lit up his face.

"I know your eyes, those are the eyes of—" I cut him off with a sharp look before softening it as he nodded. "You have no money, you say? That is no problem." He winked at me and began to stuff a sack with Southern Pears. As he handed the sack to me, he leaned in close, his lips next to my ear.

"My Queen, take this gift as one of gratitude. It was your father who saved me from my masters, long ago." He leaned away and lifted his sleeve to show me the Feroxian slave symbol burned into his skin. My eyes widened. I had forgotten that Feroxians, not just the Feron line, still kept actual slaves. I had forgotten that so many more had suffered under Richard's and his father's rules than just their subjects. I clasped the man's forearm, a symbol of friendship. A grin lit up his face.

"I will not forget this kindness, sir." With that, I turned away and was swept into the crowd of consumers once again. With my purpose in the city fulfilled, I found my way out of the city's eastern gate. It would be three more days until I reached home, but I knew that the man's gift would make the journey far easier.

Chapter 10
Adam's Thoughts

It had been three weeks since I had last lain eyes on Vita. When her hands pushed me from the window, from the stony castle walls, I hadn't realized I had fallen until her image was overtaken by the sight of stone. Because of her staying behind, because of her bravery, I, along with Bjorth, and all of the rest of our company, had gotten to our horses and out of the country, just as Vita had wanted.

But just because she had wanted it did not make it any easier.

I knew she didn't need my protection; she had already told me as much many times before. But knowing that she would be alone with that monster who called himself a king, that was enough to drive me mad. His hands could be touching her, his eyes could be searching her skin, and just the thought, I realized, made me want to run my fist through a wall. I was supposed to be her protector, at least that was what Andor had made me promise when he left for that final scouting mission.

"Adam, you will not be coming with us," Andor said, and my face had taken on a surprised look, merely a facade for the hurt I felt underneath, "I want—no, I need—you here with Vita. You must promise me that you will do everything in your power to keep her safe, alive. I have told you these words before, but they must be said again: 'You are destined, fated, to be the Hingst to her Kongeorn, so you must give all you can for her.' Is that understood?" I remember nodding.

I had seen ghosts, spirits, all my life. No one had ever explained it to me. No one had ever told me how to use it to my advantage. I didn't even know if this was a curse or some sort of gift. To see a dead loved one when the veil to the Etter was one thing, but to see the dead everywhere you went was unheard of.

Every time I opened my eyes, I prayed that the next time I saw Vita, it would be as flesh and blood, not as a spirit.

She was all I could think about on the journey home. Her, her safety, her smile. I loved her smile, the way it crinkled around her eyes. All my thoughts could not be torn away from a feeling that I had too long suppressed. She was my queen, my best friend, but, I realized in those traveling days, I could not live fully without seeing her every day.

At night, lying under the open winter sky, I pulled her dagger from my boot, holding it in my hands, and pictured her. Her eyes in their icy blue could freeze you in your place. And her features, though sharp, accented her warrior's poise. She walked with such confidence, such like I could never compare to. Though she was short, she was strong, and she made sure everyone knew it.

But her exterior was nothing compared to the complexity of her interior. Some days, she was an inferno, ready to burn, to devour, anything and anyone in sight; other days, she was an easy summer breeze, laughing at nothing, and bringing warmth with her wherever she went. She could be cold, too. She could isolate with a glance, or invite with a grin. She could build me up with a touch and make me crumble with its absence.

I loved her.

And if I loved her, how could I have left her? How could I have abandoned her to be kept in the company of a demon?

Because she told you to.

I could have stayed and fought tooth and nail, but that wasn't what she wanted. It wasn't what my queen wanted. It wasn't what my queen ordered.

And I realized then, underneath those stars, not nearly as bright as her spirit, that I would go to the drop off of Jordklode for her. I would give my life for hers. And I would do it gladly if it was what she wanted.

With those feelings beating against my skin, trying to break out, I smiled a sad smile. I had to trust her. I had to trust the Mother. Vita would find her way back to me. She would have to, because I wouldn't have realized these truths if she wasn't.

And until then, I would prepare Redefalk for her return. I would make it known that the queen was alive, and that she would never abandon her people. Especially me.

Chapter 11
Will of a Kongeorn

My pace had slowed dramatically after exiting Fere. With the pears on my back and food off of my mind, some of the pain I had grown ignorant of began to return, though in a different way. My movement again became hindered, but only because I grew increasingly tired. I could feel the energy being sucked from me, no matter how long I rested or how many pears I ate. Any strength that had been granted to me had been worn out, and I soon discovered why.

With only another day and a half to walk, I discovered one of my many needle wounds, this one on my right breast, had grown hot to the touch. From it leaked a yellow substance and a clear fluid. Panicked, I saw bright red streaks stretching out from the blackened wound. Reaching for information deep inside my brain, I remembered. As I lay against the trunk of a tree, so close to my destination, I realized one of my many wounds had become infected.

You should have known you wouldn't make it.

The image of Avery's face, cackling at my cries, appeared before me, stifling my will to keep going. Terror seized me, and though I fought, it knew how to make me stumble.

Forcing myself to my feet, I began to shuffle east, praying that somehow time would slow for me. I shuffled along the road, ignorant of any person, place, or thing that happened to pass me by. Before long, I forgot I was moving; before long, my mind was lost to memory.

Look around you. First, it was your brothers. It was your father. Then your mother. Now you. Soon, all will be erased. You are all grains of sand, and you are all washing away. The wave has only begun, and it is already ushering you out to sea. You will perish. You will fall. And you will never rise again.

Richard's face, sneering as he looks me up and down. He reaches out for my infected breast. I swing at him, but I am too slow. He wrenches me forward and forces himself upon me. I am powerless again. I cannot fight him. I lay limp. He bites and scratches and claws away at me until he has finished. The scene flashes, and Richard holds my face hostage in his ringed hand. He forces me to look down at the swollen belly he has made of me. The skin moves with the demon inside and I lurch forward.

I was caught by a polished oak door, one that seemed familiar. My hands clutched my chest, trying to hold myself together. Tears of agony, of sheer horror raced down my face. Falling to the ground, I let out a scream. Looking beside me, I was able to see a face, my face, in a small puddle. Sunken cheeks, pale skin, short, greasy hair, and icy eyes that had lost their bite. Beyond the puddle, a blurry figure ran towards me. Before I could decipher who it was, my eyes closed, offering a peace long denied.

⚒

My eyes open to Nothing. I see Nothing; I hear Nothing. I feel Nothing. It envelops me in something that doesn't exist, that which I have never experienced. Not floating, no. There is no water. Nothing.

Though there is Nothing, I find myself able to do, to be, Something. Forcing all my effort, I can move my body, flit my eyes, and sight graces me once again.

What I thought was Nothing is instead far more. It is every color I have ever seen, and those I have not. Colors that can only be expressed when one closes their eyes and grabs hold of their greatest emotions. Colors resembling the coolness of blues, but with the intensity of reds, can be seen when I bring forth my loneliness. And when the fear kicks in, the immensity of the black couples with the unsureness of gray. But these colors, like everything, soon fade as well, leaving me alone again, with Nothing.

Water. Warm water, trickling down my chin, entwining in my hair, breathing life into my dry and wanting body. Yes, there was water, but also cotton and wool, both encasing my sore limbs. Scratchy, yet dense, the wool kept what little body heat I had close to me, while the cotton, soft and light, was easy on my burnt and punctured skin.

Even more, there was motion near me. The sound of a washcloth being submerged in water and emerging full of life-giving liquid. It was then squeezed, expelling excess moisture and then applied to my feverish skin. The rag smelled clean, a luxury which had escaped my senses for weeks. Even more important, even more essential, was that which, or rather who, held the rag.

Several rogue streams of water escaped from the rag, racing to douse the sheets below. But they were stopped as a cool, calloused hand wiped them away, and, instead of moving away, stayed holding my scarred cheek. My caregiver let out a sigh, full of sorrow, something like mourning, and I felt another plop of water on the same cheek before it too was gently wiped away.

The Nothing again surrounds me, cloaking me in its breathtaking design. The landscape is also Nothing, as am I. But, there, in the distance, I detect the faintest difference. It is not light, no, but a darker darkness. Surprised to see something in this mass of Nothing, I will my body to move closer to the dark, to the one thing I am able to take hold of. It shines brighter than the sun, and it is louder than the waves, and I run to it, embracing the sensation of Something.

The water returned. But it was not as pleasant as the last time we had met. Instead, it stung, cleaning out the scars and wounds and burns all throughout my body. The wool and cotton had gone, but were replaced by another fabric, one which I could not name. And it was only covering my breast and nether, a boundary and wall to the washcloth.

As had already been done, one of those crucial walls was removed from its place, revealing the wound which had almost killed me. Another time, the water was dipped into and transferred to my skin, only slightly warm in contrast to the air around me. In my right hand, however, was something far warmer. Investigating, I brought my body to respond, and my fingers twitched, feeling those intertwined with them.

Next to me, my caregiver gasped and dropped the rag, which landed on the stone below.

"Vita," familiar, but far away, the voice was far away, "Vita, come back to me." A wet hand touched my check, just like before. *Before. Before.* More and more sounds and sensations returned to me. Wind whistling by, a tree branch bending to its will and scratching the window. The far-off clatter of swords, the whinny of horses. And next to me, quiet sobs which belonged to trembling hands, which belonged to a familiar voice.

"Vita, Vita," over and over, he whispered the name. *Vita. My name. My name is Vita.* Again and again, his voice trembled with the sobs. Trembling and shaking, mourning and praying. He was praying for me.

Vita. I heard Ahava's voice.

What? I mustered.

I think you've slept long enough. Your people need you.

I know.

Adam needs you.

…I know…

The last barrier which had kept my eyes from opening, from seeing, was overcome, and they slowly lifted, like a curtain on a stage, for me to take in the sight.

His face was red, and his hair was disheveled. His eyes were clamped shut, shutting out the world, leaving only enough room for tears to slip through. He'd let his stubble grow far more than a shadow, and he was paler than I'd ever seen him.

Trying to speak, I found my voice gone. Instead, I pulled more strength and squeezed his hand in mine. His eyes opened and looked up, green and verdant. His lips moved, as if trying to speak, but hopelessly failing. To make up for it, he lifted my hand, minding my healing wounds and bruises, and brushed his lips against it. Gooseflesh prickled me head to toe. Adam saw this and covered me back up, thinking the cold was to blame.

If only he knew.

Slipping off again into unconsciousness, my mind replayed a memory, one that swaddled me like a blanket, reminding me of the feelings I had for so long tried to hide.

"Congratulations to the happy couple!" I had toasted yet again to Amund and Karina the night of the wedding, then proceeded to down the ale in seconds. At that point in time, I had lost count and—frankly—didn't really care how many drinks I'd had. Celebration was in order, and who was I to shy away from a challenge?

"Vita, I think that's enough ale," Adam's voice came out of nowhere. I turned to my left. *Nope, not there.* Then I turned to my right.

"There you are! I thought I heard the sound of a party-pooper. You're just mad that I can drink more than you." I laughed and stood for absolutely no reason. Adam jumped at this opportunity.

"Time for bed." He gripped my elbow and ushered me out of the roaring hall, guiding me toward my room.

"Um, no, no, no," I rambled, "I am *not* a little child person that you can just—*ugh*, I was having fun!" Drunk me was a whiny and childish me. Adam knew that just as well as sober me did, and he also knew that I could get into trouble when I wasn't fully *present.* Adam wasn't a big "celebrator," and so, whenever I would "celebrate," he would always take responsibility for me. Da and Mami appreciated that; sober me appreciated that, but drunk me definitely did not.

"Well, sleep is fun, too; and come tomorrow morning, you're going to be wanting as much of it as you can get." Though he had an incredibly legitimate and relevant point, I ignored him completely, mainly because I was too focused on the color of the walls. The different ways the light from the lit sconces hit the shadows at different angles was completely astounding. Also, the shadows were moving, so that was pretty unprecedented for drunk me.

Finally, Adam managed to get me to the entrance to my room. Like the gentleman he was, he took my shoes off and laid me down on the bed. I, of course, like a child on a sugar high, was not about to go to sleep. And, of course, drunk me believed she had a wonderful idea.

"Hey Adam, close the door and come here." He did so, trying to accommodate me so I would go to sleep and, incidentally, stay out of trouble. He stood at the side of my bed, an amused look on his face.

"Yes, Stormy?"

"Come here, I have a secret for you." He rolled his eyes and did as I asked. When his face was just inches away, drunk me did something sober me would never forget. I reached up and brought his face to me. Our lips locked for the first time. I brought him closer to me, almost pulling him onto the bed before he broke away.

"No," he caught his breath, "Stormy, this isn't right. You aren't *you* right now." Ever the gentleman, he turned and tried to leave, but drunk me was not about to let that happen.

He couldn't have known it, but that night proved to me that even at my most vulnerable, I could trust Adam. And now, I trusted him with my life.

Later that night, I awoke again from the pain-induced stupor. Adam slept beside me, above the covers, always the gentleman, even if he did not need to be. *Even if I do not want him to be.* His hand was stretched out to me, and I gazed at it, feeling the urge to take it in my own. Instead, however, my attention was drawn elsewhere. From the darkness, she emerged, clothing herself in the Luna's light, but not needing any of its celestial elegance to enchant my eyes.

Sister. Her voice caressed my thoughts. Though it was sweet, I felt that, beneath her loving and charming facade, her purpose was entirely more sinister.

Why have you come?

You offend me, Sister. Can I not look upon my only charge to make sure of her health? Her voice dripped the sweet lies, and I saw past them. Drawing upon my mental strength, I pushed my own thoughts harder.

I will ask only once more. Why are you here? Silence followed. Ahava knew she couldn't lie to me for long, and I could see in her ghostly eyes that she didn't want to. Eliciting an ethereal sigh, she approached the bed and sat next to me. The mattress failed to sink beneath her form.

Sister. This is your first sign. What was done to you, neither the Mother, nor I, could stop it. But it confirmed what we already knew. Jakel…he is working through Feroxia's king. And has been for each of the past several generations.

I did not reply. Her words made perfect sense to me, every single one of them. The pieces fit perfectly, almost too perfectly.

What is asked of me?

That's not how this works. Frustrated, I snorted inwardly. Of course that wasn't how it worked. We never receive a sign *and* directions. It is never that easy. We have to extract them for ourselves.

Fine. I suppose I will wait it out. Wait until Jakel and Richard come to me. Though I wished it could be that way, that I could bide my time, wait in the safety of the keep, I also knew this was not what Ahava and the Mother wanted from me. And Ahava had a job to do.

No. You will not just wait. That is not what is purposed. As soon as the words came into being, Ahava clamped her pale hands over her mouth, eyes wide. She knew what I was doing. To prove it, she pointed a translucent finger at me accusingly.

You, you are so…ugh! No wonder Father speaks with such pride about you. Her comment struck me unexpectedly, but also brought a smile onto my lips. I raised one of my thick eyebrows, waiting, as I internalized her words.

I suppose the Mother planned for this as well. She waved her hand, trying to change the subject and save her pride. *Very well, I guess I can tell you what you need to do. You are to follow the path you have already lain out in your mind. As much as I hate to ask this, I must; war is necessary. Death is necessary. That is all I will say.* With a loud huff, she faded away, as if the words were all that had composed her glowing form. I thought on them, those words. And I knew. Kongeorn's time as a hired hand was well over.

Ahava continued to visit me every night as Adam lay sleeping beside me. Some nights, she would act as if it was duty that brought her. I, however, could see past it. I could see the worry in her eyes and the pain that she swallowed as she looked down at me.

One of these nights, she dropped the facade. As I opened my eyes to see her, I could tell something was different. Her eyes were kinder, and her motions were less planned.

What brings you to me this time, dear Sister? I felt a tickle on my hand as Ahava laid hers on it.

The Mother did not send me, she replied, eyes trained on where her ghostly hand covered mine. *I came of my own accord.*

Instead of asking her why she had come, I waited. I waited patiently as Ahava looked back up at me.

I worry about you.

You needn't.

Father said you would say that. She half-smiled as she said it.

How is he? My heart began to beat faster as I asked the question. Of all the things that had happened, of all the falling, over and over again, the one thing that still haunted me was his loss.

He is happy. He and Mother are happy. Where they are, there is no pain, no sadness. They ride in Sol-lit meadows and spar without a care in the world. Ahava moved her thumb over my hand, sending a chill up my spine.

And Amund? My mind flitted to Karina, whom I had not seen since leaving for Feroxia. Surely, she would be showing.

He patiently awaits the birth of his child, Ahava answered slowly, thinking carefully as she did so, *though many of his thoughts have been with you, as well.*

With me? I looked at her incredulously.

He thinks of how he treated you in the past and wants to know if you have forgiven him.

Those transgressions were forgiven long ago. Tell him that. My heart ached for Amund. To think he still felt guilt for treating me as less hurt me, but I hoped that Ahava would put Amund's worries to rest.

She smiled and nodded, *I will make sure he knows.*

What about Einar? I didn't know why I asked the question. The hate I had felt for my brother had slowly faded with time and distance. As I learned more about the evil from the world, I began to understand that Einar wasn't unique in his madness.

Interesting. Ahava eyed me before continuing, *He has found peace. When our mother turned Videm on herself, she set into motion a chain of events that freed Einar's soul from the evil that gripped it.*

How is that possible?

Ahava hesitated, withdrawing her hand from mine.

I'm not at liberty to say. But what I can say is that Richard is not the only person you've encountered whose soul was tainted by Jakel's power.

She stood, making no sound. I didn't want her to go; it occurred to me that we had so much more to talk about, so much more that didn't have to be Jakel, nor the dichotomy of good and evil. I wanted to know her as my sister, not just as a conduit of the Mother.

Wait, I scrambled for a moment before faltering, *you know, I wonder sometimes.*

Ahava stopped moving and listened to me, her ghostly hair unmoving as a draft blew in from an open window.

Sometimes I wonder. I wonder what it would have been like if you had lived. Would Da and Mami still be alive? Would our family still be here? Would I have gone through all of that? Who would I be today? My chin trembled as I thought about what Ahava could have been for our family. She would have been the heir, the one that my parents spent their time grooming.

Vita, her ethereal voice was a sigh as she drew near to me, *everything, though it is painful and confusing and difficult to understand, is exactly as it needs to be.* She looked deep into my eyes, and I felt that same tickle on my cheek as Ahava placed her hand there. I wanted to believe her. I wanted the confidence that she had, the confidence that it was all worth it. That somehow, we would rise higher. But none of that kept me from wondering about the 'what-ifs'.

If it is really that important to you, I can show you what it would have been like. Ahava closed her eyes, and I followed suit before being flung into what could only be described as a lucid, vivid dream.

I can see myself, hair long and braided back, in a crouched fighting stance, sword in hand. Opposite of me is Ahava, whose long brown hair is braided back as well. I lunge forward, and she blocks before twisting away and landing a blow on my thigh.

"C'mon, V," she laughs, twirling the dulled blade in her hand, "you're gonna have to be quicker than that!" I frown before faking right, then slicing left. I manage to graze her tunic as she jumps back. She only grins in reply.

We exchange more blows, and I—in a frustratingly-familiar turn of events—end up taking most of the hits. Then, just as I spring again, a voice shouts from behind us.

"Hey," the voice comes from Adam, who stands at the fence, "if you two are done, I have something to discuss with my wife.*" I feel myself stiffen at*

his words and can't help but smile inwardly. The feeling is wrenched away, though, when I see Ahava walk toward the fence and kiss Adam on the cheek.

"That's alright, we were just finishing up," Ahava says, climbing over the fence and taking Adam's hand.

Ahava took her hand from my cheek, and my eyes flew open. My gut twisted as a feeling of betrayal, of embarrassment, washed over me. I looked away, not wanting to look Ahava in the eye.

Vita, I told you, everything is as it needs to be. Adam was never meant to be my husband. He was never meant to love me. I am not the Kongeorn to his Hingst. You are.

I wanted to ask her more questions. What did she mean by that? How did she know that he loved me, if he loved me?

But the Sol was rising, and Adam was beginning to stir beside me.

Ahava made to leave, but before she did, she drew closer to me, leaning down. I felt a tingle on my forehead, where she kissed me gently. I closed my eyes, taking in the moment of sisterhood, but when I opened my eyes again, Ahava was gone.

That morning, after eating a piece of nutbread and letting Adam help me into suitable garb, I limped down the steps, only somewhat attempting to take it easy. Adam held my arm in check so I would not fall. But as I found solid ground beneath my feet, with no more stone steps to descend, I shook him off. Turning to him, I took down my hood so the healing cuts and bruises could be seen by all.

"I do not need you," thinking better of it and the pain which struck as I said the words, I elaborated, "at the moment." I held his eyes and then turned away, towards the many who had gathered in the bustling square. They had expected me to address them from the steps, which still loomed over us all. It would seem that, in the two months they had not seen me, they had forgotten how their queen operated.

"My family, my friends, my fellow Kongeorn," at first, my voice was shaky, still recovering from staying silent so long, but soon, it grew stronger, "you must know of the rumors. 'The Queen of Kongeorn is dead.' I say to you, 'No!' They tried to murder me, to snuff out my light, but I would not allow it.

"My family, my friends, my fellow Kongeorn," my eyes scanned the crowd. They met those whom I had known since birth and touched upon those whom I'd never seen before. They all, however, returned my own fury in their eyes, "I would not let them. Every day was but one day closer to my return, to the glorious morn that would come upon seeing the flags of my father, and his father, flying above the Keep Redefalk! We do not give in; we do not lay down to die. We fall to rise higher!" To this, a great cheer arose. It continued on, and I let it, at least for some time, before gesturing and asking for quiet.

"My family, my friends, my fellow Kongeorn, we are at war; there is no doubt of that. But it is not for my sake, no, not for revenge. I saw the people of Feroxia. Their eyes dimmed, with no life to light them. Their children did not run, did not smile, did not laugh. And they all bore the bloody mark of oppression, of a king who would just as easily murder each and every one of us.

"They are coming. But we, I, will not let them hurt the people, the family, that I love. Yes, we will fight, but I will be there alongside you." The crowd began to buzz, to grow with excitement. Silence and stillness gave way to chatter and fidgeting. "I will *not* let myself die. I will *not* lay down until every man knows he is worth something in this world, until every woman knows that she is equal to man, that she is capable of anything, until every single child knows that they can be whomever they want, regardless of sexuality, upbringing, or gender!"

And to my ears came the sound of eternal support, the sound of opportunity, the sound of bloodlust.

It was not long, however, before I was forgotten among them. Like colossal waves crashing over us all: the emotion, the rage, the fear, the agony, all of it, turned the crowd away from me, a feeling I was all too used to, and yet, was not expecting. Instead, the crowd washed away, and I, as always, was left again to my thoughts.

I turned away from the direction the battle cries were coming from and resigned myself to solitude. I padded, aimlessly, through the crowd, nowhere to go and no one to see. In the back of my mind, however, a sensation grew.

At first, it was only like the drops from an icicle slowly melting. Then, it reared its head, showing that, in fact, it was a newly defrosted river, charging ahead to make up for lost time. My eyes began to flit back and forth, unable to comprehend where I was, what I was doing. The silence roared in my ears, and I covered them to stifle it but to no avail. Again and again, an immense pounding, followed by sounds far louder than thunder, bombarded my ears, my mind. My eyes could not see, but still took in sight, the sight of needles and fire and acid dripping green over a hole in my chest. And I felt it too, the pain, all over again, as if new. My right hand flew from my ear and clamped down in a fist before my heart, as if that would staunch the flow of pervasive agony, which, I feared, would never end.

My skin was aflame, as were the walls, and every thought I had ever voiced was suddenly seared into nothingness, into impossible darkness. Crashing. Crashing. Banging. Crashing. Throbbing. A thud. My legs gave out, and I hit my head hard on the ground.

The initial sounds were fading, but their echoes still persevered, tormenting me, coaxing me into a stage of vulnerability and total unconsciousness.

The sounds around me persuaded my eyes to open. Around me, above me, the exotic faces of unfamiliar persons chattered. But there was one who gave me comfort. *Adam.*

Intensity had made a home in his eyes as he scrutinized me, still on the hard-packed mud of the square. My head was in his lap, and I could see that, despite the people surrounding us, his eyes were brimming with tears.

"My Queen, it is welcome news that you awake," one of the foreign voices wrenched my eyes away from Adam and to the face of a middle-aged man with skin the color of clay, but tinted blue. Subtle, but once noticed, fascinating, to the eye. I wanted to reply, but could not find my voice, and instead, looked back to Adam, who, as always, knew what I was going to say.

"It is a pleasure, sir, but if you would be so kind, I believe the Queen is in desperate need of rest and, possibly, a bath." I smiled to the best of my ability, approving of Adam's words. The blue man merely nodded in understanding, then offered a hand in helping me up. The others around us dissipated as Adam thanked the man for his kindness, said he would call upon him later, and brought me up the steps.

"Who was that?" I asked, finally finding my voice as we neared the closest bathing room, where a guard was standing by. As we neared, I deduced that Adam either didn't hear me, or wasn't going to answer. *Rude.* I inwardly rolled my eyes. The guard, seeing my condition, immediately let us by, and informed us that no one had been in all day. Adam told him to make sure we weren't disturbed, that I was tired, and needed peace. *Well, he's right about that, at least.*

Upon entering the bathing room, I felt gratification at meeting warm steam head on. The springs of Northern Jordklode allowed for several bathing rooms in Redefalk, where anyone could clean themselves, or simply relax. There were also private and designated bathing rooms, or even tubs, however, for those who did not like the idea of an all-inclusive bathing room. I, at the moment, did not care.

I did not care as Adam took my muddy cape from me and bid me sit so he could remove my boots and socks. A flash of insecurity, of fear from a memory repressed, flew through my mind as he looked me in the eye, asking permission to remove the rest of my clothing. The thought was chased away by the memory of the night of Amund's wedding and the complete weakness in my bones. I nodded hesitantly. I was like a child as he pulled my tunic up over my head, arms going with it. For a split second, I thought about covering my breasts, but my limbs simply had no strength. Adam's eyes were not searching or prying. When my trousers had been discarded, I tried to move to the bath, but found every movement near impossible. I wouldn't ask for help, and Adam knew it.

Gently, he slid an arm underneath my legs and behind my back, lifting me from the slick stone floor. Just as tenderly, he entered the pool himself, not caring for his own trousers or tunic, before placing me on one of the benches near a mosaic wall. I studied the wall, remembering having seen it before, but not having seen it so clearly as then. It depicted the same tree from my fireplace, with roots extending towards Heaven.

Behind me, I heard the sound of clothing hitting the wet floor. Only somewhat panicking, I turned abruptly, irritating my breast wound in the process. But my heart caught in my throat as I saw. Adam had removed his own shirt, but kept his trousers on, and was reentering the pool, this time with a washcloth and oil in hand. He waded to me and, without speaking, poured the oil in my short dirty hair and began to lather gently. Relaxing calmness swept over and throughout my tired body. Though I had spent the vast majority of the past week asleep, my body had yet to rebuild its own strength, to ascend back to where it was before the *experiments*.

Adam's hands removed themselves from my hair, rinsing in the warm water below, before returning with the washcloth. He made small, meticulous circles along my back, careful to avoid the nastiest scars, the ones which refused to heal. I felt every motion of his fingers, each of the five places their tips touched. And with the warm water around me, as well as Adam's fingers cleansing me of both dirt and fear, I felt myself starting to slip away from consciousness.

At some point, I must have slumped, or gone limp, yet somehow Adam had managed to rinse my hair out, dry me off, wrap me in a blanket, and return me to my room, where a fire crackled in the fireplace. Before he could leave me to my slumber, I lazily reached out, weighed down by fatigue, both physical and emotional, and asked him to stay. Of course, he obliged. My final action before succumbing to sleep was interlacing my fingers in his own and bringing our hands to meet my heartbeat.

Chapter 12
The Western Sol Sets

My eyes opened as the familiar fingers gently probed my shoulder. Adam's green eyes examined me, making sure I was truly awake, comprehending. In his eyes, I saw shining tears, which got my attention. Before I could ask, he answered.

"Bjorth," his voice trembled, "has passed." My mind flashed through countless thoughts: the 'why's and the 'how's. The ones which brought tears to my own eyes were the memories. My godfather had always known my innermost thoughts and wishes. He had given me my first sword. He had been my friend, my teacher: the person in my life that I hadn't realized I needed so much until— until he was gone.

"Take me to him," I ordered, numbness overcoming me, stretching out my soul until I was far away. I could not feel the ground below my feet as I walked unsteadily with Adam's support. I could not feel the movement of my legs as they took steps on their own. I could not see anything, only the face of the last father I had left.

"My little Euna." Bjorth had taken me in his arms, smiling and warming me in the midst of the snowy landscape, "if I made the decis'ns, you'd be comin' along, but I don'. Sorry, love." He set me back down as fresh tears escaped my eyes; the four-year-old me began to wail, wanting so desperately to go along with the boys and my godfather.

It was the same: where they went, I could not follow. My eyes focused in on the furs beneath my feet, the same furs I had been in awe of when I had received my first sword. I looked up, tears blocking out my vision. Through the salty water, I could see a large, blurred form lying on its back. Ignoring the pains of my body and following the pains of my soul, I rushed over to the blur. The tears fell, allowing me to see his face.

His red hair had become almost completely white, and his smile lines had expanded into wrinkles. For the first time, Bjorth looked old, tired. His hazel eyes were still open, as if searching for sight, for the Etter, for my father. A sob wracked through my chest. Just then, I felt Adam's hand on my back, trying to soothe me. But I knew, just as much of a mess as I was, he would be in no better of a place.

Kneeling beside me, there was no doubt that he was rolling through the memories, through the acts of love and kindness this man had shown us both. The day of Adam's arrival, Bjorth had been the first one to speak with him, to make him feel welcome. We mourned, the both of us, tears making trails down our cheeks. I leaned into Adam, my hand resting on my godfather's barrel-like chest, as more and more people began to file into the room.

I heard all of their voices clearly, individually. Karina was sobbing. Gyda was praying frantically. A little boy named Leo told his mother that there had been black smoke, and that the smoke had made the "Big Man's" breathing stop. And then there was Simon, the man who outlived so many, the young and the old. I could hear his words as if he were speaking them into my ear.

"From this, we fall. But we will rise again." And from my own mouth, more words joined the fray.

"Take care of him, Da." My voice trembled, and I moved my shaking hand to his eyes, closing the lids. I turned my face into Adam's chest and let each sob shake us both.

He's happy, Ahava spoke. *He and Father are wrestling and sparring, and he knows they will never be separated again.* More tears spilled over onto my cheeks.

I heard a new voice behind us. One of the younger message runners approached me, his footsteps soft on the animal skins. He knelt beside me and whispered a prayer before addressing me.

"My Queen," I recognized the voice belonging to Erik and opened my eyes, "there are dozens of, um, people gathered in the square. One of them is asking to speak directly with you." I sniffed and rose with Adam's help. Then, still leaning on my counterpart, still teary-eyed and heartbroken, I followed Erik to the front steps. Just below us, as Erik had promised, stood a large crowd of people. Something about them was familiar, but I could not place it.

"Queen Vita of Kongeorn." A woman in the front took notice of me and stepped forward confidently. Her golden eyes flitted up and down, as if to swallow me in their depths. And after searching her myself, I found the familiarity. Her skin held a somewhat blue tint that I had seen before, or perhaps I had dreamt it? I shook off the thought and addressed her directly.

"You are correct." I kept my delivery short and sweet to hide the tumult of emotion still crashing against my walls. Her eyes again flitted, this time around my head, almost looking through me. Though perplexed, I kept silent and waited for her to speak. To my surprise, she did not. She only continued to eye the periphery of my head, moving her molten eyes every few seconds. When those eyes looked just above my forehead, she inhaled sharply.

"My Queen, I have come in advance of my father and brother. We are of the Ordliqt Tribe from the far north. Your *misfortunes* have struck a chord in our hearts, and we wish to offer you our swords." I stared at her blankly, unable to comprehend her words. Such a proposition was unprecedented, and had me acting cautiously. Something in my expression must have tipped the woman off, as she added, "We have our reasons, and I would share them with you, if we could discuss them privately." Her words comforted me, even if I still felt on edge. I complied and led her inside and to the right, the opposite of which would have led us back to the body of my godfather.

I opened the doors to my bedroom and gestured for her to enter. Her head and those molten eyes immediately rested on my fireplace. Seconds later, she knelt before it, hands tracing the polished wood. *Don't judge her. Don't judge her. Don't judge her...* As if hearing my thoughts, her head snapped back to look at me, eyes glowing.

"Vita of Kongeorn, you underestimate yourself; you think it was by sheer coincidence that the history of our world is in the sleeping place of the one who will change it forever?" *Wait. What?* She rose and approached me, her shadow making me feel like a child. She placed a finger to my left eye, then to the place just over my left breast, where my wound had yet to completely heal. "We heard of the tragedies of your people, then of your own agony. And I knew. I knew the only way you would survive, that you could survive, was if the Mother was with you. And it is confirmed as I look upon you now." My breath came shallow and fast as my heart frantically beat its own tune, complimenting her words. Again surprised at this blue woman, I remained silent and tried desperately to understand.

After a few moments, her shadow seemed to shrink and become less profound, and her eyes dimmed. She began to walk out.

"We are here because you are the future; the Mother and Kongeorn will make something new of this world, and we plan to be a part of it." With that, she began to exit.

"Wait," I called, snapping out of it, "what is your name?"

"Ayla." She smiled a kind smile and departed from the room.

I sat down on my bed and just stared at the rug under my feet for a few moments. My eyebrows were furrowed and my nose was scrunched. *What just happened?* Of all the possible things that I could have experienced on that day, *that* was perhaps the most outlandish.

Whatever Fate had in store for me next could never surprise me. But then again, I'd been wrong before.

As I had grown up, everywhere I looked, there were men. Sometimes contemptuous, sometimes arrogant. For so long, I wanted to be like them. Da was a charismatic leader, loved by his people. Bjorth was a wise and courageous warrior. Amund was next in line for the throne, and women seemed to throw themselves at him.

I wanted to be like them. From where I stood, they had all the power. They got to be who they wanted to be without question. When I refused to wear my hair down or ride my horse side-saddle, people talked. To be a powerful, proud woman was to be a scrutinized woman, even in a society as progressive as ours.

Nana, when she was still in the World of the Living, warned me about such things. She called them, 'Necessary Obstacles.'

"Now, V," she said, braiding my hair, "there will be people who believe that there are only two kinds of human: man and woman. And they will scorn any who don't fit into their pretty little boxes. But let me tell you what: the Mother doesn't give a *svat.*"

"Nana!"

"Eh, just don't repeat it, child," she continued. "If you grow up and find you don't want to marry a man then don't. If you want to cut your hair or wear trousers or love another woman then do it.

As long as you don't hurt anyone, it doesn't matter what you like or do."

"So, if I want to marry anyone, I don't have to?"

"Yes. Your father may want you to marry a man of his choice, but you can always say 'no.' And if they don't take 'no' for an answer then you can hit them in the knees with a club." Nana finished my braids and smiled down at me.

"But Nana," I narrowed my eyes at her, "you just said not to hurt anybody."

She looked away, as if to check to see if anyone else was listening. Then, she looked back at me and said, "In this case, you can."

After that, I stood up, walking toward the door, ready to go play with my brothers. Before leaving, though, I stopped, turned, and look Nana deep in the eye.

"I am not going to ever marry anyone, Nana. I can take care of myself."

I smiled softly as I thought about the memory. For so long, I had been ready to be on my own. Thinking about it then, though, I knew that I wouldn't have survived without Adam. Over the years, I hadn't cared for romance, whether it be from a man or a woman. Maybe that had been because I had the only person I needed by my side. If I was going to keep going, to get through the next few months, I was going to need Adam more than ever.

Pushing the memory and the thought away, I stood up, albeit painfully slow. There would need to be arrangements made for Bjorth's funeral. *Funeral. Bjorth hates that word.* I started to correct myself with a revision of tense, but thought better of it.

There was no time to waste. Out of respect for our departed, Kongeorn funerals were as soon as possible after the death. Pyres were built for the burning of the body. The burning ensured that the souls of the dead are lit and remembered in the hearts of the living for all time. Like many cultures, we wore black to the funeral to mourn, and wore black until the flames themselves went out. After that, life would return to normal, or at least as normal as could be expected.

I had Oliver, along with a handful of new army members, build the pyre out in the Levend, the holy clearing where burnings took place. Once it was completed, they brought out Bjorth, wrapped in his warrior's cloak, looking every part the fighter I knew him to be. But, because of the cold, unfamiliar hands holding his sword and the white, foreign hair crowding his face, he did not look the part of my beloved godfather. I turned away from the image and made my way back to my room to dress in my mourning clothes.

Inside, all was silent; not a voice could be heard within or without the stone walls. In my mind, however, the noise more than made up for it.

He's dead. I could have done something; I should have done something.

This isn't your fault. A small voice countered but to no avail.

Of course it is. You should have known. Everyone around you dies; it's only a matter of time. And you *are to blame.* You *should have known Einar's plan.* You *should have gone scouting with them.* You *should have* died *with them.*

"I did!" I screeched aloud, clamping my hands over my ears, trying to stay the noise. In that moment, my wounds roared to life, festering in their scars. Skin boiled and popped, while tissue melted away. I collapsed onto the rug, just feet from my bedroom door, and assumed a childlike position. The ghosts of tears clutched at my eyes, which were squeezed shut. My fingers clawed at the rug beneath me, dust gathering beneath my nails.

Then hands enveloped me. They poked and they prodded and they found every nook which had gone unmolested by Avery's, and by Richard's, touch. This touch soon turned to the excruciating agony of boiling water tossed onto my skin. And then, to my horror, I realized I had been thrown into that water.

Just as the pain began to become bearable, air flow was cut off. My lips had been sealed, and my lungs begged for the oxygen they craved.

Vita! A distant voice called my name. *Vita!* It grew closer with each second, and the breath returned to me. The voice came ever closer until it was right above me.

"Vita!" He did everything but shake me. "Vita, please!" Mustering any strength I had left from the ordeal, I wrenched open my eyes. Immediately, the pain and the noises ceased. I was soaking wet, and Adam held me to him. He kissed my forehead when he saw me release the death grip I held on his soaked through shirt.

I began to shake, whether from the draft that came from nowhere, or from the realization of safety at hand. Adam took it as the former and lowered us until all but our heads were submerged beneath the hot spring's water. I laid my head on his shoulder, exhausted. In turn, he smoothed down my matted hair and placed his lips on the crown of my head. I fell asleep with them there.

"Vita, it is time for the burning."

The heavily accented voice roused me from my dreamless slumber. I laid on my bed, in warm and dry clothes beneath warm and dry covers, facing a warm and dry fire. My eyes opened to take in Ayla's cool blue skin. She gently rubbed my left shoulder. Once she knew I was truly awake, she retracted her hand, leaving my skin wanting still for the friendly warmth of her touch. Reluctantly, I rose and looked down, finding the same black garments I had planned on wearing. I smiled to myself. *Of course he knew.*

Ayla helped me up and kept my arm in hers as we made our way out of the keep and to Levenend, where a large crowd of people stood waiting. They parted as we passed; I attempted to straighten as we walked through them. At the front of the group, Adam stood, eyes glued to the pyre where my godfather's body laid. I stopped next to him and Ayla released my arm.

Out of the darkness, Simon appeared, looking as old as Omnia, itself. Oliver handed our elder the holy torch, Elmia. His frail hand reached out shakily, but as he grasped it, the shaking ceased, and Simon took on the look and persona of a young man. Throwing down his walking staff from his other hand, he then strode to the pyre and tilted the flame. The fire caught and spread. Like a serpent, it snaked between logs and branches, over Bjorth's body. The orange glow flitted and fluttered, ever sweeping. It grew higher into the sky, a beacon and testament to the man with the orange hair and scar. As the flames crackled, his laugh blew the leaves of the surrounding trees, and his eyes outshone the stars, and his heart's light caused the Luna to shine brighter than she ever had before.

I gazed at the glow, unable and unwilling to look away. The flames waved at me; Bjorth said his last goodbye and joined my father in the world of love and light. I stepped forward, wanting to see beyond the flames, needing to see what he saw, where he was. Not caring for any others' thoughts of me, I reached out for the flames, yearning to feel something beyond this sorrow. Instead of feeling the heat of the fire on my hand, however, I felt the warmth of another on my opposite arm.

Adam grasped my forearm, and I resigned myself to be pulled back into the crowd of mourners. But he did not pull me back. To my surprise, he stepped up next to me and intertwined his fingers in with mine. Of its own accord, my hand brought itself to my heart, bringing his in tow. I turned myself to him and rested my head on his chest, all the while watching the sparks of eternity's song disappear into the stars.

By the time the Sol had risen, the fire had yet to go out. Most of what remained was ash, but for a few stubborn pieces of cloth and wood. Neither Adam, nor I, had moved. I elected still to remain frozen, even as the fresh rays of Sol threatened to thaw me. The rays were briefly interrupted as two robins flitted above the tree line, first a brown female, then a vibrant male. My eyes followed them until they disappeared to the West.

"Vita," his voice strained after so long staying quiet, "the flame has died. A new day begins." I felt a cool emptiness as his heat separated from me. Wanting still for human contact, I kept my hand in his and reluctantly left behind the remains of a man once known as the Western Sol.

The two walked away as I watched them—my daughter and the man I had always hoped she would love—as I sat, perched on a high branch of a tall birch tree only feet away. In this form, I was nothing more than another part of the background, another brushstroke on canvas. The way they walked together made me proud of the decision I had made, of the way they had grown together over all this time, especially that of my absence.

It was always my hope that they would be close. Kongeorn always needed Hingst, and bringing Adam into our home had been my way of ensuring that union. I looked at the two of them, content. I waited for a moment and, just as I had expected, Adam turned his head, finding me in the trees, and nodded ever so slightly.

The Hingst to her Kongeorn. *I smiled.*

I turned as the final embers flickered out. I rose and stood atop the tree canopy, waiting for my own best friend. The winds changed direction, and before me, he stood, the same way he had been when I named him the godfather of my only daughter. Everything I had asked of him had been more than fulfilled.

"Andor?" He spoke, unsure of himself, of the renewal and revival of his soul through the ritual. Unlike his features at his time of death, his face was smooth and young again, his beard red and flaming.

"Took you long enough, cousin. I thought you'd never arrive." We both chuckled and embraced. Bjorth clasped my shoulder and took on a solemn look.

"I'm sorry, I should've been there with ya." Once again, he burdened himself with that which he could never carry. I smiled.

"I know. But if you had come with us, and if you had perished then, Vita would not have had you as a guide. Feel no guilt; you have done far more than I could have ever wished." I turned toward the rising Sol, towards Home, and left the world of the living to the living.

Chapter 13
The Demons Run

Adam made the executive decision to spend the day resting, even though that was what I had been doing for the past several weeks. Of course, he could not be dissuaded. With that in mind, I retreated back into the brightest corners of my consciousness, the ones where memories of childhood flourished, bathed in the sunlight of simpler times and simpler mindsets. I thought upon the faces in those memories, the ones both remaining and departed from this world. To my dismay, the latter seemed a far larger number. As each of the lost faces passed by my mind's eye, they paled and faded into wisps of grey, completely devoid of lively color.

Those who remained, like Gyda and Karina and Adam, did not turn grey, but instead, were magnified in color. Gyda's dusky shades framed all else of her memory to me. The raven and midnight colors of Karina's hair tinted out every other and became my mind's memory of her. And then there was Adam. Though he strode next to me, my memory of him was a moment from what seemed like so long before. His carefree face, frozen in laughter, was in reaction to some event only moments prior. I couldn't remember what that moment had been, only the face he had made to express himself.

His eyes were squinted shut, and his mouth agape in the midst of a guffaw. His sharp nose was scrunched, giving more depth to the few freckles he had there. And, as I focused on the memory, it too began to fade. My heart stopped, worried at this, afraid it was some sort of foretelling. My terror, however, was banished by the sudden reappearance of his face, only different in the color, which had been transformed into a vibrant emerald.

As my heart again regained its normal pace, I departed from my mind's eye to the real world, which found myself and Adam at the open doors of my bedroom. Inside, on my bed, sat Simon. Next to my fireplace, on the other side of the room, Trond stood inspecting the carvings of the artwork. And, to my surprise, Hakon sat slumped against the far wall, head in his hands.

"Vita," Simon addressed me, a cue for the other two to perk up, "I have taken the liberty of calling a private council. Karina and Gyda are on their way as we speak. To add, I have invited the one from the North, Ayla; I believe you two have already met." With that, he gestured a seemingly frail, yet dark, hand to the opposite corner, where Ayla leaned against the wall. Had Simon not said anything, I would never have detected her presence. With my eyes on her, however, she came forward, embodying a person far more normal than the one I had witnessed before in the same room.

"Ah yes, you are just in time," Simon welcomed the quite-pregnant Karina and the always-bedraggled Gyda. Both women passed Adam and myself and sat down to make themselves, especially Karina, comfortable. "Now that we are all here, Adam, son, please close the doors." He did. "Now, there has been much talk of war in the last few weeks, especially after our dear queen made her debut back into the world. However, we must really discuss this idea and make a decision upon it." He looked me in the eye, and I took the hint. It was my turn to speak, to give my opinion, my orders. I elected first to provide my story. It was imperative that they knew what had happened, what would happen. I took in a shaky breath, and let my eyes close, and waited for the memories to burst forth from my lips.

"While I was held captive by the Feron King, I was tortured. For fourteen days, I was tortured by a member of the Cruor Allicit." As I spoke those words, I realized I hadn't really spoken them before. I hadn't told my story, not even to Adam. "And yes, my heart seeks revenge, but I am not willing to put countless lives at stake for my own personal vendetta. I will, however, say this: while I was there, while I was escaping, I paid witness to the state of the Feroxian people." I paused, collecting myself for what was to come. Out of the corners of my eyes, I noticed the demons from before: the needles and the acid and the gaunt faces of children as I prepared to reveal them to the world. "The entire population had also been under the 'care' of the C'All. Each man, woman, and child shared a look of absence in their eyes. Their clothes were not nearly enough to provide warmth, and all which made life worth living had been taken from them." Again, I paused, both to take inventory of the demons and to gauge the reactions of my fellow council members.

Simon's eyes stared through me, as if he, the most wise and experienced, did not know what to think of, nor how to comprehend, this information. Trond's brow was knitted in knots, and his confused hands groped at the polished wood behind him, trying to find refuge from the words. Hakon had since looked up, and then stared at the wall, fists clenching and unclenching continuously. Both Gyda and Karina displayed the same look; their eyes trailed the floor, but never stopped moving, as if trying to outrun all of this. I looked over to Ayla, whose eyes had again begun to glow gold, fierce and tempestuous, though her body language suggested she was in the eye of the storm.

As for Adam, I could not look him in the eye, though I knew his were on me. They bore into me, and beside me, his hands were in fists, shaking, trembling. He was the first to move.

"A C'All? They tortured you with a C'All?" his whispers convulsed in my ear. Needing my full attention, he moved himself in front of me. "Did he touch you?" He meant Richard; he wanted to know if…though his voice was lowered, his words tore through me, ringing clear. I knew what he was asking, but I didn't want to answer. I didn't want to admit that I was broken and used and dirty. I couldn't. Eyes still lowered, feeling like a child being scolded, I refused to answer. I crossed my arms, closing myself off.

"Did he *touch* you?" This time, Adam's teeth were clenched, and his tone pained. The memory of that blurry, numbed night faded in and out of my sight; I mustered the slightest nod. I couldn't lock it away any longer, I just couldn't. Without hesitation, Adam backed off, silent. Something like rage radiated off of him in waves, pushing me away.

　　　With everyone else still silent, I was again left to my thoughts, giving the demons the perfect opportunity to lunge. With ferocity, the needles dove back into my skin, forcing me to my knees, punishing me for bringing their secrets to light. The acid, in turn, burned away at my sight, causing my world to go blank. My ears heard that same accent slither in behind me, shoving my top half onto the stone below. Pricks and pokes came from every direction. For the first time, my limbs began to move of their own accord, pulsating and shuddering. The accent grew louder and louder, thicker and thicker, and then, Nothing: the darkness of my unconsciousness had returned for me.

　　　"Vita, Queen of All, why do you fear them? They have made you stronger, more powerful than any other, and yet, your fear them." The voice fills my mind, just as my lungs are filled with water. I am still struggling, trying to fight the man from before, the one who promised a kiss, but gave me death.

　　　"Tsk, tsk," he clucks his tongue at me, like I am a misbehaving kitten, "My Queen, the more you struggle, the more this will agonize you. Let the wave crash; let the light go." 'Let the wave crash.' Where do I know that from?

The Nothing slowly allowed me to escape its binding tendrils. My eyes fluttered open; cool stone pressed against my cheek. Ayla's eyes were the first to draw my conscious attention.

"*Diqe dem Sgoer*," she exhaled in her native tongue, her eyes slowly fading back from their brilliant hue, "we had no id—"

"We cannot let what happened to me and to those citizens happen to our people. A life without spirit or free thought is no life at all. We must fight, not just for our own people, but for those of Feroxia." Though I felt bad for interrupting Ayla, the intensity of the feeling in my heart brought tears forth to accent my words. I had never been so sure of anything in my life. Not a single thing, and I would protect that sentiment with my dying breath. Each face, after recovering from the initial shock of my waking, as well as my declaration, expressed agreement.

"It is decided then; we are at war."

I cannot remember who said it, but the declaration pounded through my head, reminding me of the die that had been cast. Our next move, I knew, would be to gather troops, to train, and to formally declare war. For the last, my own words would be needed, but not yet, not until our own people knew, and that would have to wait until the morrow. For now, we would adjourn and take solace in the last moments of peace we would experience for a very long time.

Each member of the council exited my room as they had entered, except for Adam, who had already absconded somehow. Worry flashed in my heart, taking into account the waning light outside. I must have been out cold for most of the day. But where had Adam gone? *And why would he leave?* His absence and possible reasons behind it flung more painful thoughts into my mind.

He knows now that you are broken, ruined.

He cannot stand to look upon you.

He cannot stand to be near you.

He cannot stand to love *you.*

The last thought broke through the stillness which had placated me for the time being. I had to find him, if not to prove the voices were wrong then to make sure he hadn't done anything rash.

I strode down the hall, leaving my bedroom doors wide open, a rude gesture to some in our culture, and began the search. First, I tracked down the most obvious place: his room. To my dismay and partial relief, it was empty. I then found myself half walking briskly, half skipping to the baths. Inside, I found neither Adam, nor embarrassment—okay, maybe a small amount—when I took in the sight of a young couple *together.* Neither of which, of course—thank the Mother—was Adam.

I did, however, scamper away as quietly and discreetly as possible, took off my right sock and gently placed it on the door handle. Turning away, I knew my face to be tomato red and my thoughts to be somewhat voracious. After making it far enough down the hallway, and out of earshot, I let out the breath I had been holding and wheezed, laughing silently, hand covering my mouth. I squatted to compress the noise, but couldn't contain the sheer awkwardness of the brief encounter. *Yikes.*

Once I had contained myself, I stood and went on my way again, planning on riding out to the Edge, where Adam went to think sometimes. I dismounted the stairs at the front of the keep and sidled to the stables, where I found my own horse to be missing. Upon further inspection, I discovered that she had been taken out to the pasture, even though this was not her scheduled time for it. Dagny grazed more readily in the mornings, rather than evenings, so I found it strange that she should be taken out against my wishes.

And because I needed Dagny if I was to ride out to the Edge, I traversed to the pasture, where I found my horse, but she wasn't alone. Next to my beloved horse was the silhouette of a woman with long black hair. I carefully climbed over the fence and approached the woman. Before I could speak, however, she did.

"Vita of Kongeorn." *Wonderful, someone else knows me before I know them. Why does this always happen to me?* "I expected you would come." *Of course you did.* I eyed her carefully, noting her short stature and intensely golden eyes, much like Ayla's. Instead of maintaining the same bluish hue, though, this woman's skin was pale, almost gray in color. And, though her initial appearance caught me off guard, Dagny seemed to enjoy the strange woman's presence. To prove my point, Dagny nuzzled the woman's shoulder, pressing her for more nose strokes. *Okay, I guess I'll bite.*

"Who are you, and," I added, "why does my horse like you so much?"

"Your animal enjoys me because we have much in common." *Okay, what?* I closed my eyes and prayed that this woman hadn't just wandered in after eating special mushrooms. Seeing my exasperated expression, though, the woman elaborated, "We are both children of the Mother. And we both love pears." From her worn satchel, the woman pulled an Ostenian pear, like the ones that had kept me alive on my journey home. The woman, yet again, noticed my focus. Instead of explaining herself again, she let her eyes wander around my face, another similar behavior to Ayla. It wouldn't have surprised me if they knew one another.

The slivers of silver Luna light mingled with the last wisps of Sol light, capturing the woman's expression. Her brow knitted above her eyes, which grew more intense as she studied me, as if to decipher my own thoughts. She stepped toward me, away from my horse, who followed her movements. Up and down and up again, her eyes travelled, studying me ever closer, inspecting the very fabric of my soul. I straightened, incredibly uncomfortable in the situation, as usual. The woman circled me once, then twice, and then once more before stopping before me and reaching out her pale hand.

"Perse." The name slithered from her tongue, enticing my own hand forward, despite the awkward feeling in my disposition. My hand, of its own accord, continued to reach out, until our skins made contact. The woman, Perse, immediately stiffened, as if in pain, a small gasp escaping her parted lips. What she had experienced, I could not know, only that it had affected her drastically in some way. Reacting finally, I retracted my hand from its embrace with hers. Perse's glazed eyes melted back into attendance as her limbs felt movement again. The only aspect of her which remained in a frozen state was her lips. They remained parted, as if trying to breathe all the air from around her, as if to intake the Luna light, itself.

"I—" she panted, seemingly exhausted, "I am so very sorry; I did not mean… That is to say—I should have warned you." I raised an eyebrow. *Warned me of what?* I glanced over both shoulders, alert to any possible danger. "The Mother has given me the ability of Putavit; with a touch, I—I can see any part of your past, or future, that I share in." I blinked several times. *I could have used a warning, or maybe an introduction. But nope, she just had to jump right in.* After a moment or so, I realized that I was still blinking rapidly. I cut it out before this woman, this Putavita, thought me crazy. *Who am I kidding? She probably already thinks that. Then again,* she's *the one who can read my memories with a touch.* I chuckled inwardly.

"So," I tried to speak, still attempting to process the event and the information, "you saw into my past." It was neither statement, nor question, rather somewhere between talking to myself and validating what had just occurred.

"Yes." Perse started speaking quickly, attempting to explain herself as fast as possible, which I could definitely relate to "Because we have something in common in our pasts, I have access to those memories. But, I can't—I don't know how to—control when I see the events. So, yes, I am so very sorry; memories are supposed to be private unless freely shared. So, that being said, I apologize. Again." She spat the words from her mouth, and they flowed like a strong current to my ears, where the information was still too much to handle. I stood silently before her abilities made at least a small amount of sense in my mind. I looked at her, eyes fresh with a new view behind them, something of a novel understanding, which drew forth a new set of questions.

"What did you see?" I spoke softly, afraid of what she would say, of what part of my past that she had felt a kinship to.

"Well," the strange woman bit her lip, chewed for a moment, and then continued, "I saw a 'Z' with a pommeled staff down the center. I saw the needles and the instruments, and I heard the voices." Her eyes lowered, as if ashamed. "I felt the scars and the agony and the self-hatred. All of it, I felt all of the torture." Her golden eyes still refused to meet mine. Understanding, I put my hand on her shoulder, minding to keep away from her skin so she wouldn't have to feel all that I had felt again. Her eyes finally glanced up for long enough for me to establish a connection. My nose prickled, telling me that tears were on their way. I took my hand back and moved it to my chest, where I gently pushed away the fabric covering the one physical wound that I thought would never disappear.

"Mortem," I whispered, flinching slightly as the word touched my lips. Perse smiled sadly and lifted the hem of her shirt. Beneath, the majority of her torso was crisscrossed in scars upon scars, making it nearly impossible to decipher where one began and the other ended. In addition, her belly button, I noticed, was not there. Instead, a sunken stretch of scarred flesh acted as canvas for the raised tissue just above, which was formed into the image of a "Z" with a pommeled staff down the middle.

I reached out, wanting to show that I understood, but stopped my hand just short, afraid for Perse. I could not force her to relive that which I experienced every time the demons came out to play. My hand returned to my side, and Perse's shirt again covered her torso. After a long time of silence, all of the Sol's rays had given way to the light of the Luna.

"What brought you here," I began. "Was it that which we share?" I didn't know how else to word what I wanted to ask.

"Yes," she nodded her head solemnly, "sit, and I will tell you my story." I did as she asked and prepared myself.

"My full name, my given name, is Persianukya. I was born south of here, in one of the seventy provinces. My mother and father were from the far west, where the sea keeps us from going. They are from Oeste. They came here shortly before I was born, and we made a life. Papa noticed my changes before Mama did. He saw the way I would refrain from human contact, the way I would shy away from the bodies of passersby. He knew that which the Mother had given me was unlike anything in Jordklode. So we hid it, which was why I never learned to control it.

"The morning of my thirteenth birthday, I awoke to the sound of my mother screaming, her cries jolting me from unconsciousness. Two men crashed through my door and into my room. My mother was held back by two more, and my father was restrained by even more of them. One of them, the only one not in action, had his eyes on me. His were pale, and his hair stringy. Upon his command, I was snatched from my bed and pulled to him. They stole me away. I never saw my parents again.

"The man, I later learned, was of the Cruor Allicit, and wanted someone, a young nobody, to be his next experiment. I was that young nobody. I was experimented upon. Nothing like what you experienced; it was slower, more spread out. He wanted me to live. He spread out the visits so far that I would be nearly healed by the next visit. That wasn't what broke me, though.

"That which broke me, the aspect of it all that made me pray for death, was that same *gift* I thought could somehow keep me alive. Every time, every single second that he touched me, I could see all the others that he had hurt, killed, ruined. And I could feel his hatred for them, for everything that wasn't his precious C'All. I decided, one day, to just give up.

"I let the darkness that had so long been in my periphery saturate all of me. I felt the pain ebb and seep away as the darkness spread. It was over, finally over.

"But then I woke up.

"I was face down under a tree somewhere, where, I didn't, and still don't, know. I laid there for days, and then someone found me. I recovered in body, but my mind was still in jagged pieces. That, I believe, is something no healer, nor priestess, nor witch, can mend. But then I met him.

"Amal was the son of the woman treating me. And one day, he touched my hand and held it. I found we had a common thread. As a child, I had been fascinated by the sounds of storms. Apparently, so had Amal. When he took my hand in his tiny one, I became immediately surrounded by the clashes of titanic bolts of lightning and the rumble of gods. The pattering of rain brought me to my senses, and Amal's compassion, even at such an innocent age, inspired me to *try*.

"A few months ago, Amal was running errands for me and his mother when he came back to us with the news of your family's deaths. Amal's hand brushed mine as he said the news, and I again felt the shaking of the booming thunder, but saw also two eyes I shouldn't soon forget. I had to find them, find you."

Perse finished her tale and took a deep breath. Her story had brought my heart closer to hers, but I still didn't understand why, exactly, she had wanted to find me.

"The Mother," she decided to enlighten me further, "sent me to find you, and to offer you the services of my gift, my new gift. I can communicate with the Etter; I can show you what your future holds." My brow knitted then raised. Again, this woman had me at a loss for words. "Give me something to look for in your future, in what has been predicted based on your decisions thus far, and I will show you the outcome. That is why I am here. That is the duty the Mother has placed upon my shoulders." *Anything. I can ask for answers to anything. I can see how the war will play out, how Amund's child's rule will impact Jordklode. I can see Jakel's end.* My heart sank. None of those were what I actually wanted to see.

Perse bid me put my hands in hers, which I did reluctantly. She closed her eyes, but did not ask me to do the same. I watched her face as it became still, peaceful. It was completely the opposite of when our skins had first come into contact. Her words were silent, but her mouth still moved, calling to whomever it was she called to. Without warning, I felt a sensation overcome me.

Falling, further and further down, into darkness, unable to stop or slow. The darkness fades to reveal a scene of blood and war. I see a woman with the eyes of a warrior, with the heart of a wolf, deadlocked in battle with an armored man. In fact, she is so focused in her fighting that she does not see the other attacker coming from behind.

Down comes her battle axe, again and again, in slow motion, upon her opponent, but her blows are only distracting her. I watch, breathless, waiting in suspense as the attacker's sword comes down for her. His sword, however, is stopped, by the sword of someone I know.

Adam.

He blocks the blow and pars, all without the woman seeing her own salvation. Adam continues to fight, blow for blow, moving himself further away from the warrior woman, until he has gone so far that he cannot see her unless he turns around.

But then he hears it. An involuntary scream. And, against his warrior instincts, he turns away from his battle, to look for the woman, to make sure the sound did not come from her. To his relief, it did not. She turns to look back at him, to wink, but her face contorts as she sees an enemy's sword run through his chest.

Oblivious to the battle around her, the woman with the icy eyes and the crooked nose runs to Adam, and she does not care for the consequences.

I pulled away from the vision, the nightmare, Perse had placed before me. Her own eyes were widened in shock, rimmed with tears.

"I—I'm so sorry; I could not have known this would happen." But I could not hear her. My heart began to race, to pound harder and harder against my rib cage. A lump formed in my throat.

"It will *not* happen." I said, more as a comfort to myself than a true statement of doubt. Perse merely shook her head.

"It *will*, for things such as this future are nearly impossible to change." My head reeled. If Adam was lost, if he died, I would be alone. Everyone I considered family, save for Karina, would be separated from me by the Veil to Etter. But that wasn't just it. Something inside me took the sight of Adam's death as more than those which had already happened. Something about it, something inside me, clicked. And then I realized.

I ran from Perse, from the reality that had been set before me. I sprinted to my room, shut the doors behind me, stripped off all the clothing that trapped me in sweat and encased itself painfully around me. Only in my nightclothes, I clambered into bed and hid beneath the sheets like a child from a thunderstorm. Before long, I again began to sweat, so I threw off all the blankets. Trying to sleep, I tossed and turned and rolled until I finally sat upright, nearly hyperventilating.

Chapter 14

Scars

I padded along the wooden floors to his room. The vision had been too real and, though it was only a distant possibility, I could not help the pull to his chambers. I had to make sure he was still there, still alive, still breathing. Only that premise mattered, not the darkness everywhere, cloaking me in night, not the creaking beneath my feet, not even my nightclothes, which barely covered my torso. The vision, though the context seemed far-fetched, was far too real for me to return to sleep.

I inched open his door, painfully aware of the silence within. Without realizing it, I closed the door and made my way to the bed, where I could see his slumbering figure. A tear dropped down my cheek at the rise and fall of his bare chest. Adam was alive. *For now.* The thought crossed my head and my heart beat faster, like a child's at the sound of thunder.

In my mind, I recalled every memory of him: from the first "hello," when he was just a scrawny boy with messy black hair and shy green eyes. And then, the first time he bested me at swordplay. My twelve-year-old self had never expected the quick foot work he used to trip me up. I had simply lain there in shock, looking up at him. Me, completely helpless before him, the only person I had never felt that with. And then, we were riding horseback just after my fifteenth birthday. As Dagny raced ahead, I glanced back to see Adam and the look on his face, a look that I would become blind to. I remember my heart had skipped.

And then, there had been Amund's wedding. The ale had been too strong, but I drank it anyway. And he was just trying to get me safely to my room, where the fireplace had beckoned, so incredibly alluring. Unlike myself, Adam knew when to stop drinking. But he had still been light enough to the point of letting his guard down.

Just like that, a slip in his attention, and I had kissed him. And to my drunken surprise, he had returned it. I didn't let go until the morning Sol rose in the sky. All of our lives had been spent side by side in so many different ways: as childhood friends, as confidants, as sparring partners, as best friends, and, I finally had the courage to realize, so much more. And just like a part of myself, I could not lose him.

My family was already in the ground, in the Etter, far from my touch, from my sight; he could not be allowed to join, at least without knowing the way I felt. As my thoughts gave way to the present moment, I again took in the sight of Adam in an entirely new light. And like all things, it, too, was darkening. My breath grew increasingly shallower as I saw before me, yet again, the bodies of my family.

Just like a phantasm. *Each lay in their own pool of crimson. Mami and Da embrace, Amund's bloodied hand is reaching for something, his wife, perhaps. Bjorth is covered by animal skins. Elof and Geir sport demented curves of smiles, and Einar is nowhere to be seen. But then, the corpse I never want to lay eyes on catches and holds my watery gaze. His green eyes are still open, and my mouth opens to scream in agony.*

"Wha—Vita—" Adam shot up and grabbed me by the waist as the wail escaped my lips. "What's going on? Are you all right?" Without warning, without thinking, I buried my face in his chest. He stopped talking, puzzled at my behavior. Gently, he sat down on the bed, taking my shaking frame with him. He brought my legs up off of the floor so I curled into a nice little ball as he stroked my hair. It was like I was a child who had just had a nightmare. Completely vulnerable. Choking back sobs, I began to explain.

"Y—you were dead," deep breath, "I saw you, and you w— were d—dead." He then pulled my head from his chest, seeing the tears roll down my face. He studied me. As always, his eyes transported me to another memory, another time. The last time I had cried in front of him had been after Bjorth's death. But this time was entirely different.

"Believe me, please," I pleaded with him. Helpless, I felt the world crushing me and forcing tears from my eyes. Adam said nothing, yet looked at me with an emotion I had never seen on his face. *Pity? No, anything but his pity.* He thought I was crazy.

"Believe me when I say this: you are not just my family, but my soul. We have shared everything from the day you came to us. Meals, training sessions, hunts, days, nights, all of it." Still no words came from his lips, but his emerald eyes looked away when I mentioned the night we once spent in each other's company. We had not spoken of it, but I knew he had not forgotten, nor could he forget. It hadn't escaped my noticed how much more tender his touch had been after my return from captivity, how much longer his glances stayed on me, how much more heightened his emotional intensity was in my presence. No, none of it had escaped me. Risking the rest of my dignity, I said, "If you won't believe me, then comfort me."

Silence thundered as I felt the blood rush to my face. I wanted it, he wanted it—he had wanted it for some time, it would seem—and it could not wait. Still, he stalled, stared, until I felt myself roll to leave. Grasping my naked shoulder, Adam pulled me close, keeping me from escaping. My chest lay atop his and our legs intertwined.

"I would never doubt you." He brought his lips to mine. After a moment, he pulled away and looked me in the eye, asking for my permission. It was given. Then, more intensely than before, our lips met. I lay down, never once moving my eyes from his. Each motion made and each breath taken became sacred. Before long, my nightclothes were strewn about the floor, and Adam adorned my neck with careful kisses. Meticulous, yet passionate, every touch left us closer than before. He traced my skin with thoughtful fingers, as if to memorize every curve.

He studied every inch of me, careful around those places where needles had buried themselves. At the thought of each, the pain came back, but I was shielded from it as his lips found each scar, banishing the rotten nightmares from each.

It was as if he knew my every thought, my every wish, for it was done. He ran his hands up and down my wounds, physical and emotional, leaving bursts of warmth in his wake. Before long, our hearts beat as one, faster and faster, as our skin melted together. Together, in the most intimate and secret of ways. The actions which our souls had longed for, had been destined for, were being fulfilled.

When all was done, when we both lay exhausted, covered in sweat, and glowing in the radiance of the other, I lay my head on his chest, the way I had before. I listened to his heart beat steadily. And his breathing made my head rise with his chest. I felt him skip a beat in his breathing and I looked up.

"What did he do to you?" His green eyes were calm, but it felt like they were reaching into mine. Like they were trying to make another connection. I sighed, not wanting to go back to where the demons could get me so easily. But I needed to talk about it.

"After the last night of torture from the C'All, I couldn't move. I just lay, writhing in pain, on the floor. Halfway through the night, Richard walked in. My limbs were unresponsive. But he moved them anyway. And I did nothing. I just went numb. I didn't even try to fight back." Adam moved to take me closer to him, surrounding me in familiarity. His warmth was a stark contrast to the frozen memory in my head. He kissed the crown of my head, and I felt a drop of wetness fall into my hair.

Being alone was no way to live life—to fight any war. If I was going to be the person I wanted to be, I couldn't just put it all on myself. I couldn't bury it. And I was lucky because I had someone who cared, someone who would listen. Someone who would fight this war with me. And if we were to survive the coming battles, perhaps my father and mother would have another grandchild to watch over from above. But that did not matter, for I had my soul next to me, comforting me for the night. And while I slept, no dreams came to torment me, none to make the arms around me feel suffocating, nor any to ruin the calm in my heart.

Chapter 15
The Sapien of the North

The next morning, I awoke far later into the morning than anticipated. My head still rested on Adam's chest, which rose and fell steadily. The only signal to his consciousness was one of his hands playing with my shortened locks, which had grown some in the past month. I closed my eyes again and let his fingers continue to explore, eventually accidentally snagging one of the locks and tugging. I flinched, and Adam cursed.

"Sorry," he whispered, trying to recover. I turned myself to see him, and shook my head, chuckling, before sitting up. I scooted back so my back was against the headboard; Adam did the same. I tilted my head over, expressing my unwillingness to get up with a gnarly groan. Adam, in turn, chuckled at me and shook his head before going silent.

"So," he sighed, "what now?" I knew, even if he didn't explicitly say it, what he was talking about.

"We continue on as we always have to the outside world." I chose my words carefully—not for fear of hurting his feelings, but out of caution for the consequences if our partnership should become common knowledge. "They have no reason to know the details of our personal lives." Adam nodded in agreement before leaning over and kissing me.

"Then we have to get going. It definitely isn't normal that the queen and one of her advisors are both missing well past sunrise." With that, to my annoyance, he turned away, stood, and stretched. I tore my eyes away from the shifting muscles of his back, and planned a sneaky route back to my own room. I picked up my nightclothes and dressed quickly before running back over to Adam, pecking him on the cheek and absconding.

I made my way along the wall of the hall, trying to make myself as small and hidden as possible. The doors to my room were in sight, and I found myself moving slightly faster.

"Well, hello there, young Missy!" Gyda's voice met my ears and I froze. Something in her tone, the way she sauntered through the words, made my heart beat faster. "Now, where did you wander off to last night, hm?" I turned around, and her eyes hovered over me, scrutinizing me, before she broke out into a grin. She winked at me. "I'm sure glad you got some exercise. 'Bout damn time you two got together; Karina owes me a pretty hefty sum, and the middle name of her babe, too." She burst into laughter. I whipped my head around, making sure no one was nearby to hear us.

"Gyda, you cannot let people know about this. If word gets out, Adam could be targeted just as much as me." The old woman ceased her laughing alarmingly quickly before looking me directly in the eye.

"Oh, darlin, I wouldn't tell a soul who didn't already know." Happy with herself, she turned on a heel and sauntered away leaving me open-mouthed and dumbfounded. *She wouldn't tell a soul who didn't already know? Who else knew?* I almost ran after her, but found the need to be in my room and getting on with the day far more pressing. I found some clean riding pants and a tunic before donning my boots and freshening up. I glanced to the mirror, taking in my reflection. I was different. I was a survivor, and I had my people behind me. It was time to get down to business. I made my way to the flat area past the pasture where Ayla and her tribesmen had settled, despite our offering of rooms in the keep. Not at all to my surprise, Ayla awaited me at the edge of the camp.

"You appear rested." A smile played on her lips. *You've got to be kidding me! How could she possibly—you know what,* svat *on it. I don't even care.* I did, but I wasn't going to show it, at least not excessively.

"Ayla," I cut to the chase, circumventing the *other* subject, "when do the rest of your tribe get here, as I am sure they, if they are like you, already knew to come." I smiled, wondering what surprise could come from my blue skinned friend. But the answer did not come from her.

"My Queen, we have already arrived." Behind Ayla, another blue figure emerged from a tent. He had the same features as the woman before me, but was masculine in nearly every other way. Other than that, his features also seemed fairly familiar to me.

"Have we met? I apologize for the awkwardness, but I feel like we've met." I squinted, feeling somewhat embarrassed, but far more curious. The man smiled and nodded.

"I am surprised you remember, even if it is just an inkling of a memory. I was there after your speech to the people, when your injuries caused you to collapse." Thinking back, I nodded; it made sense, even if the details were still fuzzy. I then realized that I had never gotten his name. Before I could ask, however, he displayed the same foresight as Ayla.

"My name is Mehmet. I have the honor of being Ayla's brother and the son of our leader, Roald." Svat, *that makes a ridiculous amount of sense. Of course they're family.* I offered my hand to shake, and Mehmet took it, affirming our official introduction. Before I could think of what to say next, the siblings looked to each other, exchanging a glance, before Mehmet returned to the tent, and Ayla bid me follow. *And I thought* one *of them was weird.* I followed, nonetheless.

The tent, on the outside, seemed just large enough for a few people to sleep in. Its blue was a shade darker than the skin of my newfound friends. As I entered, however, to my amazement and complete shock, I found the tent was bigger on the inside. My jaw dropped, while my eyes nearly popped out of my skull. I'd never seen anything like this. I turned around and ran around the tent, checking to see that I wasn't crazy. The tent was a four-sided pyramid on the outside, about six feet on each side and ten feet tall. On the inside, however, there were entrances to several different rooms, each a different shade of blue. The main room, or cavern, it seemed, was at least one hundred by one hundred feet and about that high as well.

I ran to the farthest back wall of the tent and pushed tentatively. Like a normal tent side, it gave. I blinked several times, completely at a loss for what to say, what to do. I just stood there, eyes flitting around, taking it all in, before I noticed that I hadn't taken it *all* in. Near the back wall, where I had tested the give of the "fabric," Ayla stood with Mehmet, in front of them, an old man with that same blue skin and a snowy white beard, even though he was bald at his scalp.

"You are certainly not the first to do that, Vita, I promise." The old man's voice caught my attention and refused to let go, as if he could say anything, and I would believe it. I stepped forward, collecting myself, then catching myself.

I knew this man.

In the histories I had learned from Trond, there were legends tied within. Just over one hundred years before, the tribes of the North and Feroxia were at war. At the head of the Northern tribes was a Sapien, a man of prolonged life who had once walked side by side with the Mother, and had been deemed worthy of the title. He had been given abilities by the Mother, as he would use them wisely, never to be corrupted. His name had not been translated for our scholars, so we knew him only as "the Sapien."

He was said to be the oldest human alive, with a direct tie to the Mother and the power to carry out Her will. The stories said that his eyes glowed, unable to hide the power of creation, the light, that flowed through him.

I looked at the man in front of me and saw the glow of his eyes, as clear and bright as Luna light. His hair was long and white, and his dark skin was wrinkled, though nothing about him seemed weak.

Looking upon him, I knew that the old man before me was the Sapien.

I dropped to one knee, head bowed in the presence of someone who had walked, had talked, with the Mother. It was an honor to even breathe the same air as Her.

"You will not kneel, Vita of Kongeorn, you will never kneel before any." The old man's voice rose me from my knee. I knew of nothing else to do, no way other than that, to react. Ayla's abilities, and I imagined Mehmet's, as well, were no doubt a gift from the Sapien, and I felt embarrassed for thinking them weird, strange.

"We are all strange, Vita, all for different reasons. But strange does not always mean something negative. You, yourself, know this to be true. Therefore, do not feel guilt. Instead, pick up your eyes from your boots and engage in a conversation with me." Though I still felt somewhat guilty, I obeyed him and looked up at him, shuffling forward at the same time. I wished to apologize for my behavior, for how childish I seemed. I wanted to explain to him that I wasn't ever like this, that I was strong and confident, not submissive and scared. But my tongue was still unable to speak. So, he did it for me.

"Your behavior is not reason for embarrassment; and there is no reason to worry, as I know very well your level of perseverance, of fierce heart. Elsewise, I would not be here." He paused, signaling a change of subject. "Yes, you know me as 'the Sapien,' but my children and my tribesmen know me as 'Roald,' and that is how I would like you to know me." *What a minute, his children? He couldn't mean—oh, but he does. Ayla and Mehmet are the Sapien's—Roald's—children? That makes a lot of sense, actually.* Finally, I found my tongue.

"Sir, it is an honor—more than that, a dream—to speak with you, for you to be here. And your children, as well." My voice was filled with genuine wonder, with awe. Roald grinned.

"And I must say, it is an honor to finally come face to face with the she-wolf, herself." I froze. *Did he just say 'she-wolf'?* He nodded, as if to answer the question posed in my mind. "Your reign has been a long time coming. And when the sign was given, I knew your time had come." I was again silent, retreating back into the mode of ignorance, of inability to speak.

"When I spoke last with the Mother, She told me there would be a massacre, a tragedy, a tall, proud family torn asunder by the betrayal of one member. She told there would be a war, a queen's war. But Vita, She said you were the key. You and your Adam. She has seen that which could happen, and every scenario ends with the world changing drastically. I could not stand to miss it. So when I heard of your family's deaths—and I grieve for you—I knew the time had come to stir. And here we are." As I took in Roald's words, a large weight, even greater than the one I had felt at the last council meeting, sank down onto my aching shoulders. If what Roald said was true, then Ahava had been right as well. We were at war; there was no changing that, but that didn't mean death was certain.

"Then you have come to help us?" The question seemed obvious, but I needed to be sure, to know that someone so powerful was actually on my side.

"*Vill oer steige.*" Of the vast languages of the North, this phrase was one I would recognize anywhere. From my mother's last words to me, to those that kept me alive in the den of those most evil to now, staring into the eyes of an influential ally, I knew that would be our only choice, the only way to go about it. We may fall, yes; everyone falls. But it is those who get back up, those who climb farther and farther up the mountain, who will come out on top. War was imminent, but no one, no matter who their god was, could stand against us. Yes, we could fall, but Mother knows what would happen next. We would rise even higher than anyone would have dared to think.

Part Two

Chapter 16
Back in the Saddle

The weeks trudged on.

Karina and I spent less time together than I would have liked in preparation for the birth of her child. I tried to visit with her once a week, offering words of encouragement.

"I don't know if I can do it without him, V," she said to me. "This was supposed to be *our* baby, our future, but he's gone."

I could tell that Amund had been on her mind constantly, and I felt guilt creep through me at the thought that I had been distant towards my sister-by-marriage in the past months. To make up for it, I offered what I could.

"No matter where you go or what happens, I know Amund will be with you."

More often than not, my time with Karina was cut short by my other duties, namely: training.

Training began for newer recruits soon after Roald had voiced his desire to help us, and it was headed up by someone I felt was more than qualified: Ayla. Her presence on its own was enough to make some of them think twice about whispering behind her back, yet some still made the idiotic decision to do so. One particular morning, a new wave of recruits, mere children with wide eyes and hopeful hearts, waited in our newly constructed barracks for their first day to begin. A buzz of electricity simmered through them as I watched from behind. I smiled as Ayla made her appearance.

"Listen," her voice cut clear through the noise, completely silencing each and every member of the sizable group, "you are here for a reason, each and every one of you. I do not know your individual reasons, but I do know that you are—and will be— fighting for us, alongside us. We will not be easy on you. Ladies, I stand before you a woman. You will train the same as the men because that is who you will be fighting. We will *not* go easy on you. Because war is not easy." Her gold eyes flashed back to me, a smirk emerging on her lips. *Oh, great.* She gestured back to where I stood, causing the group to shift and train their eyes on me.

"Your queen will also be training. She will not, as the ruler of Feroxia does, sit in her room in luxury. She, like you and the rest of our soldiers, will be fighting and training and getting dirty." I confirmed her words by nodding. Because I had not fought, nor trained, since before my own trip to Feroxia, I felt the need to build my way back up, to ease my way back in. We had time, and I would not waste it by diving back in and making a mistake immediately, causing me to re-injure or rip open old wounds. For that reason, the recruits she was talking to would be my comrades to start out until I got my *mojo* back.

Until then, I would spar with new recruits, condition with new recruits, and spend most of my day in the presence of new recruits.

At first, they kept their distance, but finally, finally, one of them had the courage to approach me.

"It is an honor, Your Majesty—"

"No, we are comrades, equals. I'm not your queen out here. I'd prefer that you speak to me as you would to anyone else. Please." I cut him off. Surprised, yet seemingly understanding, he nodded, dark skin glistening with sweat.

"I apologize. It is only that I never introduced myself to you, and I thought, as you said yourself, we are comrades." He stuck out a dark hand. "My name is Nir." I shook his hand, grateful to finally speak with one of my fellow trainees. None of them, before that moment, had had the courage to even look at me. It felt nice to know that at least one of them thought I didn't bite.

"It is a pleasure to meet you, Nir. As we have some time before sparring starts, I would love to speak with you some more." Coming from my mouth, the phrase sounded more like a question than a suggestion, which I suppose it was. He readily agreed, and we found a shady spot to rest and swap stories.

"My brother and I," Nir began, "are from the southern edges of Kongeorn, near Sur. Our farm was ransacked by Feroxian mercenaries. My father and mother were killed; we lost everything. So, Niko and I traveled up here, hoping to join the cause against Feroxia. You really have no idea how much it means to the both of us to feel safe, to feel like we have something to live for." I nodded. I knew all too well the feeling of which he spoke.

Over those weeks, I trained hard, completely apart from my friends of the past, from Adam. Sometimes, I would sneak away from Ayla's watchful eye, to the stables, where I would find Dagny. Once we were clear of the fences, I'd send her into a canter and just enjoy the feel of the wind in my hair, the scent of home, where dewy grass greeted me with each stride. I just let the world fall away. The worries and the fears and the demons, all of them, sent running by Sol's rays. Dagny ran faster than the darkness could ever hope. I didn't bother to guide her: she ran free, and I closed my eyes.

Rides like those, when I was unshackled from memories, living just in that time, those were the times I felt closest to Da, to Mami. In fact, it had been Mami who had given me my first riding lesson. She may have acted the part of disciplinary, but she was just as wild as the wilderness she loved to ride through.

She was the one who taught me that being a woman didn't have to be dresses and makeup, that it could be riding and fighting, as long as it was my choice. It didn't matter which I chose, or if I did both.

At the end of the day, Adam and I would meet in our corner of the bathing room, completely exhausted. The days flew by so quickly that the coming of nights gave us whiplash, leaving no energy for encounters like that first night. We simply had no time for affection, but we did take turns sleeping in the other's bed, grateful for the quiet company. One of these nights, I fell asleep waiting for Adam to show up, as would happen sometimes. When he did finally arrive, it was not what I was expecting.

Adam slammed open the doors to my chamber, instantly waking me from the beautiful, beautiful sleep I had been under.

"Vita! Karina is having the child!" I barely understood his words. Then, as they began to make sense, I moved frantically to get out of my bed. The sheets caught around me, encasing me and tripping me up, causing me to land on the floor with a hard thud. *Svat.* I cursed under my breath. Adam, of course, was no help: he just leaned against the doorway and laughed while I got untangled. As I walked by, brushing off my tunic and smoothing out my hair, I paused and punched him hard on the shoulder.

"Ow," he whined, "that's gonna leave a bruise." I rolled my eyes, knowing that he was just playing into my annoyance. I quickened my pace, not waiting for Adam to catch up. He did.

Though it was probably hours from sunrise, the halls were bustling the closer we got to Karina's room. I could hear Gyda inside, helping everything along. Then, to my horror, I heard the most agonizing scream. Blood chilling, limbs alert, I felt around for my dagger.

"Child," Simon hobbled up behind me, "that is not needed here." He smiled, revealing several gummy spots where his teeth had grown too old and had decided to jump ship. But he was right; I was so used to torture, to pain, that I couldn't understand and differentiate its sounds from that of life. Just as another scream erupted through the air, Daniel's wife, Moa, poked her head out of the door, and scanned around before her eyes landed on me.

"Vita," she ordered, "I need you in here." *Wait, what.* I was no good with children, nor with childbirth. I barely knew how it worked. Okay, that was a lie, but still. I shuffled to the door, terrified of what I would see inside, afraid of how different Karina would look to me after *this*. Moa yelled at me to be quicker about it, and, like a puppy who had been scolded, I hurried in, shutting the door behind me. My breath caught in my throat as I saw my brother's love lying in her bed, a sheet covering her lower half, sweat caked all over. She looked as if she had just fought the most powerful fighter in all of Jordklode. Moa yelled at me *again*, and I shuffled, this time a bit quicker, to Karina's side.

I got on my knees as Karina's sweat covered face turned to me, tears in her eyes. She reached her hand out to me, and somehow knowing, I took it in my own. Her face then contorted in agony, and she screamed yet again, squeezing my hand in a vice grip. Though I didn't say anything, I knew my face told it all. *Ow. Pain. Ow. Much pain. Ow.* Luckily, mere moments later, her grip subsided, and her face relaxed.

"H—how long has this been going on?" I stumbled over the words, feeling as if my tongue was the size of an orange. Karina scrunched her face again, unable to answer. I looked around for an answer from anyone. Moa finally spoke up, answering my question and others, all while attending to the lower side of the bed, where all the action was happening.

"The contractions started about six hours ago, but we only called Adam and told him to get you in the last hour because the baby is ready, or almost ready, to come into the world." I heard Gyda grunt in agreement as she was examining Karina. She suddenly jumped up, nodded to Moa, and spoke. "Karina, honey, now you are going to need to push when I tell you, yes?"

Karina mustered a nod in reply and gripped my hand. I looked around, incredibly confused.

"What, why—wait, what's happening?" I was completely ignored as Karina's face contorted, and she turned to look at me, or rather, through me. Her eyes never left mine. I saw her mouth a word, a word I knew to be my brother's name. Her eyes then clamped shut and Gyda screeched.

"Push now, Karina!"

And, to my knowledge, that is exactly what Karina did, all the while squeezing the life out of my hand. After about ten seconds, Gyda told her to take a rest. Karina relaxed. But I almost jumped as I felt a new hand on my shoulder. I turned around and saw, cloaked in pride and glory, my oldest brother. He had tears in his pale eyes. He squeezed my shoulder and was gone. *Thank you.* He reappeared on the other side of the room, my mother patting him. She looked up and winked at me. *Your father was always this worried. But Gyda knows her stuff.* My focus was then redirected to my throbbing hand as Gyda once again told my beloved sister-in-marriage to push.

It went on like this for hours. Off and on, no pain and pain—for me, not Karina; I'm sure she felt it the entire time—with my brother watching from the Etter anxiously. Finally, after a particularly long push, Moa shouted.

"It's crowning." She grinned as Gyda assured Karina that it wasn't much further. Another hour later, after all the pain and the struggle and the sweat and the tears, Gyda handed Karina my niece, whose cries shook me to the core. As Gyda cut the cord, I found tears in my periphery. Amund stood and rushed over to his bride, who could not see him. Tears streaked down both of their cheeks. I got up to go, just as Gyda and Moa had. This was a private moment.

"No," Karina pled, hoarse, "don't leave me." So I knelt again and watched the child as she fed at my sister's breast. Both Mother and Father smiled at the beautiful creation who had just come into the world.

"What will you name her?" I asked, to the both of them. The child then opened her eyes and looked not at me or her mother, but at her father as he stood silently. Her eyes. Just as all the Kongeorn before her. Her grandfather, her aunt, her father, all had the same icy blue eyes as she.

"Nina," both parents whispered. Amund bent and kissed the child's forehead. *Take care of them, Vita; I have every faith in you.* He then stooped to kiss his bride on the top of her head. As he did, Karina paused, frozen, and began to sob. Amund, testing the power he had in our realm, cupped Karina's chin and wiped away her tears with his thumb. She smiled, tears still flowing freely. And then, Amund backed into the shadows and back into the Etter.

I knelt beside my sister and my niece, still trying to convince myself of all that had just happened. After the child was full, she closed her eyes and fell into a peaceful sleep. All I could do was stare. Soon after, Karina's own eyelids began to flutter, exhausted from the effort of giving life. I stealthily got to my feet and left the pair in peace.

Once outside, I nestled myself under the crook of Adam's arm, showing, for the first time, affection for him in public. I knew many in the small crowd of friends noticed, but I didn't care. I kissed his lips. I needed him to see, before leading him back to my room. I closed the door behind me and waited for him to show that he knew. He made no such gesture, only sitting on the bed and waiting for me. Sighing and feeling a large wave of emotion rolling in, I approached him.

My fingers tingled, and I felt the sudden and fatal presence of those demons who had been held at bay by the constant motion and action of past weeks. The first touch in so long felt just as sharp as when the first razor had cut into my flesh.

They dragged their nails across my flesh as I padded forward, feeling the sting of the acid, the wounds opening back up, blood flowing from the cuts, the millions of cuts. As my flesh fried, my mind saw the little baby girl that had come into the world. I saw the same things that happened to me happening to her. My nails, in reaction, bit into my palms, hard enough that I felt blood pool and drip. Her screams made me, still under Avery's knife, reach up to clutch at my ears. I frantically looked around, searching for an escape back to reality, away from my newfound greatest fears.

There, in the distance, a flame, warm and flitting and inviting, was surrounded by smooth, polished wood. The stories on the wood brought me, ever so slowly, back to my world, out of my own terrorizing mind. Adam still sat on the bed, not hearing Nina's screams, nor my own. He couldn't see the blood gushing from my palms, nor the acid eating away at my skin. Instead, he looked at his bare feet, hands clasped, elbows resting on his knees. I needed him to look at me. I couldn't stand to be left alone in my own head anymore. And I felt, as I looked at him, the dam burst.

"Look at me. Please, just graze my eyes with yours. I'm sorry." He looked up, and the words came faster from my tongue, "For all that I am and for all that I am not; I am sorry. I wish I could've been, could be, the leader that we need. But I'm not. I am alive only through luck. I was lucky that Avery left. I was lucky there were clothes at that mill. I was lucky that old woman didn't rat me out. I was lucky that man gave me pears. I was lucky that I had enough stubborn will to just keep moving my feet. That's all I was; that's all I am. And luck runs out. I don't want you to be involved, or anyone to be involved, when that luck runs out. Adam, can't you see? Whatever it is you love about me, it's a mistake. I am broken. I am damaged goods. I have scars that can tell you as much. I am not capable of giving you anything that you want because I have nothing to give. Please, stop looking at me like that. I'm not worth it." Tears were rolling down my cheeks; my throat was sore from fighting back sobs. He made a move, as if he were going to take me into his loving arms and prove me wrong, but I couldn't let him.

"No," I sighed shakily, "no. Why—how—do you try to love someone who wishes they weren't alive, someone whose dreams make them wish for death's cold scythe, someone whose only reason for not ending it is because they are too much of a coward to? Why do you try to love me? I wouldn't. Adam, I know that we have the same soul, but my body and my mind and my spirit can only take so much. I won't let myself take your soul with it. I can't."

"Stormy, why are you so full of shit?" He chuckled; why was he chuckling? "You keep saying you're damaged, broken, that nothing redeemable resides in you. Have you looked around? These people would not be here if not for you. I would not be here. I would be somewhere in Hingst territory, acting like a complete ass, chasing after women who wouldn't want me. You have brought people together. Not with luck, Stormy. But with love and passion and perseverance. And as for the scars, I love them, too. They tell a story, each one. Like the one on your nose there: it tells the story of the only time I got the best of you." He waited before speaking again."What brought all of this on? Tonight, I mean."

"Nina," I whispered, barely audible, "she's so pure and innocent and the best thing in this horrible world. All I want is for her to be safe. I want her to look around when she can understand and know that she doesn't have to fear for the lives that she cares about. I would gladly die an infinite amount of deaths to ensure her happiness. But I can't. I can't bring her father back, nor her grandfather, nor her uncles. And I can't make this world worthy of her. No matter what I do, people like Richard and Avery will still be lurking in the shadows of her nightmares. No amount of training, of recruits, of praying, will fix any of that."

He waited for a long time, thinking on his next words, before speaking again.

"You're right. The world will never be worthy of her. There will always be people like Richard and Avery, but we can make sure they, themselves, are sent back to Hell where they belong. We can't control who lives or dies after we, ourselves, are dead. We can't purify the world. But we can—and we will—leave it better than we found it." He reached out, and I let him pull me close. We laid back across the bed, facing each other. I closed my eyes and tried to subdue the sobs.

"Stormy," his voice wavered, making me open my eyes, "I know that I will never understand what you have been through; and I cannot make the pain go away, no matter how hard I try. But you are never, and will never, be alone. As long as I am living, you will never be alone. So please don't let the darkness consume you. I would never forgive myself if it did." His voice broke at the end, and I saw a tear drop from his eye, stopped on the fall by the ridge of his nose. I moved closer to him, until only our clothes separated us. Reaching behind him, I brought his head to mine, so we were forehead to forehead. I breathed out.

"Not even death could separate us."

Chapter 17

Heart of a Lion and the Body of a Mouse

The next day, after our needed day of rest, we both awoke refreshed. Outside my window, the blossoms of spring greeted each caressing wind as it sashayed by them. The delicate white petals clung to the newly rejuvenated branches. One frosty flower, however, lost its resolve and drifted down, further and further down, until it was out of my sight. Beside me, Adam stirred, taking my attention away from the window. His eyes were still puffy from worrying about me, from sharing in my emotions. I smiled drowsily and ran a hand through his pitch hair, content in the moment, happy to remain in the moment. It had been a year or so since my family had made their way into the Etter, but I finally knew that at least one of my foundation rocks refused to crumble, that he would keep my house above the flood waters and strong in the face of the storm to come.

I knew in my heart that we still had a ways to go with our war preparations, that new recruits needed training, that more swords needed forging, that green minds needed testing. But I also knew that we had the favor of the Mother, a favor that, though I hadn't personally felt, many drew strength from. It was only a matter of time before we would be ready, and before justice could prevail.

Reigning my attention span back in, I searched Adam's face. There was some sort of peace in his expression, the kind one sees just after the birth of a child or marriage to a beloved. I smiled again, ready to start the day. The blossoms outside still beckoned, and beyond, some trainees were getting an early start. Seeing this, I scrambled from the bed and to the window to get a better look. The trainees were, to my pride—and shameful surprise—all women. Their work ethic gave me strong hope for my people, for the future. But it also made me feel guilty about still being in the comfort of nightclothes. So, with an enthusiastically fast routine, I became ready for the day.

Adam in tow, I made a beeline for the kitchens, where I picked off a few ham slices and grapes before gulping down a cup of water and hurrying out to the training fields in earnest excitement. By the time we had gotten out there, however, the action of the day had already begun. I let Adam go to his own training when I spotted Ayla in the midst of the organized chaos. Sprinting over to her, I knocked into her playfully.

"It would seem you have renewed excitement for life, yes?" A glint of knowing smugness passed over her eyes for mere seconds, but I noticed it, nonetheless. I assumed she was talking about finally showing my affection for Adam, but I chose to make it about Nina, instead.

"Exactly, because the future is on its way, and there's no stopping it; we're doing this so the world can be safe for Nina and children that have come before her and will come after her. And that, Ayla, Daughter of Roald, excites me more than anything." Her eyes brightened, as if the Sol had come out from behind the clouds, as if my words had held a candle to her irises. She took my rerouting for a grain of salt, not the least bit offended, and smiled kindly. She then touched my shoulder and turned back to her trainees.

I, too, found myself turning to the trainees, curious. I surveyed our newest recruits. Da had been known to do this at any given time. *Oh, how I miss him.* Nothing would change that, but dwelling on the longing would not change anything either. As I perused, I was overcome with pride at seeing the many women in the ranks. I decided then to get to know them and their stories. I knew all too well that having a friend, any friend, was a necessity.

One of the women in particular caught my eye. Her shoulder-length brown hair was pulled back, revealing determined green eyes and a look of the same. Though she was small in height and stature, her movements were quick and powerful, exploding with every step, as if she aimed to prove herself with each blow. And, as far as I could tell, she did.

I approached the pair as they sparred, the small woman on one side, a seasoned veteran on the other.

"It would seem you have your hands full here, Hakon," I chuckled with the quip. Upon hearing my voice, both ceased what they were doing and dropped to one knee. I rolled my eyes. "Oh, for Creator's sake, when will people learn that I hate that?" Hearing this, both rose. Hakon gestured toward the woman.

"You're right about one thing, Vita: this one is quite the fighter. I've never seen anything like it." Next to him, the woman blushed a deep red, and I could tell she was fighting a grin of pride behind her humble facade. I nodded to Hakon, giving him the signal that I wished to be alone with this woman. He, knowing this to be a gesture once used by my father, already knew its meaning and departed from the scene, most likely to yell at another new soldier.

Realizing her trainer had left her with the highest in command, the woman once again assumed the most humble and respecting position. I, of course, wanted none of that, so I physically took her skinny arm and raised her from one knee. Face to face, I could see that my person was only slightly taller than hers, yet she carried herself like it was irrelevant. Had I not been someone she felt deserved reverence, I imagine she would have looked at me with straight defiance, with a challenge in her gaze. Yet, because I was someone whom she thought deserved reverence, she kept her eyeline down. Again, this was not what I wanted.

I offered my hand to her. "I'm Vita." I hoped she would understand my meaning, my gesture of equality, and drop the facade. I wanted to see what others saw when she looked at them. I wanted to befriend her, not subjugate her. Lucky for me, she made it easy. Taking my hand with a firm grip, her eyes met mine, daring me to look away first.

"Hanna," she replied with confidence, the kind I could only wish for. Her voice was steady, unshakable on its own. I could already tell Hanna and I would get along well. I glanced around for a possible practice weapon of my own and found a blunt longsword in the grass a few feet away. Picking it up, I glanced over my shoulder at Hanna.

"You ready?"

"Definitely."

I came at her with fervent speed, relying on quick jabs rather than the explosive power I used against bigger opponents. Fake left, slash right. Parry up, swing low. Parry right, jab left. And on and on it went. Nearly every movement was blocked with resilient accuracy. At the end of what must have been at least twenty minutes, the two of us were covered in sweat and gasping in the air. I put my hands on my knees, trying to regain my breath.

"Don't do that," she said, pausing to take in oxygen. "Put your hands over your head and straighten up; that way, your lungs can fully expand." I did as she said and found that she was right: it was far easier to breathe. I smiled at her, thankful for the advice. I'd have to remember that one. After we both caught our breath, lungs working normally again, I decided to say something.

"You fight with aggression, assertion," I said, complimenting her. I had never met anyone so small, so humble, yet so confident in themselves, and so ready, so determined, to prove themselves. Hanna was truly unique, and the kind of friend I knew I'd be grateful to have.

"I prefer passion, actually." Her reply initially caught me off-guard, but once I understood the glimmer of humor in her voice, I relaxed. Even though she may have meant it as something of a joke, I knew the word *passion* fit her fighting perfectly. That's what she did; she fought with passion. She took every movement seriously and made it worth something. And that was more than I could ever say for my own fighting. For me, all of this was second nature, like keeping one's balance. I had grown up being disciplined in this very subject area, but that's all it had ever been for me: discipline. I didn't have that same passion, that same intensity. And, as I invited Hanna to eat dinner with me and my other new friends, I realized that passion was crucial to my success, both as fighter and queen.

I smiled at Hanna as I turned to survey the rest of the training. As I walked, however, my attention was stolen by one of my favorite people running towards me.

"Vita!" Pierre exclaimed, bringing joy to my heart. "I have a letter." He stopped abruptly in front of me, panting for breath. I smiled at him and took the letter before patting him on the back.

"Thank you, Pierre." I grinned, grateful for the joy he could bring at a moment's notice. "What have you been up to today?" He lunged at the question, as if he had been waiting for me to ask it.

"Vita, I wath looking at my mapth when Thuri brought me thith." He smiled with pride, pumping up his chest. He gave me a thumbs up, and I returned it, signaling he could go back to his favorite pastime. I unrolled the parchment and began to read:

My Queen:
We have been scouting the borders of Feroxia, just as you
Asked us months ago.

We must report that their army is mobilizing.

Our spies indicate that they will arrive in the Disputed Lands in
Three weeks.

Ju'jer vallen.

     The words of my clan told me that this was no forged letter. If our scouts said this, then there would be no time to lose. I folded the letter and put it in my undershirt before sprinting to the barracks.

     Once there, I searched for Adam, for Hakon, for Ayla. I found all three of them as they watched Nir spar with Hanna. I ran over to them, feeling the urgency in my bones as it burned.

     "A letter," I panted, "from our scouts." I revealed the letter and presented it to Adam, who read it aloud. Once he had finished, the entire training ground had gone silent. All had heard his relay of the words, and, if they hadn't, the word would spread to them soon, no doubt. Ayla took off to find her father and brother. Hakon went to find Simon. Adam and I went in search of Gyda and Karina.

     Gyda had responded with several curses, her hair seeming to grow more unruly with every word. Karina, on the other hand, held Nina closer to her chest and remained silent, thinking. We led them to the council room, where the others of our group awaited us. I made my way to the middle, and all seated themselves. Tension quickened the pace of all our hearts, mine feeling as if it would escape with my words.

     I rotated, taking in the expression of each member. We had all known this was coming, but it was still a surprise to finally hear the words, to finally know there was no going back from this. My eyes rested on Nina, my innocent niece, the only heir to the throne. Karina's gaze, however, was on me, her eyes growing wet with unsure tears. The sleeping child in her arms was of the upmost importance. She would need to be secure before we went any further.

"I think we can all agree," Simon spoke up, "the child must leave us." As if she approved, Nina stretched her tiny limbs, releasing a tiny cry of content.

"I know of a place." Adam stood from his chair unexpectedly. "My people will watch over mother and child. They will be safe in the capitol of Hingst." The way he said *his people* was strained, as if they were only his by default, which was what he had always believed. The time that he had been with us had proven that he was just as much Kongeorn as the rest of us. He looked to me, emerald eyes searching for my consent. I nodded, unable to speak. It was understood, then, that no one—not even Pierre, nor any letter carrier—could know where my niece was to go. Hakon stood.

"I will take them. There is no need to draw attention to a large party leaving. I will meet the army on my way back." Again, all I could do was nod. Time was of the essence. Hakon then helped Karina stand, my niece in her arms. She rushed to me, embracing me.

"Be brave, sister." I can't remember which of us said it, but it would apply to us both. I leaned down to kiss Nina's forehead. Amund would be with them, there would be no reason to doubt that. The party left, and with them, any reserve that had been holding me together. My lungs started to collapse, to fold, but I forced breath into them, determined to last through this meeting. The demons were infiltrating through the windows, but I blocked them out. I tuned out their snarls, their moans. Words needed to be said.

"I have seen our fighters, and I know that they can be ready in the time given. Every single one of them. There will be a feast tonight, and tomorrow, we put together our army. We march on the Disputed Lands in two days. Gyda, you will need assistants; we will find some for you. You will not be expected on the front lines. As for you, Simon and Roald, it is your choice whether you want to join us, but I will say that I would prefer your leadership here, at home, in my absence. For now, all of you, take the time to be with family and friends. Training for the rest of the day will be suspended." With that, I turned around and departed, Adam following close behind me.

"Where do you think you're going?" He poked me, ever the sunspot in my life. The demons were still following, but they seemed to fall away each step I took. Without looking back at him, I replied.

"No idea."

"Well, then, I'll decide." As soon as the words were spoken, I felt myself being hefted up over his shoulder, reminding me of my days as a rag doll little sister. The rug flew by beneath me, and I couldn't help but giggle as I was jostled up and down. I jokingly pounded on his back until he set me down. We had come to one of the back doors of the keep, ones which led out to our spot, to the Edge. I stuck out my footthen pushed Adam, causing him to trip and fall over it. I sped away as fast as I could, laughing, feeling free, oh so free. I could hear him behind me, his longer strides letting him catch up.

"If you think you're going to win this race, you're wrong!" He shouted at me. With no intent of stopping, and not even knowing where we were racing to, I kept running. After a few minutes, I could hear him just behind me. I turned my head to see him, to see the playful hunger in his eyes. He lunged for me and knocked me over.

"Told you, Stormy." I ignored the potential bruises and laughed happily. I rolled out from underneath him and got up to run through the adjacent brush. As soon as I cleared it, though, I stopped cold. I shouted for Adam. He emerged from the bushes, ready for me to tackle him. What he found, though, was far more terrifying than any prank I could possibly play.

Only ten feet from us, the Edge glared, red and black and daunting. We certainly had not run thirty miles. There was absolutely no way. That left only one explanation.

Both of our eyes had widened in disbelief, completely taken aback by this discovery. Afraid to take my eyes off of the crumbling earth, I retreated back through the bushes; Adam followed suit. The terror in each of our hearts was unrealistic, was unlike anything either of us had ever felt. We walked back, still trying to understand what had happened, and we walked closer together, nearly touching. By the time we had returned, it was well past midday, nearly time for the feast. As we emerged from the forest, the sight of people bustling around seemed to shatter the feeling of fear. It snapped us out of it. We quickly resolved to talk about it with Simon later, to leave our knowledge in the furthest corner of our minds, where it could not reach and wreak havoc on other people.

Around us, children squealed and skipped around, fingers already sticky somehow. Horses were grazing contentedly, while their riders conversed near the fence. Ayla's blue people milled around and mingled with my own. Though the reason for this feast was utterly heart-stopping, the energy a feast provided, both physically and spiritually, gave rest to the many who feared the outcome of this war, including myself.

At the end of the day's preparation, all of us, veteran and green, migrated from the barracks to the meal hall. Instead of sitting on the dais, however, I planted myself right between some new friends of mine: Hanna to the right of me and Nir to the left, Adam and Ayla across. We all dug into our food, absolutely famished from the day's events, as always. Out of the corner of my eye, I could see Hanna putting away serving after serving. *And I thought I ate a lot.* Adam, across from me, had been restraining himself, but when our eyes met, he knew the challenge was afoot.

As children, we had played a game to see who could drink their milk the fastest. It was never pretty, especially when one of us accidentally snorted it through their nose. As years went by, the milk turned to water and the water, to ale. And no matter the drink, I never backed down from this challenge.

To be expected, neither did he.

We both reached for our cups and, counting silently in our heads to three, threw the drinks back. I downed the ale as fast as I could, taking care to breathe through the nose and disregard the troublemaking streams of escaping ale running down my chin. I slammed my cup down on the table, only to find Adam doing the same. I rolled my eyes: ties were no fun. Snapping me out of my annoyance, Nir exclaimed next to me, making room for two more, a man and woman. The man, I gathered, was Nir's younger brother, Niko. The resemblance was certainly there, but Niko, being six years Nir's junior, certainly hadn't grown to his brother's stature yet. The woman, I learned, was Yara. I introduced myself and felt myself being drawn into her story.

"My name, Yara, is taken from my three-greats grandmother. Long ago, she was taken from her village, near Creat, and was sold into slavery. But, because of her resilience, she escaped to this country. And my family has lived here ever since." Her red skin nearly glowed in the dimming light, making her story enchanting to all who sat near enough to hear. After her story was told, we all dissolved back into our own smaller conversations.

After all the food had been eaten—rather quickly, I might add—and as the noise grew to a roar, I found myself drawn away from my friends and to the quiet of the side courtyard, near one of the mourning fires that had been kept lit by an unknown person since my father and brothers' deaths. The cool night air and fresh smells were a welcomed change from the crowded and sweaty dining hall from which I had come. I soon found myself standing under the moonlight, merely feet from the mourning fire. To my surprise, a woman already occupied the space in front of it, feeding the flames with long-burning wood. My approach was unbeknownst to her, and, deciding it would be best not to sneak in the shadows, I made myself known.

Instead of speaking up, I merely walked around to the other side of the flames where the woman could see me clearly. Upon stopping, I realized that I had seen this woman before, the day I had heard the news of my family's deaths. She was the one with the pendant round her neck, the only one who had acknowledged me. She did the same again. Looking up at me, her golden eyes seemed aflame in the reflection of the fire. Just like before, she fingered the pendant at her breast. I could see it more clearly then; it was in the shape of a small egg, but engraved with the image of flames. Its smooth, marbled surface kept my gaze entranced. The woman, on the other hand, let her gaze fall back to the flames, seeming to forget me entirely. Suddenly feeling like an intruder, I turned to leave. I passed her, but stopped when I heard the sound of her voice.

"*No night is too dark, my love—no, my love—when your flame is here with me.*" The song, though its melody irritatingly out of reach, resonated with me then. The last note she sang bent down, as if it had been broken. I turned back around to see the tears streaming down her face and a dagger in her hand that I hadn't noticed before. Her lips again began to move as her hand hovered in front of her chest.

"If this hand were not my own, and, if I were not a coward," she paused, as if this had been something she had spoken countless times, "it would grant me with Death's sweet kiss. Would that I could look upon my heart in my hands; would that I could escape from these sleepless nights." Finally and fully recognizing my presence, she turned and offered me the dagger.

"You know that which I see: the nightmares and faces and ways that it could end. Please, I beg you, let me join my husband, let me look upon him again." I searched her face and saw the sunken cheeks, the dark circles, the glass over her eyes. Looking down, I could see the scars on her wrists as her sleeves revealed them. I reached out for the hand with the dagger. Taking it from her, I threw it to the ground and heard it clang against the stone. The tiny glimmer of hope that had been in her eyes when I took the knife then disappeared into melancholic disappointment. She turned to leave, but was stopped as I grasped her wrists. Before gauging her reaction, I pulled her into an embrace. I cradled her head and wrapped my arms completely around her skinny frame. As sobs racked her body, I only held her tighter.

I didn't know how much time passed, but I could feel the woman begin to relax into my embrace. Not only that, but I could feel the catharsis, the dam of being alone for so long breaking and flooding everything around us. Soon enough, she put her own arms around me before pulling away so we could see each other.

"There are no words," she mustered feebly.

"Then you don't have to talk. It's okay," That's all I knew to say. I couldn't know what she was going through, nor what she was feeling, only that she could not be allowed to be alone any longer. I put my arm around her and discretely led her inside to my chambers. There, I helped her in and laid next to her, offering a comforting presence until she fell asleep. Eventually, my own exhaustion kicked in, and I, too, gave in to sleep.

Chapter 18

Warning: Does Not Play Well with Others

I awoke to the feeling of a wet nose sniffing at my cheek. *Wait, what.* My eyes flew open to take in the sight of a black and white hound pup. Seeing me alert, the pup turned his attention to my sleeping charge. He placed a small paw tentatively on her chest, and then, getting only a small sigh in return, began licking her face furiously. She began to stir, a smile growing on her face as the pup began to whine for her attention. When finally her eyes opened, she furrowed her brow momentarily before scratching the pup behind the ear. Noticing me, she spoke up.

"Aidan had a dog like this when we first met. Her name was Rosie." She managed a small smile as she looked down at the pup. "I wonder how he got in here." I wondered the same and looked to the door, which was strangely open. *I thought I closed that last night.* Scanning the room, I found the explanation.

In the corner of the room, the shade of a man I vaguely remembered sparring with stood with his translucent eyes trained on the woman. He, too, sported the same sad smile. I assumed it was Aidan, trying to help his wife overcome the immense grief that had overwhelmed her. The pup barked happily, causing the woman to smile bigger. This was reflected in Aidan's own expression. He glanced over to me, jumping slightly as he realized that I could see him. After he recovered from the initial surprise, he relaxed again and mouthed the words, "thank you." I nodded back at him before turning my attention back to the woman.

"I never caught your name," she said, but then turned and looked at me. Her hands stopped scratching the pup's ears, which he did not appreciate: he pawed at her hand. "Y—you're the queen. I didn't realize. Oh my goodness. I am so—"

"You have no reason to be sorry, absolutely none. What you have been going through is not your fault. At all. And my job is to help those who need it, whether they ask for it or not." I smiled, extending the wordless offer of friendship.

"Well, whatever the case, I apologize for not introducing myself," she paused, "my name is Solvei." Now that I heard her name, her person rang a bell; I had known her younger brother in the training fields years ago. He had gone to Nae as an ambassador years back and gotten married. That's how I knew her. Because I had finally learned her name, this tender of the fires, I knew she would be a part of my circle, someone who knew what it was like, someone I could help.

Before I could send Solvei off with a clear conscience, I had to ask her one last question.

"Is there anything I can do?" Her answer surprised me more than anything thus far.

"I want to be a part of this, all of this. I don't want to feel powerless anymore. I want to fight." I, though taken aback, accepted her into our army without question. Of course, I had to gauge her ability first. So we, along with the pup, whom Solvei had given the name Asher, made our way to the training grounds, which were being used already. I picked up a blunted sword and handed another to Solvei. The pup was content to lay under a tree near us for the time being.

I started with footwork, stepping to and fro, seeing where her own feet went. They mirrored mine almost exactly. Then we sparred. Sweat stained our brows as we slashed and parred, blocked and stabbed. Solvei lunged at me, her sword flying in from my right. I went to block the move, but found my feet flying out from under me. I landed on the ground with a hard thud.

"Well, *svat*." I chuckled, impressed and slightly embarrassed, "That was—that was certainly interesting." We both laughed as she offered her hand to pull me off my bottom. I was more than relieved to know that this woman could hold her own, could more than handle herself just with the fire at her breast. It put my heart at ease, as well, to see her openly grinning afterwards.

That day went quickly, packing all we would need, all the provisions our fighters, our healers, would require. Pierre had drawn a map of the most useful terrain, the most strategic to our cause. The most important, however, was erasing any evidence of Nina, in case, Creator forbid, we lost this battle and Redefalk was taken.

Watching Karina and Hakon ride off with my niece that morning had felt like I was losing another family member, another person my life could not be lived fully without. My heart wept anxious tears, while my mind told me it was all for the best, for the future. Nothing, though, could convince my heart that I would see Nina again. And that was what worried me most of all. In fact, that was the thought, the horrid feeling, that persisted through all of my activities, my duties, until we departed for the Disputed Lands.

We were to travel west three hundred and twelve miles until we marked the boundary of ours and the Disputed Lands. Once there, we would wait for word from our scouts and adjust to where the Feroxian army would be stopping. We wanted to halt their progress before they got to Kongeorn land, where our civilians would, no doubt, be in incredible danger.

As we progressed, we received word from our scouts. At the end of every two days, a letter would arrive via Trakni—a dappled gray bird about the size of a crow. They were unique to Kongeorn, but there was no guarantee that Feroxia wouldn't be using them as well. This was why our schedule was the way it was and why our clan words were written at the end of each letter, changing the dialect and spelling with every new Luna. "*Ju'jer vallen.*" Unless told by a scout or member of the council, the words would mean nothing to any given being. The words were protected and protective. And that's how we knew whom we could trust, what information was true, and what was false.

It took us, with our four thousand, seven hundred and seventy-two warriors, all of two weeks to reach our destination. Along the way, we dined on Myank, large fish that could feed about fifteen people in one sitting, along with Sorve, large elk that maintain small antlers. We ate well nearly every night of the trip.

One night, however, all prey was scared away from our hunters, myself included. Oliver, Adam, and I had been on the trail of a herd of Sorve when a great rumble surfaced from the earth, telling tale of a large animal, or animals, nearby. Instinctively, we all crouched down among the tall grass in the meadow we had been in. The Luna above us gave light to see through the night's darkness. Perhaps half a mile from where we crouched, a tree was being trampled over. I held tight to my bow, arrow notched. Once the tree had been downed, nearly obliterated, one of the rarest creatures to ever prowl Jordklode came into view.

His hair shone silver in the moonlight, giving off an elusive shine. Unlike our horses, he stood, at his withers, perhaps six feet tall. And from his rump, a constantly moving streamline tail, much like a lizard, whipped back and forth. His massive size was something few had ever observed, especially this close. Unafraid, the massive Srontes cantered ever closer, until he was hardly twenty feet from us. We three refused to move, to even breathe. Such creatures were known for their tempers, for their inability to "play well with others." If we were detected, we would be trampled. The animal's nostrils flared: once, twice, three times. As if catching wind of a larger, or more formidable, animal, the Srontes whinnied, turned, and cantered away.

I heard Adam exhale in relief next to me. I then realized I *hadn't* been breathing and took in a large gulp of air. Safe and in awe, the three of us stood out of our crouches and headed back to camp.

That night, we ate only the fruit which we had collected the previous day.

Finally, there came a letter, one day before our three weeks was to end. I stroked the Trakni's feathers before taking the letter from its curved beak. It cooed at me as I read:

Kongeorn:
Feroxian army has made it to Disputed Lands.

Camp is to be made on Nubilum Hill,
overlooking the Valley of Mork.

Ju'jer vallen.

As I finished reading, I looked up to see Hakon, having found us and returned successfully, trotting in on his black horse. I smiled to him in greeting before returning to the urgent business at hand. I announced the news, the instructions, to my commanders, each of whom relayed the message to their respective warriors. The Valley of Mork was an hour's walk from where we were camped. I resolved to uproot all of our warriors, along with our healers, and move to the eastern hill of the valley, Verum Hill. Opposite of it was Nubilum Hill, where our enemies would arrive surprised to find us on the morrow, ready for battle.

The trek to Verum was one full of anxiety, of restlessness. The noon Sol did nothing to still this, only giving us more energy and more drive to get to our destination. I knew we were ready; I knew this group of people, so different on the outside, all had the drive, the need, to fight for their nation, their friends, their families.

This revelation comforted me as I rode in solitude, several feet ahead of the rest. I refused to speak to any of our warriors just yet. I needed to think of something, anything, that would ease my own worries.

No matter how many mental barriers I put up, I could not keep the image from my head. Adam was there, lying lifeless on the ground. His emerald eyes wide open, even in death. My toes tingled and my mouth went dry every time the image came to mind. I could not let him die. Perse said I couldn't change the future, but I would try. I would try with everything I was. And with that in mind, I came up with a plan. Adam wouldn't like it, but that certainly had never stopped me.

That night, the Luna's light draped us in a calming quiet, in the aura of protection we needed. In our tent, I laid with my front towards Adam, studying his features, etching them forever into my mind's eye. His eyes were closed in sleep, dreaming of things I could never know, things that would be of no help to him when the Sol rose. After tracing his face with my eyes time after a countless time, I finally ended up closing my own eyes, giving in to the sleep I desperately needed.

I rose with the Sol the next morning, antsy in heart and limbs, unable to stop moving. I realized as I readied my clothing that I had forgotten my blood cloth. Svat. *At least my blood won't be the only one on this get-up. Oh well.* I dressed in my battle tunic, my pants, and my boots. I stuck my dagger into its sheath in my right boot, and tried to tame my hair. It had grown since I had been home, down to my shoulders. My braids would not be as long, but they would keep the majority of my hair out of my way; and it would make it all the more difficult to grab me. That was always a positive.

What wasn't a positive was how quiet Ahava had been. In the previous months of training, she hadn't appeared once, not even when Nina was born. That, in itself, worried me. *Oh sister, now would be as great a time as any to give me some of your divine advice!* The irritation showed through the sweetness in my tone, no doubt. And yet, there was still nothing on her end. I rolled my eyes and continued to get ready. I was polishing my battle axe when the announcement came.

"They're here!" I didn't know who had yelled it, but all of our members mobilized, putting on their weapons and getting into battle formation. I, leading Dagny, moved to the front of the crowd.

Chapter 19
The Battle of Red Moon

The sun's rays peeked over the hill to our east. In the morning light, the armor of Kongeorn's fighters blazed and bathed in oranges and reds, no doubt a foreshadowing of the battle to come. On the rise opposite our own stood the Feroxian army. Their reds, in both armor and banners, did nothing to disguise their unrest. Taking this into consideration, I turned to Adam.

"I believe you should say something." He looked down at me. Though I was still a good head shorter than him, his demeanor gave me the authority.

"This is true," I said to him, knowing words to an army before a battle were near as important as the training in the months before. I pivoted and mounted my horse. Dagny shifted as I put my weight onto her back. It would be my first battle, and Dagny could detect my restlessness. The inexperience on my part, however, would not be shown. I turned Dagny around to face my warriors.

"Do you see it? Do you see the way they squirm? The way they shift from foot to foot, not knowing what to do with themselves? Because I do. I see their cheap, western-made armor. I see their light, polished swords. I see the tent, far beyond the front lines, out of harm's way, where their king, their commander, hides. In the shadows of luxury, he cowers. His men fear us, just as he does. Now tell me, brothers and sisters, why would they fear us?" The response was an overwhelmingly colossal outcry. The call for blood had been made, and the cry for war had been announced.

"Do you know why they are scared, other than of our axes and arrows?" I basked in the sight of my warriors, willing them to have the hunger, the confidence they needed to have. "They have a craven for a king. They see he has abandoned them to the safety of his tent. But, where is your queen, your leader, your commander? She is here. On the front line, ready to bleed, ready to kill, ready to die, for her people, for Kongeorn, for you!" Another cry to the heavens startled the horses from the opposite rise. "So fight with me, brothers and sisters! So that those we have left behind, and those that we have lost, know they need not fear. Let us fight so that no man, woman, or child should ever fear the cruelty of the Feron line!" As my people screamed, I raised my voice to the sky, to my father and mother, to my brothers, to the Mother. They heard us, no doubt. In fact, it was reasonable that all of Jordklode heard our battle cry.

Knowing the battle was soon to commence, I dismounted Dagny and sent her away. Having the knowledge that she would be free, even if I was not, was a small prize. Then, knowing my next words, I turned to Adam.

"I need you," I lowered my voice, "to listen to me carefully and, at all costs, obey." He nodded, following my eyes as they searched his face. "When the battle commences, all of the Ferons will want to be the one who kills the Kongeorn Queen. You must, if it comes to it, let them. Do you understand?" Adam looked as if he were about to argue. I silenced the words on his tongue with a commanding look.

"You will run, hard and fast, to the tent of the king. Mehmet will be behind you. You will find a way in. You must end his life. I don't care if a battle axe is coming down upon me, or if swords are finding my back, or if I am on the ground being raped. You will kill the Feroxian king." Adam's emerald eyes were shadowed by his dark brow. I knew what he was thinking. He would never leave me to die, to be injured, which was why I explicitly ordered that he do so. Perse said I could not change the future, but I was surely going to try.

"If you don't do it, I will have to, and that would be embarrassing for the both of us." After donning my she-wolf cloak and minding the teeth, I took his free hand and squeezed before saying, "I'll race you."

With that, the trumpets of red sounded, and the painted faces of my people matched their sound. The battle had begun. Slowly, then increasingly faster, and faster, and faster, we began to run, to sprint toward revolution, toward freedom from fear, from nightmares. Adrenaline and anger surged through my veins, vehemently pumped by my warrior heart. Adam and I broke away and kept pace with each other as we raced ahead. We both kept our eyes straight ahead, confident in the person next to us, sure in our abilities, certain in our cause. The first Feroxian soldier came at me directly, and we clashed. I parried his sword with my battle axe, and then taking advantage, kicked his feet out from under him.

As he fell, my axe moved of its own accord, separating head from shoulders. I had no time to celebrate, for another opponent came at me from the right, a brave young soldier who was overly ambitious. His rapid, ostentatious swings told me so. It was not hard to dodge him then to slash at his right hand, removing the problem. He fell to his knees, clutching at the bleeding stump. Without pause, I heard a battle cry from behind me and turned to see two men, both of them quite big, going for Hanna. I made a move towards her, to aid her, but stopped myself as I witnessed her passion at work.

She ducked under one of the men's swords, then the other's, until they could not find her. She then took that opportunity to drive her own sword into the undercarriage of one of the men. The other saw this and slashed at her, but hit his fellow soldier in the stomach instead, slicing it open, entrails spilling out. Some of them made their way into Hanna's hair. This did not faze her; while the stunned comrade thought on his injury of his fellow Feroxian, Hanna ran her sword clean through his chest. He, too, fell.

Knowing Hanna was in good hands, her own, I turned again, trying to spot any of my own friends. Nir was going back and forth with a large, pale man, his brother at his back, defending him from attack. To my left, Yara was running her short sword through the ribs of a fat soldier. Solvei's battle cry could be heard for miles as she decapitated an older soldier who had been in her way. And then there was a different woman, one I had never seen before, whose sword had been dislodged from her hands. Without hesitation, she grabbed her dagger from its sheath, lunged at her opponent and buried it in his eye.

I swiveled again, looking for more of my friends, and found a break in the fighting, a path leading directly to the hill where the wretched coward quivered in fear. Not seeing Adam, I ran towards it myself. He had one job, and, if he couldn't do it, then I would. Or, Mother forbid, I would die trying. I sprinted through the gaps, barely differentiating between my own warriors and the Feroxians. I did not swing my axe, but dodged every slash. I had my eye on my target, and I would get to it. To him. Out of my periphery, I saw Adam making his way up the hill, as well. He was sparring and slashing furiously, desperately trying to push through the mass of men he had encountered. And, to my heart's terror, he was alone.

I stopped. I turned. I ran to him.

The men were packing in around him, trying to get a piece of him, any piece they could. I flew into the fray, furiously swinging my battle axe to and fro, doing as much damage as I could, as much as would let me get to the middle of the crowd, to Adam. The crowd became thicker, harder to cut through, harder to get by. Out of nowhere, an elbow made contact with my brow, splitting it open and sending me to the hard ground. Dazed, I tried to rise. The crowd had thickened further, and I could hear the anger, sense the hatred all around.

In the distance, the demons emerged, cloaked in black smoke. Their onyx-jeweled eyes locked on me. I froze. Fear surrounded me as they did. Bodies in the physical world milled around slowly now, like molasses. They were unimportant. Why was I on the ground? Where was I supposed to be going? I heard a voice, calling my name, then a small touch, like a pat on the back. Suddenly, reality snapped back. My name was being called, shouted, screamed, at me. I turned around at the second blow, not enough to injure, but enough to get my undivided attention.

"Vita," her blue lips screamed at me, "get up! Get up and save him!" That was my reminder, my trigger. Without the need for help, I rose and pushed the crowd, slicing down any red in my path. Ayla covered me from behind, ensuring that no cowards stabbed me in the back. I continued to push through. Denser and denser, the bodies became. Finally, I saw the circle's break and dove into it. Adam had just fallen to one knee, a large wound, blood oozing, from his collar bone to stomach. I looked for the swordsman who had done it. When my eyes caught his, red sword in red hand, I saw in crimson. I stalked towards him, a look in my eyes that froze him in place. He knew what he had done. I brought my axe up, and he brought his sword to block my swipe. My force, my anger, my hunger for revenge, sliced clean through his unworthy steel. Defenseless, he stood there, begging for mercy.

I gave him none.

I swiveled, finding myself in the middle of the circle, along with Adam's bleeding body. He was struggling to get up.

"Stay down, Adam of Hingst," Ayla shouted to him, "now is not the time to rise higher." She then commenced to thrusting her short sword into three separate men in a row. I half smiled and began my own body count. Soon enough, Ayla and I were almost back to back, Adam in between us. Not even my need for revenge surpassed the overwhelming need to protect my soul then. Every man who came up against me fell to the ground. *Thud. Thud. Thud. Clang. Thud.*

And then, suddenly, there was complete quiet, save for the moaning of the dying.

I turned my attention outwards, to the battle field, still seeing red. And then I realized it was because the blood from my brow was seeping into my left eye. I blinked, forgetting it instantly as my attention was turned to Adam. He lay on the ground, pale and quiet. I rushed to him.

Reaching out, I ripped open his shirt, finding a deep cut from his collar bone through his navel. I removed my own shirt and applied pressure, not caring for how apparent my scars would be, how immodest my nudity was considered. Adam's eyes opened and focused on me. He smiled and shakily managed a thumbs up. He was responsive; I exhaled, relaxing. Ayla came up behind me, saying something.

"There are far more red bodies than blue. The blue await your words." I tore my eyes away from Adam, who was breathing steadily, but kept his eyes closed, completely exhausted. I realized just how fatigued I was, as well.

"Have any of ours who are healthy enough to walk look for anyone who is alive, but injured. If they are ours—and they can be saved—get Gyda to them. If they cannot be saved, make it quick. The latter applies for all Feroxian soldiers who remain alive." Ayla nodded in understanding then ran off to spread my orders. I exhaled again, ready to be enveloped in sleep. Not even the promise of a beautiful sunset, like the one taking place before my own eyes, could make me look away from my soul though.

It wasn't until the Luna rose, red from the day's bloodshed, that I was given help in moving Adam back to our camp. There, I was given a tunic to keep out the coming chill, and Adam was seen to. Once he was situated under Gyda's or one of other medic's knowledgeable gaze, I, placated, made my rounds to see the damage that had been done.

Neat rows of bodies had been made, up and down, up and down. Though it pained me to see the faces of men and women I had trained with drained of color and laid to rest, it relieved me to know that there were so comparatively few of them. The enemy received no such mercy, nor care. The soldiers in red had been left to rot by their commanders, by their king. This action, or lack thereof, kindled life into my already ashen fury. What ruler could ever abandon their people, in life or death? The thought of myself doing such a thing made me feel I was spitting acid. Without asking or telling anyone else, I made my way over to the battlefield.

The first body I came upon was one I vaguely remembered cutting down. It belonged to a young man, reckless and ambitious. His right arm was missing its hand. Mechanically, and devoid of emotion, I dragged the body to a dry part of the meadow, one without blood and sweat. I went back for another, and then another. After the first few, my war-weary comrades caught on. Solvei began to drag other bodies, while Hanna picked up loose garments and belongings. We were silent under the pale red Luna light, somber. Before long—that is, before the Sol came up—nearly all the capable members of my army had added to the funeral pyre. I estimated five hundred to six hundred red bodies, nearly six times what we had lost. Even surrounded by so much death, there was a small victory.

We then made our own fallen into a separate pyre. Among the faces were ones I remembered clearly. Niko, his dark face peaceful, had fallen defending his brother from attackers. He had been sixteen years old. Nir refused to let anyone touch him and carried him in his arms to the pyre, laying him down softly. Ayla shadowed them both.

A man I had never thought could fall had fallen as well. Hakon the warrior, the last of my father's generation, had fought his last fight. This time, it was Gyda who was distraught. She had been diligently working with Yara to attend to the injured, but once she saw Hakon among the dead, her gaze became less fiery, less focused. I did not have the heart to ask her, nor anyone else, why her heart was so frozen by his loss.

When all the dead had been accumulated into the pyres, I began trying for a spark. Ayla, appearing from behind me, placed a hand on my shoulder, stopping my rigorous attempt for friction. She put her blue palm over mine. Between them, a warmth grew until it was red hot. Her hand uncovered mine, and there in my palm was a small flame. I looked Ayla in the eyes, amazed at this work, this miracle. She looked from me to the pyres. Taking the hint, I walked forward.

Everyone's eyes looked past me now; I was only an instrument. Some had tears in their eyes, some stood stoic. But all, like me, felt the pain of loss and showed it in their own tells. Ayla's eyes began to change colors, from chocolate to gold to hazel and back. Nir clenched and unclenched his jaw, attempting to keep the tears from flowing. Solvei fingered at her pendant, eyes trained on an unseen point on the horizon.

The red Luna above us guided me to each pyre. I approached the enemy first; true, they had been our foes in life, but in death, they were just like us, just like those we had lost. It was not our job to bring judgement upon them now.

With flame in hand, I reached out and touched the tattered Feroxian banner, causing it to immediately catch fire. I retreated and watched as the pyre lit up, more quickly than I would have anticipated. The stench of burning flesh accented the odor of misery in the air. And then I turned and approached our own funeral pyre, the one which played host to people, to souls I had dined with, laughed with, trained with. My eyes flitted around, finally resting on Niko.

I trudged forward, to the outermost part of the pyre, where he lay. I took his hand in mine and kissed his forehead. I took off my she-wolf cloak and placed it over the brave young warrior. As I backed away, the pyre began to light, releasing the souls of those who had perished that day. One could almost see them dancing up through the red moonlight.

Chapter 20
The Chalice is Half-Full

We later learned that the Feroxian army had retreated back with their king, all of them cowards. We rejoiced in our victory, but still mourned for those who had been lost. Ayla took it upon herself to take care of Nir in his time of mourning. There was something more between them, I knew that much, but all that mattered to me was their safety and happiness.

We stayed at camp for about a week, tending to those who had been injured. The majority of my time awake was spent at Adam's side. Gyda had given me instructions, knowing I would follow them exactly, just as Adam had done for me months before. Like me, he spent most of his time asleep, exhausted from healing, from feeling the agony of one's skin and muscle stitching back together. *Now we match.* The trivial thought popped into my mind one night as I used my clean cloth and a bucket of fresh water to clean his wound. I was careful, just as he had been. Sometimes, despite my efforts, the contact of cloth to his reddened and scarring skin made him wince in pain. These were the moments that I hated most. Every so often, Yara would drop by with medicine that would help to speed up the healing process and give Adam restful nights of deep sleep, where his pain could not follow. I was perhaps more grateful for this than him, knowing he was safe, healing, eased the sorrow in my heart at least a small amount.

After he had fallen asleep again, I made sure someone I trusted, usually Mehmet or Solvei, was nearby in case he awoke. With this somber time of freedom, I visited others who had been injured.

I walked, a phantom in the world of the living, from tent to tent. Sometimes I entered, and sometimes, I did not. I followed only my wandering feet. Though I slept well some nights at camp, I was still emotionally exhausted. I was waiting, time and time again, for the demons to come back; that was nearly worse than their actual presence. Onward, night after night, I walked. Occasionally, I would stop at a fire and speak kind words of encouragement to those nestled near it, but I could not break myself from this fog that grew stagnant and putrid in my mind, in my heart.

I walked on. And on. But then, my wandering legs stopped in front of a tent that housed several different injured warriors. One of them was the woman I had seen on the battlefield, the one I had never seen before. I remembered that she had lost her sword and had killed her opponent by stabbing him in the eye. She had taken a nasty blow to the side of her skull. Gyda had shaved that side of her head and attended to the wound with her homemade salves.

The woman opened her eyes and looked at me. They were a deep brown, full of confidence, hunger. She had seen so much with those eyes, and I was willing to wager on it.

"You may enter, Vita." Her words surprised me; I had never before been addressed with my first name upon meeting someone. My certainty in her past was growing. I treaded lightly, careful of the bodies resting on the floor. The woman moved into a cross-legged position so I could sit on her mat with her. I sat and assumed the same position. "My name is Nitocris." *Alrighty then, right to the point. She obviously doesn't like to mess around.*

"Nitocris," I addressed her, "I saw you fighting during the battle. You stabbed a man in the eye." I was careful in my tone. This woman gave me no expressional tells. I didn't know how to approach her. I waited nervously for her to reply.

"My sword was on the ground, but I know my way around a good dagger." She smiled a pointy grin. There was the tell. She was a proud woman, confident in herself. I could respect that.

"And where did you learn your way 'around a good dagger'?" I asked her. "We certainly didn't go over that in training. You have experience." The way the last words came out of my mouth sounded somewhat like an accusation, which they almost were. I was fascinated with this woman, drawn to learn all I could about her. And I daresay she took the hint.

"My Queen," her voice was dripping in sarcasm, "your wish is my command.

"I was born a slave in northern Daygn, not far from here, to the South. At the age of fourteen, my master sold me to a brothel. There, in the brothel, the head whore, A, looked after us. She taught us what we would need to know to survive. Never let a man touch you without consent. Never let a man finish inside you. And if you get pregnant, make him support you and the child. Those were our guidelines, and they were followed without hesitation. If a man were to try to break one of these rules, we were given permission to strike them.

"My good friend at the brothel, Meri, was three years older than me. Thirteen years ago, a man broke all three of our rules with her. She was broken, distraught. He hadn't even paid her. When she gave birth, and we saw it was a baby girl, I, along with three other women, took justice into our own hands. We went to his house. We demanded for him to support the child; he refused, calling us liars. So we came back the next day, and the next. We returned every day for eight days. On the eighth day, when he began to slam the door in our faces, I pushed past him and into the house. When he tried to stop me, I stabbed him clean through the eye. After we fed him to the fish in the lake behind his home, we took all the money we would need to help Meri raise her daughter.

"Twelve years after that, when Meri's daughter started her bleeding, we all decided that this life was nothing for a young girl. We looked at what we had become. So we decided to escape with the girl in tow. We would run to Kongeorn, where all are accepted. But, somehow—I still do not know—our plan was found out. The owners of the brothel came to us and, before our very eyes, raped Meri's little girl. Rage flooded through every single one of us, Meri had the most, though. She attacked them, the men who had provided for us. And she was cut down, throat slit from ear to ear. When this happened, I looked to the other women. I looked to A.

She nodded, and we charged at them. I picked up the little girl in my arms and ran, hard and fast, as far north as I could without stopping.

"When we got to the Disputed Lands, we found a group of soldiers. The poor girl could not even speak, nor walk, she was so traumatized. I spoke to one of the soldiers, and for once, I was terrified. There was something about him, like he wasn't truly there, like nothing I could do, no knife, nor poison, could kill him. But I pled for his aid anyway.

"He laughed at me.

"He laughed at me, and from my arms, he took the battered little girl. He broke her back over his knee. I screamed at him, begging, pleading. Meri's little girl was still alive, but barely. She needed help, and I needed to get her to a healer.

"Again, he laughed at me. He turned to leave, dropping the precious child on the ground. When she cried out, he crushed her skull beneath his boot." Nitocris paused after that, seething with rage at the memory.

"Men like them, they wear the Feroxian flag. They are brutes and monsters and think they can walk all over us, take whatever they want from us. I have had enough. No more. I knew the minute that I heard of what you had done, escaping from a man like the ones who had oppressed us for so long, I knew that being by your side, fighting behind you, was the only thing I could do to make Meri and her daughter's memories worth anything." Her voice cracked, but she wasn't crying, not at all. She was furious, filled with holy anger. Her story had given me the same; it had hardened my heart against what I already knew to be evil. And, like Nitocris, I knew there could be no more. No more walking like a phantom through the camp. My warriors needed a leader, and that was exactly who I had promised to be. It was exactly who I had promised to be.

As I walked back to my tent, I thought about Nitocris, about her determination, about who she was, about her story. It reminded me of a time long before, when Adam wasn't the only person I was attracted to.

I was a teenager, no older than fourteen, when Da brought in a foreign blacksmith to teach ours a few tricks. The blacksmith's name was Cara, and—upon first meeting her—I was absolutely enchanted. She had black hair, cropped close on one side and long on the other. Up and down her arms, she wore ceremonial tattoos. When she spoke, it was such authority that I couldn't help but listen.

I began to come to the forge nearly every day just to see Cara at work. She was strong and muscular. For a week or so, I convinced myself that I just admired her, but when I started to *feel* new things in new places, I realized that I was attracted to her.

Though I'm sure other people could see it, I never told anyone except Adam about how I felt about Cara. At that point, I'd only had one or two crushes, and they had all been on junior members of the legion—and Adam, though I couldn't even admit that to myself.

When Cara left, I was heart-broken. I had been convinced that, one day, I would marry her and work in the forge with her. She was the first woman I'd ever been attracted to, but she wasn't the last.

The next morning, I walked the boundaries of the camp, taking care to shake hands with every warrior, able and injured. They all saw me, back straight, head held high. 'Yes,' my body language told them, 'we lost brave men and women. But we also have gained the upper hand. We are Kongeorn, and the world, especially the people of Feroxia, will know it.'

As I walked by, people's heads looked up at me. And as I departed, their heads stayed up, proud of what they had accomplished. It was not enough to win the battle; we had to *act* like we had won the battle, and were going to win the war. Otherwise, everything we had worked so hard for would crumble down around us.

That's my girl. Finally, a voice had returned to me, but it wasn't Ahava. Instead, it was Da. I could hear from the tone of his voice that he was proud. My chest puffed out, and I walked with my head even higher. Yes, even higher.

It took another week for our injured to be well enough to move again. By that time, Dagny had returned to me. She was safe, alive, and that was yet another small victory for me. Adam's horse, Tyr, was also more than happy to have Dagny back. For those who were not strong enough to make the trek on foot, horses were provided. Adam rode his horse, but was unable to canter; his stitches were still too fresh, and the risk of ripping them open was too great. Our pace on the journey home would have to be slower.

Of course, every night, I slept beside Adam. I couldn't tell if it was the pain or something else, but he refused to speak to me. For this reason, I felt alienated, and decided to leave him be. If he wanted to share something with me, then he would. For the time being, I resolved to be the leader I had promised to be.

Every day, I rode ahead of the group, scouting, along with Dana. We both checked for signs of dangerous fauna, possible enemy troops, and breaks in the terrain that would make for easier travel.

The trip back home took a grueling three weeks. When I had travelled the distance before, I hadn't stopped, simply out of pure stubbornness, and I had been alone. Traveling is always faster alone. But it certainly isn't more enjoyable.

On the way back, we stopped through Fere, the city I had stopped in before, for provisions. The majority of our warriors stayed outside the city, while a select few—Hanna, Solvei, Yara, Oliver, Dana, and I—went inside to comb through the merchants for those who had bargains for food and provisions. The crowds here were all too familiar for me there. My memory of Fere was slightly distorted by the experiences that had come from before. As I searched for deals, I heard a familiar voice.

"Pearz! Pearz! Zweet pearz from Ozter!" My eyes lit up, and I pushed through the crowd to get to his booth. I shoved and apologized, shoved and apologized, until I reached the sweet smell of pears. The man from before glanced towards me, then away, then back again.

"It iz you!" He shouted, then realizing his volume, brought it down to a near whisper, "You are not in trouble thiz time?" I chuckled and shook my head no. I then explained why there was a large mass of people, armed and unarmed, outside the city's thick limestone walls. The pear man chuckled. When a break in the conversation came, however, I found myself growing somewhat somber, serious.

"I wanted to thank you for your kindness...last time." The sincerity of my thank you brought tears pricking at my eyes. I looked down at my fingers, which had begun to absent-mindedly touch the rough wood of the booth. When I looked up, the pear man was smiling with tears in his own eyes.

"I never expected for you to zay zuch a thing to me, let alone remember me. I zuppoze you are juzt like your father." He reached out and clasped my hand. While he did so, I pulled an item from my pocket. I offered it to him. His hand let go of mine as his eyes grew exceedingly wider. As if I had presented him with a venomous snake, he jumped backwards, catching the eye of a few passersby.

"It's for you. Had you not been so kind, I would be dead. My father would want you to have it." Silent, the man slowly inched forward, again inspecting the seemingly worthless trinket in my hand. If, like him, the possessor of this object knew of its importance, they could do great things. Of course, being from the

South, this man knew very well what the rusting metal tooth in my hand could do.

"Are you zure? I am no royal, and I have no experienze with zuch thingz." I nodded my head, and again offered him the tooth. The reasons he thought I should not give it to him were the exact reasons I wanted him to have it. With this object, an evil or proud man could summon the darkest powers of the guardian Kongeorn. But a man such as the one who stood before me, a man like him, would treasure both the powers and the item itself. That was why I was giving this man the Dagv'arder. That was why I had taken it from our room of treasures, brought it all this way, and offered it to a stranger. Because I knew it would be treasured, not used.

Finally, the man took the Dagv'arder from me and held it to his chest. I smiled, knowing I had made a good choice—for once. Before I could turn to leave, however, to go back to my army, the man spoke up.

"My Queen, if you ever again find yourzelf in Fere, pleaze ztop by and vizit me. If I am not here, I will be back zoon." I again smiled at the pear man, content with this ending, the kind Da would tell when I was a child. Everything was wrapped up in a little bow. Everything was as it should be.

Chapter 21
Scalding Cold

I made my way back to my people, taking the time to purchase clean bandages from a healer's cottage not far from the city gates. When I passed back through to the outside world, I turned back briefly to take in the scene of ordinary life before me. It was a scene that I hoped would never change for these people. I hoped that what we had done the week before on the battlefield would at least make headway against Jakel—and those that followed in his ways.

When our large party reached the outskirts of Redefalk, many of the warriors, elated, began to sprint. A greeting party would be waiting, we knew, and the promise of seeing those that had been left behind would be worth the aching feet and sunburned skin. Mothers from our group ran to embrace their children. Fathers did the same, some of them embracing their own husbands or wives. Brothers and sisters embraced. Daughters and sons grinned from ear to ear as they ran to greet their parents who had stayed behind. It was joyous, but there was sorrow.

A man walked up to us, to Adam and me, and he asked where his husband was. I asked his name, and was told. My heart broke all over again as I told this man that his love would not be returning. He stared off into the distance, numb, as if there was no noise, nor movement going on around him. He was in his own little bubble, unfeeling to the world. My toes tingled, uncomfortable in not knowing what to do, how to comfort this man I had never met. Luckily for me, however, Dana was there, too. She approached the man, taking him under her arm and saying his name. They were relatives: how though, I didn't quite know.

Adam and I walked our horses to the stables and groomed them in their stalls, side by side. Dagny whinnied when I tried to leave, reminding me that I owed her. Remembering, I jogged to the tack room and found one of her dried apples. I jogged back and fed it to her, stroking her neck as she ate.

"Good girl," I whispered, scratching her nose. I closed the stall behind me and waited for Adam to finish with Tyr. As I waited, however, I realized that he wasn't actually in Tyr's stall at all. He had left.

Without me.

Such a thing shouldn't have hurt; it shouldn't have stung the way that it did. I should have been able to brush it off, like any normal adult could do. But the demons wouldn't let that happen. *You didn't do enough.* I began walking to the bathing pools. *He thinks you could have spared him the scar.* I shed my sweaty, dusty riding clothes and entered the placid pool. *You weren't fast enough.* The water cast ripples out in front of me as I waded deeper, all the way until it was to my chin. *You almost let him die. You almost killed him. And now he can't stand to look at you.* I submerged myself under the water, trying to drown out the voices, but they only grew louder, along with the pounding of my heart.

Right now, he's probably with another woman, just to hurt you. Ba-bump. *You hurt him, now it's your turn.* Ba-bump. Ba-bump. *You were lazy, stupid, slow. You should be punished.* Ba-bump, ba-bump, ba-bump. *You shouldn't even be alive.* Ba-bump ba-bump ba-bump ba-bump.

My head broke through the surface of the water, and I gulped down air. Despite everything my heart was believing, despite every word the demons had said, my body refused to let me give up. And I suppose it wasn't just *my* body.

"Vita!" She threw her completely clothed arms around me. "You had me scared to death." Hanna's green eyes were wide and full of worry, of fear. It hadn't been my own body that had pushed me back above the water, it had been Hanna who had pulled me up. My breathing evened out, and Hanna finally let go. "Please don't do that again. Please. Whatever it was that you were thinking—"

"It's okay. I'm okay, I promise." I offered a half-smile, but she wasn't entirely convinced.

"Vita, if you make me worry like that again, I'm going to have to beat some sense into you with a club or something." The image of her trying to even handle a club made me chuckle. At this, she smiled too. "Are you sure you're okay?" I listened, trying to decide if the demons had gone back to their hiding place or were still present. From what I could tell, it was the former.

"Yeah, I'm okay." Hanna, almost pacified, let go of my arms, which she had been gripping during the entire conversation. She didn't leave, however, as—I suppose—she was afraid that leaving me alone would result in more self-imposed danger. I knew she meant well, but I also really needed a bath. So she stayed, looking away most of the time for privacy's sake, while I washed away the grime of travel. Only did she leave once I had been escorted back to my room and explained to her several times that I would be okay.

Once she had left, however, I found my heart warming at the thought of a real friend, of the knowledge that there was someone willing to give their valued time and energy just to make sure I was okay. That warmth drove out the icy doubt I had felt earlier about Adam. That warmth was my comfort as I drifted off to sleep.

A woman, clothed in all white, bound with rope, marches through a crowd of onlookers. They jeer at her, call for her death. Her green eyes are focused on nothing; her tanned face shows no emotion as she makes her way to the stake. The men who wait for her have torches in their hands, meant to execute her, meant to light the fire which is to burn her alive. Still, she remains stoic. Still, she does not show fear.

The next few mornings were quiet, save for the chirping of birds. I, for every one of these, awoke alone in my own room. I spent most of my days talking to my warriors, both healing and healed. I hadn't talked to Adam in days. Any time we crossed each other's paths, he refused to even look me in the eye. And so, the pain in my heart, the ripping of my soul, became so prevalent that the only way I could deal with it was to push it away, push it deeper and deeper down into my depths, hoping that it could become easier to ignore.

It wasn't.

Because every time I saw him, saw the look on his face when he looked at me, all of the voices in my head, the ones that I had fought so hard against before, came to life.

You're nothing.

Obviously, you're no queen to him.

You were a tool, all this time, nothing more than an instrument.

He's just like your brothers. He's found his life, his fight, and now, he's going to leave you, too. Just as they did.

And why would he want you? Look at yourself! Scars all over, even without the breaking, your nose would be bird-like, impossible to ever be beautiful. And don't even start on your personality. What man wants a woman who can't keep it together? What man can deal with all the svat you have? What man wants to spend his time in the same bed as a psychopath?

There were moments when I didn't even want to get out of bed. Not because I was nothing without Adam, no. I didn't need a man to function. But his cold shoulder had been one that had kept me sane before. He had talked me off the ledge time and time again. Yes, I had friends, like Hanna and Solvei, who could help me see the bright spots. But they didn't know how deep down and how tied in all of the darkness was. Adam knew, though. He and Mami and Bjorth. But it seemed that all of them were far from my reach. Two were dead, gone from my sight, from my touch, until my own time came. And the other wanted nothing to do with me. To say I felt lonely would be a gross understatement. But then again, lonely wasn't anything new to me.

Lujy 27th, 533—

Why is it that one can be in the midst of doing something they treasure, and yet, still feel empty? I do not mean to sound sappy, nor cliche, but it seems to me that the happiest of us are the ones who are most talented at living in the present moment. Needless to say, I must find someone like these and have them teach me their ways.

—Octavia

Chapter 22

Catharsis

As the dinner fires were dying down, and my company resorted to trivial conversation—the 'who's and the 'what's, rather than 'why's and 'how's—I felt my mind growing somber. The smiles of those around me weren't as uplifting as before, nor as contagious. I resolved to say good night and go to my room, where I could surrender to the one saving grace I had felt lately: sleep.

As I walked, the brisk night air accompanying me, my thoughts wandered away, too far away to reign them in. I thought on Nina, how fast she must have been growing. I thought on Ayla and Nir, a blossoming romance in the works, no doubt. I thought on many things, many people, but all the thoughts came crashing to a halt when I saw my bedroom door ajar.

Cautiously, I approached, mindful of every sound that chanced by my ear. Upon peering inside, I saw a stranger on my bed. I say stranger, but that was only how he had been to me the previous weeks. I entered, and he stirred. He still refused to meet my eyes. As I watched him sitting on the bed, I saw him clench his jaw, a tell-tale sign of his temper planning to erupt forth. Treading lightly would not do; and I had had enough.

"What is it?" I said with no amount of sympathy, crossing my arms and sending up a mental wall. Now would finally be my chance to know why he had been so distant, so cautious of me. But it would take some coaxing to get it out of him. He still hadn't looked away from the fire in the fireplace, and hadn't said a word, besides. I would pull no punches. I was done feeling alone without explanation. I wanted an answer. *Now.* "Have I done something?" *That'll get him.* And it did. His head looked up at an alarming speed, as if he were about to break his neck.

"Absolutely not. Never," he paused, trying to form the right words, "if anything, it is what *I* have done, or rather, not done." *Finally.* Relief flooded over me, but his words cast a shadow of doubt in my mind. Such self-incrimination had destructive effects, and I would know. I waited for him to elaborate, one eyebrow raised. He enlightened me, "I couldn't kill him. He was right there, and I couldn't kill him. I'm weak, I have no right to even fight beside you. He was there, feet away from me, and I let him get away, after all he did to you."

The relief I had felt before morphed into determination; I was not about to let him feel the self-hatred I had felt. My soul was stitching back together, and I refused to let half of it hurt so badly.

"First of all, the blame does not fall on you. He was, no doubt, heavily guarded, and they were not *that* close to you. Besides, you were completely surrounded." Even as the words came out of my mouth, I knew I had said the wrong thing. Though the words were the best I could think of, as they were the truth, I knew they wouldn't work. It would be harder to absolve Adam of his guilt.

"No! The blame falls on me. *I* let you stay in his damned castle. *I* let those things happen to you. *I* let that sick son of a bitch get away with his head. This is not some pity party, Vita. Blame must be set on someone, and I am taking it." His voice has risen in volume until I felt as if the entire hallway could hear him. He stood. His eyes burned with intensity, with something like hatred. I didn't know what to say, and I didn't give myself time to think. In that moment, only emotion consumed my mind, overtaking it and throwing logic and caution to the wind.

"*You* didn't decide anything. *You* didn't *let* those things happen to me. *I* did!" My own temper had been added to the vortex circling in the room, and I could not hold it at bay. "It is not your duty to protect the oh-so-helpless Queen of Kongeorn. *I* got out of that damned keep on my own."

"But you wouldn't have had to escape on your own if you had listened to me in the first place. And none of this would have even happened if I hadn't agreed with your father to stay behind—"

"Adam! Just stop talking! You need to get over the fact that *you cannot protect me.*" He stopped. Silence swooped into the space between us. It doused my flaming temper in icy water. I came to my senses. The words I had said weren't fair. If anything, I had always been the one to try to control him. I had been the one to try and twist his future, to mess with fate's plan.

"Really?" he whispered, his tone foreign to me. Not gentle, no. Not hurt, either. Something else, entirely.

He turned, slowly and cautiously, as if trying to calm a skittish horse. Then, to my utter surprise, he enveloped me in his arms, pulling me close, and rested his chin on my head.

"I know we've been through this, and I know what you'll say," he exhaled softly, "but I will always feel guilt at not being able to protect you, even if you don't always need protecting." He turned his head so his stubbled cheek rested on my hair. "I've seen what it's done to you; even when I didn't know what 'it' was."

My eyes welled with tears, not ones of anger, but of bitter sweetness. It was like I was finally being given permission to let myself be vulnerable. I didn't need to save face. I didn't need to be the strong queen, the focused ruler. I could be the survivor, the patient who needed to heal.

Adam loosened the hug and leaned back, looking down at me.

"C'mon," he held my hand in his, "we're going to find someone who can help you more than I can."

I hesitated as he made to leave the room with me in tow. I didn't know if I was ready to talk about it. But then, I felt a push behind me, gentle and guiding, and I knew that—even if I wasn't completely ready—that it needed to be done.

Adam led me out to the main portion of the keep, where our many visitors were staying. We weaved between the temporary and permanent living spaces until we came to a squat hut with a single light shining through the window.

"Adam," my voice shook, heart beating, "I don't know about this, what if she—"

"Vita, she knows your heart, and she knows how to help, far more than I do. Please, just trust me."

With that, Adam knocked gently on Gyda's door. There was a faint commotion inside, followed by indiscrete cursing. Finally, the door swung open to reveal the older woman in her robe of wool. Her toothy grin quickly turned somber when she saw the looks on our faces.

"Don' tell me yer with child?" She gestured between us both wildly, clearly exasperated.

"No, Gyda, we simply wanted to talk. May we come in?" Adam's amused smile set Gyda at ease as she made room for us to come into the small hut. I made my way to her bed to sit down, easily navigating between the low-hanging shelves, while Adam repeatedly bumped his head.

Gyda sat down beside me, and Adam came to rest next to the bed, leaning against the wall.

"So what can I help with, you two?" Gyda's eyes looked patiently between the two of us before resting on Adam. He must have made a gesture or mouthed something, because her eyes soon widened in understanding. She turned to me.

"I know it might be difficul' and hard at times, but the only way to really help you is for you to talk abou' it." She placed her injured hand on my shoulder, trying to soothe me. I could only look down at my own hands.

"If it makes it easier, I can leave," Adam's voice softly suggested. I looked up.

"It wouldn't offend you? If I asked to be alone with her?" I searched his eyes for any sign of anger or dissent, but found none.

With the decision made, Adam kissed the top of my head and ducked out of the hut, leaving Gyda and me alone. I turned my eyes to her, to the soft wrinkles around her eyes, to sprigs of wayward hair jutting out from her mane.

"I knew what was happening," I started, feeling it was the only place I could begin, "but I felt so detached from it. And I felt—"

My voice broke as my throat seized up. From my periphery, the darkness was closing in, the demons edging closer, and I could see Richard's face, and I could feel every movement.

But then, I could feel Gyda's hand gently rubbing my back. I wasn't in that castle anymore: I was home, in Redefalk, safe.

"I felt so—I felt so helpless. And I—I'd never felt like that before. I should have fought harder, I should have pushed through the fear, I should have—"

"Vita, child," Gyda gently interrupted me, "there are always goin' to be those 'should have's' and 'what if's', but they can'ot change what really happened. And what really happened was not your fault."

"But I could have been more careful, I could have listened to Adam—I thought something like that could never happen to me—I shouldn't have been so naive."

"We all have those moments. It's human nature to distance ourselves from tragedy and pain. Now, Vita, I need ya to look at me, in the eyes." It took me a few moments, but I managed it.

"What he did to you does not define you. *You* define you. And so, as hard as it may be, it is best for you to forgive 'im."

"What?" I scoffed at her. *Forgive him? No. No, I want him dead, I want to see the pain in his eyes when I take his life.*

"You misunderstan' me. Forgiveness is not saying what someone did to you is right. No, it's not condonin' their actions. Forgiveness is letting go. Forgiveness is freeing yourself from the bondage of that memory."

I looked at Gyda, thinking on her words. I had only ever known forgiveness as something you do to absolve someone of blame. But this forgiveness, this was purer, and it was what needed to be done, even if I couldn't quite understand it.

Chapter 23

Simon and His Unicorns

The next morning, my eyes opened to dust dancing in the weak Sol light. I smiled as I felt Adam breathe in next to me. I turned my head and found him there, exactly where he belonged. I remembered the events of the previous night, remembered the way I had finally begun to let go, remembered those who had helped me to do so. Adam stirred next to me. Turning over, his eyes slowly blinked open.

"Good morning." The smile still played on my lips as a tone of peace waltzed through my words. Hearing this, Adam became a bit more alert, observant.

"Do you want to talk about it?" His eyes searched mine. "You don't have to, of course." I twirled one of his locks around my finger absentmindedly.

"Not now. But when I need to again—and I know I will—I will be sure to pull you aside. I promise." I meant it. The past few weeks, burdened with this dark trauma, this fear, had felt like three hundred years, and I was glad that the tension had been dissolved, and that things were at least out in the open and out of the confines of my mind.

Adam leaned in and kissed me.

"I'm ready for the next steps. I know it may not be easy, but I'm ready to try." I rolled over to get up out of bed. As my feet hit the floor, however, one of my pinky toes came in contact with something that wasn't wood at all. Instead, it was cool leather, dry and out of place. At my feet, the missing book from our buried collection lay. The *Dead Waning* cover was cracked and worn in several different places, a sign of being exposed to the elements. How it ended up in my room, let alone at my feet, I had no idea.

My longer-than-usual pause made Adam's curiosity come to a head. He scooted towards me and leaned to look over my shoulder.

"*Svatus kud,*" he exhaled, "how does that even happen?" I turned my head to give him the "Obviously It Rode In On A Unicorn" look. Sarcasm is an art, my friends; even without words, it can be achieved. After receiving an equally sassy eye roll in return, my mind's eye flew back to the Edge, how its red and black lights had come creeping in even further: far too close for comfort. How I had forgotten about this, I didn't know. As my eyes found Adam's scar, I cut myself some slack. No wonder some thoughts had gotten shoved aside.

This time, I turned back and looked at Adam with a more sincere, telling look.

"Simon?" he asked.

"Simon." I nodded.

After we had both dressed and made ourselves relatively presentable, I sent Adam off to get us food—as we had our priorities to take care of—and bring it to the library, where Simon spent most of his time, along with a couple of other geriatric cases we knew.

When I arrived at the double doors, I could hear them inside, chatting away.

"Oh, and yer so sure of yerself, Roald," Gyda cackled within, "ya can't even produce a proper poultice wit'out yer magic!" Annunciating her "p's" was Gyda's excuse for spitting all over people when she was messing with them, which was why I usually stood or sat outside a three-foot radius. I decided to enter, which was met with no evident surprise out of any of the three.

"Vita." Roald nodded a greeting, while Gyda did a fake salute, and Simon merely smiled. *Of course he knows.*

"May I join you?" I asked before pulling up a chair.

"Only if Adam offers us some of that food he's bringing you," Simon quipped jokingly. I rolled my eyes inwardly. How did they always know everything? Out of the corner of my eye, I could see Simon struggling to keep his answer to *that* question inside. I turned my eyes away from him, exasperated, and silently rejoiced as Adam arrived with the food and the book.

He set both down on the table in the middle of us all. I hadn't expected there to be reactions, especially because Simon usually never gave any, but the movements and noises that came as a result of Adam simply placing the book on the table made me incredibly anxious.

"*Sqover rette uns,*" Roald exhaled the words, and though I didn't know the direct translation, there was no doubt that it was a call to the Mother.

"*Iza.*" Simon actually flinched and shifted away from the book. It was interesting that his word choice was the only southern word I knew, and it was their equivalent to *svat*. Gyda, unlike the men, sat still in her chair, unruly hair punctuating the panic in her eyes.

Adam and I exchanged a look of cautious fear. The book hadn't been our true reason for coming to them, and yet, it brought more terror onto their faces than I ever thought I'd see.

"Wh—what is it?" Adam mustered when he realized I couldn't. We waited in tense silence. After a few minutes of staring at each other, Simon spoke up.

"Where did you find this book?" *Oh so you don't know the answer to that one, huh?* "Vita, I am quite serious." My eyes widened, feeling like a scolded child.

"Well, it was ours, but we buried years ago, near the Edge. And then, when we went to unbury it, along with the other two books, it was missing. Then, this morning, we woke up, and it was at the foot of my bed." My eyes flitted from person to person, attempting to gauge their reactions. Simon, more to character, held no emotion on his face. Roald nodded after every few words, and Gyda listened intently, frizzy head cocked to the side. Adam, next to me, held his breath until I finished my story. He exhaled as I did.

Simon, not at all to my surprise, was the first to speak up.

"You are sure this is still your book?" I looked questioningly at the old man before catching the disrespectful look. As sure as I was, I looked to Adam. Like me, he also seemed confused. "Have you even thought to look at the pages?" It seemed like such an obvious question that I almost blurted out that we had—of course, we had. Again, though, a look at Adam told me that I was wrong.

Svat. *That's embarrassing.* I looked down at my hands, watching my fingers intertwine, and shook my head slowly.

"Chil', there's no shame in gettin' ahead of yerself. Happens ta this one all the time," Gyda attempted to raise my spirits by making a quip at Roald's expense. He merely rolled his ancient eyes at her and turned his attention back to the book. Though I appreciated the attempt, I still felt altogether stupid. Nothing new.

"Vita," this time, it was Roald who spoke, "put aside the feeling in your heart and *look* at what you have in front of you." This gentle call to action was all I needed. I turned my eyes up, shedding the skin of my younger self, and set my eyes on the book.

The dust-colored leather cover was flaking, peeling off. Where the title, *Dead Waning,* had been in red ink, now there were only hints of letters. The corners had been eroded away. Where binding used to be, strong and dark, now it had almost given way completely to the substance which held it together. Nothing about it could be considered pleasant to look at. And yet, when I opened the cover, the pages inside were pristine. They were bright white, crisp with clean edges. Even when we had buried our copy, pages had been ripped, and all had been at least somewhat worn.

"Now tell me, Vita," Simon interjected into my observations, "is this your book?" My mind puzzled, I shook my head. This was like some sort of horrible street magic I had seen as a kid when Da took me to the South. A man dressed in all black had taken my favorite doll and placed him into a sack. But when he opened the sack, my doll was gone. A four-year-old had never been so loud as I was. Mortified, the man in black made my doll reappear and had apologized profusely. But I had a feeling then that our copy of the book was not coming back.

"Roald," Simon turned to address his equal, "do you know of this book, of the story it tells?"

"It's just the story of lion and his cub," Adam interjected, "but when the cub grows up, he wants his father's pride, so he gets the other lions to chase his father away. That's all it is."

"No," Roald shook his head, "that is not all it is. This is an allegory. It tells the tale of Jakel casting his Mother out of Omnia. It was disguised as a children's story to help young ones to understand. What worries me is the author. Even the Mother does not know who wrote this book."

Adam and I stared, wide eyed, at Roald. This was news to us. If this book was an allegory with an unknown author then that made it all the more sinister. In southern cultures, spells could be attached to books if their stories represented something else. If the author of *Dead Waning* was from the South—or even had the capabilities— then this book could be more dangerous than we knew. I retreated into my mind, trying to think about what this meant for my people. The book had come to me, and if it was dangerous, then I had brought danger to my people. I began to panic.

"Vita," Gyda's voice snapped me back to reality, "you mentioned the Edge. What about it?" Seeing me still reeling from a venture into my own mind, Adam took the question.

"When we were younger, we would ride out to the Edge, which has always been about thirty miles away from Redefalk—"

"No, when I last paid it a visit, it was at least sixty," Gyda interrupted.

"That's not the point," I spoke up. "Now it's got to be only ten or so. It's getting closer." Nothing. No one said a single word. I waited, trying to get comfortable under the weight of what we had just unearthed.

"Jakel grows more powerful," Roald's voice had become grave, and his eyes took on the molten gold I had known his daughter's to. "If he is allowed to spread his power, the Edge will only loom closer. It is his domain. As he takes souls, he takes land."

I could not speak for the rest of our time in the library. It felt as if there was cotton in my throat, drying it out and prohibiting my speech. It was agreed that we burn the book for good measure. It could not be allowed to maintain existence. Gyda took us back to her hut to make a purifying incendiary. As she went to work, I could not help but feel Emilie's yellow eyes on my back, baring into me. Once we finally got out of Gyda's hut, I breathed a sigh of relief. However, my throat still remained too dry for speech.

When we arrived at the holy clearing, at Levend, I set the book down, almost afraid that it would bite me. Adam sprinkled on the incendiary powder then lit it aflame with the torch that stood watch over the clearing. We watched it burn, and, as it became ash, my throat again became capable of speech. Thankfully, I took Adam's hand in mine and watched the flames dance.

⚒

"Why have you not shown yerself to 'er yet?" My best friend questioned me as I watched over the couple burning the book.

"What makes you think I haven't?" I shot back, ready to explain and defend myself. Bjorth looked over quizzically.

"She could use yer help, you know. The things you never told 'er would come in handy now." I shook my head and chuckled.

"Like Ahava? They've met, but not because of me. Any help that Vita has gotten has come from those who willingly give it—that or she has had to look to herself. They see her and offer help, offer themselves because she gives them something that they haven't felt in, perhaps, a quite long time."

"An' what is that?"

"Hope."

"Well your wife certainly di' not agree wit' that." He chuckled and crossed his arms triumphantly, thinking he had bested me at my own game.

"Oh, you mean that time with the mirror? I was there, but Dagmar wasn't. The only time she's shown herself to Vita was when Nina was born. Like I said, Vita looks inside herself. She finds the lights in her darkness and makes them brighter so she can see. Vita is so much stronger than she thinks."

The big red man was silent.

"An' what do you think?"

"She always falls, but she knows how to rise higher, if only she realizes she can."

Chapter 24
Do Not Disturb

After we burned the book and made sure it was completely ash, we buried the ashes for good measure. There would be no risks taken with whatever the hell this was. I exhaled once it was finished and done with. Sweaty and exhausted, Adam and I decided to go for a swim. The hot springs just north of Redefalk would be a welcome recess from the day's responsibilities.

The hike was short, but trying. The pools were high on a mountain that Redefalk sat at the base of. Our own bathing pools took water from these in the cold winter months, when the underground water was too cool. But those pools were nothing like the original up where we were.

I took off my boot and relished the feeling of moss beneath my toes. A splash next to me signaled that Adam had wasted no time in entering the pool. I rolled my eyes. He always had to be first in. After slinging our garments over a dry rock, I entered the water next, slowly and mindful of my scars. This water was hotter than what I was used to, and the new skin could hate me for this. But, to my relief, the steaming water eased the ache from my muscles and left my scars alone, save for a small initial sting.

I lowered myself until only my head was above the water. Adam, of course, was nowhere in sight. I rolled my eyes. I waited for him to try to sneak up on me. He didn't. I began to panic; perhaps I had been wrong. Maybe he hadn't jumped in, maybe he had been pushed and hit his head, or pulled in, or maybe the smoke that had killed Bjorth had gotten to Adam too. I began to breathe in faster than I could breathe out, confusing my lungs. My throat began to tighten in my panic. Then, I felt a hand on my shoulder.

"Vita?" Adam turned me around as I gasped at his touch. "What happened?"

"You just—you scared me." I breathed in and out slowly, trying catch my breath and restore the damage done to my nerves. Adam took me in his arms and petted down my hair. Eventually, I regained composure—and dignity.

"Sorry," I said.

"Why are you sorry? You didn't do anything wrong." He looked down at me.

"I guess I'm just hard to deal with," I chuckled, "between the fits and the easy scaring and the temper..." I trailed off, hoping Adam would say something to ease my worries. He didn't speak, which, of course, made me worry. I opened my mouth to apologize again, but, before I could say anything, Adam spoke up.

"You can be sorry all you want, but dealing with you isn't hard because I love you. The fits remind me that I almost lost you, and the spooking reminds me that you have seen so much more than I could ever imagine, and the temper reminds me of myself, so what's not to love? You have every right to feel the way you do, but that doesn't mean I'm going to sit by and do nothing while you hurt." He kissed each of my temples before making his way to my lips. I smiled at him, thankful that, of all the people that had been wrenched away from me, Adam wasn't one of them. I leaned against him, letting the moment stretch on forever.

Of course, no moment lasts forever. After about ten minutes, the bushes to our left began to shake. Both on guard, we reached for the daggers in our boots at the edge of the steaming pool. We didn't need them though. Through the brush, almost melting into one another, were Nitocris and a woman I barely recognized as Kalliope, one of our healers. They, ignorant of us, made their way to the pool just right of us. Adam and I looked at each other and stifled giggles. We stealthily exited the pool and donned our clothes, leaving the two to some well-deserved private time. Just before I got to the brush, Nitocris looked up at me and winked before going back to planting kisses on the woman in front of her. *Smooth.*

I smiled as we walked away. I thought about the two women, and I thought about myself. Had Adam not been there, through all of it, there was a real chance that I would have been with a woman. Both options had always intrigued me, but the obvious choice, as I looked back, had always been Adam.

Once out of earshot, Adam and I began to laugh hysterically. Then, I went silent, stopping in my tracks. Adam saw this and, concerned, circled back to me.

"What's wrong?" A smile tried to poke at my lips.

"Do you think *we* are that ignorant? Have we ever left the door open? Or what about in the bathing pools? *Svat*, what if—" He cut me off with a hand over my mouth and a chuckle on his lips.

"Honestly though, you wouldn't care if we were caught, would you?" I gave him an offended look then shrugged.

"Probably not." I laughed and sprinted away towards the keep, not waiting for Adam to catch up. Hopping over snarled roots and dashing between trees, I let responsibility fall away. The dull winter sunlight streamed through the barren canopy, casting shadows on the patchy forest floor. Adam was just far enough behind me that I could hear, but not see, him. I halted and, with a tricky smile playing at my lips, ascended the closest tree. Though its branches were bare and sparse, I was well hidden at this height. When Adam made his way to where I had been, he slowed, warrior instincts kicking in. My heart pounded as his head swiveled this way and that. Finally, he sighed and laughed. I narrowed my eyes. *What are you about to do?*

Probably keep going, I'd say. The voice startled me, and I, losing my balance and cool, fell from the tree and onto Adam. *That one hurt.* I rolled my eyes and looked up. There, in the branches just above me, sat Ahava, reveling in her divinity. Shooting her an annoyed look, I made sure Adam was okay and helped him up.

"Try sticking to the ground next time, Stormy. For my sake." He feigned a broken arm and a limp before stopping and waiting for me to follow. I did. When I looked back over my shoulder, however, Ahava was gone, and I was left to walk in confusion. For Ahava to reveal herself now, that in itself was thought-provoking. *Why now,*

Sister? Why come to me now? And, of course, to my growing irritation, there was no answer.

In the past months, there had been nothing from the Etter, not from Ahava, nor the rest of my family. Even before the battle, no advice. Where were they? I half expected to turn the corner and see them, but that, as we emerged from the dormant wood, seemed only a fantasy. I decided to let the issue be, knowing that no answer would reveal itself anytime soon.

As we walked aimlessly, my eyes focused on random items and places. A rusty nail here, a pile of wood there. Every now and then, a thought of some organized merit would pop into my head, only to be snuffed out by my short attention span. For the time being, I resigned myself to be incapable of thinking. Observing was enough.

A roan mare pranced about in the yellow pasture with her blanket-covered foal. A few men and women sat on the fence, each having their own conversations. On the other side of the fence, children ran about. Their laughter chimed in the brisk air, warming the atmosphere and giving chase to the cold, just as they did with their wooden swords. The hound pup, whom Solvei had named Asher, bounded behind the children, content to follow. He stopped as they passed the tree his owner sat beneath. He barked happily. Taking a moment, he jogged over and licked her face. Content with this, he turned and bounded again after the children. Solvei rested under the tree, watching just as I was. Her gaze landed on a couple over near the stables. I followed her gaze and took in the sight of

Ayla and Nir, nestled together, reading a book. Each smiled in their comfort, in the presence of the other so close to them.

My heart grinned at the sight. My people, as far as I could see, were happy. The smiles and the laughter and the warmth they shared with me in that long moment was all it took to break my thoughts from their mute solitude. *This is all I wanted.* Tears pricked at my eyes, imagining Da and Mami above me, watching, *proud.* They were proud. And all was as it should be.

But what should be is not what was.

The calm, sunny atmosphere was broken by the sound of urgent pounding hooves. A rider raced into Redefalk, bearing the Kongeorn garb. Behind him, another horse followed, its rider slumped over. I recognized the first rider as Fritz. The second, then, would be Engel. Fritz glanced around frantically before finding me. He and his horse cantered over. The other horse followed.

"We are all that remain." I took Fritz's words as a shock. We had sent out eight scouts. For only two to return meant horror in my heart.

"Solvei, get Gyda and Yara to tend to Engel. Adam, the horses need to be cared for. See that it happens. Fritz, walk with me." My orders were followed without question as I let my queenly mantle rest again on my shoulders. After Fritz dismounted, I took his arm and gently led him away from all the people in the field. My voice lowered.

"What happened?" We stopped at the far fence, the one that separated the training grounds from the pasture. Fritz ran a shaking hand through his hair.

"We were camped as we have been. Nothing had changed. We had just gotten news of an execution in Ferida. It had been more brutal than the rest, with torture before it. Sash had returned to us with this news after witnessing it. But she had been followed by Feroxian men. She was taken down by an arrow to the back. Then, Anima was cut down where she stood. And Hagen finally saw what was happening, so he charged at the attackers. But there were so many. He fell. Then Siegfried fell trying to avenge him. Andreas and Aris told Engel and I to ride, to tell of what had happened. They, too, perished."

"How do you know this?" I asked. If they had ridden off before the brothers had been taken down, how did they know it had happened?

"We did not leave immediately. We had to set fire to our maps and letters. If we were to be compromised, we needed to know Kongeorn was safe, at least. As we did this, Andreas was beheaded by a short-sword, and Aris was cut down then trampled to death. As we rode off, Engel was hit by one of their arrows." Fritz looked down despairingly. Putting an arm around his shoulder, I asked him two more questions.

"The execution was a dumb man. His tongue had been removed long ago. But he was big. His crime was helping us escape from the castle the first time." My eyes widened in sorrow. My big friend. Such innocence did not deserve what had been done to him. I took in a shaky breath. Fritz answered my final question soon after.

"They know nothing of the heir. They think you are the last Kongeorn." I nodded my head. That was good. Nina was at least safe. I patted Fritz on the back and relieved him of his duties. He would be a mess for the time being. What he had seen does not rest easy on the soul.

Heart heavy, I went in search of something, anything, that could save this day. The air stung. And the atmosphere had lost its glee. Sorrow again climbed into the sky, expanding with the storm clouds. Human and animal alike had absconded back to shelter in preparation for the oncoming storm. The lightning would spook horses, while the thunder would send children running to their parents.

I, however, would revel with the cold droplets of rain, with the angry winds. Even as a child, they had ignited in me something more than I could say, and now, it was even more powerful.

My earliest memory, from just after my third birthday, blurry, but I knew it by heart. A storm had come, late in the cold winter. Static electricity crackled and snaked. My brothers had run for the cover of the keep, forgetting their smallest sibling. I stood in wonder. Chubby cheeks smiling, I waddled to and fro, eyes to the sky. The way the clouds rolled and churned, swept and contorted, fascinated me. I reached up. Higher, I wanted to be higher. But the best I could do was stand on tip-toes and reach out a pudgy hand. Even when the first lightning bolt skated across the sky, I continued to reach. The following crack of thunder delighted me. The fit of giggles and singing and dancing that ensued was the only way Da had been able to find me. As he held me to him, I continued to reach for the sky, for the storm.

And just because it was *strongly suggested* that I stay inside during thunderstorms didn't mean I did so. I would always find a way out, giving my Da acute anxiety until he had learned to accept my childhood obsession. I did catch a few colds, though.

Later, after Adam had arrived, he too observed my love of storms. After the first time he observed my behavior, he began calling me "Stormy," as he still did every day, especially on days when the sky opened up and the thunder rocked the world below.

I reached out a hand as the first rain drop plopped into my palm. I half smiled at the simple action, and smiled wider as more drops of water cascaded from the sky to our earth below. Tilting my head up, I reveled in the feel of each tiny droplet, and chuckled inwardly at each fat drop. I had come to realize, long before this, that raindrops were like people. There are different sizes, speeds, and shapes. But, when put together, a great flood can occur; life can be given or taken. It was just up to us which kind we would be.

I breathed in deeply, taking in the smell of the wet gravel below and the rain above. Eastern winds would carry the scent of pine our way after the storm. They always did. And, as always, I wasn't allowed to stay out in the storm for long.

"C'mon, Stormy, I think that's enough." Adam gestured, shielded from the rain by the overhanging roof above the steps. I took one more look back at the sky and ascended. Following Adam, I let out a small shiver. Once inside, I felt the chill far more strongly.

Knowing this, Adam led me to my room, where he had lit a fire in the fireplace. I removed my wet clothes and replaced them with dry ones before claiming a spot before the flames. Adam laid down and put his head in my criss-crossed lap. I stared into the dancing flames, watched as they shifted to their own beat. Like flowing water, they separated, then came back together, a single being made of many. I exhaled.

"What happens if I don't defeat Jakel?" My eyes still rested on the flames. Adam turned his gaze to me, puzzled.

"What do you mean if *you* don't defeat Jakel?" His brows knitted together in confusion, a challenging tone hinting in his voice.

"What if I don't kill him, or even Richard? I can't just let them continue to exist." I sighed, feeling the weight of the world return and settle on my shoulders. Adam sat up.

"You assume that this is a now or never situation. And you assume that you are alone. Two very wrong assumptions. You've never been alone, especially not in this fight. There have been countless warriors and scholars and rulers before you who have tried this same thing. Remember King Chaka of the Second Province? His crusades tried to bring the Mother back. Even though he failed, others picked up the mantle, just as you have. If *you* don't defeat Jakel, there will be someone else who will try, someone else who will fail. That is just the nature of fighting for a cause." Adam shrugged. It irritated me that he seemed to have this all figured out. And he knew it. He smirked at me before adding, "Besides, who would I be if I wasn't ready to clean up your mess?" That did it.

"My mess?" I chuckled. "You forget *I'm* the one who saved your sorry ass at Red Moon, thank you very much." I crossed my arms playfully. Adam, ever so slowly, inched forward until the tips of our noses met.

"Are you sure you want to challenge me, Stormy?"

"Wouldn't be anything new, but doesn't losing get old after a while? I wouldn't know." Hearing this, Adam scooped me up over his shoulder and jogged to the bed before depositing me on it.

"The only thing I know about losing is it just makes you hungrier for winning."

Chapter 25

Charcoal and Waltzing

I woke up in the middle of the night.

The starlight barely cast through the windows. The only path for me to follow was the one my feet made for themselves. Before I left the room, I draped an extra fur over my chilled shoulders. Outside my room, in the still dark of night, even the sconces seemed dim.

Silence. Like music.

Like a melody I'd heard as a child, it welcomed me, beckoned me. My feet danced slowly to their own unheard tempo, taking me with them, down the hall. Even my steps were drowned out by the heavenly notes. Ghosts of memories waltzed by.

My father and mother, laughing together, arm in arm. Amund, in all his ten-year-old glory, bounding around with his dulled sword. Elof and Geir, hiding behind a plant, watching as one of their pranks took another victim. Nana. My amazing Nana.

She rocked back and forth on her toes, a tell of excitement. Excitement about what, I didn't know, never knew. She always kept the reasons a secret, but let her emotion become contagious. And contagious it was. My own toes rocked back and forth on the rug, feeling the fibers underneath. To and fro, one and two. To and fro, three and four. Right foot forward, then back; five, six. Left foot forward, then back; seven, eight. Sweet silence, pure and unadulterated.

Down the hall, my silent melody carried me. Farther and farther, until I came to a door that I remembered fondly. Reaching out, my fingers stopped just short of the polished wood. He was gone. Even if I opened these doors, it wasn't his room behind them anymore. Yes, everything was in the same place: the furs still lined the floors, and swords adorned the walls. But he wasn't there. And he would never be, never again.

I turned away, afraid to face the empty room. Afraid to admit it was empty.

I kept walking.

The melody was gone, replaced by the kind of deafening silence that rings in the ears. The kind that one avoids. I ran my fingers over the wall, easing the volume to a comfortable hum of silence. And I walked. A left here, and a right there. A few dead ends and turn arounds. And then, I didn't know what brought me there, but there I was.

Da's thinking room, the place all his important decisions had been made. A room I had never been allowed to enter. A room I had forgotten about.

I opened the door. To my surprise, there came no creak from the hinges, no noise from the heavy oak door. Inside, there were three walls and a large window taking up all of the fourth. In the middle of the room, two chairs, nothing particularly special about them.

I shut the door behind me and dropped the fur. My bare feet could feel the smooth stone. As I walked, my feet found the scuffs in the floor where my father had paced back and forth. He always paced when he was worried. He said it helped get nervous energy out of one's system. I closed my eyes. Skin to stone, I took in a breath, the scent of leather and old books and a hint of pine. It smelled of Da. Even after all this time, a piece of him was still here.

Opening, my eyes looked to the far wall, where a bookshelf held countless leather-bound books. On the middle shelf, to the far right, near the window, I saw a set of books with different bindings. As I ran my fingers over the bindings, I noticed each had a name engraved in it. *Dagmar* was the first. Then *Amund, Einar, Elof and Geir.* Even Adam had a book. But where was mine? I turned around, thinking I had missed something. Then I saw. In one of the chairs, a stick of charcoal and another book lay together, both having gathered dust.

Sure enough, when I picked up the book and dusted off the binding, I found my name: *Vita.* Curiosity and, more than that, the need to feel close to Da made my fingers open the book. The first page was another rendering of my name, with intricate swoops and swirls. I exhaled in wonder, taking a seat cross-legged on the floor. I turned the page.

A drawing of an infant, eyes closed, in the arms of their mother, drew my eyes. I tried to process and turned the page. More drawings, beautiful portraits of a growing baby then a chubby toddler. And then, another page and another age. The girl drawn had a gap-toothed smile and a hooked nose that was scrunching as she smiled. I flipped by more pages, seeing the child grow into a teenager. Then, a new page, where the girl had become a woman, and her nose had taken on a crooked shape. I knew this woman. I had seen her in mirrors and pond reflections. I turned the page a few more times, taking in the art at my fingertips. About three-quarters through the book, I came to an unfinished drawing. The woman, sword in hand, hair braided back, was in a battle stance, about to spar with an unseen partner.

Amazed, I jumped up and ran to the book shelf, taking the rest of the labeled books down. I spread them out on the floor around me, taking turns looking through each. The one with my mother's name had an image of her with flowers in her hair, laughing. As I looked through my mother's book, I was surprised at how much we had in common. One of the most common poses Da had drawn her in was a fighting stance, an axe in her hand. I had never known my mother to be a fighter, but I had heard the stories.

Mami's name, before she had married Da, had been Dagmar the Just. Like Da and myself, Mami had risen in the ranks of our army. She had saved Da's life more times than he could count, or—at least—that's what he told me. The reason she stopped her fighting, gave up her warrior life, as I understood it, was she wanted a family. It was not that she felt an obligation, but that she wanted children of her own to love and protect. And, as her family grew, her ability to take time for herself dwindled. By the time I had been born, my mother had taken to politics and to making just decisions where Da was unable or asked for her help. They were a team, and he always worshiped the ground she walked on. His drawings of her proved this.

I looked at the other books. Amund's had one of him putting on his battle helm. Einar's was nearly empty, save for several drawings of a sleeping infant. Elof and Geir shared a book because they were nearly impossible to tell apart, and they were inseparable. There was not a single image of them without a smile on both their faces. Then I opened Adam's.

The first picture was one of him from when he first came to us, a lanky eight-year-old. He, too, grew as the pages flipped by. The last drawing Da had done was of Adam in his own fighting stance, a mirror to my own. I smiled. Da had secrets, like everyone else. But this secret was one that I needed to see then, even if he couldn't tell me himself. I closed all the books except for mine and returned them to their spots on the bookshelf. I then returned to mine.

Picking it up, still open to the incomplete picture, I held it to my chest. As I did, a piece of paper fell out. My eyebrows knitted together. Had I accidentally ripped a page? I then saw that this was no normal piece of paper; it was a letter. Gently placing the book beside me, I picked up the letter.

My V,

You have grown up so fast. I can still picture you in your mother's arms,
Snoozing away as I sketch.
From your first tooth to first sword to now and forever,
I have been so proud of you.
Everything you do, I can see me in it.
Which is why it is so hard to let you go.
You're a woman now, and that means it's time for you to find your match.
Though something tells me you've already found it.
I see the way you look at Adam, and the way he looks at you.
He's everything I have always wanted for you. That's why we
Brought him here, to us. He was always meant to
Be the Hingst to your Kongeorn.
And I know it is only a matter of time before you realize that, before
You're ready to love and be loved wholly.
But that doesn't mean I'm ready to let go of my little girl.
And I suppose you aren't so little anymore. But you will always be to me.
And though I know you won't be going anywhere, that we won't be far apart,
I still can't understand how time has gone by so fast.
And it will, no doubt, keep going by.
So take care to slow it down,
As much as you can.

This is my blessing, V, and you will always have it.

Love,

Da

The tears free flowed from my eyes. I put the letter down beside me, careful not to crumple or rip it, and brought my knees to my chest. I felt my heart would burst forth into my hands. Sobs racked at my ribs. Breathing failed me. I just, I *missed* him.

I missed his rough hands, the calloused fingers that would always wipe hair from my eyes. I missed his scruff, the beard that grew more and more grey with each passing year. I missed his arms, the ones that would hold me close after a bad nightmare. And I missed his eyes, the ones we shared, and his voice, how it could calm me and bring me down from the highest ledge. I missed him, my father, the man who had told me that it was okay to not have friends who were my age or my gender. The man who taught me who I was. The man who promised to love me, no matter who I chose to be. The man that would never leave my heart.

She sat in my study, crying and crying. I'd seen her like this before, but I never thought I'd be the cause. And that was what killed me, truly. My baby girl, my little V, my strong girl, she was heartbroken, and she was letting it all go. Letting it all go. And that was okay. Because she would be okay, and that was what mattered, more than anything, that my Vita would be okay.

The Sol was beginning to rise, shining through the wall window. It had been hours since all my tears had dried, since the sobs had subsided. With a renewed heart, I got up, taking the book with me. I set it back where I had found it, with the charcoal beside it. The letter, however, that I kept with me, holding it close to my heart as I picked up my fur blanket. After I closed the doors to Da's study behind me, I exhaled heavily, breathing out the last of my sorrow. I then made my way back to my room, where Adam still lay snoring.

Before waking him I folded up the letter and placed it above the fireplace, where it would be safe. Turning, I was ready to attack the day.

"Adam," I whispered. When he didn't respond, I grinned devilishly. "Oh, dear, however will I wake him up?" I took on the voice of an innocent lady before pouncing on my prey. I leapt onto the bed, aiming so I wouldn't do *too* much damage.

"Ugh," Adam groaned, rubbing his eyes, "Vita, what the *svat*—"

"Oh hush, you're fine. C'mon, we've got work to do." He glared at me, but eventually followed suit and got dressed as I did.

"So what's on the agenda for today?" He raised an eyebrow at me. I raised one back.

"Sparring." It came out as a challenge, a challenge that Adam would always be up for. He nodded before slowly straightening. He looked me up and down, unmoving. I knew what this was.

"Yeah, fine, I'll race you there." I broke into a sprint out of the room, Adam close behind me. We flew through the halls, looking nothing like a queen and her closest council advisor. I leapt through the front doors of the keep and sprinted for the training yard, refusing to look behind me. He was always right behind me. The weapons rack grew closer, our destination. I puffed out air through my mouth and breathed it in steadily through my nose. *Creator, help me. I have not run in a long time.* Luckily, Adam hadn't either. And also lucky for me, I got there first. Unlucky for me, it was not a victory with honor. I doubled over, trying to catch my breath. As I did this, I saw Hanna walk by.

"Hands off your knees," she fake barked at the two of us. I rolled my eyes at her smile. At least I had won.

After recovering from the running, Adam and I grabbed a few swords and commenced to sparring. We knew each other's movements well enough to keep the fight going for over fifteen minutes. Our footwork was nearly identical, and we knew the other's movement tells. If Adam adjusted his right hand on the sword, he'd go for a jab; if he adjusted his left hand, it would be a slash. By the time we called it a truce, we both had sweat running down our faces. My hair would be matted even in the meager braids. I gave him a thumbs up and we caught our breath.

"I feel old," He managed.

"You are old," I countered.

"Well, this old man is going to get us breakfast." He straightened and walked in the direction of the meal hall, glancing back over his shoulder at me to stick his tongue out. *Old and a child at the same time, now that's talent.*

I spent the rest of the morning observing those who had decided to come out and practice. Everyone who was in our army practiced at least once a day. If one was an overachiever, like Hanna, it was more like three times a day. I walked around, munching on whatever food Adam brought me throughout the day, giving tips to newer fighters, and pairing up those I thought would make good opponents. My favorite of the day was the pairing between Oliver and Nitocris.

Oliver's cool well-oiled machine was an interesting balance against Nitocris' fiery, explosive aggression. Seeing them duel it out was similar to watching a wild wolf against a well-trained dog. Equally dangerous, but very different. And it certainly made for an interesting fight, one that I was glad to not be in.

At the day's end, we received word from one of the scouting tribesmen Roald had sent to replace the ones we lost. Feroxia was again on the move. And it looked like, this time, they didn't care if we knew. *At least we're on the same page, then.* I made the announcement that we would set off for the Disputed lands in two days, particularly for the Ridge of Cincinnatus, which overlooked a great deal of abandoned land. No civilians needed to be hurt. I had Pierre send a letter to Feroxia that we wished to battle at the Ridge. The next day, this site was confirmed. By the War Laws of our world, the destination had been decided.

And then, we were on our way.

Chapter 26
It Ends

Similar to when we had traveled for the Battle of Red Moon, the trip took us six days. After we set up camp a little ways off the ridge, I sent out a group of scouts, both Kongeorn and Ordliqt, to wait for the appearance of Feroxians. Before the Sol had risen entirely in the sky, we had our answer. Because we were, for the most part, well rested, we sounded the horns of war. It had worked in our favor to begin the battle just as the Feroxian army had arrived before, so we opted to do it again. We lined up just as before, ready.

The Sol peeked out from the hills behind the Feroxian army, casting its rays onto all of us. I closed my eyes and took in the warmth. I could feel the excitement among our men and women, the need for movement becoming contagious. The winds shifted towards us, carrying with them the smell of horses, of sweat. I turned to Adam and nodded. I guided Dagny to the front of the line and began to speak.

"This, today, is where it ends. This, today, is where we decide the fate of our world, of our people, of those we love." I took a deep breath, "We all come from different places, we all believe in different gods, and we speak different languages, have skins of different colors. But, here, today, and every day that comes after, we are one. We are united here, on this day! United we are, and though some of us may fall, all will rise higher!" I raised my axe in the air and turned my face toward the heavens, toward my father and mother, toward Bjorth and Amund. I let out a battle cry and felt my blood begin to pump faster. As my people continued to cry out behind me, I turned to face the opposing hill, where all was silent, unmoving. The king's tent was there, behind them all. But the soldiers were still, and they were afraid.

My own people quieted, awaiting my command. My eyes flashed, ready, confident. Again, I raised my axe in the air and let out a battle cry before breaking Dagny into a run and charging ahead. Upon seeing this, the opposing army began to move, breaking formation. Some turned and ran, others charged toward us. None of them, however, were riding horses.

As I charged, I saw a line of horses carrying guards at the king's tent. *Of course he puts more value in his own life.* More fury bubbled in my stomach, and I slashed down, my axe meeting the chest of a Feroxian soldier unlucky enough to be in front. I steered Dagny to the flank of the army and jumped from the saddle. I hit her behind, sending her away. I had enough to worry about and had to be sure Dagny would not be in the way.

Three Feroxian soldiers, all men, came at me, swords slashing vehemently. I parried with the first, slashed and kicked back the second, and cut the head off the third. The first two returned for more, and received it. The first took an axe blow to the side. My axe, however, was stuck in his armor, so, as the second came for me, I took a page from Nitocris' book. Snatching my dagger from my boot, I kicked his sword arm up, dislodging the weapon. I then hopped on him and stabbed my dagger through his eye. As he fell, I dismounted and pulled the blade from his socket before sticking it back in my boot and heaving my axe out of the first one's side. Red splattered on my face, but I only smiled.

I circled around, looking for other opponents, or for my own people that may need help. As I did this, I saw one of our own fall.

Mehmet slashed and parried, but the many men around him were simply too numerous. In the middle of them, he fell for the last time. His sister, though, his sister refused to let this be. I saw her rush headlong into the circle of men, not caring for her own fate. From where I was, I could see the glowing of her molten eyes as they looked upon each who made the mistake of standing in her way. My heart broke for her, but I had to keep moving.

To my right, I saw Nitocris and Solvei acting as a tag team, cutting down man after man and covering each other.

Ahead of me, Hanna followed behind Dana and Oliver, finishing off those that they dropped to the ground. Her person was covered in blood. *Not her own. This is certain.*

Knowing I had watched for too long, I sprung back into action.

I pushed forward, trying to make a path through the middle to divide the red army into two halves. Different soldiers ran at me, flailing around like nervous teenagers. They were all cut down. I counted fifteen slain by my hand before my pace slowed.

I came to a big soldier, one with arms the size of tree trunks. Looking up at him, I smirked, reveling in the challenge. I breathed in, then charged at him. Surprised, he stepped back. Taking the chance, I brought my axe down on his left leg, hitting the knee and sending blood shooting into my face. I spit it out and continued to bring down my axe upon the giant, who apparently didn't feel pain. He stumbled backwards then stepped back to me. Again and again. He just kept coming back, blow for blow.

As I swung, I felt the hairs on the back of my neck stand up. The feeling intensified as I heard a sharp clang of sword on sword right behind me. It seemed eerily familiar, but all fighting does. All fighting consists of moving, blocking, dodging, slashing. I continued to strike the man until he collapsed, shaking the ground and landing on a comrade, who let out a scream that could shatter glass.

I swiveled to check on my own people and caught Adam's eye. I smiled and winked.

He began to smile back, confident and alive, but stopped abruptly. My gaze traveled down to the sword, coated in crimson, protruding through his chest, his armor. His emerald eyes opened wide, glazing over slowly, never leaving me. He began to fall, slowly and heavily. I sprinted through the chaos. Nothing else mattered. The fighting around me was silent. No clanging of sword, no grunting of those fighting for their lives, no battle cries. No, not anymore. I saw nothing else. Nothing else mattered in those long, stretched out moments. I ran, faster, harder, feeling my lungs burning, feeling the desperation build.

The man who the blade belonged to didn't have a chance. He looked up from his kill, malice in his eyes, to see the fire in mine.

He half-heartedly swung at me, knowing it was already over.

I caught his inferior blade with my left hand, not feeling the bite of the steel, and separated his head from his body with my axe in the other. I turned back to Adam, who was barely breathing.

I dropped my axe; I knelt beside him.

It wasn't right. Yes, I had seen it, but it wasn't how our lives should have been. He shouldn't have been wrenched away from me. We should have reveled in our victory and gone home. We should have announced our plans to wed, and I should have asked Simon to give me away in place of Da. We should have been wed before our people as we had been before the Mother so long ago. I should've grown as our child did inside me. We should have celebrated the birth of our child. And we should've watched the kingdom prosper under the rule of my niece. We should have grown grey together.

But what should be is not what was.

There my soul lay, in my arms, bleeding and bleeding crimson. I felt myself dying with him as I screamed in agony. I pled with the Mother to do something, anything. I wanted to go in his stead or go with him. I willed all I had to go into him, all the power the she-wolf had given me. When his breathing stopped and his emerald eyes dimmed, my agony turned to numbness.

The world around me slowed further as I said a final goodbye to my soul and kissed his forehead. Laying him gently beneath me,

I began to rise, a holy fury building in my soul, or where it used to be.

For my people, I would end the war. *Tears change nothing.*

For my father, I would end it. *Nothing can change the past.*

For Adam, I would end it. *But I can decide the future.*

I remember my comrades looked to me, but I do not remember giving orders. They followed anyway, Nir to my right and Ayla to my left. They had both lost loved ones in this war. They had both come into this with hope and confidence, but now, now that was turned into the cold grip of revenge, of sorrow and exhaustion. They followed closely until I arrived at the Feroxian king's tent, where I bid them to stay outside. I thought they would argue, that they would insist they come with me. Instead, they merely stood in silence, sentinels on the hill.

I laid down my axe and walked in, the tent flaps closing behind me. All was silent, the kind of silent where your ears ring. The same kind I had felt since I saw that sword pierce the heart of my soul.

Deaf to the king's false courtesies, I saw his mouth move without any foul sound. He would be gloating, of course. He'd be bragging about breaking me, and then breaking my people. Tears of fury fought to free themselves from my eyes, but I refused. *You know what to do.* A voice curled around behind my eyes, shading my sight to a crimson color.

I bid Richard to come closer. *Do it.*

He stepped forward. *Kill him.*

Again, I asked that he come closer. He did. *Do it now.*

Finally, we stood inches apart. I, clad in armor and blood; he, clothed in silk and arrogance. I looked him in the eyes, relishing in what was to come, relishing the thought of wrenching this fiend from life. A grotesque, contorted smile spread on my face as I took my hidden dagger from its sheath in my boot and sent it into his ribcage. Blood spurted from his mouth as I twisted and wriggled it. I wanted it to hurt, I wanted him to see the demons as they came upon him. I brought his ear to me and whispered.

"Let my grief be the last thing you feel." Letting go of his body and my dagger, I let his carcass hit the ground with a *thud*. I watched as his blood ran from wound and mouth, watched as his grey eyes lost their life, glazed over, became void. And then, I knew it would be over. *Finally.*

Seeing their king fall, his many guards unsheathed their swords and formed a tight circle around me. They looked down at their king, confused. I knew what must have been circling their minds. Were they truly free? *You no longer answer to him.* What would become of their lives then? *You can go to your families, rebuild your lives.* There was no time to think as Ayla and Nir came in, armed to the teeth. A decision had to be made, and it was. Dropping their weapons, most of the guards looked at me, wide eyed, and ran out of the tent. The yellow flaps of the entrance fell closed behind them. I turned back to see one soldier, one who had stayed.

He was different from the rest; he held no fear, only anger and jealousy, it radiated off him in waves, almost powerful enough to knock me backwards. Ripping off his helm, he exposed darkness, a cloud of smoke. There was no face, only two onyx coals where his eyes should have been. In that moment, the film behind my eyes cleared: I knew who I was facing.

"Like a wave," I offered.

"Washing over grains of sand." His voice was smoother than I thought, like a song without words. The smoke shifted, forming a dark face, the face of Jakel. The Sol light streaming in through the cracks in the tent dimmed as darkness enveloped me.

I swung my arm, motioning for Ayla and Nir to leave, to get out, but they wouldn't budge. *Can't they hear me?* I screamed at them. I could not have any more blood on my hands.

Still, though, they stayed. *Why won't you listen to me?*

Turning, my eyes met with the two burning onyx coals of the devil before me. I had no weapon to vanquish him with, and I had no knowledge of killing a Prince of the Darkness, anyway. So, I stood, head held high, waiting for him to attack, waiting for him to make the first move, hoping that it would offer me some clue. My heart pounded against my chest, wishing he would get it over with.

Except, he didn't. Instead, he laid down his sword and spoke.

"What purpose has my Mother given you? Has She even told you what you're fighting for, what your people are dying for?" The pitch face smiled, raising his gauntleted hand in a gesture of inclusion, pausing, he sighed. "You know, I didn't tell Richard or Alfred to do those things to those people. I didn't have to. They asked for power, and I gladly gave it to them. And I could give it to you, too." A shiver ran down my spine as the face again began to change, to morph in the smoke. This time, it was transformed completely into one I had never wanted to see again.

"Don't you remember me, my sweet? Don't you remember how much fun we had with my toys and tools?" As he speaks, with Avery's voice, my reality flits away, leaving me once again in that stony, barren room, skin burning, flesh tearing. I can still smell the acrid odor of my own flesh being burned away.

"Oh, now you see," the voice swirls through my head as I stand, unable to move, paralyzed, "you were such a good patient, that is, until you deserted me." He reaches out a pale, stretched hand and caresses my face before digging in with his dirty nails and pulling my skin from my skull. I screech in agony, remembering and feeling the same pain, but this time, in the very core of my being, where only my grief had reached. Just as it peaks, the scene again changes.

Suddenly, I am five again, trying to run with my brothers, trying and falling. With mud all over, I try to get up, but Einar, eyes as black as the burning coals, kicks me down again. He stuffs mud, more and more of it, down my throat. I try to breathe, but the mud hardens into rock, urging my lungs to gasp and burn for air. My vision grows dark at the corners. The scene again changes.

This time, however, I am in a place, a memory, where I had been only minutes before. I am clutching the body of my beloved. I am begging for Adam to come back to me. Looking down, I see his eyes snap open, only to reveal black coals.

Again, the scene changes. I am watching my mother die. I hold her head in my lap, and she opens her eyes: black.

I am sitting in front of my father as he tells me stories of our people, of Kongeorn. I look around. Amund's eyes, black; Einar's eyes, black; Elof and Geir's eyes, black. Even Adam's eyes have turned. But then I look to Da. His *eyes are still the same icy blue. He winks at me. I feel confusion circling in me, an itch that I can't quite reach. But why?*

Now I stand in a meadow, where dead flowers and grass encircle me. The bodies of those I love lay before me. Elof and Geir. Amund. Little Nina. Ayla. Bjorth. Nir. Niko. Gyda. Hanna. Solvei. Mami. Adam. Even Da.

"So you see," the smooth voice, the voice of Jakel, says. He appears in front of me, in the form of a man I have seen only in a nightmare. With pale skin and black eyes, he says, "Death comes to all. You are all but grains of sand, so easily manipulated by waves such as I. You are corrupt. It is in your nature. You have known it all along. And now, you are alone. *" He smiles, extending an arm out to me. "But you don't have to be. Come with me. Be my warrior queen. And we shall make Kongeorn reign forever."*

I look around at their faces, at the pale eyes of the dead. Each one of them had paid a price, whether it had been their own death or the grief that came from someone else's. I think in that moment that I can change that, that I can stop their pain.

But I can't bring back what they've lost. I can't play God. I can't best Death. I am only human, no power to change what has already been done. But I can change what is to come. I can choose.

"No." The voice does not just come from me. It is the voice of every innocent person who has died for peace, who has died in the name of love. Love for their child, their parent, their sibling, a friend, or a partner. I can feel the power of the voices behind me, the ones who resist. The bodies are no longer lying lifeless in the meadow, but standing behind me, with me.

Looking to my left, I see the face of my sister, of Ahava, as she stands with me. My sister. She has never really left me. She takes my hand and stares down Jakel.

I feel something appear in my other hand. The Sword of Gauthier, the Mother's Blessing that I have carried with me all this time, appears in my hand, glowing.

"Have we met?" Jakel is genuinely confused. He thinks he has access to everyone I love.

"No, but I know your Mother," Ahava raises her voice, "and I know the atrocities you have committed. I know the evil you do, and you will not take my sister." Ahava squeezes my hand before she begins to speak with an ethereal voice. Her words, though I cannot understand them, shake me to my core. More voices join themselves to Ahava's, and the people behind me move, forming a protective line in front of me. Jakel, wide-eyed, scared, *looks between the two of us. I manage a smirk. He's panicking now, trying to think of a way to stop his own destruction.*

"Beautiful, merciful Vita, do not let them do this! If you let them—" The last words I hear and understand are spoken,

"Avani, your Mother, binds you to the hate you have sown, for you will reap it." I can't tell who says it, it may even be me, but I can feel the power of those words, the power that comes with unity. *I swing the sword in front of me, aiming for the Prince of Darkness.*

Jakel's porcelain facade begins to crack, and he emits a shriek of agony, which only serves to further break him apart, as if he is made of glass, into several different pieces. I see that he has eight gaping voids, from pieces already missing, pieces of himself that he has installed into monsters like Richard and Einar. Jakel's five remaining pieces begin to fly and whirl around, as if in a massive windstorm. I see many coming towards me before I am thrown from the vision.

I awoke, a throbbing in my head, to see Nir and Ayla running from the tent as it began to be torn apart. The pieces of Jakel ripped at the canvas, shredding it. Then, like the wind, they were gone. Silence erupted in that moment, as I laid on the ground.

The war was over. Jakel was gone. It was finished.

I tried to get to my feet, but was stopped by a searing pain in my abdomen. Looking down, I took in the sight of a gash, deep into me, that had been made by one of the pieces. My breath caught as the pain seeped through my mental barrier, ebbing like the tide on a beach. I laid my head back on the welcoming grass, wincing slightly, a small smile on my face. *It is finished.*

Chapter 27
Mirrored Images

I awoke to the sound of crows squawking. My ears rang, and my head pounded. Opening my eyes, I saw the twilight sky. Get up, *a voice, somewhere inside, said to me. I obeyed and slowly rose from my place in the dead grass. Around me, I saw the bloodied bodies of countless men, soldiers and civilians alike. Their eyes frozen open toward the sky. I began to remember something: a dream, it felt like.*

I had died. I had left the world of the living, and I had done so in the arms of the woman I loved. Where is she? *I swiveled, searching for any sign. In the distance, I saw what remained of the king's tattered tent. Feeling something in me shout, I started to run for it. Countless bodies blurred by as I pushed to the tent.*

Silence. Walking in, my body tense, I saw the corpse of the Feroxian king, a demon in human flesh. To his right, I saw her.

Her chest rose and fell, weak and slow. A deep wound opened her abdomen, and her blood pooled around her. Her eyes were closed, as if asleep. I rushed to her.

I prayed for it to end, to be with those I loved, with Adam, and Da, and Mami, and Bjorth. Just when I felt peace encompass me, the pain leaving me at last, a feeling inside wrenched my eyes open. Above me, kneeling, was my soul.

Her eyes opened as I placed her head in my lap. Though something about her was different.

He had changed somehow. His eyes.

Her eyes.

One blue and one green.

They took me by surprise, but I let it go. There was a reason I was alive, and I could not just let her die. I began to kiss her. Anywhere and everywhere. Her forehead, her lips, her neck. Just to show her I was there; maybe she could hold on until the healers arrived. When I searched her face for another place to kiss, she smiled sadly. I bought my forehead down to touch hers.

I looked into his eyes before me. He was here. All I needed was right in front of me. It was truly Heaven. Mustering the last of my strength, I whispered, "I'll race you there."

Her eyes closed, and my world shattered. Pulling her head to my chest, I begged for her to come back, to come back to me. You've come back to me before; you can do it again. You can do it again. Please. *I never thought I would have to live without her, and I already knew that I never could. I held her to me, weeping into her hair for hours.* Why couldn't I have died with you?

When her body grew cold, and no more tears would come, and my throat was raw from sobbing, I lifted her in my arms. I carried her out into the meadow and turned toward the adjacent wood, following the wind. It cradled us as I walked. It blew strands of bloody hair away from her face, and I held her body closer to my own. I trekked until a clearing came into view, one that let the soft light of the Luna bathe the soft grass. It was there that I laid her, there, in the light of the Luna. Pushing a strand of hair from her face, I kissed her for what I hoped would not be the last time.

There was nothing left for me here. This world doesn't need me, not like it needs her.

I carefully extracted the hidden dagger from my boot, the twin to Vita's. My mind rushed through all of my memories of her. I thought back to when I first spoke to her.

She had been standing out in the middle of a rainstorm, dancing, singing. Her chunky cheeks grinned with pure joy. Up until then, I had never seen anything like it, that joy. And then, she invited me to dance with her, out in the storm. And I did.

I thought back to when she had tricked me the night of Amund's wedding. She had caught me off guard, kissed me. And I couldn't tell her no. I hadn't wanted to tell her no.

I even thought back to my favorite memory of her. Late one night, just after her eighteenth birthday, we were in the midst of studying the Disputed Wars. We had been pouring over textbooks for hours and hours. And then, when I thought I couldn't take anymore names and dates and strategies, Vita had perked up.

"I have an idea," she had said. That was all it took. That, and the spark in her eye that she would get whenever she felt like getting into trouble.

"Yes, please," I had replied, willing to be anywhere but there.

We ended up in riding north, to a small lake called Fe. We splashed and swam and stayed until dawn. I could still remember the icy fire in her eyes when we found a rope swing on the shore. That was Vita.

And then I thought on when she had stumbled back home, to Redefalk, after being gone for so long. I had thought I would lose her then. I stayed awake for days, watching, waiting, praying. I tried to bargain with the Mother. 'If you let her live, I will do anything, anything.' *I prayed the same prayer for hours on that battlefield, but the Mother's favor had run out. And that meant my time had run out.*

My face lifted until my eyes could see past the tops of the trees. The Luna light shone on my face as I positioned the blade. I could see Vita's eyes in the light of that Luna. They were bright and overpowering. She was waiting for me. My mind focused on that as I prepared my body for the coming pain. One last breath, and I began to thrust the steel—

"Stop." *A voice rang out from around me, from within me. The thoughts of Vita snapped out of my vision. My hand dropped the dagger, unable to disobey. I turned around frantically, looking for anyone or anything. There was nothing.* "The sword will not kill you, my son." *The voice rumbled again, this time far more gentle. Still frantically searching, I called out,*

"Where are you?" I waited for an answer. My heart beat fervently, trying to catch my attention. It wanted me to get back to the task at hand. This time the voice was quiet and from a more targeted origin.

"I am in you. I am the I Am, the One who has created and still creates." *Confusion swirled and thickened within me; my heart beat harder, now urgent in need to finish what had been started.* "Adam, have no fear. Calm your heart." *Without warning, Her commands were heeded. I could not disobey. As my heart was calmed, it seemed to be stilled completely, releasing the fear. A wave of images, of memories, swept over me.*

I saw as Vita clutched me to her, begging to take my place.

I saw a dark figure, towering over Vita as she stood her ground. I saw a beautiful woman—who I at once recognized as the same ethereal woman from the cave at Mayken—at Vita's side, cloaked in a bright white aura, unafraid of the demon. And finally, I heard the words, the same words that would be etched into my heart.

"Avani, your Mother, binds you to the hate you have sown, for you will reap it."

"W—what?" My mind swam, trying to make sense of it all. Why is this happening? What is happening?

"That, Adam, was My way of saving people I love more than Myself." *The voice paused, as if collecting itself,* "I could not expel Jakel from time and Omnia altogether, but I could, with help, bind him to those bloodlines he invested in." *I knew the name Jakel. He was the son of the Mother, the one who tried to exile Her, the one Vita was charged with stopping. Then, I understood.*

"It is not finished, is it?" I asked, hoping this was all a joke. My stomach dropped, and tears prickled.

"No, Adam, it is not. And I am afraid I must ask you to do one last task for me."

My heart again began to pound, to swell and contract, not out of fear, but anguish. Desperation. All I wanted was to be with my family, where there is no more pain, no more tears, where I was destined to be. I just wanted to be with her.

"I know, and I understand. I, myself, am anxious for when you can be reunited with those you love. However, you are the only one I can trust with this." *I inhaled sharply, bracing myself for what would be more painful than the death I had prepared for. Kongeorn had won the war when Feroxia's heirless king had been slain. My people were safe, the line secure in my wife's niece.* What else can there be?

"Though Ahava bound Jakel, broke him into pieces, she, nor I, can destroy those pieces, not all of them." *I realized that the woman in the vision, the same woman from the cave, must have been Ahava.*

"*Am I to destroy the pieces?*" I asked, puzzled. *It didn't make sense. None of this made any sense.*

"You can't. As my instrument, you will be unable to. I am unable to harm any of my children, even those who deserve it. As my instrument, you will share that burden. But you can guide those who can destroy the pieces. And even then…" *She trailed off, worrying me. 'And even then?' There's more? Why is there still more? Further, my stomach dropped, taking my broken heart with it.*

"I am afraid so."

"*Why me? Why not save Vita? Why isn't she your instrument?*" I *wasn't special enough, not like her. People looked up to her, people loved her. If anyone could do it, she could.*

"You are the Hingst to her Kongeorn. All this time, you both have played your parts. And for that, I thank you. You see, Adam of Hingst, Vita fell at my son's hands. I cannot rely on she who has been marred by a piece of darkness. And besides, you wouldn't let me choose her, would you?"

I looked around, confused, before understanding.

"No," I said, shoulders sagging, "I wouldn't. She deserves the peace she's found."

The Mother said no more, and I sat down on the soft grass, a growing pain in my chest as I thought about the woman I loved and all she had sacrificed.

As I sat, feeling only sorrow, I saw an image, clear and striking, appear in my mind's eye. Her raven hair had just grown where it covered her scalp fully. And her peaceful smile was everything pure and innocent about an infant. And her eyes, they were as blue as those in my dreams every night. I was to pay a visit to the heir of Kongeorn, to little Nina.

Before I left for my task, a task that I was unable to abandon, I saw to Vita's body. It had become cold and pale, nothing like the woman, the queen, I loved. Blood covered her torso, leaking through her leather. Her sweaty hair crowded her scarred face. Though she was gone, a smile remained on her lips. I always loved the way she smiled. The way her eyes crinkled.

I resolved to give her a proper funeral for a Kongeorn, because I knew that was what she would have wanted, to be recognized as a warrior. Using my own dagger, I painstakingly severed branches and limbs from trees and constructed a pyre fit for a queen. When the pyre was finished, I laid her upon it. She wouldn't have wanted flowers, she never liked them anyway—something about 'Death makes them less beautiful.'

Before I could find something to start the fire with, I felt a burning in my hand. Looking, I saw a smoldering ember, searing my palm. I did not feel the pain, but fixed my eyes on Vita, my Vita. I placed the ember deep within the pyre, which soon ignited. The inferno before me was nothing compared to the fiery spirit that had left this world with my soul. Thinking of her, I remembered the words she always whispered to herself: "Fall to rise higher."

With these words, along with countless more questions, circling my mourning mind, I made my way to Favre, the place of my birth. Its rolling green hills showed none of the scars that were seared into the Disputed Lands. Vita was right, Favre was the safest place for Amund's child. She was always right.

In the night, I crept along the battlement, easily staying quiet, stealthy, in the shadows. No one heard or saw me. I did not know where the child was, but I had faith I was being led by the One who did. I finally came to a door, plain and splintery. Pushing passed it, I saw Karina laying in the bed.

Beside her, in a small crib, Nina. I walked to the crib. There, standing over the child who shared my soul's eyes, I recognized the power of the Mother *guiding me as I laid a hand over her sleeping eyes. Into her flowed the light of the Mother and the future of Jordklode, of Omnia.*

Index

Oster—famous for their pears, which are known around all of Omnia as sweet. Most of their peoples are farmers, but they are becoming more reliant on diplomacy than ever before.

Signy—usually plays second fiddle to Oster and does not share in the wealth very often. However, Signy's textiles are some of the finest in Jordklode.

Nae—famous for its democratic government, which was the first in all of Omnia.

Nox—famous for its export of horses, which its wranglers capture and/or breed just south of this nation, in the southern wetlands.

The vast, remaining land in Jordklode belongs to fifty-four different clans, each too small to be considered a nation. Some of the more powerful clans include the Ordliqt, Drake, Daemon, Straq, and Andreas tribes.

Northwest—Oeste—812 miles long by 843.75 miles wide. This continent is a collection of large islands, the largest of which being Vindex. There is a strict hierarchy in Oeste, with the the rulingpower, the Apendy race, residing only in Vindex. The rest of Oeste's people live in

Aurum—famous for their gold work, which can be jewelry, statues, or furniture.

Argentum—famous for their silver, which, similar to Aurum, can be made into jewelry. However, their silver is also made into weaponry.

Aes—famous for carpentry, this is where nearly all of Oeste's wood goes to be made into decor or furniture, sometimes even ships or fireplace mantles.

Semel—only farmers reside her, where they grow the vast majority of Vindex's food.

Unguis—this is a purely academic area, where anyone who is wealthy or devoted enough may go to learn any subject they can imagine.

Tandem—this is the halfway port and resting point in the Aniac Ocean between Jordklode and Oeste. Money is often exchanged here, making it a favorite spot for pirates to raid. This danger has been decreased in recent centuries because of how guarded the island is.

Sparget Chain—only native peoples, reclusive and religious set foot on these islands. Those who inhabit the chain are aggressive and do not take kindly to anyone, which is why the chain is avoided by all but an ignorant few.

Southwest—Ungula—156.25 miles long by 187 miles wide. Ungula is a set of four small islands, two bigger than the others. The only people to reside here were the Lost Nation, who had been guided by the Dragonae guardians. Not much is known about these isles. Rumor has it that, unlike the other guardians, these Dragonae kept their conscience and still continue to guide their peoples.

There are several different races in Omnia, based on where they are from geographically.

In Jordklode, those south of Oster tend to have dark skin. This includes the nations of Nae and Nox, as well as the tribal lands south of them.

Oster's people are a mix of all races, though their rulers have olive-toned skin and dark features. This is the same in Signy and the 70 Provinces of Dagyn.

Feroxia's people tend to be a mix as well, though the vast majority are ghostly pale, with fiery red hair; this includes the Feron line.

Hingst people, though culturally similar to Kongeorn, are quite different in appearance. They maintain tanned skin and dark, almost raven hair. Their rulers also sport light eyes, usually hazel or green.

As for Kongeorn, they are the most diverse nation in Omnia, with all of the above traits and those not yet listed. The ruling line of Kongeorn, which is known by the same name, tend to have chestnut or blond hair with light eyes, either purple or icy blue.

The tribes in the far north, like the Ordliqt tribe, sport blue-tinted skin, along with color-changing eyes.

In Oeste, those who reside and rule in Vindex, the Apendy, have orange or green skin, depending on the light. They typically have dark eyes and pale hair.

Aurum, Argentum, and Aes all have the same root from which their people came. Their people tend to have reddish skin, with any number of combinations for hair and eyes.

Semel's people are a mix of those from Aes and Vindex, so its people can sport the orange/green skin or the red, or somewhere in between.

Tandem has no specific root. Anyone in Tandem is never there for more than ten years, even if they have a family there. All races can be found in Tandem.

Unguis is the same as Tandem in this respect.

In the Ungula Isles, there is only one people. The Lost Nation's people are unique in that their skin completely lacks pigmentation. They are grey, almost like the underside of a cloud. Their eyes, however, are a constant gold or red, depending on sex. Women's eyes are gold, while the men's are crimson. As for hair, it tends to be dark and curly.

Animals

The Northern and Southern regions are quite different from each other as far as climate and fauna go.

Northern Jordklode

This climate is comparable to our world's North America and Europe, where there are cold winters and hot summer, with spring rains and fall foliage.

Polecats/Weasels—Similar to our own, but are always jet black with bright yellow eyes, making them seem inherently evil. They are sometimes thought to be messengers of Jakel.

Pidges—These birds are similar to our own crows, but are significantly smaller in size. However, in flocks they are still quite intimidating. They are thought to be messengers of Jakel.

Srontes—These are horses, but sport the tail of a lizard-like creature. In every other aspect, they are horses. They are, however, typically more difficult to domesticate, which is why they are not ridden in Jorklode.

Myank—These fish are native to the rivers and lakes of Northern Jordklode. They grow to about 6 feet in length and can weigh around 80 pounds. When caught, they are used as meals for large groups.

Sorve—These are Northern Jordklode's deer/elk. They maintain the antlers of a white-tail with the stature of an elk.

Our world's wolves, horses, squirrels, red foxes, and beavers also inhabit this part of Omnia.

Southern Jordklode
This area has a climate similar to our world's South America and Africa, along our Equator. It is hot nearly all year round, and has far more rain than dry spells.

Negan—These are gators from the Wetlands of Drake. They only grow to about three feet long, but have vibrant yellow and green scales. They also have two front teeth that protrude like a sabertooth. Their blood is used in witchcraft.

Tanzi—A vibrant-colored bird, this animal is about the size of an emu and is easily domesticated, making it the far South's favorite pet/guard dog.

Duay—this is a mix between a frog and a bird. It jumps and flies. It has slick skin with a beak and feathers only in wings. If caught, it is treated like a delicacy.

Our world's horses, white foxes, doves, and serpents of various kinds also inhabit this part of Omnis.

Oeste

This land is both mountainous and dry at once. Where it is mountainous, it is like an oasis. That area is in Aes, Tandem, the Sparget Chain, Semel, and the middle of Vindex. All is dry desert, with oasis-like coast around the edges of each island.

Chandri—instead of horses, Oestians typically ride these animals. They are similar to camels, but have no humps and have completely white hair.

Kinay—This is the largest serpent known to man. It is a desert snake that grows to 60 feet long. Because it is so fearsome, it is subject to legend and myth. In reality, it really just prefers to be left alone. They hide under the sand and can often be mistaken for actual sculptures from ruins. They were Oeste's guardians once.

Diday—This is a large jellyfish-like creature. They live their entire lives close to the surface and can grow to be 120 feet in diameter. For this reason, many of the poorer aborigines, especially in the Chain, make homes on top of these creatures.

Our World's horned toads, eagles, hawks, and tropical fish also inhabit this part of Omnia.

Ungula

This land is the land of the Lost Nation. Dragonae, sea turtles, vibrant glow-in-the-dark plankton, and Caya trees reside here with them. The climate here is very much like our tropical rainforests. The life that finds its way here thrives.

Caya trees are enchanted trees that adapt to their caretaker's needs. For the Dragonae, they produce fire fruit, the purest form of sunlight.

Dragonae are ridiculously intelligent, with their own beliefs and philosophies. They were one of the original companions, but, unlike the original Luposi wolves and Kinay, they were believed to maintain their consciousness.

Not much is known about the history of Oeste or Ungula in 792, when Vita's story begins. Her history books only show two historical events in Oeste and none in Ungula.

0

Creator creates the five guardians of man, who are born on the island of Creat.

Once they are created, they are given a population of twelve people to look after and guide. Six men and six women. The guardians are told to teach their people to do the following things:

1—Trust the Mother and develop a relationship with Her.

2—Treat each other with justice, equality, and compassion.

3—Abstain from greed, hate, and jealousy.

4—If a wrong is done, punish with less severity than is deserved.

5—Remember kindness in all situations, but give the decision to the Creator when it is required.

6—When one has found their soul-partner, they may bond in two ways; first, they may bond publicly, through a wedding, this is optional; secondly, they must bond before the eyes of the Mother with a Total Embrace of Mind, Body, and Soul.

100

After 100 years of training together, the clans split apart. Hjort and Egern went south and grew their territories there. Ulv went west to establish their own territory. Kongeorn and Hingst remained together in the East, where they established their civilizations.

203

The first Apendy king, Arrajin I, is crowned.

401-406

Wars of the Southern Nations begin. After fractioning off into seventy different provinces, the clans of Hjorth and Egern fight to establish dominance. Oster, Signy, Nae, and Nox become the southern superpowers.

499-502

Barbarian Wars begin. Kongeorn and Hingst's alliance allows them to gain more power in trade and land, which expands their territory into previously unclaimed lands. This war was mainly just them against tribes that had previously splintered off. There were only three deaths in this "war."

525

Octavia's adventures begin.

569-575

War of Feroxian Creation occurs. An ambitious clan leader from the nations which splintered from Ulv rises to power and takes over the surrounding tribes in the West. Kongeorn stops them from mass killing more innocent people by signing the Treaty of Niagn. That clan leader was Pridbor I, the first king of Feroxia and the Feron line.

634-638

The Apendy king, Harust, makes a trade agreement with the 70 Provinces of Daygn, opening up its markets to Jordklode.

682-699

Unclaimed Wars occur. Bloody wars between Ferons and several tribes in the North. Kongeorn's king, Cain, gets involved and gives this land to the tribes instead of Feroxia. This strengthens the animosity between Feroxia and Kongeorn.

792-794

Krigar (Queen's) War occurs. Vita declares war on Feroxia after the deaths of her family and after King Richard keeps her hostage. There are *mass casualties* on both sides.

Kongeorn

Adelaide and Gauthier (married 179)

491 years pass

Cain, born 670, marries Gabi in 693

Hendrick, born 695, marries Shea in 735

Bjorth, born in 740

Kay, born in 697, marries Adolf in 710

Saga "Nana," born in 699, marries Paul in 722

David, born in 722

Hans, born in 724

Johan, born in 725

Magnus, born in 727

Max, born in 728

Niklas, born in 730

Andor, born in 740, marries Dagmar in 765

Ahava, born in 765

Amund, born in 766, marries Karina in 792

Nina, born in 793

Einar, born in 768

Elof and Geir, born in 770

Vita, born in 771

Hingst

Gemane and Agathe (married 190)

480 years pass

Daniel, born in 673, marries Regina in 694

Drax, born in 694

Franc, born in 698

Luci, born in 700

Gertrude, born in 702, marries Jorge in 724

Yara, born in 725, marries Ava in 750

Abraham, born in 726, marries Noellah in 749

Dodd, born in 750

Delilah, born in 751

Adam, born in 768

Asher, born in 760, marries Giselle in 780

Feron, of Feroxia

Pridbor and Alexa, married 575

Pridbor II, born 575, marries Alice in 600

Ben, born in 601

Bradford, born in 602, marries Calla in 620

Clark, born in 622, marries Dahlia in 640

Damon, born 642

Dane, born 644

Diana, born 646, marries cousin, Earnest, in 662

Edmund, born 663, marries Alicia in 684

Eli, born 686

Ezra, born 688

Fitzroy, born 690, marries Fleur in 710

Gabe, born in 710

Alfred, born in 710, marries Odette in 747

Richard, born 759

Aaron, born 577

Baldwin, born 578, marries Jenna in 608

Susanna, born in 610, marries Nic in 622

Earnest, born 624, marries cousin, Diana, in 662

Thank you for reading this book!

We encourage anyone to share their thoughts and experiences wherever they can. Feel free to do this by leaving a review on any reading platform, such as Kindle or Goodreads.

About the Author

S. N. Jones (aka Sydney Jones) has been writing for as long as she can remember. This love has bloomed with the help of her English teachers, family members, and friends. Jones currently attends Western Kentucky University, where she plans to graduate in May 2021 with a degree in Public Relations and Spanish. When she isn't writing, Jones spends her time going out for Indian food and ice cream with friends, listening to podcasts, and spending time with her family, especially her two nieces.

More from Zenith Publishing:

Don't Blame the Reckless by Maddyson Wilson (2019)

Not Always Blu Skyes by Gabrielle McMaster (2020)

More than Us by Ryan Jones (2020)

Rise of Knight and Sword by Miriam Wade (*coming 2020*)

A Love Across Time by Genevieve Jane (*coming 2020*)

Made in the USA
Middletown, DE
14 January 2021